Extraction

Dietrich Stogner

To my friend.

Thank you for sharing books with me.

Thank you for talking about books with me.

Thank you for standing with me during the best and worst days of my life.

Thank you for always reading my writing.

Thank you for dedicating so much to helping me with my craft.

Thank you, Josh. I would not be who I am today if not for you.

Chapter 1

Aldo was grateful his face was no longer bleeding. The tile beneath his feet was of a quality that seemed unlikely to tolerate mud, let alone bodily fluids.

Exhaustion had a way of making everything more potent. More than a fortnight had passed since his nose had shattered into a mess of bone and blood, and the pain had dulled to an occasional spiked reminder. He'd gone nearly three days without sleep, and as the exhaustion settled over him like a heavy blanket, the throbbing became a constant drumbeat reminding him of broken bones and cartilage sitting in entirely the wrong place.

He'd been standing for nearly an hour. The guard had brought a bench to the immaculately manicured garden. The eleven-year old girl that had accompanied him was quietly snoring on it as he waited. But Aldo didn't sit. Instead, whenever anyone offered him water or the attentions of an anatomist, he simply shook his head and said the same thing he'd been repeating since he arrived.

"I need to see Mistress DeLuca."

Aldo knew how he looked. The homespun cotton clothing he wore was not of Vetticcian cut, and even if it hadn't been spattered with mud and blood, it would have done an outstanding job of informing anyone with a pair of functioning eyes that he had no place within five miles of the DeLuca Family estate. They had tried to escort him away upon his arrival, but he knew the words. He was meant to be here.

Not like this, though. He shook his head wearily. *This is a bad idea.*

The staff held muttered conferences between each other for a brief period, but finally settled on escorting Aldo and Auggie behind the sprawling palatial home, through a series of gardens like interlocking cells of a beehive, divided by tall stone walls covered in creeping ivy and flowering honeysuckle. By the time they'd passed through the tenth gate, Aldo was quite lost. There they left him to wait, struggling to stay on his feet.

He was surprised they'd let him keep the dagger. Surprised, but grateful. His hand hadn't left the hilt since they'd left the ranch.

When the gate to the north opened up, Aldo lifted his tired eyes to the pair of guardsmen carrying a small white oak table. Two more followed behind with a pair of chairs. Like many of the senior Families of Vetticci, the guards had distinct uniforms, brightly colored patterns making them seem more like peacocks than trained soldiers. The rapiers at their belts would be sharp, though.

The quartet arranged the table in the center of the garden, setting the chairs in place. An older man, dressed in black clothing with silver thread, followed them out, wordlessly setting a clay pitcher and a pair of cups on the table. He spent a moment adjusting the placement, looking over the entire setup, and nodding to the guards, who had assumed positions around the table, faces blank and eyes unblinking. Moments later, Mistress Toni DeLuca walked through the same gate.

White, close cropped hair framed a face with hard grey eyes and an expression that had forgotten what smiles looked like decades before. Her sapphire blue dress wasn't in line with Vetticcian styles. It was *the* style. When a woman of her wealth and breeding wore something, the rest of the massive city-state followed. Her heels clicked on the paving stones as she walked up to the table, and sat down, pouring herself a cup of water.

"Pratchett."

The man in black stepped forward. "Mistress."

"Have an anatomist sent from the Pallia Clinic. Should these two be permitted to leave, I'll not have them looking as if they've been dragged across cobbles." Her voice was even and soft, but beneath the velvet lay sharp cold steel.

"At once." Pratchett vanished through the gate, and DeLuca gestured at Aldo.

"Sit." Aldo did, and DeLuca said, "You are not Nicolette Saffman."

"No, Mistress."

"Is she dead?"

"I don't believe so, but I can't be sure," Aldo said. "She's in custody. The last I saw her was sixteen days ago."

"That's unfortunate." DeLuca's voice never changed, but the temperature in the garden felt as if it had dropped several degrees. "She had several very specific directions. I don't know how many she shared with you, but the most crucial was that this entire operation remain unseen."

Walking a very tight line now, aren't you? Aldo swallowed, nodding. "I know. She told me. And I can promise you, the Vorchese know nothing about..."

"You should be very, very careful about promising things of which you have little knowledge." DeLuca crooked a finger towards one of the guards, who leaned down for her to softly speak into his ear. He nodded, and vanished through the gate. Once he'd gone, DeLuca turned her attention back to Aldo. "Quite a bit can happen in sixteen days. If we're lucky, Miss Saffman is dead. If we're not, well." She poured some water into the cup. "There will undoubtedly be blood to spare."

Aldo could feel the eyes of the guards on him. *One wrong word, Aldo. One wrong word and there's no going back.* "If you'll let me explain, Mistress DeLuca, I hope to be able to assuage your concerns," he said. "At least most of them. My name is..."

"Aldo Marini. Born 28 years ago to Stiliano and Rinna Marini in the Ruins. Recently working as a day longshoreman in the cannery district. No siblings. No spouse or romantic partner. Your last residence was the Pier 34 bunkhouse." Her eyes did not break contact as she recited the information, and Aldo felt as if he very much understood how it felt to be dissected. "You were convicted of trespassing and vandalism at the age of fourteen." Tilting her head, DeLuca said, "Do you know what I find interesting, Mr. Marini?"

Aldo shook his head. "No, Mistress."

"The recommended sentence for trespassing is three weeks upkeep labor on the Myre Road. The recommended sentence for vandalism is a fine equivalent to six times the value of damaged property," she said. Extending a blood red fingernail in his direction, she said, "You have fourteen fishhooks tattooed on your forearm. I'm curious as to why a fourteen-year-old boy is sentenced to nearly a decade and a half on a penance barge for trespassing and vandalism."

"It's complicated."

"I doubt that," DeLuca said. "Very few things truly are. But ultimately, that's not the most important question. There is one thing I need to know right now, Mr. Marini, and your answer will determine how many more beats lie within your and your sleeping companion's hearts."

Toni DeLuca leaned forward, fixing hard grey eyes on Aldo Marini. "Mr. Marini... where is my bull semen?"

Chapter 2

Four Weeks Earlier

It was raining.

Aldo had to decide whether to keep the rain off of his head, or off of the fish. It wasn't much of a decision. The large horde of seagulls that crowded the barnacle-crusted piles lining the long pier shrieked in a constant, unending din, small black eyes watching for any opportunity to dart in and nip chunks off the fish. The cannery looked for any reason to skim a handful of coral off of the total. Aldo knew he'd be soaked to the bone with the canvas over the catch rather than his head, but he'd long ago learned that suffering often yielded profit.

The end of the pier had a small pavilion set up, a sheet of angled canvas directing the fat, warm raindrops into the black water of Pallia Bay. The bumboats crowded around, sailors passing the corusca cod up to the porters waiting to fit as many as possible in baskets held by canvas straps crisscrossing their backs. They had to be careful loading the fish. Too many, and the shimmering muscled bodies of the two to three foot long cod would mash together, deforming the meat and dropping the price. Too few, and the mile-long walk wouldn't yield enough ducats to fill their bellies.

Aldo carefully arranged five of the fish in his basket, and tucked the waxed scrap of canvas he'd scrounged around the edges. His black hair was already plastered against his face, his beard beaded with droplets, as he turned and followed the stream of porters beginning the trek uphill. When they reached the road running along the shore of Pallia Bay, he broke left while the rest split right. Several sent glances his way, brow furrowed. He didn't return their stares.

The easiest route to the cannery was along one of the cobblestone roads that wove its way through the dense warehouses and tenements nestled close to the bay. However, Aldo had quickly learned that this popular route, like every road throughout the massive city-state of Vetticci, was jammed full of loudly shouting and chattering Vetticcians, pushing and jostling their way through. That wasn't unusual for the city, but it did slow down the porters, turning a mile walk into nearly a ninety minute slog. They all knew the alternative, and chose the road.

Aldo had to pull off the basket and feed it through the narrow gap between a tenement and a sailmaker's shop. He lifted his leg over the rusted iron grating extending two feet off of the ground. When his boot came down, it squelched in the sewage piled up against the grate.

Vetticci was shaped like a massive bowl. The bottom was the sprawling Pallia Bay, dotted with hundreds of ships, from the bumboats bobbing drunkenly between the larger ships, to the large freighters laden heavy with cargo waiting for a dock large enough to accommodate them. Once the dark water gave way to the countless docks and piers extending out into the bay like spindly fingers, the cobblestones road that ringed the waters began the uphill slope.

Four miles up the hill were the shining white estates of the wealthiest families of the city. The size of the houses, as well as the size of the occupant's accounts, decreased more and more as one traveled downhill to the bay. The sewage of the city all channeled down the countless greywater alleys carved between the buildings, tracing stinking routes between cobbled-together homes before dumping its noxious contents into the bay. In a city in which nothing held more value than a square foot of vacant space, the greywater alleys were too foul for anyone to lay claim.

They were perfect. Aldo considered shoes full of shit a fair trade for being first.

Aldo slung the basket back over his shoulder, and began wading uphill. The ground was slick with the unspeakable lumps floating around his boots, but he had no difficulty keeping his footing. He was grateful for the driving rain. The heavy humidity in the air helped somewhat to smother the odor.

The din of the crowd was reduced to a dull roar. Vetticci was never quiet, but in this foul escape, Aldo could hear himself think. He didn't like that part. The moments he was alone, not distracted by the never-ending chaos of the city, he could remember. He didn't like remembering.

When he emerged back onto the road, fifteen minutes later, he was only a stones throw from the Sanni's stand at the cannery. He took a few moments to stick his feet and boots under the water pouring off the corner of a rooftop, washing most of the shit away. None of the other porters had made it up the road by the time he quietly ducked through the gull netting, and came to a halt in front of the buyer's wooden table.

The short, swarthy man scowled up at Aldo. "Again?"

Aldo shrugged, and set the basket onto the table. He pulled away the cloth, and laid the five fish side by side on the battered and worn wood. Sanni's brow furrowed, and he waved a hand to a butcher in a stained leather apron, who pulled a long knife from a bucket of alcohol and trudged over.

Sanni lifted the gills of each fish with a chopstick, studying each with a practiced eye. He prodded the flesh gently, and after a few moments, grunted. "Accepted." The butcher nodded, and began gutting the fish with quick darting slashes of the knife. Long fillets were laid on the tray of a scale, and once they were done, the heads and tails went into a bucket on a separate scale. Sanni glanced over the results, lips moving silently as he ran the calculations.

"Sixteen pounds for salt and canning. Twenty-one for the chum." As he spoke, several workers pulled them off the scale and disappeared into the cannery. "Comes to eighteen ducats. Minus processing fee, weighing fee…"

Aldo tuned him out for the buyer's droning litany. He'd heard it more than enough, and to his credit, Sanni didn't bleed him any more white than most of the buyers in the cannery district. He glanced around, spotting the first of the other porters shoving past a cart with a broken wheel. The porter saw him, and offered a grin. Aldo nodded, and turned back in time for Sanni to announce, "Six and a half. You want script or coral?"

"Coral," Aldo said. He'd get the full amount in script, but it could only be spent at the cannery's shops. They were overpriced. For over three hundred years, Vetticcians had used ducats, coins cut from rare coral as currency, and there wasn't a soul on the entire continent of Alddarri that wouldn't eagerly accept them.

Sanni nodded. He pulled the lockbox from its spot beneath the table, and fiddled with the cheap but effective lock. Aldo's eyes flickered down to the lock briefly. *Three tumblers, maybe two. Brass.* His fingers twitched slightly, but he pushed the thought aside. Lifting the battered wooden lid, Sanni peered inside and said, "I'm out of red. You okay with white?"

Aldo nodded, and Sanni counted out twenty six discs of bone white coral coins, pushing them across the table for Aldo to count as well. Sanni's eyes lingered on the handful of fishhook tattoos visible on Aldo's right wrist as he counted. Satisfied, Aldo stashed them in his leather purse, returning it to inside his stained tunic. "Time for one more batch?"

Sanni glanced back at the clock over the cannery door, and shook his head. "Ten minutes to shift change. Even you don't move that fast."

"I wouldn't bet against him." Aldo glanced over as Henri came through the netting flap, lifting his basket up on the table. "Evening, Aldo. You smell like shit."

"So do you, but I come by it honest."

Henri offered a toothy grin. "You want to grab a drink after Sanni robs me blind for one missplaced scale?"

"Did that scale fall off after you kicked these poor fish all the way up the gods-damned hill?" snapped the buyer, lifting up one smaller fish. "These look like they've been trampled."

"Plenty of good meat still. And, I don't stink like the greywater drains."

"I give a shit how you smell?" Sanni muttered a few curses, and returned to looking over the four fish Henri had dumped onto the table.

"So, that drink?" Henri asked Aldo. "I'm buying. Or are you babysitting tonight?"

Aldo snorted. "If you're buying, I can do both."

***

Aldo had once heard the term "an acquired taste" in reference to the fermented eel heads that were a popular snack with a certain type on the docks. With that said, he'd yet to meet anyone who'd managed the impressive task of actually acquiring a taste for green. He sniffed the wooden mug the bartender had set before him. It smelled of rotting fish, but no worse than usual, so he took a sip of the brackish dark green drink.

Aldo didn't know who had first come up with the idea of distilling liquor from the slimy seaweed that got caught in the rudders of the ships leaving Pallia Bay. While the unsettlingly viscous beverage lacked certain qualities, such as any flavor one might actually want to put in one's mouth, it was strong and cheap, the pair of which redeemed it enough to ensure a steady demand for the product down close to the docks.

Aldo took one more long, careful sniff. Everyone claimed to know someone who had gone blind from a contaminated batch. While Aldo had yet to make the acquaintance of such a tragic figure, it had almost become a tradition to check for a strong metallic scent peeking its way up through the odor of barnacles and decomposing carp.

"Are we safe?" Henri settled onto the crate that served as a bar stool next to Aldo. The older woman behind the bar scowled, but filled a mismatched mug with the same leaf-green elixir, setting it in front of Henri, who produced a grey coral disc with the air of a prestidigitator performing a miraculous illusion. She made it vanish with equal alacrity.

"We're drinking green. There's not all that much safe about it."

"I have other drinks," Mae said. Mae had been a fixture in the cannery district since Aldo was a child. Her bar tended to migrate somewhat. She was not blessed with the bloated bank account necessary to actually lay claim to a permanent spot, so instead, each night, she found an empty section of road close to the highest concentration of longshoremen with a few extra ducats, and constructed a bar out of the crates from which she pulled bottles of cheap booze.

Henri raised a dubious eyebrow at the woman. "Are they more potable than this swill?"

"I didn't say that. I just said I had other drinks."

"Are they cheaper?"

"Well now you're just being unreasonable."

"It's not bad," Aldo spoke up, taking a sip. He winced. "Okay, it's not worse than usual."

"A ringing endorsement," Henri said, toasting Mae and Aldo alike. Mae offered an obscene gesture in return.

Aldo had never asked Henri to get drinks, but that hadn't stopped the terminally cheerful man from asking Aldo. The first day Aldo had shown up to try to find day work on the docs, Henri had seemed determined to fill the position of Aldo's shadow, particularly once he'd spotted the twin rows of blue fishhooks tattooed on Aldo's scarred and muscled forearms.

He'd never said anything about them. Aldo had been warned of those who would go out of their way to demonstrate their lack of prejudice against those who'd served time on the penance barges, earning a fishhook on each anniversary of their arrival to the prison ships. But Henri had never been particularly offensive, and despite the fact that Aldo generally brought back more coin than he did, he seemed to have little issue paying for drinks.

Henri glanced up, making sure Mae was facing away, and pulled a small wax paper envelope from his sleeve. Aldo shook his head as he sprinkled the smallest amount of the grey dust into his drink, where it dissolved instantly.

"She's gonna kick your ass if she sees that."

"I'm getting drunk tonight. I'd rather do it with two drinks instead of ten." Henry returned the packet of powdered isleweed to his sleeve. The dried and crushed herb had little effect on its own, but combined with an alcoholic beverage, it intensified the intoxicating effects. Bartenders hated it. Drunks loved it.

"Another, Mae." Henri pushed another pair of ducats across the table.

"My thanks," Aldo said, tilting his mug towards the other man.

"Should be having you foot the bill," Henri said, his laughing eyes showing he wasn't serious. "How many runs did you pull today? Six? Seven?"

Aldo held the mug out for the viscous emerald pour. The liquid made the sound of a dead jellyfish plopping onto a soggy pier. "Nine."

"Nine." His friend shook his head. "Ever hear of such a thing, Mae? Nine runs?"

There is a school of thought that bartenders should offer counsel alongside cocktails, providing sage wisdom and a neutral listening ear. Mae's expression made it clear that if such a school existed, she had not only declined admission, but had done her level best to burn it to the ground and hang the bodies of the teachers as a warning to others. She grunted, and began polishing the plank of battered wood that served as a bar.

Undeterred, Henri waved his mug around while he continued to speak. "I got three runs today, and I mark that a day well spent."

"You know, you could show up a touch earlier," Aldo said.

"What a thoroughly horrible idea," Henri said, making a face. "I don't want to do more than three runs. Sure, maybe during the summer, when the weather isn't so much of a cod's asshole, I'll do four. Five if I'm feeling salty. But three is enough to fill my belly, pay for a flop, and ensure that I can contribute to Mae's long career of service with a smile."

Mae offered another gesture selected from her impressive lexicon of obscenity.

"See, right there. Think of the loss to the city, the blow to our cultural landscape should I abandon my patronage of this institution." Henri toasted to Mae's back. Glancing back at Aldo, he said, "I suppose this work is nothing, compared to..." He trailed off at Aldo's raised eyebrow, and cleared his throat. "Sorry."

Aldo shook his head. "It's fine." It wasn't, but Aldo had long since resigned himself to enduring the curiosity of anyone who hadn't spent time on a penance barge. "And yes. This is easier."

Any further discussion was interrupted by loud cursing behind them. A passing longshoreman glared at the pile of elbows and skinned knees that had just shoved past him and tumbled up to the bar between the two of them. Auggie grinned up at Aldo, showing crooked teeth and more freckles than seemed possible. "I was waiting for you."

"What about me?" Henri asked, offended.

The eleven-year old girl turned and considered him. "You gonna buy me dinner?"

"No, but it's nice to be noticed."

"Hey, there you are." Auggie turned back to Aldo. "How about it?"

"It's been three days since you turned up, Auggie," Aldo said, raising an eyebrow. "Where have you been?"

"Doing my best to make an honest living, follow your example. I found work." She leaned against his arm. "Hungry, hungry work."

He snorted, but asked, "Mae, what do you have tonight?"

"Not much," she said, peering into an open crate. "Dried cod, a bit of bread that's not too moldy. Zucchini. Had some clams, but they sold out by noon."

Auggie made a face. "I hate zucchini."

"Everyone hates zucchini," Aldo said. He slid a pair of coins across the table. "Whatever you can put together, Mae."

"And a drink?" Auggie asked hopefully.

"All the water from the drain barrel you can drink."

She made a face. "That's worse than the green."

"Proof positive you've never tasted green," Henri offered. He belched, and made a face. "Tastes worse coming up." He considered for a moment, and offered Auggie his cup. "Care to try?"

"Drain water sounds good," Auggie said, backing away as if he was holding a snake.

"So this work." Aldo tilted his head as spoke. "How illegal is it?"

Auggie shrugged. "Not like I can carry fish like you. The Sovrano always needs runners. Her capos have coin, I have legs."

Aldo shook his head. "I told you, nothing illegal. I'll keep you and your friends fed, but find honest work."

Mae snorted from behind the bar. "Aldo, no disrespect, it's noble as the sun what you do for those kids, but where are they going to find honest work that won't put them in a chum bucket?"

He glared at her. "Think honest work was what earned me these decorations? I'd rather end up chum then walk the deck again. Auggie's smart. She can do better than I did."

"I asked, Aldo, honest," Auggie said. "The fishing boats are full up. The cannery doesn't want kids. I go north of the district, some guardsman'll blacken my eye and slide me back down the greywater alley, and that's if he's cheerful." She hesitated, then stuffed her hand in her pocket, coming out with a strip of cloth the color of a summer sky. "I got the Sovrano's colors. Safer wearin' this than sticking my arms in the guts of the cannery."

"She's not wrong," Henri said. "Not like you and I would be ruining our knees carrying fish uphill if there were jobs to be found anywhere else. Given her size and general foul disposition, it's got to be near impossible for this little minnow."

"I learned a new word from Mae. Wanna hear it?" Auggie asked.

"Make sure you shout. It's a long way from all the way down there."

Auggie gestured in Henri's direction.

"Both fingers, Auggie."

"Mae, stop teaching her things." Aldo rubbed his forehead. "I don't like it."

"Even if I get pinched, it's three lashes." Auggie rolled her eyes. "Had worse at temple. Anyway, it's not like a foreman'll be gentler." Mae passed Auggie a pile of food on a scrap of paper, and the girl stuffed an improbably large chunk of salted cod in her mouth. Around the mouthful of food, she grinned up at Aldo. "Thanks."

Aldo watched her carry off the food, and muttered a curse. "I'll be back," he said, and rose to follow.

***

It wasn't easy to catch up with Auggie. The crowds in the streets had yet to begin to thin out, and the gangly girl darted around skirts and breeches alike, slipping in and out of Aldo's view. She had hidden the food in the folds of her cheap tunic, sneaking bites as often as she could. If she hadn't ducked into a narrow slit between a pair of warehouses, he wasn't sure that he'd have been able to reach her.

When he poked his head in, she was waiting, her young features rearranged into something she clearly meant to be ferocity. In her hand, she held a shard of broken pottery, half wrapped with strips of cloth.

Aldo raised an eyebrow when he saw her. "What the hell is that?"

"It's my knife."

"A knife," he said. "It's made from a piece of roof tile."

"Just means it'd be more embarrassing if I stuck you with it," she said, grinning as she lowered the chunk of fired clay.

"Fair enough."

"Why you chasing my wake, Aldo?"

"I wanted to talk to you."

"We did talk."

"I talked, but you didn't listen," he said. "This is important."

She rolled her eyes, but shrugged as she sat down, back to the wall, and pulled out her food. "I'm eating while you talk."

"That's fine." He stepped into the alley with her, but it was far too narrow for him to sit as well. Aldo pushed aside the discomfort at the tight spaces. "Auggie, running with the sovrano's crew..."

Her mouth was full of pickled zucchini, so she couldn't reply, but Auggie started shaking her head as soon as he began speaking.

"I know. It's not easy finding honest work."

She swallowed, wincing as the spices burned her tongue. "I hate zucchini." Smacking her lips, she looked up at him. "What do you want me to do? I told you. No one else is offerin' coral. Not less I want to end up on the Street of Shivers. Not sure even they'd take me."

Aldo blanched at the thought. "For your sake, I would hope not."

She toasted him with another piece of squash. "You've been good to me. Kept my belly going empty more days than not. But that doesn't give me a roof. Doesn't give me a new tunic when this one rips or starts to rot. Doesn't keep coral in my pocket for when the guild guard needs a bribe to let me be." Auggie shrugged. "I'm eleven. I have all my fingers. All my toes. I can work, and no one's gonna give me an inch if I don't. You know that."

Aldo scratched at his beard. "You remember when I first met you? You were hiding in the greywater alley. Ankle deep in shit, hiding from some house guard that was looking for the book you stole."

She grinned. "I was good at second story work."

"You were shit at second story work," he shot back. "You got into an artificer's shop. Of course, you set off every alarm they had. Broke a window. Grabbed the first thing you saw and ran."

"It was my first try!" Auggie said. "Besides, a book's worth more than a tidy stack."

Aldo nodded. "It was. But that's not my point. You remember what you were doing when I found you?"

Auggie lowered her eyes, not responding.

"You weren't looking for a place to stash the book," Aldo said. "You were reading it."

She stuffed the last bite of zucchini in her mouth. "So?" she mumbled.

"So?" Aldo raised his eyebrow. "Auggie, I can't read. Henri can't read. Ninety-nine out of one hundred people in this city can't read. You're eleven years old, and you can do something half the merchants in the Trade District can't do."

Auggie shook her head. "Barely. My momma didn't get to teach me more than a bit before the fever put her in the chum. Takes me forever to sound out the words. Don't know what half of them mean."

"That matters less than you might think," he said. "A few more years, a bit more practice, and you can find work. Real work. Away from the docks, away from the Nest. In the Trade or Artisan Districts, maybe even at one of the colleges. A few years proving your worth, you could even find an apprenticeship."

She made a face. "Ink-stained fingers and ledgers. Sounds boring."

"Get a bit older, you'll find the value in boring."

"Doubt it."

"Gods-dammit, Auggie," Aldo snapped, his voice echoing off the stone walls, and she looked up in shock at his tone. "I'm trying to tell you something. I need you to hear me."

To his surprise, she didn't argue.

"There was a time I thought I had a future at the colleges. A time where I was told by those who were meant to do right by me that I do something more than survive, day by day," He pulled up his sleeve, revealing the pale blue fishhook tattoos one by one. "Instead, this is what my future held. I wasn't much older than you when I got my first of these. Care to count them? You can read, surely that's not that far beyond you."

Her eyes darted from hook to hook. "You lived. You made it back."

"That future I had didn't," Aldo said. He meant for his voice to sound strict, but even he could hear the weariness beneath the words. "I spent fourteen years sick. Hurt. Starving." He held up his hands, his time on the penance barge mapped out in the scars on his hands. "Bleeding from the thousand bites the hooks took from my flesh. And most don't come back. Seven out of ten go into the cold black each year. There's always more to take their place. I don't want you to be among them."

Auggie stared at his hands, but shook her head. "You worry too much."

"And you don't worry enough," he said. "You're my friend, Auggie. You make me laugh, and that's not easy to do. You're funny, and you're smart. Smart enough to know that ink would serve you far better on your fingertips than under your skin."

She nodded. "I hear you."

"Do you?"

"I do, Aldo, honest. But it doesn't change anything."

"Auggie…"

"No one's gonna hire me to spend ten minutes sounding out each word," she said. "No one's gonna take time to teach me. You're the only one who actually cares. I don't know why. Not really, but I know you do, and it means a lot. But even if you're right, even if when I'm old and boring I can find that kind of work, that does nothing to fill my belly now."

Aldo snorted. "You've eaten more in this alley than I have in a week."

"You know what I mean." She pulled out the pale blue cloth. "You look out for me, but I can't ride your wake all day. I wear this, and I'm under the sovrano's colors. Laying hands on me is disrespecting her, and not many in the city'd think that a smart idea. I can earn coin." Auggie shrugged. "Maybe even get her people's help finding a job like you say once I'm old enough."

"I thought you said it was boring."

Auggie offered a toothy grin. "I didn't take these colors to get into trouble, Aldo, honest. I took them cause it's my best chance to stay out of it. Tell me I'm wrong."

Aldo ran his fingers through his hair, scowling. "I don't like it."

"And you can tell me that every time you buy me dinner."

"I thought you were going to be bringing home more coral than you could carry," he said.

"Free food tastes better."

He snorted. "You're impossible." Aldo rubbed his forehead. "Okay. If I can find you something, something that doesn't involve you breaking the law, will you consider it?"

Auggie nodded. "I got no interest in wearing shackles. You find me honest work for honest pay, I'll hand back the colors." She tilted her head. "You know someone?"

"Got a little coin. Maybe enough to win a friend or two," Aldo said. "Might take a bit. Just promise me you'll keep your head down, be careful."

She scrambled to her feet, and gave him a quick hug. "I promise, Aldo. Nothing bad's gonna happen."

***

"Something bad happened."

Henri blinked blearily, accepting the cup of strong tea and pressing a coin into the vendor's palm. "Aldo. It's just so gods-damned early."

Aldo counted up the cluster of children and teenagers milling about the cart, eyes darting between them. He scowled as his sixth count failed to reveal the freckled girl. "Uh, food and tea for twelve."

The vendor nodded, and began rolling fried dough and clams into scraps of paper. He'd been a regular at this pier since the first day Aldo dropped half of the previous day's pay feeding the group of hungry children that showed up.

"It's been four days." Aldo shook his head. "She's never missed breakfast. Not for the three months I've been here. And now four in a row?"

"So maybe she moved on." Henri winced as the steaming brew burned his tongue. "Headed to the trade district or the Nest. Maybe even the Ruins. It happens. She's not your kid, Aldo."

"I know that," Aldo snapped. "But no word at all? Not even a quick stop by to give you shit one last time?"

"Okay, yeah, that doesn't sound like Auggie." Henri blinked a few times, and said, "Oh. I forgot. After you left last night, someone came by asking for you."

"What does this have to do with Auggie?"

Henri shrugged. "Far as I know, nothing. She said she wanted to talk to you about a job."

"What did you say?"

"Oh, I told her your address, where you sling fish, a list of your greatest fears, you know, the basics." He snorted. "The fuck do you think? I told her you weren't there, and she was welcome to politely fuck off."

Aldo nodded. "Thanks." He scanned the children milling about, spotted a half dozen more, and passed the vendor the rest of the coin in his pocket. "If she moved on, fine. I get it. But I just want to know she's okay. Running with a sovrano's people..." He shook his head. "Auggie's far too good at finding trouble."

A younger child, waiting impatiently for his food, looked up. "You know Auggie?"

Aldo's eyes widened. "Yeah, we do. We're friends."

The boy couldn't be older than eight, with dirty blonde hair sticking in all directions. He gave them a dubious look. "You're old. Why would Auggie have old friends?"

"Don't worry about that. Do you know where she is?"

Sticking out a pudgy hand, the boy flashed a toothy grin. "Yup. Tell ya for a red."

"You've been standing in the sun too long," Henri snorted. "I could buy this cart for a..." His voice trailed off in shock as he watched Aldo drop fifty ducats in the boy's hand, the red coral coin disappearing in an eyeblink. "Aldo!"

Ignoring him, Aldo said, "Where is she?"

Eying the children around him nervously, the boy said, "She got pinched. Three nights ago. She's coming here, to the piers. Today."

Henri was still staring at Aldo, stunned, but that got through. "Wait. Why is she coming to the pier? Didn't they do the lashes at the adjudication?"

He shook his head. "Didn't get lashes. Got time. Two years. She'll be old like you when she's done."

Aldo didn't hear what Henri said. Blood thundered in his ears as he spun, scanning the waters of Pallia Bay. Dozens of fishing boats were heading out for the day's fishing, sails filling with the summer breeze blowing down from the hills. It took him a moment to see the one boat coming in. It was a bumboat, one of the flat, awkward rafts driven by an artificer fin used to transport goods and people from the fleet to the docs and back again. The bobbing boat was still about two miles away, but Aldo could easily see the red tunics of the men standing at the prow.

"Shit. SHIT!" The children all took a step back, and several onlookers turned to stare at Aldo's outburst. He spun toward the vendor. "The penance boat. Where does it pick up?"

"What?"

Stalking forward, Aldo grabbed the vendor by the shoulder, bodily spinning him around to face the water. The man squawked in protest, but Aldo pointed out towards the bumboat. "That boat. Which pier does it pick up at?"

"I don't know!"

"You've been here for weeks, overcharging me. Don't fucking tell me you don't know." The thick corded muscles in Aldo's forearm tightened along with his grip, and the vendor winced. "Where?"

"Uh, pier 224 or 225, I think!" The shorter man waved a hand to the west. "Next to the greywater drain!"

Aldo released him, and started in that direction, but Henri stepped in front of him, pushing him a few feet away. "Aldo, what the fuck are you doing?"

"I don't know. Something."

Henri shook his head. "Even if the kid is telling you the truth, it's done. That boat's twenty, maybe thirty minutes out. She's already in the stock wagon, on her way down here now. There's nothing you can do."

"You don't know that."

"The fucking thing is locked!" Henri snapped. "Not to mention the fucking guards, neither of which have a key! You're going to get yourself sent back out there too, and it's not going to do a gods-damned thing for Auggie!"

"Then she'll have fucking company," Aldo said, his voice hard, shoving Henri out of the way. His friend spilled back onto the ground, spilling his tea. A burst of guilt flashed through Aldo, but he pushed it aside, and began to run.

Okay, now what?

Aldo ran through the morning crowd, ignoring the curses and objections from those he bumped. It took nearly five minutes before he smelled the greywater drain dumping the offal from a city into the bay. Coming to a halt, he clenched his fists as he swung his head from side to side, searching for anything to yield inspiration.

Think, asshole, think.

Closing his eyes for a moment, Aldo imagined himself rising up off the worn cobblestones, high above the warehouses and alleys, far into the sky, until looking down on the city from above. He saw the greywater alley he used to save time, running a block west of the main road running through the heart of the cannery district, tracing a straight line down to the piers. He took in the pots loaded with squash and tomatoes crowding the rooftops, the vendors shouting out to bleary-eyed longshoremen making their way to the piers for their first run, clutching their canvas...

His eyes snapped open.

That's a really fucking bad plan. A voice from his past swam up in his head. *But at least it's a plan.*

Aldo pushed through a cluster of people, running the block to the familiar iron grating at the mouth of the alley. Without the rain, the stink of the flowing sewage made him gag, and his boots squished with every step, but he ran, heart thudding in his chest and nausea blooming in his gut by the time he burst out of the alley five minutes later.

Saani was still setting up for the day, stringing the nets up, when Aldo ran up to him. "Fuck off. I know the boats haven't started..." He wrinkled his nose, and turned to stare at Aldo. "I know I said I didn't care how you smelled, but that's foul."

"Are you selling rot today?"

"What, you don't smell bad enough?"

Aldo resisted the urge to grab the buyer by his stained lapels. "Rot. Are you selling?"

"Yeah." Saani pointed over towards the front of the cannery, where small casks were being stacked. "You're taking up farming now?"

"How much?"

"You don't own a flat. The fuck you need rot for?"

Aldo pulled out his purse, and dug out a pair of coins. "If you tell me you're making more than twenty a cask, I'll call you a fucking liar. Here's 25. I need one."

Saani paused. "Forty."

"Fine."

Saani raised an eyebrow, but took the coins. "Grab one and go. Don't use too much, you'll burn the roots."

Aldo ignored him, running over and picking up the first cask he reached. The wood was cheap. The canneries bought warped and cracked casks from the assorted distilleries throughout the city, ones that were no longer fit to age spirits. The cask was covered in a thin layer of beeswax, sealing the noxious contents from the outside world.

Saani asked him a question, but Aldo was already running back down the alley. As soon as he'd stepped through, he muttered a curse under his breath. *Too fast. Too gods-damned fast.* He was making mistakes, acting oddly, drawing attention.

"Not like I have a fucking choice," he said under his breath.

You do. You're just picking the stupidest option.

His eyes darted from building to building. Many of the warehouses lining the main road were two or three stories tall, and while storage and flats on the highest floors tended to be cheaper, they also ran the risk should a fire break out. As such, residents often had a rope coiled up near a window to allow a quick exit. Most were neatly tied. However, occasionally neglect or simple apathy meant that they didn't haul it back up after dropping it.

You hope.

He'd passed three buildings, his stomach sinking as he saw rope after rope neatly bundled and tied thirty feet above his head, but finally, he spotted a thick hempen rope, the end soaking in the noxious flow in the greywater alley, extending up to the roof. Rushing over, he pushed aside his nausea and fished the end of the line out, wrapping the end four times around the cask and tying a knot as tight as he could. Taking a deep breath, he grabbed hold of the rope and began clambering up.

It had been months since Aldo had been forced to climb lines. But he quickly found his muscles remembered the grip, and without a heaving deck and blowing rain doing their best to loose his grip and send him tumbling into roiling black water, he quickly scaled, pulling himself up to the third story roof. Grabbing the ledge, he pulled himself up just enough to peer over, scanning for any occupants that he might be disturbing. The good news was that the rooftop was absent any company.

The bad news was why.

Very slowly, Aldo pulled himself up, squeezing into the space between two of the dozens of hives that packed the rooftop. Fat yellow honeybees bobbed drunkenly in the air around his head, and a pair lit on his arm. When he saw their coloring, he let out a long breath. There were thousands of apiaries on rooftops throughout the city, with several different breeds. The honeybees were the most amiable.

Slowly, as a few curious bees buzzed around his head, he pulled up his cargo. He tried not to think about whether he was too late, whether he'd run to the other edge of the roof and see the back of the stockwagon disappearing far down the road, nearly to the pier already. When he thought about it, it made him want to rush. The cask knocking softly against the building's side combined with the growing number of curious bees made it clear that would be a poor choice.

When he had the cask in hand, he quickly untied it, and stepped gently between the hives to reach the other side. Leaning over the edge, he looked down at the street below. The first few longshoremen had already begun their morning trudge towards the cannery, while carts and tents were being set up for the day's commerce. Aldo could count fewer than ten people in the area beneath him.

"Make way!"

The cry drew his attention in a heartbeat, and Aldo spotted the stock wagon less than two hundred feet away. The wagon was heavy, the iron bands cradling it above the wheels straining. Normally, that would be an indication of heavy cargo, but Aldo knew that wasn't the case. Instead, the stock wagon traded thin pine planks for heavy banded oak walls. There were no windows, and the only door was barred, a heavy lock bouncing off the outside with a steady, rhythmic thudding sound.

At the front of the stock wagon, a pair of guild guards sat, reins in hand, loudly calling out to give people the chance to step out of the way of the heavy prison transport. Two other men in studded leather armor walked alongside, scanning the crowd with hard eyes. Their half-spears were in their hand, short two-foot lengths of hickory topped with eighteen inches of sharpened black iron. People gave the vehicle a wide berth.

"Okay." Aldo took several quick rapid breaths, took in as much air as he could, and held his breath as he pulled a cheap dagger from his pocket and began prying at the lid of the cask. Between the wax and the nails, it stubbornly refused his attentions for a few moments, but finally the wood gave way with a creak, and the lid popped off.

The canneries of Vetticci were tasked with processing thousands of pounds of fish daily, chopping them up, laying the chunks in beds of salt, and sealing the dried cod and mackerel into tin cans. They were also famous for not wasting a single bit of the fish. Heads, tails, and bones were shredded and sold as chum to the fishing boats heading out to ply their fortunes in the crowded waters.

The blood and organs, however, were set aside for weeks in huge sealed vats to ferment. The resulting sludge was known as rot, and was a rich fertilizer. In a city of five million people with a distinct lack of cattle, being able to stir the rot into the countless pots from which vegetables were grown was invaluable. However, for two reasons, it was sealed in a waxed cask until used.

The first reason was the smell. Even holding his breath, the scent of putrefaction and fermentation clawed its way into his nose, and the bees around him promptly departed to find their fortunes in less aromatic environments. The second reason...

You know how stupid this is, right?

Yup.

Aldo grabbed the cask, and swung it in a flat arc, sending the noxious blended offal in a wide arc to rain down over the street. Several vendors and passersby cried out in disgust as it splattered over them, but the majority of the contents splashed over the wagon, the guards, and the horses. The men cried out, pawing at their eyes as the stinking mixture streaked down their face and clothes, and the horses whinnied and stomped, tossing their heads and sending sheets of yellowing rot splattering out. The guards had only a few moments to try to wipe their faces clean before the first squawk.

At first, it was only two or three gulls swooping down, drawn by the pungent aroma, but within five seconds, hundreds of the black-winged birds came flying in from all directions, their screeching drowning out the cries of the guards. They snapped at the putrescent mixture, their beaks darting out and drawing scarlet lines wherever they struck horse or man. Screaming erupted from all directions as people broke for any cover nearby, waving their hands frantically overhead to try to beat back the shrieking mass of gulls.

The horses were well trained. They'd clearly been distraught when the rot had splashed over them, but they'd held steady. Whatever breeding or training allowed them to do so shattered like glass under a hammer. On of the black horses reared up, an otherworldly scream exploding between teeth that snapped at the impossible swarm, and the entire wagon jolted hard to the side.

The drivers, which had released the reins to shield their eyes, were nearly thrown off. One of the pair was older than his companion, and at the sudden motion, involuntarily reached out to grab the reins. Before he realized his mistake, an orange beak snapped shut on his eyebrow, ripping a small gobbet of flesh free, and as he clamped his hand back over the bloody wound, the horses burst into a gallop. Both he and his companion went tumbling over the side, and to his horror, Aldo saw the younger fall under the wagon's wheels.

The vehicle jolted up as it rolled over the guard's hip. The horses each chose a different direction to flee, and the sound of splintering wood punched through the symphony of shrieking birds and screaming men. The front right wheel broke free, and the entire wagon rolled to the side, obliterating at least a dozen birds in a deafening crash.

Aldo was already moving, throwing the rope over the side of the building and clambering down. Miraculously, he somehow had avoided the rot spilling on him or his clothes, but as he ran up to the wrecked wagon, he plunged into the cloud of bloody feathers and snapping beaks. It was chaos. He could make out several people curled up on the ground, covering their faces as best they could as birds drew bloody furrows over their flesh and tore at clothes soaked with the fermented offal.

Aldo kept an arm up, shielding his eyes, but while wings beat at his head and several nips tugged at his clothing, he wasn't what the swarm had gone feral for. He climbed up onto the wrecked wagon, muttering a quick prayer of thanks that it hadn't fallen the other way. The wood was scratched and splattered with both blood and white shit, but he found the lock, gritted his teeth, and focused.

It had been a long time.

The lock fell open in his hand.

He threw the heavy lock to the side, and ripped the bar free. As soon as he did, the door came flying open, smashing into his knees and throwing him back off the wagon to crash down to the cobblestones. A seagull wasn't quite quick enough, and he felt a sickening crunch beneath his back. His head bounced off the stones, and lights popped in Aldo's vision. Through whirling birds and blurred vision, he saw a burly man, pull himself from the open door.

The first man out of the wagon cursed wildly at the chaos, leaping down and running through the swarm, waving his arms wildly to disappear. The second person out was also a man, thin and lanky, but his wild eyes fixed on Aldo. Unlike the first man, his wrists were shackled with heavy iron bracelets, and he jumped down, his knee coming down hard on Aldo's gut. Aldo gasped, and the thin man drove the chain linking his fists into Aldo's throat, choking him.

"The key. Where's the key?" Aldo could barely make out the words over the din, but shook his head violently. That was apparently the wrong response. "Fucking guild bastard," he snarled, pressing down until Aldo couldn't draw breath. Aldo beat at him weakly, but between the blow to his head and the man's position, it did no good.

Black began to creep in on the edge of his vision. He couldn't see past the bloodshot eyes glaring down on him, the rough iron digging deep into his throat, couldn't tell if Auggie was free, if she was safe, but in an instant, the weight was gone, and Aldo choked air in desperate gasps. He rose up and saw Auggie bring the fist-sized rock down twice more onto the now insensate man's skull before throwing it aside. She spun to Aldo, and yelled his name.

Aldo struggled to his feet, his throat howling, and croaked out, "We have to run!"

Auggie nodded, grabbed his hand, and the pair took off running, leaving the wreckage and din behind. It took several blocks before the noise faded, and Aldo nodded towards a dark alley, barely big enough for the two of them to squeeze into. He grabbed her shoulders. "Are you okay?!"

Auggie's hair was streaked with gull shit, and there was a cut above her eyebrow oozing blood, but she nodded. She opened her mouth to say something, but Aldo saw her eyes shift to over his shoulder and widen. She shouted his name, but before he could turn, a hood dropped over his head and face, plunging his world into blackness. He lashed out behind him, but strong hands seized his wrist, twisting it painfully behind his back, and a sharp chemical scent filled his nostrils. Moments later, his world went dark.

Chapter 3

When he woke, his hands weren't bound. The hood was gone,
Aldo found himself slumped in a wooden chair, sitting before a pub table. He pushed himself up and looked around, blinking
the chemical sting that lingered in his eyes.

"Sorry about the hood and all that." To his left, a tall man with bone
white skin and pink eyes leaned against a polished bar. He had a small
knife out, and was cleaning under his nails. When he spoke, his voice
was cracked and high-pitched. He was smiling at Aldo, but it didn't
touch his eyes.

Aldo didn't say anything, but slowly took in his surroundings.
He was in a pub, but of a quality that he'd never set foot in before.
The floor was shining parquetry, and oil lanterns lined the walls. The
collection of the bottles behind the bar included wines, brandy, and
whiskey, and Aldo was certain that green would not be permitted to
come within a thousand yards of a place like this.

He also noted the lack of any windows.

Behind the bar, a short plump woman polished a pair of crystal
glasses. She'd turned when her companion had spoken, and her eyes
lit up. "Ah! Welcome back, Aldo." She set down a glass, and poured
crystal clear water. To his shock, she plucked a chunk of ice from
somewhere beneath the bar, and slid it forward. "Stop picking at your

nails and get the poor man a drink, Speaker." She offered a warm smile. "The insomnia hoods do make the eyes and throat burn. Water helps the latter. Cooler the better."

The man she'd called Speaker brought it over, and held it just out of reach, forcing him to lean forward to accept it. He watched Aldo with unblinking eyes the color of bloody meat. Aldo had never seen the like.

"Where's Auggie?" His voice was raw, and he sipped at the water.

The woman pointed behind him. A long bench ran the length of the wall. Auggie was sprawled on it, sleeping beneath a wool blanket. "Afraid with her slight build, it'll take a bit longer for the hood to wear off. She'll be all right, though."

"Will she." Aldo started to rise to his feet. He froze as the tip of a length of blackened steel kissed his cheek. He hadn't seen Speaker move.

"We should talk, Aldo." She set the cloth and the other glass on the bar, and came around to pull a chair across from him. Speaker was a statue, unblinking. "First, introductions. My name is Lia Parvotti."

The temperature in the room dropped nearly ten degrees. Aldo swallowed, and sat back in his chair. "You're the Sovrano of the Ruins."

She nodded, offering a slight smile.

That fucked you right through the breeches, didn't it?

The city of Vetticci was ruled by the Five Families, representing the wealthiest handful of the city's elite. Just below them in power was the peerage, a few hundred families who had access to the kind of money to make numbers meaningless. They dictated Vetticcian trade policy, diplomacy, extended guild contracts, set tax rates, and made law for the nearly five million people that made up the massive city. But in the slums and tenements that surrounded Pallia Bay, the sovranos held sway. Where the Families used coin to exert their will, the sovranos bought their power with blood.

"This is my adjutant, Speaker Birch. He's here to make sure you stay calm."

"I'm calm."

"I appreciate the assertion, Aldo, but you acted quite impulsively this morning," she said in a gently chiding voice. "Until I'm certain that was a momentary lapse and not a character flaw, I do believe Speaker will remain."

"I wouldn't have had to be impulsive if your colors meant anything," he snapped, before he could stop himself. "Auggie was wearing them when she got pinched."

Speaker giggled, a high-pitched titter that made Aldo's skin crawl. "He's funny." He slid the blade back into his jacket.

"He's angry."

"That too."

Parvotti nodded. "It's a fair criticism. Your young friend was supposed to be running messages. Two of my more foolhardy boys thought she'd be less likely to draw attention running a pound of Dezma powder to the artisan district. Told her I'd issued the command as a test. I had not."

Aldo shut his eyes briefly. "That's why they gave her time." The spines from the Dezma urchins that carpeted the bottom of the bay could numb the skin for stitches and surgery. But when it was discovered that the venom could be extracted and concentrated, it left thousands across the city addicted to the silvery powder. Even possessing Dezma powder was illegal.

"Indeed."

"Those two should have stood for her at the adjudication. Bought her time."

"That would be difficult," she said, her tone mild. "They're in chum buckets on one of my fishing boats. And your friend was going to be handled." Parvotti gestured at Speaker. "At the time you were drawing every hungry bird for miles, my friend here was negotiating to purchase her release. She would have been on the barge for a week, maybe two before she was back home."

"Do you know how many things can go wrong in a week out there?" Aldo could feel Speaker's eyes on him, but his anger punched past his caution. "If you'd ever spent a day on deck, you wouldn't think that a solution."

"It's certainly a better option than ambushing a prison transport," Speaker said.

"Aldo, however you feel about what happened to Auggie, that's not why we're here. You took a small problem, planted it in the soil, and grew a giant fucking headache for me and mine," Parvotti said, her voice growing a bit harder. She pulled a small piece of paper from a pocket, as well as a pair of spectacles with mother-of-pearl frames. Peering down at her notes, she said, "Three guards from the Bronattas Escort Guild with injuries. One will most likely never walk again. Sixteen Vetticcian citizens injured. Two horses injured. And three prisoners escaped."

Leaning forward, Parvotti said, "That's the real surprise. You pulled our young friend out of that wagon, but the two men riding with her were not young juveniles led astray. They're dangerous men, and it's going to cost blood and screams to bring them to heel."

She held up the paper. "Do you know what this is, Aldo? This is an invoice. A very, very expensive invoice, and one that the Bronattas fully intend to collect. In fact, they've offered a tidy stack of coral to whoever hands over the parties responsible."

Aldo shook his head. "I didn't mean for any of that to happen. I just wanted to keep Auggie off the barge."

"What you meant when you cast the line and what you pull from the water are often very different." She considered him. "The annoying part is that your plan was oddly brilliant. If you'd actually given it more thought, I have no doubt that you could have figured a way to spirit your friend away without laying waste to an entire block of the cannery district."

"So why am I still here? Why are either of us?" Aldo asked. "You could hand us over, make a nice turn for the day, and earn favor with a guild. Wouldn't cost you a thing."

"Another interested party has need of your services. They've asked me to broker a deal. I've agreed." Standing up, Parvotti said, "Say yes."

"It doesn't sound as if I have much of a choice," Aldo said.

"Life is nothing but choices." She headed towards the door. "But either you leave with my new friend, or you leave with my old one."

***

Speaker Birch didn't follow his employer out of the bar. Instead, he plopped down in a chair, and called out, "Come on in, then!"

The door Parvotti had just left opened once more, and Aldo turned to face the woman who stepped through. His eyes widened. She was tall, at least a handspan over him, and wore a sleeveless leather tunic that left her thickly muscled arms bare. She wore the close cropped hair of a guild mercenary, but Aldo saw none of the tattoos that would accompany such a posting. A rapier hung from her hip, the driftwood hilt worn and faded.

She nodded at Aldo, and glanced over at Speaker. "I appreciate the sovrano's assistance, but I'd like to speak with Aldo alone."

"Would you." He didn't look up at her.

"I would."

"Hmmm." Speaker blinked slowly, like a snake eying a mouse. He seemed to weigh the options, but finally rose to his feet, his long limbs unfolding from the chair. "Deal was, if he chooses not to help you, I get to deal with him as I see fit. Not quite sure how I'll know what my schedule for today looks like if I'm not here to see his response."

"There's one way out of this place," the woman said, her voice taking a hard edge. "You're welcome to wait outside, but an audience wasn't part of the arrangement."

Speaker smiled, a wide toothy grin, and gave an exaggerated bow. "You and he walk out that door together, I'll go find lunch. Either of you walk out alone, we go another way." He glanced at Aldo. "Makes no difference to me which way you go. Savvy?"

"He gets it." She jerked her head. "Now get the fuck out."

His smile was unwavering as he walked past, closing the door behind him. The woman swallowed, and said, "Not sure I like that man."

"Might be a poor choice of a business partner, then," Aldo said. "I know you?"

She shook her head. "I tried coming to see you last night, at that knockdown pub your friend was at. I was planning to try to find you at the docks today, but things went a bit sideways." She offered her hand. "My name is Nicolette Saffman. I have a proposal for you."

Aldo didn't take the hand. "A proposal?" He shook his head. "No, see a proposal involves sitting down across a table, having a drink, discussing terms, all of that. But the most important aspect is the ability to say no, and you've cut that line quite neatly. This is an ultimatum."

Nicolette narrowed her eyes. "I didn't put you in this situation. And if I hadn't shown up, you honestly think you'd be here right now? Or do you think it more likely that pasty gentleman with bloody eyes would have already put you in a bucket or back on a barge?"

"You may not have created the problem, but you're damn sure willing to take advantage of it," Aldo snapped.

"We're Vetticcian. If we're not looking for the angle, we're not fucking breathing."

"Poetic. Now how about you turn that tongue to telling me what you want from me?"

She gritted her teeth. "This isn't how I wanted to do this." Nicolette ran a finger through her short hair. "I've been contracted to do a job. I need your help. The job pays. A lot."

"I'm actually going to get paid?"

"Even split."

"Of how much?"

"Eight hundred white coral."

Aldo snorted. "Tell me another one."

Nicolette raised an eyebrow, but said nothing. Aldo's eyes widened.

"Eight hundred thousand ducats. You could hire an entire guild-insured crew for that," he said. "Gods, you could contract an Iron Eye battalion for a fucking week."

"I know," she said. "They can't help me. You can."

"Who the fuck is your bankroll?" Aldo didn't expect an answer, and was surprised when he got one.

"Toni DeLuca."

"Fuck you."

Nicolette grinned. "I take it you know the name?"

"Spent fourteen gods-damned years on a boat with that name on the hull." Aldo said. "They own half the city."

"That's an exaggeration." She shrugged. "At best, five percent. More than enough that this payout won't make too much of a dent in their accounts."

Gods, Aldo. What the fuck did you walk into? "Okay." He nodded slowly as he walked to a table. "I think you're full of chum, but given I only get to keep a pulse as long as you're happy with me, why don't you tell me about this job." *Until I can figure out how you're trying to fuck me.*

"Not the rousing enthusiasm I'd hoped for, but it's a start." She sat down across from him. "First, just a quick confirmation. You are Aldo Marini, correct?"

He nodded, and she said, "The same Aldo Marini who served a fourteen year sentence on a penance barge for the charges of burglary and theft?"

"You're truly terrible at introductions."

"I'm not judging, but I need to be sure. Aldo's not exactly a common name, but there's more than a few of you scampering about the city."

"What happens if I'm not who you're looking for?"

"I'd imagine an awkward conversation with the sovrano."

Sighing, he pushed up his sleeve, displaying his tattoos. She raised an eyebrow, but nodded. "That works."

"If you know how many fishhooks I have, you should know that I'm not particularly eager to earn any more."

"I don't blame you," she said. "Not that I have any experience to bring to that particular discussion, but the few stories I've heard about the barges do not recommend it as a vocational pursuit." She shrugged. "The good news is, there's no risk of you going back to the barges from this job."

"Everyone says that," Aldo scoffed. "The people grows fat on fish pulled from the water from those who had the perfect plan."

Nicolette shook her head. "Oh, my plan's not perfect. It's pretty good. But it's not perfect."

"Then how can you say that there's no risk..."

"It's not in Vetticci."

Aldo raised an eyebrow. "It's outside the city?" She nodded, and he asked, "Where?"

"North. The Dominion."

Aldo came to a halt. "The Dominion."

"Big country? Lots of farms, between us and the Breaking?"

"I know what it is." He shook his head. "They hang people in the Dominion."

"Yes, but they don't have penance barges."

He blinked. "You might be insane."

"Would I know if I was?"

"What's the job?"

"A ranch. Cattle," she said.

"We're stealing a cow?"

"I'm not that strong. The package is small, easy to carry. It just happens to be in a cold storage room. At the center of the ranch, in a cave with one entrance that's locked quite securely."

"What kind of lock?"

She shrugged. "Fairly standard. It's Vetticcian, I know that. Probably College-made. But nothing too fancy. The problem isn't the lock. Well, the lock's a problem, but it's not the big one."

"What's the problem?" Aldo asked.

"The sixty guards and thirty scent hounds they use for security."

Aldo's eyes widened. "How the hell does a cattle ranch afford a small army for security?"

"Careful budgeting, I assume," She pulled a flask from a pocket, and took a drink. She offered it to Aldo, who shook his head. Shrugging, she put it away before continuing. "I've seen the ranch a few times now. I'm good at this, Aldo. It's what I do. I've plotted out near a dozen jobs in my time, come out clean from every one. But I can't figure out a way to pull off the job without someone on the inside, working on the guard force."

She tilted a head towards Aldo. "That would be you. We get you a job with the guard, that gives you access to the cold storage. Considering what earned you a place on that boat you're so eager not to return to, I don't expect the lock to pose much of a challenge."

"Wait." Aldo raised an eyebrow. "You want me to get hired on as a guard."

"Yes."

"Oh, sure." Aldo nodded. "Makes perfect sense. What professional guard force wouldn't want to hire a man with no experience, no training, and a conviction for theft?"

She grinned at him. "I have thought about that. But you have a connection."

"I have a connection? What does that mean?"

"You know the guard captain."

He shook his head. "No, I don't."

"I'm fairly sure you do."

Aldo stood up, and went behind the bar. "What do you think the odds are that the sovrano would be mad at me taking a drink?"

"I'll leave coin for it."

He selected a bottle off the shelf that looked expensive, and filled a glass. It felt odd in his hands. There wasn't much glass in the city. He held it carefully as he returned to his seat.

"Look, I don't know what you've heard. But I don't have any connections," Aldo said. "I got sent to the barge when I was fourteen. Given the depressing survival rate, I didn't form any lasting friendships. I've been out for six months. The only people I know are longshoremen and a bartender who doesn't overcharge for her terrible liquor. If someone owed me, I would have cashed that in. You've got the wrong guy."

"You'd better hope not," she said. "If I do, we're both in a world of hurt, although you a touch more than me." She considered him. "You really that eager to go back to hauling fish?"

"It's a good job."

"It's carrying heavy, stinking fish in the hot sun for hours on end."

"It's honest work. Plus, it's a hell of a lot easier than my last job."

"Fair," she said. "But you're wrong. Someone does owe you. Owes you big. And that someone is currently the captain of the Vorchese ranch guard force." She tilted her head. "His name is Stiliano Marini."

The strength bled out of Aldo's legs in a heartbeat, and he gripped the bar to keep from losing his footing as the blood thundered in his head. He shut his eyes for a moment. Aldo was certain that if the big woman had buried her fist in his stomach, it would not have hit as hard as those words. His hands were shaking as he slowly set down the glass. "He's alive?"

She nodded. "He is."

"You're sure?"

"I've shaken his hand. Last month."

He ran trembling fingers through his hair as she silently let him come to terms with what he said. Aldo shut his eyes for a moment, remembering his own panicked breathing as he waited for a door to open, to hear a voice that never came. He took a deep breath. "I can't."

"He owes you," she said. "I don't know everything that went down when you got caught, but even the bits and pieces I've managed to gather... He owes you big."

"You don't understand." *A hard voice and a crashing gavel. "Total penalty assayed, one hundred seventy months."* He pushed the memory deep down.

"He's your father."

"The fact that you think that matters a single solitary shit means you really don't understand."

"Maybe not. But I can understand the reality of where you're sitting. Even if you weren't in the sovrano's bad books, it's not going to take long for the guild to send a sniffer. They'll ask around, put coin in hands," Nicolette shook her head. "Your plan was creative, but it was rushed. How many people saw you running like a shark was on your ass? How long before they talk to someone who knows you, who saw you buy that shit you dumped?"

Aldo muttered a curse. "Saani."

"Who's that?"

"The buyer. The one I bought the rot from," he said. "He knows me. Knows I bought it ten minutes before..."

"Is he loyal to you?"

"Is anyone?"

Nicolette spread her hands. "What I'm saying. Even if you walk out of here alive, you've got a day, maybe two, before the guild knows your name. That transport was insured. You know what that means."

"Few months, they'll move on."

"You confident you can stay hidden that long? From a guild sniffer?"

Aldo took a long drink in lieu of a response.

"What I'm saying," Nicolette said. "You need to get away from the docks. Preferably, out of the city."

"And I suppose you can help with that," Aldo said.

"Hadn't planned on doing the job from here," she replied. "I've already arranged for transport in a trade convoy heading north. Paid for two, in the optimistic if apparently foolhardy belief that you'd be interested in the job."

"Let me guess. I just have to say yes." He eyed the woman carefully. "This worked out well for you, didn't it?"

She blinked twice, then scowled. "Congratulations, you've seen through my diabolical plan. I managed to convince a child I've never met to get scammed by a pair of peers all in the hopes that you would end up leaving a city block in ruins with a cask of rotting fish and your lack of impulse control." Nicolette shook her head. "The inside of your skull must be a terrifying place. I'm offering you a way out of the pit you dug for yourself."

"And furthering your own interests at the same time."

"Fucking right I am. And if you were in my shoes, you'd do the same gods-damned thing."

Aldo wanted to argue the point. He couldn't find an angle. "I really fucked this up."

Her glare softened. "You've had a bad day."

"Can't remember my last good one."

"Yeah." Nicolette tapped her fingers against the tabletop for a moment. "Look, I don't feel good about strong-arming you into this. I really don't want to step into a job this dangerous with you looking to bury a knife in my back. So here's the deal. I paid for two people on a Iron Eye-escorted convoy heading north. Let's walk out, and tell that barracuda in a skin suit out there that we're happy partners, that you're completely on board. Come with me. Get out of the city, at least for a while. Long enough that you fall off the guild's radar."

He raised an eyebrow. "And then?"

She leaned forward. "Give me a chance to pitch the job. It's a two day trip to get through the Myre and to Lofland Fork. Once we're there, if you're not convinced, you can be on your way. You'll be out of Vetticci. You can find work in Lofland Fork, or make your way to one of the farms. You'll be poor, but at least you'll be safe."

He stared at her. "Why would you do that? You have me over the fucking yardarm. If you walk away, I'm dead."

"Because if there's any chance you're going to say yes to this job, you and I have to trust each other. If our professional relationship kicks off with me blackmailing you into helping me, that's never going to happen." Leaning forward, she said, "I don't know what happened between you and your father. Considering you ended up spending over a dozen years pulling fish out of the sea when you were fourteen, I'm guessing it was nothing good. I'm not asking you to reconcile, to forgive him for whatever it was he did. But this is a chance for you to be done with all of it. The docks, the sovranos, your father, me, hell, Vetticci. Once this job is done, you can disappear. Live whatever kind of life you want."

Aldo didn't say anything for quite a while, and Nicolette was smart enough not to press him. She stood up, stretching as she looked around the room. As she looked over the bottles behind the bar, he said, "I'm not saying yes."

She glanced back over her shoulder, and Aldo said, "But you're right. I need to get away from here before they find me again. And I'm not saying yes, but I'm willing to hear a bit more."

Nicolette held up her hands. "That's all I'm asking."

"I have a request." He nodded towards Auggie, who was still sleeping. "We have to get her out of the city too. They'll already be hunting for her. She's an escaped convict, with a price on her head. Lofland Fork, you've been there?"

"Several times."

"Think we could find a place for her?"

She nodded slowly. "Between you and me, I think we could put together enough coral to buy her an apprenticeship with someone. Set her up for a life. Won't be exciting, but..."

"She'll hate it," he said, and Nicolette chuckled. "You didn't say."

"Say what?"

"You just told me where and that my father was involved. You didn't tell me what we're stealing."

Nicolette nodded. "I was going to get to that." She stepped forward, and offered her hand. "Do we have a deal?"

Aldo shook her hand.

"Do you need anything from your place? I wouldn't suggest going back there, but maybe we could have someone break in."

Aldo shook his head. "I keep my money on me. Nothing else worth going back for."

"You have an account?"

He snorted. "I have about eighty ducats to my name. Don't think that's enough to walk through the Bank's door."

She grinned. "When this job is done, they'll come to your door."

He shook his head. "And you're serious. Eight hundred thousand."

"Four hundred is your share."

"What in the gods are we stealing?"

"Bull semen," she said. "You ready to go?"

Chapter 4

The city of Vetticci had been established nearly thirteen hundred years before Aldo made the somewhat unfortunate decision to rain fermented offal on a prison transport. During that time, it had experienced its share of upheavals, both natural and self-inflicted, but the one ignominy that it had yet to endure was that of invasion. While several mercenary guilds and city guard contractors had, on occasion, claimed responsibility for the city's apparent invulnerability, no one took them too seriously. They knew it was the Myre.

The tangled, massive woods that surrounded the city on all sides not occupied by shoreline was a fixture in every story, play, or song that came out of Vetticci. A hundred miles wide at its narrowest point, there was very little actually known about the Myre save for the snippets of rumor and information that came from those who had attempted to explore it, the few of which actually returned with enough information to publish and enough blood remaining in their bruised and lacerated bodies to allow them to live long enough to do so.

Indeed, one of the proudest achievements in Vetticci history was the successful construction of the Myre Road, a narrow, winding path that stretched from the walls of the city through the dense woods, reaching all the way up across the border with the Dominion. The

Myre Road had become a lifeline for not just Vetticcians, but for anyone outside the city who had business with the families or the Bank of Vetticci, which was to say, everyone. The road was always packed full of convoys bearing currency shipments and luxury goods north, with wagons sagging under the weight of grain, fruit, and meat creaking their way south. It was among the number of one of these northbound convoys that Aldo Marini and Nicolette Saffman rode, although their particular method of conveyance was proving difficult.

"The caravan master said that it was less about steering him and more about understanding him," Nicolette offered, not for the first time.

Not for the first time, Aldo extended several fingers in a gesture certain to trigger a brawl back in Mae's.

"You yelled at me when I did that," Auggie offered from the back. She sat between two bolts of cloth, a length of blue silk wrapped around her face. Nicolette had been certain that the convoy escorts wouldn't betray her presence there.

"There's no understanding this monstrosity," Aldo said, his forearms burning from the effort of yanking the reins one way or another. "I'm almost certain that walking would have been preferable. You couldn't have found a horse?"

Nicolette nodded cheerfully. "It's Vetticci. I could have found you a Suviveian yak to ride if we needed one. But we didn't need one, horses cost more than a small ship, and Edgar here is doing just fine." She leaned over to pat her donkey on the neck. He brayed softly, but continued plodding forward at a steady pace. "Besides, the last time you were near horses, it didn't go well."

Aldo had seen Edgar respond well to such physical affection, and had thought that perhaps Stuart, his steed for the journey north, would enjoy a nice pat as well. Stuart nearly bit off his fingers. Currently, the donkey was gnawing at the corner of the wagon they were meant to be riding alongside, screaming at any of the occupants who tried to dissuade him. Aldo was well aware that donkeys did not scream, they brayed. No one had seen fit to inform Stuart of that fact.

Aldo yanked sharply, and Stuart reluctantly stumbled back alongside Edgar, snapping his yellow and mismatched teeth at the other donkey. When Edgar didn't respond, Stuart sullenly lowered his head and began plodding along in a relatively straight line.

"This is taking some of the wonder out of my first trip through the Myre," Aldo said, watching his mount with narrow eyes.

Nicolette snorted. "The Myre smells like a rotting corpse upon which Edgar here relieved himself, and it'll kill you if you walk more than a quarter mile past the treeline. Romance was never going to be on the menu."

Auggie peered over the edge of the wagon. "How much will you give me if I walk a hundred paces in?"

"If you hop out of this wagon, I'll feed you to Stuart."

Auggie made a face, but sank back into the bed of the wagon. Their plodding pace had slowed enough that the wagon, the last in the long line that made up the caravan, had widened the distance between itself and the donkey-riding pair. Once that gap had reached a certain point, Aldo looked over at her. "Now?"

Nicolette frowned, and craned her neck to look behind them. The Myre Road was relatively straight, so she could see the next convoy, nearly half a mile behind them. It was customary to keep a respectful distance between each managed convoy. She nodded slowly. "Yeah, I think we can talk for a bit. Any topics in mind?"

"I'm fairly sure Stuart would eat you both."

Stuart screamed.

Nicolette grinned. "Stay your knives, Confessor. I'll answer your questions."

"Good," Aldo said. He glanced back at Auggie. "You know this falls in the 'you didn't hear any of this' category, right?"

Auggie made a face. "I'm not an idiot."

"You agreed to carry Dzema powder for two men you didn't know. I'm not saying you're an idiot, but we need to work on your decision process."

Auggie rolled her eyes. "I can keep my mouth shut."

"Good." Aldo returned his attention to Nicolette. "The first of my many questions is you're joking, right?"

Nicolette shook her head. "Nope."

"We're not stealing bull semen."

"We are."

"We're not getting paid to steal bull semen."

"We are."

"We're not getting paid enough to buy a gods-damn sloop to steal bull semen."

Nicolette frowned. "These aren't technically questions, they're just a string of false statements."

"It's been nearly two days, Nicolette," Aldo said. "Two days since you dropped that particular bit of information. Two days since we've been able to talk. So can you please just explain why we're getting paid that much to steal semen?"

"What's semen?"

"That sounds suspiciously like you hearing something, Auggie," Aldo said. Auggie stuck out her tongue, but did not repeat the question.

Nicolette chuckled. "You ever hear of Vorchese beef?"

"No, I've not... wait." Aldo frowned as he thought. "That's the name of the ranch, right? I think you said that."

She nodded. "The Vorchese Ranch, in the Snowsill duchy of the Dominion. Owned by Petyr Vorchese and his family for nearly two hundred years. Used to be cattle, goats, chickens, and pigs, and it used to be like any other ranch in the Dominion. But Petyr's father had a bit of a gift for animal husbandry. About sixty years ago, he successfully bred the first of a new type of cattle. Predictably, he named it after himself." Nicolette pulled a leather pouch from her tunic pocket, and pulled out a small strip of dried beef, about the length of Aldo's pinky. She offered it to him. "Here. This is from a Vorchese cow. Bought a bit on my last trip to the ranch."

Aldo accepted it, raising an eyebrow. The meat had an odd coloring to it, with yellowish streaks running through the grey meat. "I think it's gone bad."

"That's just what it looks like. Try it."

Aldo shrugged, and took a small nibble off the corner. As he chewed, his eyes widened. It was beef, all right. With every moment, the flavor gained depth and richness, becoming juicy and savory in his mouth. He swallowed, raising an eyebrow. "Damn. That's very, very good."

"Don't like it too much," Nicolette said. "That piece you're holding is twenty-five ducats worth of meat."

Aldo coughed as he nearly choked. "You're joking."

"Nope," Nicolette said, returning the rest to her tunic. "The pouch was five hundred. To be fair, they cut me a good deal."

Aldo stared at the remaining strip in his hand. "It's good, but why would anyone pay that much?"

"The flavor isn't what makes it special," Nicolette said. "There's something about Vorchese beef. That piece you're holding, right there?

That's enough food to last you three days. And I don't mean as a ration, emergency portions or anything like that. You finish that piece, and you won't be hungry for three days."

"How is that possible?"

Nicolette snorted. "You figure that out, you're smarter than the College of Naturists or any of the hundreds of experts that the Families have hired to figure it out. It makes no sense to them. But they've tested it, over and over. It's 'inexplicably nutritionally dense'. That's the term they use." A bug buzzed near Nicolette's head, and she waved it away. "Milk and cheese too, although they're not quite as effective. A shot glass of milk will only last you a full day."

Aldo nodded. "So the cows are valuable."

"They're gold mines with fur and hooves," Nicolette replied. "And the Vorchese family knows it. They'll export the meat, milk, and cheese. But they won't allow anyone outside their ranch to breed the actual cattle themselves. They've got the market cornered, and they have zero intention of giving it up."

"They won't sell the cows," Aldo said.

"Well, they've sold a few," Nicolette said. "About five years ago, the Vorchese wanted to expand their operations. More land, refurbish the ranch facilities, that kind of thing. They approached the Bank about a loan, but one of the wealthier families in town had a proposal. They funded over five million ducats worth of work on the ranch in exchange for three female calves. Took over a year of negotiation, but as far as I know, those are the only cows the Vorchese have ever sold."

"Three females," Aldo said, nodding slowly. "No males."

"Exactly," Nicolette said. "Hence, bull semen."

"The DeLucas bought the animals?"

She shook her head. "No. I actually don't know. I think it's a Table member, but they want to keep their name far away from the entire business. They asked the DeLucas to manage this job."

"Why would the DeLucas do their dirty work?"

"The DeLucas are an odd family," Nicolette said. "Still follow the old ways. Puts them a bit on the outside, but I get the sense in my limited dealings that they prefer it that way. Toni DeLuca's young for a matriarch, early forties. But she's rich. Rich enough that if she wasn't a woman, she could probably buy a seat on the Table if she was interested."

"She's not?"

"I've met Toni DeLuca twice," Nicolette said. "I came away with two distinct impressions. First, if she wanted a seat on the Table, she'd have one, gender politics be damned. Second, she's a woman that understands the value of living in the margins."

Something in the woods squawked. Stuart shrieked a battle cry, and tried to charge at his fairly unimpressive top speed towards the unseen foe. Aldo used all of his upper body strength and a string of invectives to wrench the bloodthirsty mount back in line. "Walking is becoming more and more appealing," he said, teeth gritted. "Okay, so a family wants to breed their own Vorchese cattle."

"They won't call them that, of course. They'll name them something like Pallia Bovines and swear up and down they're a different breed," Nicolette said. "But yes."

"How many cattle do the Vorchese have?"

"Hundreds," Nicolette said. "They won't give an exact number, but their ranch is huge, and I've seen a few of the herds. They're massive."

"So why not just steal a bull?"

"Two reasons," Nicolette said. "First will become apparent when you see these cows. They're... not small."

"I know how big cows are, Nicolette."

She chuckled. "Not these. But that's not the biggest problem. There's something about the breeding process with Vorchese cattle. The vast majority of the newborns are female. Right now, the entire bull population of the Vorchese ranch consists of a single bull," she said. "That's one of the main reasons they use manual insemination. Too many cows, not enough bulls. Even if natural mating were an option, it wouldn't be as efficient."

Aldo raised an eyebrow. "Why isn't natural mating an option?"

"The breeding process has several issues. The lack of male births, for one. But the males that are born are apparently aggressive. Very aggressive. They keep the bull in an isolated paddock, half a mile from any other animal. Apparently if he gets a scent, he gets angry." Nicolette shrugged. "It's not worth risking the safety of a cow. So instead, they drug the bull, bring it into the harvesting building..."

Aldo made a face. "The harvesting building?"

"What do you want them to call it? 'Spunk shack' doesn't have that air of professionalism."

Stuart screamed again. Aldo felt inclined to agree.

"Anyway, once the bull is in the harvesting building, they..." Nicolette waved her hands in the air randomly. "They do whatever they do to get what they need. Apparently, each session produces enough... ah, product to inseminate up to twenty females. The Vorchese know their business, though. They're very picky about which cows are selected for breeding. So usually, they only have two or three ready for insemination. The rest of the..."

"Bovine batter?"

"You deserve Stuart," Nicolette said. "The rest of the product is placed in glass vials, and moved to a cold storage facility beneath the harvesting building. It can be safely stored there for up to a year and remain viable."

Aldo nodded. "So the cold storage is what you need me for."

"Access to the cold storage mostly, but yes," Nicolette said. "I haven't seen it, so I'm not exactly sure what lock they have on the door, but I know it's guarded by at least two men at all times."

"You said you've been there, right?" Nicolette nodded, and Aldo said, "How have you had so much access?"

"How much do you know about the Empire?"

"About the same as most," Aldo said. "It's cold and it's north of the Breaking. No one ever needed to know all that much. Kind of hard for them to wander south with a mile-wide chasm in the way."

"That changed a few years ago."

"The bridge, right?" Aldo asked, and Nicolette nodded. "We heard about that even out on the barge."

"It was all anyone was talking about. First few months after the bridge was finished, everyone was holding their breath, waiting to see if the Imperial Army would cross, but when nobody heard any war drums, everyone in the Dominion started scrambling to set up trade with the Empire," Nicolette said. "The Vorchese are no different. They've been trying to convince the Empire to send a representative down to tour the ranch and negotiate a trade deal for almost a year. You can imagine how delighted they were when SubArcheron Noya Soyavich, aide to the Archeron of Rilsko, arrived." She touched a finger to her brow. "Madame Soyavich, at your disposal."

Aldo raised an eyebrow. "Isn't that risky?" For centuries, only a long and arduous sea journey could connect Vetticci with the Empire, leaving the people living north of the yawning Breaking a mystery to nearly everyone in the city, Aldo included. Building a bridge was thought to be impossible, but the Imperial sorcerers known as the Chorale had managed to do just that.

She shrugged. "We shared a house with a Rilsovar family growing up. They fled south on a trade vessel during the Unification War, ended up settling in Vetticci. I speak it well enough. Plus, Rilsko is way up in the north of the Empire, on the other side of the Greymare Peaks. It's unlikely that trade with the Dominion is high on their list of priorities. It's a gamble, but a calculated one. In the meantime, the Vorchese family has given me tours, treated me like a visiting dignitary. I've been there three times."

"Okay." Aldo nodded. "You said that the job needed someone on the inside. Why?"

"Two big problems," Nicolette said. "First, the damn ranch is huge. It takes two hours to get from the main gate to the ranch facilities, and that's mounted. They have a huge guard force, nearly eighty men, all equipped with horses and crossbows. And even if you could get away from the guards, the dozen Lofland bloodhounds they have can track a mouse that swam across Pallia Bay. Second problem: they can't know that the semen's been stolen. Ever."

Aldo's eyes widened. "And how do you expect to do that?"

Nicolette glanced around, verifying once more they were out of earshot. She reached down into the saddlebags, and pulled out a glass vial. Inside was a murky liquid.

"Shit. Is that..."

"Yes," Nicolette said. "One of the many undesirable issue that the breeding process results in is that the semen they harvest is not always viable. They showed me the testing room. They bottle the semen, then test it to make sure it's good. If it's not, the vial goes into the trash for disposal." She waggled her fingers in the air. "They probably would have been more cautious if they knew I was Vetticcian."

Aldo nodded. "So the idea is to switch out a viable sample for that one. Won't they wonder why one of their good vials went bad after they tested it?"

Nicolette shook her head. "The testing process isn't perfect, and the viable semen doesn't look any different from the bad. They'll use it to inseminate, it won't take, and they'll assume either the timing wasn't right or a bad batch got through testing. It happens."

"But in order to make that switch..."

"We have to get into the cold storage room," Nicolette said. "They want my business, but they don't let me go anywhere without an escort. I could disable them, but I'd only have minutes to get to the cold storage, take out the guards, break through the lock that I'm wholly unfamiliar with, make the swap, get out, and try to make my way across thousands of unfamiliar acres while being chased by dozens of angry guards on horseback led by scent hounds. I wouldn't make it a mile."

Aldo considered something, and sat up straighter. "Not to mention, if they catch someone stealing a vial of semen, there's only one person that connects to."

Nicolette nodded. "That's the other reason they can't know. Under no circumstances can this trace back to the families. If there's even a whiff of their involvement, the DeLucas will contact the Vorchese and Duke Snowsill, and give us up to keep suspicion off of them."

"You really think they'd do that?"

"Shit, Toni DeLuca sat across a table from me and bluntly told me that she'd do just that," Nicolette said. "She's willing to pay a lot for this job, but only if her name stays out of it. That means we walk out of that ranch with everyone wishing us a good journey, and no one ever knows what we did."

From deep in the woods, a rapid clicking drifted out to the convoys. Stuart shied away, ears flattening against his head. Aldo tried to control him, but realized that Nicolette's mount was doing the same. "What in the gods is that sound?"

"Don't know," Nicolette said, eyeing the trees nervously. "It's the Myre. I heard it on my last trip through. The caravan master said not to worry. Whatever it is, it doesn't come out on the road."

Aldo's thoughts swirled as all three of them stared into the verdant darkness that vines and jungle formed. *Four hundred thousand...* He shook his head. It was a fortune. Enough to last for years, maybe even decades in the city. *'Course, you aren't exactly all that welcome in the city.* He glanced back at Augee, who was staring wide eyed at the eerie sounds echoing out of the Myre. *Could she even go home?* The guilds had a long memory, and while it might be possible for Aldo to exhaust a not-insubstantial portion of his payment for this job in bribing the right people until he didn't have to look over his shoulder every ten minutes.

Auggie, though? Her name was marked. She was an escaped convict, and that would take so much more than money to undo. He chewed on the inside of his lip as he considered her. *Four hundred white coral would mean she never had to go back. Neither of us would.*

The clicking faded. It took a few moments before the animals calmed down. Hesitantly, Aldo reached down and stroked Stuart's head. For once, the donkey didn't react. He could feel Stuart trembling beneath his hand.

"Okay." He patted Stuart gently, and the donkey chuffed softly. "So you need me on the inside to get access to the cold storage, and to figure out a way past the guards without anyone knowing that we got in and out."

"And to break the lock," Nicolette said. "I can get past some, but I'm guessing you're better."

"It's been a long time since I did that," Aldo admitted.

"You managed that lock on the prison transport quite neatly." There was an odd tone to her voice.

"Cheap lock. Heavy, but cheap. If this stuff is as valuable as you say, I'm guessing we're looking at a Porra lock, maybe even a Devrese. Haven't touched one of those since I went away."

She raised an eyebrow. "Sure you can still do it?"

"Only one way I can think of to find out." He glanced her way. "None of this matters if I can't get a job with the guard."

"He'll give you a job," Nicolette said. "I'm not worried about that."

"You've talked to him?"

"Not about you, obviously," she said. "But yes, I've spoken with him. Several times."

Aldo didn't say anything for a bit. He stared at the tree line forty feet away, listening to the wind rustle the dense foliage. "You're assuming a lot."

Nicolette nodded. "Kind of the way jobs like this work. But you are his only son."

"Hasn't mattered much in the past."

"I looked into you, you know," Nicolette said. "Standard stuff. Made sure you weren't connected, weren't in debt to someone that might put you in the position of fucking me over."

Aldo nodded.

"Looked into your time on the penance barge. Not a lot of available information, but I did pick up a few things," she said. "There were two offers to buy out the rest of your sentence. One six months into your term, one three years. Both got denied, of course. The buyer couldn't meet the barge's counter offer. And sentence buyers are anonymous. But given your lack of connection, it's only reasonable to think..."

Aldo grunted. "So he made an offer that had zero chance of working. Not exactly sacrificing anything." He shook his head. "I don't know if I can act like everything's fine when I see him. I'm pretty sure that I can't."

Nicolette shrugged. "Good." Aldo raised a questioning eyebrow, and she said, "I don't know how everything went down between you two. I just know that you ended up doing fourteen years, and he didn't. I've seen a fair amount in my time, but I can't think of any scenario in which that doesn't result in some bitterness. You walk in there smiling with outstretched arms, I don't know that he's going to buy that. But if you approach him, still angry but desperate? Out of options, and hoping that he cares enough about you to try to make up for what happened? That's a lot more believable."

He grunted. "Not too far off from the truth." Without looking at her, he asked, "When you saw him, was he... I mean, did he seem good? Okay?"

"I think so," she said. "He was quiet. Didn't say much more than he had to. But he's respected there. Seems to be good at his job."

Aldo didn't say anything. He stared into the woods for a bit. *This is a bad idea. But I'm not exactly burdened with an excess of good ones.* He'd spent years having the idea of hope beaten from his soul. He'd assumed it was gone for good. He certainly never expected to feel it flicker once more on a narrow road in the midst of a stinking, deadly jungle. *If it works... This could change everything.*

Nicolette said, "Look, if this works out, nothing sticks to anyone. You're there for a week, maybe two. We make the switch. The next day, I leave for the Empire as expected," Nicolette says. "You pick a fight with your father. Make it public, let people see. That way, no one will think twice about you quitting and walking away. We meet back up in Lofland Fork. Madame DeLuca's attache will meet us there, and we'll make the exchange." She shrugged. "You can go anywhere you like."

Aldo took a deep breath. "It's not a great plan." She didn't respond, and he allowed, "But it's not the worst I've heard."

She raised an eyebrow. "Does that mean…"

He nodded. "If he agrees, gets me in, I'll do what I can."

Nicolette smiled, relief plain on her face. "This is going to work, Aldo. I know it."

Chapter 5

"What do you think?"

Aldo raised an eyebrow as he took in the gate leading into the Dominion city of Lofland Fork. "This is one of their biggest?"

Nicolette nodded. They'd parted ways with the convoy at the southern gate, and she had taken the chance to change into unfamiliar clothes. The cut was severe and militaristic, the fabric rich and luxurious. The Imperial wools already was drawing beads of sweat to her brow, but she'd left off the heavy coat. "The capital's bigger. Havensport, too, I'm fairly sure. But yeah, Lofland Fork is up there. Nearly 150,000 people." From the back, Auggie audibly snorted, and Nicolette laughed. "I know."

"The Nest alone holds almost ten times this many," Aldo said. "And it's half the size."

She shrugged. "One of the benefits of life in the Dominion, I suppose. Room to stretch."

"That's for damn sure," Aldo said. They had emerged from the Myre wood six hours ago, and the road led up to a hilltop before descending toward Lofland Fork. When they'd crested the hill, Aldo's mouth had gone dry. Golden fields of wheat spilled out the the west for miles, further than he could see, battered fences tracing the border between farms and fields bigger than he could imagine. To the west, he spotted dense patches of trees, but something had seemed off. They were too regular, too precise. When they'd ridden past, Aldo realized they were precise, neat rows of pear trees, each laden with fruit yet to fully ripen.

He preferred being among the trees. The rolling fields were too open. They reminded him of the ocean.

Their convoy had joined a steady stream of wagons and carts as they came closer to Lofland Fork. The city was less a fork than it was a cross, with two roads intersecting at the center of town. Nicolette had explained that the road vanishing in the east and west connected Walshire, the Dominion capital, with Havensport, a major trade center on the east coast, while the north-south road connected Vetticci in the south to Lofland Fork, extending over a thousand miles north. "Give it two, three years, and the Dukes will have extended it all the way north to the bridge over the Breaking," one of the merchants accompanying them on their journey had grumbled. "We'll all be in for a pinch then."

They currently stood more or less in the center of Lofland Fork, a sprawling open pavilion packed full of colorful tents and shouting merchants insisting that you sample their goods. It was the first moment since they'd entered the Dominion that something had felt familiar. City watchmen in grey uniforms with scarlet armbands chatted idly on a nearby corner, hands resting on polished truncheons hanging from their belts. They passed a fruit vendor, a slender man with pale skin standing behind tables creaking under bushels of fruit, behind which an older man with similar features stacked melons.

Auggie tugged at his arm. "I'm hungry."

"You're always hungry," Aldo said, but he began to head his way, reaching for his purse. Nicolette stopped him.

"We need to change out some money first," Nicolette said.

"They don't take coral?"

"They do, but..." She pulled out a grey ducat. "Watch."

Approaching the vendor, she touched two fingers to her brow. "Morning."

"It is at that, my dear," he replied, eyes quickly assessing her clothing and carriage. "Always a pleasure to see our friends from beyond the wood come visit. How may I be of service?"

She held up the coin. "My friend is hungry," she said. Glancing back at Auggie, she asked, "What's your favorite?"

"I like limes."

Nicolette made a face. "Just limes?"

"What's wrong with limes?" Auggie shot back. "I like limes."

"Okay, limes." She turned back. "How many will you part with for one ducat?"

"Alas, the exchange rate is not what it might have been," he said, spreading his hands wide. "Three is the best I can do."

Nicolette looked delighted. "I didn't realize we got a show in this booth! You have my thanks, sir, your jokes have lightened my spirit. But we are indeed in a hurry, so if you could tell us a number that wouldn't be laughable to anyone over the age of three..."

The vendor assumed an offended expression Aldo had seen on every merchant and negotiator since he was young. "I'll have you know, this was my father's stand, may he have ascended. I would never tarnish his fine memory by exploiting my customers!" He shook his head mournfully. "It is only in remembrance of his unfailing generosity that I can offer four."

Aldo frowned. "Isn't that your father?" He pointed at the other man.

"Yes."

"He's not dead."

"It's like I can still hear his voice."

"It's still my stand, you ungrateful..." Nicolette interrupted before the older man could continue.

"The two of you clearly have much to discuss. Let's settle on six, and we will let you go back to negotiating just who owns this empire of produce."

The older man snorted. "Ivan, if you give her six for a dirty disc of coral, your mother will perish of shame."

"She's already dead."

"And now you'll know what killed her. Knowledge of your future failings."

Ivan turned a suffering glance to Nicolette. "You see what I must endure. Take pity on me. If we settle upon five, he might only harangue me for the next month, may death claim him before that day comes."

Nicolette grinned. "Five will do." She handed him the coin, and Ivan bowed.

"One moment, my lady, and I will have your order ready." She nodded, and came over to stand next to Aldo as the two men argued loudly behind her.

"That's a hell of a deal," Aldo said in a low voice. "Limes go for two ducats in the city, and they don't look like those. Dried, shriveled things."

"Long trip down," Nicolette said. "Plus, the good quality ones are gobbled up by the families. We get the leftovers."

Aldo started to say something else, but the sound of Ivan clearing his throat drew their attention. He had come out from behind the booth, and bowed at the waist. "If you could direct me to your cart, my lady."

"No cart," Nicolette said. "Just us."

He raised an eyebrow. "Shall I hold them for you? Until you arrange pickup?"

"Pickup?" Aldo frowned. "What do you..." His voice trailed off as he looked past Ivan to where his father was setting the fifth bushel of plump, emerald-colored limes in front of the stand. Each basket was piled high with the fruit.

"Change of plans, sir." Nicolette produced another grey coral ducat, and handed it to Ivan. "If you would be so kind as to see these distributed to anyone who might be hungry. Feel free to swap them out for something less tart should those in need have a more discerning palate than my young friend." She walked over, and picked four limes off the first basket. "A few for the road, though."

She paused as she realized that both Ivan, Auggie, and Aldo were all staring at her. "What?"

Ivan recovered first, quickly bowing again and again, so deeply Aldo feared he would spill forward into the dusty road. "I will see it done. Thank you."

She touched her forehead once more. Once they'd gotten out of earshot, she said, "Like I said. We need to change out some money."

"What the shit was that?" Aldo said.

"What?"

"You just..." He trailed off, glancing back at Ivan and his father, who were talking animatedly among themselves. "You don't honestly think they're going to give those away, do you? They're going to pocket your coin and sell those limes a second time. And what kind of Vetticcian gives away coin?"

"It's two ducats."

"More'n a few days I would have stabbed someone for two coral," Auggie said.

Nicolette looked uncomfortable. "It's not... I didn't mean to say..."

Aldo shook his head. "It's fine. Just unexpected." Gratefully, Nicolette handed them each a fruit. Auggie took a huge bite out of the side of the lime, and Nicolette made a face. "That's disgusting."

"Ipfs good." Mashed pulp and rind kept appearing and disappearing behind her teeth.

"You're worse than Stuart." Auggie made a face, and Nicolette shook her head, returning to Aldo. "Exchange rate's always been favorable to Vetticcians. If you can believe it, that's actually a lot fewer than I thought I'd get. First time I came through, I got a full cartload of peaches for three ducats."

If four hundred thousand would last me years in the city... Aldo blinked several times, trying to wrap his mind around the possibilities.

As they walked, Aldo began peeling the lime. He glanced around. "Compost?"

She shook her head. "They don't do that here. Just leave it."

Auggie thrust her hand out. "Gimme."

Aldo grimaced, but handed her the peel. "No compost. Seems wasteful."

"They're not growing plants from whatever container they can scrounge up, with whatever dirt they can find," she pointed out.

"Hey!" They all turned at the shout. A boy, not much older than Auggie, jogged up to them, and looked Nicolette up and down. "You Saffman?"

She glanced at Aldo, confused, but nodded. "Who's asking?"

"Nobody. Vetticcian roost keeper paid me to find a big Imperial lady, give her a message." He shrugged. "Telling me that ain't you?"

Nicolette frowned. "How much?"

"Two coral."

"Bullshit," Aldo said. "Roost keeper already paid you."

The kid grinned sheepishly. "Can't blame me for trying." He handed Nicolette a slip of paper, and was gone before she could unfold it. Her eyes darted over the writing, and she nodded, stuffing it in her pocket.

"Something I need to know?"

"Some arrangements I made. A local contact took a bit to confirm he'd be able to help." Nicolette pointed down a long road lined with warehouses. "He's down here, end of the street. But first..." She glanced back at Auggie and lowered her voice. "We need to sort her out."

He frowned for a moment. The last few days, he'd gotten used to having Auggie around. For a brief time, he had forgotten she couldn't come with them. "Any ideas?"

"The vendor? Seemed to be doing well."

Aldo took a deep breath. "I'd feel better if we knew someone here."

"Me too, but it is what it is," she said. "Tell you what. Let me go talk to him. After the job, after we've gotten paid, we come back. See that she's doing well. If we need to make a change, we'll have the funds."

He nodded. "Okay. You go see if they're willing. I'll talk to Auggie."

Auggie watched her go, swallowing her bite, and turned to Aldo, her face sullen. "I want to stay with you."

Aldo snorted. "You don't even like me."

"I don't like you less than I don't like most people."

"Praise of the highest order, I'm sure."

She folded her arms. "I can be useful."

"I don't doubt that, Auggie." He dropped to a crouch. "But this job, it's dangerous. And I need to focus. Not be wondering every ten minutes what kind of trouble you're getting into."

"So you leave me with a stranger?" Auggie asked. "I can still get in trouble here, you know."

"I have no doubt." Aldo felt the guilt gnaw at his guts, but he shook his head. "It's work. Honest work. And you won't go hungry. That's more than most in the city get."

"It's going to be boring." Auggie's shoulders slumped. "I hate getting bored."

"Yeah, we've had that discussion before." He raised an eyebrow. "Remember how that played out?" She made a face, and Aldo said, "When you're older, you'll appreciate the value of boring."

"Doubt it." She chewed on her lip for a moment. "What if they're mean?"

"I'll be back. Four, maybe five weeks. And I'll check on you. If you're not happy, we'll figure something else out. And if they're mean?" He raised an eyebrow, and pulled a thin blackened stiletto in a sharkskin sheath. Her eyes widened, and she reached for it, but he pulled it back. "No stabbing unless necessary. They hang people up here, Auggie."

"I know."

He nodded, and handed the blade to her. She pulled the seven inches of sharpened steel free, and stared at it for a moment. "It's sharp."

"Better than a roof tile, anyway." He saw Nicolette waving from the vendor. "Work hard. Be respectful. They'll do the same. We're making a deal for them to take you in. If they do right by you, you can make a home here. If they don't..." Aldo raised an eyebrow. "You're a Vetticcian, born and bred. You have teeth."

The blade had vanished somewhere within the cheap clothes Auggie was wearing when Nicolette returned. "All good?" she asked.

"You tell me."

Nicolette nodded. "Paid twenty ducats. Told them we'd do a hundred more if we came back to her healthy and happy next month."

"You trust them?"

"Fuck no." She shrugged. "But I trust they want that money. It's half a year's pay. Besides, I may have suggested some bloody consequences should we return to find her in poor straits. Everyone here seems to think Vetticcians are all just waiting to slip a knife between their ribs."

Aldo nodded, and turned to Auggie, who was doing her best to keep her face blank. "You ready?"

"You're going to fail miserably without me."

He nodded. "Most likely."

She took a deep breath. "Okay. I'll be good." Both Nicolette and Aldo raised an eyebrow, and Auggie offered a half smile. "I'll try to be good."

"Still not sure I buy it, but I'll take it."

Auggie rushed over, throwing her long arms around Aldo's waist. "You'd better come back."

He awkwardly hugged her back, clearing his throat. "I'll be back in a month. I'll see you then. Besides, more than enough to eat without hanging around the stinking docks. This place is paradise."

She let him go, and he intentionally didn't look at the streaks on her cheeks. *It's better than the city. Better than she knew. And if this job pays out, maybe it can see more than just me to a future.*

Nicolette offered her hand. "Come on, Auggie. Let's go."

Aldo had intended not to watch them go. He did anyway.

***

"You okay?"

It had taken Nicolette about twenty minutes before she returned. Aldo nodded, trying to keep the truth from his face. "Don't know her all that well. Just bought her breakfast every now and then."

"Way I hear it, she's not the only one," Nicolette said. He raised an eyebrow, and she shrugged. "I asked around. Several kids mentioned you. Something about a sucker."

Aldo snorted. "Not far off."

"That can't be cheap."

"I'm not getting them anything you can't get off the dock," he said. "Whatever cod was too beat up for the buyers, whatever moldy flatbread no one wanted from the market. Just enough to fill their bellies."

"Why?"

"What do you mean?"

Nicolette gestured down a side street. "This way." Aldo fell into step beside her, and she said, "We Vetticcians are good at many things. Charity is not generally among them. The Table makes sure there's enough food for everyone. Why pay out of pocket?"

He raised an eyebrow. "Where did you grow up?"

"The academic district," she said. "Near the college."

"Your parents were artificers?"

"Nothing so fancy," Nicolette said. "Da cleaned one of the libraries. My mother worked as an archivist, cataloging master artwork records."

He nodded. "That explains it."

"Explains what?"

Aldo jerked his head back towards where they'd left Auggie. "The thing with the limes. Why it didn't matter to you." He glanced at her. "I'm going to guess you never had to rely on Table rations."

She raised an eyebrow. "We weren't rich."

"No, but you lived around those who were, and your family had enough to get by. You shopped at the markets. You've never lined up for the food wagons." She looked a bit irritated, and he raised his hand. "Not a criticism. Gods knows if I could find a place there I'd never look back. But the food wagons aren't quite the beacon of Table generosity the families make them out to be."

"Not enough food?"

"Depends on your definition and the day," Aldo said. "They bring enough to keep people from starving. So long as they guess the number of people who show up, that is. Enough to keep us from being hungry?" He shook his head. "And a few pieces of salted fish doesn't put a roof over your head, or clothes on your back. When you're cold and hungry, you'll do quite a bit to be otherwise. When you're cold and hungry and young, the list of things you do is often not tempered by common sense or self-preservation."

Nicolette frowned. "The Table insists they give enough."

"The Table says a lot of things. Less than three out of ten kids in the Nest reach their fifteenth year," Aldo said. "They get sick, or they starve, or they get desperate. I can't help the sickness part, but the other two?" He grunted. "Course, seeing how the dice fell, not sure I managed that well."

"Wasn't your fault."

"Blame to go around. Some of it lands on me." Aldo shrugged. "I do what I can to keep them from charting the same course as I did. Best I can tell, I make not a single solitary fuck worth of difference." He cleared his throat. "Who is this guy you got a message about?"

Nicolette didn't comment on the pivot. "Used to work on the Vorchese ranch before being ignominiously fired. He's a bit angry about it, and fortunately for us, he's got some skill with a pen," she said. "He's drawn detailed maps of the entire property."

Aldo nodded. "Once we have that..."

"We'll get rooms at an inn. Tomorrow morning, you and Stuart will head north."

Coming to a stop, Aldo stopped eating and stared at her. "That donkey belongs to the convoy."

She shrugged. "You need a mount to get up to the ranch. It's two hundred miles, Aldo. Besides, they gave me a good deal. He's waiting at the northern stables for us."

"Was the deal free, gods just get this cursed creature away from us?"

"They may have been motivated sellers, yes." Nicolette grinned. "Stuart bit his arm while we were negotiating. Probably saved me a decent stack of coral."

"You know, you're heading north a few days after me," Aldo said. "I'd be willing to walk so that you can have our mount."

"Gods, no. I have a horse waiting for me."

"This seems highly inequitable."

"You're supposed to look desperate and exhausted," Nicolette pointed out. "Donkey bites will help sell the illusion."

"This entire plan was a terrible mistake."

"Maybe he'll grow on you," Nicolette said. She pointed to the end of an alley. "He's meeting us down there."

"I'm just saying, it would help sell my starvation if I ate that cursed creature during my journey," Aldo pointed out as they made their way towards a run down building. A short set of stairs led down to a door. "Anyone who can kill and devour that thing is truly at the end of his rope."

"Your call, but if it comes down to mortal combat between you and Stuart, I have to say, my money's not on you," Nicolette pointed out. There was a young teenage boy sitting on the step. "Afternoon, Jacen. Your parents know you're here?"

The young man shook his head. "They think I'm cleaning the ovens."

"Terrible lie," Nicolette said, shaking her head. "I weep when I think of the thieves of the future." She chucked a thumb in Aldo's direction. "Aldo, this is Jacen. He and his brother are thoroughly disreputable in the best possible way. He's an awful excuse for a lifter, but outside of the city, our choices are limited. He's going to keep an eye out for us."

"This is the guy?" Jacen looked Aldo up and down with a dubious expression. "He smells like rotting fish."

"Charming." Aldo raised an eyebrow. "Let's get on with it. I'm sure you have a pressing appointment being an ass to someone else."

"Oh, my calendar's full up," Jacen said, grinning.

"You two are hilarious," Nicolette said. "Keep an eye open, Jacen?"

"What you're paying, both of 'em."

Jacen returned to his slumped position on the stairs as Aldo followed Nicolette down to the doorway. She produced a key, and he could hear the thunk of a heavy lock as she turned it. Pushing the door open, she said, "Hey, Aldo?"

"Mmm?" Aldo peered past her into the room. It was dark, the windows covered in grease. He couldn't make out the interior.

"I'm sorry about this."

"About what?"

The words had barely left his mouth when Nicolette's hands seized the back of his tunic, hurling him forward. His feet got tangled up, and he tumbled to the floor of the cellar, rolling once before falling in a heap. He started to scramble to his feet, turning just in time to see the door slam shut. The lock clicked.

"What the hell are you doing?!" he shouted, slamming his shoulder into the door. He tried the handle. It didn't budge. *No no no... Gods dammit, I fucking KNEW it!*

"Message was from the sovrano. The sniffer found out who you are. The guild put a price on your head," she said through the thick wood. "It's not personal." Her voice was fainter as he heard her say, "Go get the guard, Jacen. Tell them we caught someone breaking in and trapped them."

"You *bitch*!" he screamed, hammering his fists against the door. "You absolute bastard!"

"Like I said, Aldo. It's not personal." Her boots pounded up the stairs, fading away.

Chapter 6

Aldo slammed his shoulder into the door, but it refused to budge. Spinning, he squinted through the darkness. There was a pair of small windows painted over, small pinpricks of light sneaking through the gaps in the lazy paint job, but each was less than a handspan tall. He spotted a ladder leading up to a trap door in the ceiling, and ran over to it. Scrambling up the rungs, he tried to push the hatch open, but it didn't budge. He ran his fingers over the hatch, but couldn't find a handle or latch.

"Fuck!" He dropped back down the ladder, running back over to the door. He shook the handle harder, and pounded his fist against the door. It remained stubbornly closed. Dropping to one knee, he tried to make out the lock in the darkness. It was a heavy iron bolt, built into the wood of the door and secured with thick nails, cut flush with the surface of the lock.

You have to be calm, have to focus. You fucked up, trusting her, but that's later's problem. Now's problem is going to be here any fucking minute if you can't do this. He tried to remember how far away one of the men wearing the bright red armband of the city guard had been.

His eyes traced the outline of the door. It had opened out, so he knew the hinges were on the other side. Shaking his head sharply, he flexed the fingers in his right hand, and splayed them over the iron of the lock. He tried to ignore the blood thundering in his ears and steady his breathing.

At first, he felt nothing but the cool rough metal under his skin. He muttered another curse, and shut his eyes. It used to come so easily, but it had been a long time since it was second nature.

A shiver ran through his index finger. Another through his palm. His breath caught in his throat, and he froze. The shiver faded, but he swallowed and tried to slow his breathing. After a few moments, it returned, spreading like warm wax over his hand. The vibration buzzing in his fingertips and palm felt like the tickle of butterfly wings. He tried to ignore the ticking clock in the back of his mind, and pushed as gently as he could.

The shiver continued, but spread. Not through his flesh, but through the iron beneath his skin.

Just as it had with the prison transport, it came rushing back in a moment, a dozen years melting away. Threads of vibration, loops of tension and pressure, slithering their way through the metal of the lock, feeling for the gaps, the breaks, the pieces not fixed in place, but sliding up and down in channels. After a few breaths, he could see it in his mind. Five tumblers, cylinders of notched metal holding the bolt firmly in place. He focused on the first, sending threads spiraling through to snag the tumbler. At first, the loop didn't hold, but he sent three more, and felt the tumbler shift under the metal. He eased it upward, while sending loops of tension into the bolt, tugging it to the side. From under his palm, he heard the faintest click.

One.

The tricky part had never been to move the metal. Any spacer could make a tattoo needle blur between their fingers, or send a coin spinning across a table. The trick was holding multiple threads at once. He held the first tumbler in place, maintained the tension on the bolt, and sent more loops to wrap around the second. Then the third. Sweat was beading on his forehead when the fourth click issued from the lock, and the blood thundering in his head had sent a needle of pain deep between his eyes.

Aldo tried not to think about how much time had passed, how close he was to having the door yanked open and gloved fists seizing him. His focus was wholly on the complex weave of threads, pushing, pulling, twisting, forcing the cylinders to move where he wanted, holding them in place once they'd gotten there. He gritted his teeth as he sent out another thread, seizing the fifth tumbler. He pushed hard on the cylinder while lifting the last tumbler, and with a loud thunk, he felt the thick bar slam back into its housing in the door. He'd been leaning on the door as he worked, and when it flew open, he sprawled forward, bashing his knee on the ground as he caught himself.

"Gods, that was fast." Aldo looked up, sweat stinging his eyes, to see Nicolette standing at the top of the stairs.

"You..." Scrambling to his feet, Aldo charged up the stairs, snarling. Nicolette stepped back as he did. A voice in the back of his head told him what a terrible idea this was, but fury smothered it as he threw a punch at her face.

Without missing a beat, Nicolette batted his fist aside, stepping to the right as his momentum carried him past. He stumbled, but managed to keep his footing, and spun to lash out again. Each time he'd throw a punch, she'd slip out of his path, never striking back, but faster and stronger in every way. He screamed in anger, and lunged at her, trying to wrap his hands around her waist to drive her to the ground. She snagged his arm, rotated with his momentum, and he tumbled over her hip to fall to the ground. Even as he fell, he could feel her taking some of his weight, making sure he didn't strike the packed dirt of the alley too hard.

"I knew I couldn't fucking trust you!" he raged, scrambling back to his feet and spinning back to face her. Even as he clenched his fists, he knew attacking her was pointless. Even as he knew that, he swung again.

She batted it aside. "Yeah, you said that," Nicolette said. Her expression was still calm but her voice was hard. "Funny thing, you never for a moment stopped too long to think whether or not that went the other way."

"I'm not the one who came to you!" To his horror, Aldo felt tears sting the corners of his eyes. "I was fucking fine!"

Nicolette took two quick steps forward and shoved him, sharp and hard. He spilled back into the dirt again, and she towered over him, staring down. "If I hadn't shown up, you'd be back on a penance barge, either pulling lines from the waters or as chum in the fucking barrels, and you goddamn know it."

"I didn't ask for your help," he raged, feeling how hollow the words were even as he spat them out.

"I don't give a shit." She extended a finger up the alley. "You want to walk away, do it. But don't pretend like you don't understand why I just did what I did. I don't fucking know you. I know a handful of stories about why you ended up on that boat, but I don't know you. And if you're full of shit, if you were no better at finding your way past a lock than you were finding your way to a life that wasn't going to end in blood and grief, it's my ass."

He pushed himself up on his arms. "So this was what? A fucking test?"

"Of course it was a test, you ass," Nicolette snapped. "You know there aren't any penance barges up here! If we get caught, I'm going to swing right next to you. If you're so wrapped up in your own fears that you don't realize that, then maybe it really is better that you just disappear right now. I'm sure you'll do just fine." She dropped into a crouch. "Or maybe, if you can get over yourself for a heartbeat, you'll realize that you just broke through a five tumbler lock without a pick, without a wire, all while you thought the city guard was bearing down on you."

Aldo's jaw worked back and forth as he stared at her, his stomach tightening. He didn't respond.

"I told you, I read up on you," she said. "I read the report of your arrest. You had a courier bundle that had previously been in the safe, a handful of coral, a half-eaten honey stick, and that was it. No picks. No gear. Nothing on you but candy and coin, and you cracked a Devresse safe. A glass locked, College-crafted safe." She tilted her head. "I'm not the best artist in the world, but I know how to draw a conclusion. You're a spacer, aren't you?"

He didn't answer, which was answer enough. Nicolette offered a hand. Aldo stared at it for a moment, as if he didn't know what to do with it, then slowly took it, letting her pull him to his feet.

She brushed the dust from his shoulder. "Come on. Let me buy you a ridiculously cheap drink."

***

The pair hadn't spoken as they walked back towards the center of town. Indeed, Aldo didn't say anything until they'd sat at a polished wooden table inside a sprawling inn sitting at the crossroads. The Oak's Shade was actually made up of two buildings, connected by a sturdy skybridge twenty feet over the road. A burly man was shouting orders at a pair of twin boys doing their best to appear industrious, but paused long enough to set two full tankards of cider before Aldo and Nicolette.

Once he was gone, Aldo looked up at her. "I get it. Why you felt you had to do that. But you could have just asked."

Nicolette shook her head. "I wish I could have. But even assuming I was right about you, about what you could do, I don't know anything about spacers. It's not like they're all that common. I couldn't know whether or not using it for so long could have let it stagnate, or if you were even able to do it anymore after everything you've been through." She took a sip. "Plus, it's one thing to crack a lock when everything's fine. That's not going to be the case when we're at that cold storage room. You're going to be pressed, under a clock, at risk of everything, and I needed to know..."

"You needed to know I could handle something harder to crack." He took a deep breath. "And that I wasn't going to melt down and fuck us both." He sniffed his drink. "I don't know this fruit."

"Peaches," Nicolette said. "We don't get many into the city, and they never make it down to the dock level. The Families love them."

He took a drink, and nodded. "It's good." Aldo rubbed his forehead, and said, "I kept thinking you were too nice. Too generous. Taking me out of the city without any promise that I'd agree to the job? Gods, dropping enough coin to convince the sovrano to let me walk? In my experience, people don't do things like that. Not for free."

"Yeah," she said. "I'm not proud of it. And honestly, if you were to walk away, I really will let you go."

"I know. That's not what I'm saying," Aldo said. "I don't know. It just didn't make sense to me. But what you did back there?" He shrugged. "It pissed me off, but... it made sense."

They drank in silence for a bit, watching people come in and out of the inn, barmaids carrying steaming bowls and brimming mugs to tables. Finally, Nicolette asked, "How old were you when you found out?"

Aldo stared into the golden liquid in his mug. "Eight, I think. It wasn't long after my mother passed." He scratched at a loose fleck of paint on the table. "I found one of her hairpins. My dad came in, found me playing with it, making it move without touching it. I thought he'd be mad."

"Why?"

Aldo shrugged. "You know what it's like. Everyone's fine with people with a Talent if they work for the Colleges. If they don't, well, that's a different story."

Another tray of steaming bowls went past. Nicolette eyed them. "You hungry?"

"Sure."

She waved to get the barmaid's attention, who raised a querying eyebrow. Nicolette pointed at the bowls and raised two fingers. The young woman nodded, and turned to head back to the kitchen. Nicolette's eyes lingered on her for a moment before she turned back to Aldo. "So why didn't you? Go work for the Colleges, I mean?"

"Gotta be fifteen," Aldo said. "By that time, it was too late. They won't hire anyone with fishhooks. It's why it was so important to keep Auggie off the barges. Thought I could give her the choice I never had."

Nicolette looked surprised. "She's a spacer?"

Aldo shook his head. "She can read. Not sure how well, but she can definitely read."

Nicolette whistled softly. "That's unexpected. I have to say, I'm surprised your father let you start cracking. Talents make good money working for the Colleges. Enough to provide for you both."

Aldo snorted softly. "Yeah. That was the plan, at first. He even had me practice. Brought home Dominion coins, the tin ones. Doesn't work on coral. Just metal. He'd have me set them to spinning on my palm. First one, than more. By the time I was eleven, I could keep seven coins spinning between my hands. Problem was, by that time, he'd started bringing home bottles of green along with the coins."

"When did you figure out you could use it for cracking?"

"I didn't," Aldo said. "Dad got drunk one night at some dive in the Nest. Was bragging to someone about how I was his meal ticket, how I was so gifted the Colleges would be fighting over me. Someone from Sovrano Angelo's crew heard him. He owed them money. Not a lot, nothing worth squabbling over, but they had an idea."

He stopped speaking as the barmaid approached, setting two wooden bowls brimming with stew in front of him. The scent nearly made Aldo light headed, and he stared down at the thick potatoes and chunks of beef. Nicolette pressed two grey ducats into the barmaid's hand, and the young woman's eyes nearly bugged from her head. "Keep it," Nicolette said, smiling.

"Many thanks," the young woman said. "Wave if you need anything else."

"I definitely will." Nicolette watched her leave as Aldo picked up a spoon and took a bite. It was so rich it was nearly overwhelming. Nicolette saw him. "Not exactly what we're used to."

"They all eat like this?"

She shook her head. "This place is better than most. But yeah, food isn't an issue up here. All they do is grow." After they'd eaten in silence for a bit, she said, "So what was the idea?"

He swallowed, and reluctantly paused his meal. "A lockbox. One of their junior peers had snagged one, but they couldn't get it open. It was one of the rigged ones that couriers use. You know the type?"

Nicolette nodded. Couriers often used lockboxes with a glass bulb of squid ink inside. Any attempt to force the lid open shattered the bulb, permanently marking all the contents. "So you got it open."

"Yeah." Aldo took another bite. "After that, Dad was trading my services as a cracker to three different sovranos. I don't know how much he was getting paid. I know that the only thing that changed was the quality of his drinks."

Once they'd both finished, the barmaid darted over, trading the empty bowls for full tankards. Aldo's head was feeling a bit light from the drink, but his stomach was full in a way he couldn't remember ever feeling.

"Do you mind if I ask what happened?" Nicolette asked. "That night?"

Aldo stared down into his mug. "Dad found out about a safe. Most of the jobs we'd done were in the dockyards. Maybe a few near the Ruins, but nothing on the upper levels. I don't know where he heard about it, but one night, we took a cart up to the Artisan District. It was a scribe. Dad said the safe was on the second floor. Boosted me up to the window. It's how we worked. He made sure the place was empty, I went in and cracked while he kept watch." He took a long pull. Wiping his mouth on his sleeve, he said, "I don't know what went wrong. But after I cracked the safe, I headed downstairs to the back door, where we were supposed to meet. When I opened it, he wasn't there. Two guild guardsmen were. They grabbed me before I knew what was happening."

"Had he left?" Nicolette asked, leaning forward, her eyes narrowing.

Aldo shrugged. "Don't know. I looked around as they were carrying me away. My feet didn't even touch the ground. They just had me pinned between them. I was too scared to fight or try to run. I looked around. I didn't see him."

He cleared his throat. "We'd talked about it before. What would happen if I got pinched. We had a close call one time, and I got frightened. Didn't want to go on runs. Dad sat me down, explained that even if I did get caught, he could buy my sentence. He said they wouldn't give me much time at my age, so even with the 25% fee, it wouldn't be that bad. Might not even be on a barge, might just be hard labor on the docks."

Aldo's voice was dull as he spoke. Nicolette said nothing, just listening to him with thin lips and narrow eyes. "Sat in the stockade for three days. Didn't see him. Didn't think much of it. I knew he had to be at the tribunal to make an offer on my sentence. When I got there, I told the adjudicator he was coming. He waited, longer than I thought he would. No one came."

He took a big drink. "The scribe was writing communiques for Table families. One of them was in the stack I had on me when I got pinched. Whichever family it was pushed for a higher sentence. Don't know which family, or why, but what the Table says goes."

"But fourteen years?" Nicolette said softly. "That's a death sentence."

"It didn't seem real. It was too big a number, didn't really register. Even after they loaded me onto the bumboat to head out to the barge, it still felt like a mistake." Aldo shook his head. "I figured out that it wasn't pretty damn quickly."

He fell silent after that, and just drank. The buzz in his head helped mute the memories that were trying to peek out of the cracks of the box he kept them in.

"We have rooms. Here, I mean," Nicolette said a bit later. "Tomorrow..." She considered him. "Have you changed your mind? About the job, I mean."

Aldo gave a flat chuckle. "Probably should. Most people'd call me insane to trust you after that stunt." Before she could say anything, he raised his hand. "Meant what I said. You being nice to me, doing all these favors? That's not something I can trust. You throwing me to the wolves to make sure I still know how to step?" He shrugged. "That makes sense to me. Pissed me off, but it makes sense. And a payout like that?"

"It's a lot of money."

"It's more than that," he said. "I've been under someone's thumb since I could talk. Never really got to choose my own path. But if we do this..." He shook his head. "Nothing's changed. If I walk away now, I don't know anyone. I don't have a trade. I can find work, but Lofland Fork is a bit too close to the border to be comfortable for a while." He shrugged. "It's a good plan."

"It's a chance, Aldo," Nicolette said. "A chance for you to put everything behind you, live whatever life you want, fishhooks be damned." Her expression darkened. "And a chance to take back something from your father, a fraction of what he took from you."

"If we do this right, no one will know," Aldo said.

"You will."

Aldo nodded. "Yeah. I suppose I will." He cleared his throat, and sat up. "So. You satisfied with my skill?"

"Oh yes."

"You satisfied with your plan?"

Nicolette nodded. "You do what you do. I'll do what I do. It'll all work out."

Chapter 7

Aldo Marini had been born and raised in the city of Vetticci. Until Nicolette plucked him off the docks, out of the reach of those he'd angered, he'd only set foot outside the city during his time on the barge. He'd grown up used to buildings packing every square inch of space, roads and alleys bouncing back and forth, seeking out any opening they could find, jammed thick with the throng of people that had managed to find a tiny corner of the city to call their own. When they'd first emerged from the Myre, he'd been overwhelmed at just how much the Dominion sprawled, the wide swaths of open yawning space.

It was quiet. Vetticci was never quiet. Aldo didn't know if he'd ever get used to it.

As it turned out, four days on the back of a sullen donkey with a penchant for biting managed to break the romance of his journey quite nicely.

When Aldo spotted the large wooden archway in the distance, he nearly wept. The arch was made from dried and twisted vines, springing from the fence on each side of the road to meet at a large brass "V" hanging twenty feet off the ground. Two men waited by the arch. One was leaning against the fence on the left side, eating an apple with enough gusto that Aldo could hear his lips smacking from fifty feet away. The other wore an expression that made it plain that the experience of hearing his companion's gustatory endeavors at a closer range was not what he wanted to be doing on this slightly overcast day.

Once Aldo closed within fifty feet, the apple eater tossed the core into the long yellow grass that carpeted everything for miles around, wiping his hands on his trousers. The other guard made a face. "How are you not always sick?"

"Healthy living, I suppose." Reaching behind the fencepost, the guard picked up the strung longbow that had been hidden from view. A quiver of arrows hung at his hip. Raising his voice, he shouted, "You! On the ass! Think you made a wrong turn!"

Aldo tugged at the reins to bring Stuart to a stop. Stuart brayed, took another ten steps out of pure spite, shit on the road, and finally came to a halt. Aldo climbed off, wincing as he stretched muscles battered by the animal's spine for the last six hours. "If I did, could you gentlemen do me a great service? Please kill me. I don't know what awaits us beyond the final sleep, but I'm certain it can't be worse than climbing back on this monster for one more second."

The apple eater grinned. "I've not seen a mount with that particular color. It looks like the shits my son took during his first few months in this world."

"His color matches his disposition, I assure you." Stuart snapped his yellowing teeth at Aldo, who hopped to the side with a muttered curse. "A modification, if you please. Kill this beast first, so I might die with a pleasant view." Turning back to the guards, he touched his fingers to his brow. "My name is Aldo, and it's my pleasure to meet you."

"Hello, Aldo." The second guard stepped forward, hand dropping to the leather-wrapped hilt of the short sword hanging from his belt. "Goodbye, Aldo. You've clearly made a wrong turn."

Aldo pointed at the brass V. "This is the Vorchese Ranch, is it not?"

"You've been on the Vorchese Ranch for the last three miles," the bowman said. "This is just the main gate."

Aldo raised an eyebrow. "I don't see a gate."

"It's mostly just a turn of phrase."

"An odd choice." Aldo shrugged. "In any event, I'm exactly where I intend to be."

"Might be where you intended. Not going to be where you stay. Walk or ride, makes no difference to me, so long as it's back down the way you came."

"I thought the people of the Dominion were known for their hospitality."

"Filthy rumors."

"I'm here to see someone."

"I know everyone who lives and works this ranch. Saw them today." The bowman pulled an arrow and fit it to the string. "Not a single solitary one is expecting company."

"Well, no, he doesn't know that I'm coming."

"See, that's a surprise, right there. We're not the type to enjoy surprises, are we, Luca?"

The man with the sword, presumably Luca, shook his head. "Hate them, Ian."

"Tried surprising Luca here with a new blade last year, I did."

"Stabbed him with this one."

"See? Just not our cup of tea." Ian gestured with the point of the arrow back up the road. "What we do enjoy is someone who sends a letter, waits for a reply inviting them, which they would be brandishing in the air crowing their intent aloud as they rode their baby-shit colored donkey towards our main gate."

"See, I would enjoy that," Luca said. "Minimal stabbing in that case."

Aldo raised an eyebrow. "Minimal?"

"Can't account for all scenarios, can I?"

"I suppose not." Aldo scowled. *Careful, Aldo. Don't fuck this up before you even get started.* Nicolette had warned him that it might take some convincing to reach his father in the first place. "Look, I'm here to see Stiliano Marini. We know each other, from back in Vetticci."

"Never heard him mention you."

"To be fair, you just learned my name. How can you be certain?"

"Ayuh, but he never mentions anything from the city," Ian said. "Or really anything much at all. So it's a safe wager that he's never mentioned you."

"How do you know Stilts?" Luca asked.

"Stilts?" Aldo shook his head. "We worked together. For quite a while. Haven't seen him in a long time."

"How you know he's still got an interest in seeing you?"

I don't. "I'm confident."

"Fine line between confident and reckless, friend." Ian shook his head. "You can't walk the property unescorted. And we can't leave our post. Stilts isn't walking this quarter today. You see the problem."

Aldo tried to keep the dismay from his face. Nicolette had made her best guess as to when the watch would be relieved, and he'd tried to coordinate his arrival, but he was clearly early. *Or late, in which case I'm quite nicely fucked.* "I can wait until you're relieved."

"That's not going to be until a few hours before sundown. Right now, in this moment? You're trespassing. We wouldn't be very good at our jobs if we let a trespasser continue to trespass for hours on end while we watched said trespassing trespasser do all that heinous trespassing."

Luca shook his head. "Not happening today. You pass through Galen's Crossing this morning?"

"Last night."

"Head back there. We'll see Stilts tonight or tomorrow morning. Give him your name. You can come back in two, three days, and if he wants to see you, we'll show you to him."

Aldo shook his head. It wasn't an unreasonable request, but he was on a clock. *I show up same time as she does, that's gonna be hard to look past.* "I've come a long way."

"That particular fact fits quite nicely into the 'not our problem' category."

"Ask you two a question?" Neither responded, but Aldo continued. "If you'd come all the way from Vetticci for the solitary purpose of seeing someone, would you be particularly inclined to delay any further?"

"If the choice was between that and an arrow in the right shin?" Ian shrugged. "Probably."

"The right shin?"

"Welcome to the Dominion, Aldo. I can put this broadhead anywhere I choose," Ian said. "I promise, I'm really not an unpleasant sort. But the longer this conversation goes on, the more my choices narrow to an unpleasant few."

Aldo opened his mouth to speak, but spotted something behind them. A pair of men on horseback crested a rise, riding towards the gate. They each carried a spear, and a crossbow slung over their shoulder. He tried to keep his relief from his face.

Luca glanced back, and pursed his lips. "We could have one of the rovers relieve you, Ian. Walk him back."

"Me? Why not you?"

"Because it's my name day."

"It's not. You say that every week." Ian shook his head. "Naath isn't going to be pleased if we bring a stranger on property."

"Stilts isn't going to be pleased if he actually wants to see him and we turn him away."

"Between Naath and Stilts, I know whose ire I'd rather be on the receiving end of."

The men on horseback rode up, pulling their mounts to a halt with a gentle tug of the reins. Aldo shot Stuart a look. Stuart screamed.

"Just watch him, will you?" Luca walked over and began speaking with one of the riders while Ian scowled.

"Was having a good morning until you and your ass rode up."

"I'm terribly sorry," Aldo said. "Please accept this noble steed as my most heartfelt apology."

"That might be the most hostile thing you've said since arriving."

Luca came back. "Yeah, Drew is going to assume your watch." Ian opened his mouth to protest, and Luca held up a hand. "If Naath finds out and makes noise, tell him it was my call." Turning to Aldo, he said, "You have a choice here, friend. You can leave your name, and come back in a few days. No harm. Or, we can take you to see Stilts now. But if he doesn't want to see you, I can't promise you'll be walking out of here."

"Leave your name." Ian tilted his head. "He's not joking. The boss doesn't take well to strangers. He thinks for a moment you're here to cause trouble, it won't end well for you."

Aldo glanced between the pair, seeing no indication they were anything other than serious. *Gods, you'd better be right, Nicolette.* "Let's go."

Ian shook his head, but walked over to one of the riders, holding the reins while the man dismounted. He handed off his longbow, accepting the other guard's crossbow in exchange. "Come on, then.

It's at least an hour ride. Two, given the speed I suspect your animal
will make."

Aldo looked at Stuart with dismay. "Can't we walk?"

"It's a three hour walk."

"I'm okay with that."

"I'm not."

Reluctantly, Aldo took Stuart's reins, and clambered back on as Ian
rode up beside him.

"Go ahead. The road doesn't fork." Ian gestured. "You stay ahead
of me. You try anything foolish, try to run..."

"I understand that you're just doing your job, but the only way
Stuart here will move fast enough to cause you concern is if you throw
him off a cliff."

Ian smiled. It didn't touch his eyes. "I'll keep that in mind."

***

For the first thirty minutes or so, they rode in silence. The road they
were on was lined with a wooden slat fence extending nearly six feet
off the ground. Beyond the fence were huge rolling fields of yellow
grass, punctuated occasionally by massive oak trees. The grass was
undisturbed, but after a bit, the fields to the left of the road began to
look patchy, huge swaths absent of grass, the ground churned up. Aldo
considered asking Ian, but the man's hard expression had not yielded
since they began their ride together. He stayed thirty feet behind Aldo
at all times, the crossbow set across his knees, a bolt nocked and ready.

They began riding up a hill, the road cresting over the top. Aldo
heard barking. The grass to the left rustled and parted, and a shaggy
brown dog, bigger than any Aldo had ever seen, burst out to bark at

them. Stuart brayed fiercely back at the dog, which fell silent, staring at Aldo's mount with an expression of horror that Aldo had previously thought unachievable for a dog.

He heard hoofbeats behind him. Ian drew up alongside. "If your ride is easily spooked, keep a steady hand on the reins."

"He doesn't seem concerned about the dog," Aldo pointed out.

"That's a herd dog," Ian said. "Some mounts don't react well the first time they see them."

"See what?"

They crested the hill, and Ian said, "That."

Stuart came to an immediate halt. Aldo didn't protest. He was too busy staring.

On the downward slope of the rise was a herd of cattle, about twenty, dotting the field as they grazed. Three more dogs of the same breed prowled around the perimeter of the herd.

Cattle were an uncommon sight in Vetticci for obvious reasons. Beef rarely made its way down to the poorer levels of the city. However, several of the wealthier families maintained herds in the mile-wide grass fields between the borders of the city and the tree line of the Myre. He and Nicolette had passed several cows on their trip out, and he'd seen more while they made their way up north.

The creatures looming above the rolling plains before his eyes made those animals look almost quaint.

The Vorchese cattle were massive, the shoulders of the smallest in the herd nearly ten feet off the ground. Instead of the slender legs of most cows, these stood on thick, pillar-like feet, nearly two feet around, ending in blunted hooves that sank deep into the ground. They lowered heads the size of dining tables to the ground, clamping yellow teeth around huge chunks of grass, yanking them from the soil, roots and all. Their fur was a rich, deep orange, the color of pumpkins, dotted with dark brown spots. The nearest turned its glassy eyes towards the newcomers. Ian's mount nickered softly. Stuart shied to the side, letting out a sharp exhalation between his teeth, staring intently at the beasts.

"Gods," Aldo said. "They're huge."

"That they are," Ian said. "We need to keep moving."

The cow tracked them as they rode past, chewing slowly as it stared at them, craning its head around. Aldo kept looking back, shaking his head. "How much do they weigh?"

"Varies," Ian said. "Three, four tons."

"Most bridges can't hold that much."

"Why we don't take them on bridges." Ian gestured. "Let's pick up the pace. I want to get there before sundown."

Aldo nodded, and dug his heels into Stuart's flanks. For once, the donkey didn't object, its eyes still fixed on the massive animals on the other side of the fence. "I can't imagine that fence would hold if they even leaned on it."

"Nope."

"So how do you keep them from..."

"Appreciate the curiosity, but not the questions, friend," Ian said. "Stilts tells me I can chat with you, I'll be the liveliest conversationalist you'll find this side of a pub. Until then, it's best for both of us that you keep moving."

Aldo didn't want silence. A pit was forming at the center of his stomach, growing bigger as they rode. At one point, he saw two men working on repairing a section of fence, and his mouth grew dry as they came closer. When he realized they were both young, he let out a long breath. He tried to keep his nerves from reflecting on his face.

Will he recognize me? Aldo ran a hand over his beard, glanced down at the myriad scars dotting his hands and forearms. His sleeves were rolled down to his wrists despite the warm weather. He couldn't see the fishhook tattoos. He could feel them, though. *Will he know who I am?*

After a bit, buildings began to take shape in the distance, dozens of wooden clapboard structures set up almost like a small town. A large, three story house sat at the center, heavy wooden beams framing the large doors at the front. Just past all of those was a palisade. It looked like a fort, with thick logs driven deep into the ground, towering nearly twenty feet off the ground, butted up against each other to form a huge wall that extended for nearly a half mile in either direction before curving back and away.

As they drew closer to the compound, Aldo heard Ian mutter a curse. Three men were standing before one of the smaller buildings. Two wore the same simple homespun clothing that Ian and Luca wore, but the third wore a grey tunic, tailored and embroidered with scarlet thread. He turned to look at the approaching riders, and even from a distance, Aldo could make out the scowl on his face.

"Don't say anything," Ian said. "Let me handle this."

"Ian. I was under the impression that you were on watch at the main gate," the man said as he approached. His voice lacked the rough Dominion accent. It was educated and polished.

"Yes, sir," Ian said. "I had Brennan relieve me." He gestured towards Aldo. "Visitor. Says he knows Stilts, from back before. We tried telling him to leave his name, come back after we'd talked to Stilts, but..."

"But instead you decided to bring an unvetted guest onto my ranch," the man said. His voice was mild, but Aldo could see the tension in Ian's shoulders. "That's an interesting decision."

"He wouldn't leave, sir."

"I see." The man let his gaze linger on Ian for a moment longer, then turned his attention to Aldo. "Naath Vorchese, and I'm very much at your service."

Aldo glanced at Ian. "May I dismount?"

"You may." The response didn't come from Ian. It came from Naath.

Aldo climbed down, and bowed at the waist. "My name is Aldo."

"Just Aldo?"

"Aldo Fisher." He'd settled on the name with Nicolette back in town. It was easy to remember. Neither were sure whether his relationship with his father would play well or not with the others at the ranch, so they decided to err on the side of caution. "I apologize for not writing ahead of my arrival. I can't write, and a scribe is a bit outside my means."

"So you know Stiliano." Naath nodded slowly. "Well, I can understand Ian's motivation for bringing you up here, even if the choice was not what I would have preferred."

"Please don't blame him, Master Vorchese," Aldo said. "I have few talents, but I'm assured by those who know me that being stubborn tops the list. I left them little choice."

"There's always a choice," Naath said. "But I'll let it lie for now. And please, I don't like formality. My name is Naath." He tilted his head. "I have to confess, I'm quite curious. Our dear captain says so little about his history, and here comes a man claiming to be a part of that history. I have quite a few questions."

Aldo shifted, uncomfortable. *How much did you tell them, dad?* "Is it possible for me to see him?"

"Ian, I believe Stilts was inspecting the north pastures. He should be back shortly. Go find him, let him know that he has a guest." Ian nodded, and headed to the left of the big house. Naath smiled at

Aldo. "I apologize if their welcome was a bit more brusque than you'd hoped. We aren't really the sort to have unexpected guests. We take the safety of our animals quite seriously."

"I saw them on the way in," Aldo said. "I've never seen anything quite like them."

"I should hope not," Naath said. "We're the only ranch in the Dominion that has that breed." He tilted his head. "How close did you get?"

"Not that close," Aldo admitted. "Ian really didn't let me approach the fence. I promise, he was a complete professional."

Naath nodded. "Well, while we wait, I'd be happy to show you around."

For an instant, Aldo was surprised the rancher was so willing to show him around. A heartbeat later, he realized the truth. *If you belong, you belong. If not, you're not leaving. Doesn't really matter what he shows you.* The thought did little for the pit in his stomach.

If Naath knew the apprehension he'd caused Aldo, he didn't show it. "We call this central area the Promenade. All of our facility buildings are within this small area." He nodded at the house. "I suppose it's obvious where our family home is."

"It's impressive."

"You should see what my grandfather grew up in," Naath said. "Actually, you can. We use it as equipment storage." He shrugged. "Fortunately, his experiments in breeding paid off." He pointed to a long building to the left of the house, painted clapboard with windows of greased paper regularly spaced. "Our barracks. You've met a few of our guards, but we maintain a sizable force. It's a lot of land to keep watch over." He pointed to a small cottage about a hundred feet away. "Guard captain's quarters. Where your old friend resides."

Aldo followed as Naath began walking up alongside the fence, pointing as he went. "Curing building, husbandry house." As they passed the house, the palisade loomed over head. Aldo tilted his head back to look to the top. Naath grinned. "Impressive, isn't it? Took nearly three years to build."

"What is it?"

"The bull paddock."

Aldo raised an eyebrow. "You don't keep the bulls in the field with the cows?"

"Bull. Singular. They're very rare. And keeping them with the cows would be quite impossible," Naath said. "Vorchese bulls are... irritable. They're also quite large."

"All your cows are enormous."

"The bull is bigger." Naath considered him. "Would you like to see?"

"What?" Aldo looked over, confused. "The bull?"

"We have a few observation ports cut into the palisade. There's no guarantee you'll see anything, but if you're curious..."

Aldo nodded. "If you're sure."

"Any friend of Stilts." Naath led the way. The palisade was even more impressive up close. None of the logs sunk deep into the ground were less than a foot in diameter, the spaces between them packed tightly with mud and straw, not allowing a glimmer of light to escape. About twenty feet to their right, a small alcove, maybe ten feet wide, was set into the fence. "Here."

They stepped inside. Heavy oak beams framed a small structure, extending inside the palisade and with a set of two small windows, each with metal bars. It looked like the inside of a cell. Naath stepped to one window, and when Aldo hesitated, Naath waved him forward.

"It's all right. They don't get close to this part of the fence."

"Why not?" Aldo asked, peering through the bars.

"See the flowers, planted all around us?" The tiny scarlet blooms dotted the ground like drops of blood against the yellowed grass. "Those are penny blossoms. The bulls don't like the smell. They stay away."

Aldo nodded. On the other side of the massive wall was another field, identical to those he'd passed on the way inside. He could spot the wooden barrier disappearing around the squat hill it surrounded. The interior of the enclosed area was huge, at least a mile across. Large deep furrows were scattered randomly around the slope of the hill, gouges in the earth nearly three feet deep and stretching the length of a building.

At the top of the hill was a dense copse of trees, old sprawling oaks with thick limbs. He spotted several branches bigger around than his thigh broken, dangling from the few remaining pieces of wood clinging to the trunk. As he stared, he heard wood snap. The tops of the trees swayed, and something crunched inside the dark dense cluster of woods.

He nearly had his face pressed against the bar. From the corner of his eye, he realized Naath was not watching the field, but was watching him. He felt self-conscious, and was about to say something, but a loud crack echoed over the hill, and he saw a massive shadow shift from within the trees. A low baying noise rolled over the grass, like the cry of a bloodhound, but deeper, mournful. The trees trembled again, and then went still, the shadow vanishing back into the copse.

"Feeling shy today, I suppose." Naath shrugged. "Sometimes he's a bit more energetic."

"I hope to see that one day," Aldo said. He was not entirely sure that he was telling the truth.

"Maybe you will," Naath said. "So I have to ask. What do you want of Stiliano? He's not in any trouble, is he?"

Aldo shook his head. "Does that happen? People come looking for him?"

"Not once since he showed up here eight years ago." Naath leaned back against the wall of the observation post. "He does his job, quietly and well. Men like that are worth more than I can say." He glanced over Aldo's shoulder, and grinned. "Speaking of..."

"Ian said you needed to see me, boss?"

The voice came barreling through a decade and a half, crashing into to Aldo like a sledgehammer.

In and out, Aldo. This street's clear. You need anything, give the whistle, and I'll come running.

His legs threatened to turn to water. He reached out and gripped the bar, steadying himself, not ready to turn around.

"You have a guest. An uninvited guest," Naath said. "At least I presume he was uninvited. I can't imagine that you would have neglected to tell us, particularly since we don't really allow guests."

"What? I don't know this guy."

Aldo turned around, and was fourteen years old once more.

His father had always been thin. Food was never in steady supply in the slums of the Nest, but if there had been a choice to spend coin on food or liquor, it had never been a difficult call. Aldo often ate with whatever the family they shared the flat with had managed to scrounge.

Stiliano Marini had gained weight. His chest and arms were muscled, his neck thick. He wore the same homespun cotton clothes as the rest of the guard, but a red diamond had been stitched onto his tunic's breast. His boots and the lower third of his trousers were covered in mud, and while there were more wrinkles surrounding them, the grey eyes that were narrowed at Aldo were the same.

"I've never seen this guy before in my life, boss. I don't know what's..." Aldo stepped forward, out of the shadows of the observation alcove and into the faint evening light, and Stiliano's words died in his throat. His eyes darted over Aldo, from his beard to his clothes, and the color drained from his face. His mouth opened once, twice, but nothing came out.

"Stilts? You okay?" Ian stood next to him, his eyebrows raised in alarm. His hand went to the dagger on his belt. "What's wrong?"

Before Stiliano could speak, Aldo said, "It's been a long time, Stiliano." He was shocked at how even his voice sounded.

Swallowing, Stiliano nodded, a quick, jerky motion. "Y...Yeah. Long time. How have you..." He licked his lips. "Uh. Yeah."

"Are you all right?" Naath stepped forward, and gripped Stiliano's shoulder. When his captain didn't immediately respond, he glanced over at Ian. "Get this man out of here. Now."

Ian had Aldo's arm in a steel grip before Stiliano could speak. "No. No, please. I'm, uh, I'm sorry, boss. Just surprised." He tore his eyes away from Aldo. "Would it be okay if he and I could talk? It's been a long time since we've seen each other."

Naath raised an eyebrow, glancing between the two of them, but nodded slowly. "Sure, Stilts. Sure." He pointed to the house. "Use the dining room. You can close the door, have as much time as you need."

Stiliano nodded. "I, uh, I need to lock down the northside gate."

"Ian, can you handle that?" Naath asked. Ian nodded, still staring daggers at Aldo. "Go."

"Thanks, boss." Stiliano looked back to Aldo, but he seemed to be having trouble now keeping his eyes in one place. "Uh, follow me. Please."

They walked in silence, Aldo staring at the hair that was much thinner than he remembered, at a mild limp of which he had no recollection. His days of rehearsal melted away. He had no idea what he was going to say.

In and out, Aldo.

They climbed up the steps to the patio, through the red painted doors. Aldo didn't notice the halls they walked through, or the whispered stares of a pair of chambermaids watching from large sweeping staircase. He just saw Stiliano, pulling open a door into a large dining room, windows covered in drapes, a long polished wood table in the center. Aldo walked past him as Stiliano held the door. He walked over to a chair, gripping the back as if to pull it out, then changing his mind. He stared down at the lamplight reflecting in the tabletop as the door closed and latched behind them. Finally, he looked up.

"Hi, Dad."

Chapter 8

"You grew a beard."

Aldo stared at his father. "What?"

Stiliano pointed with a trembling hand. "You grew a beard."

Aldo brought his fingers up to brush the coarse hairs. "Yeah, I grew a beard."

"It looks good."

Tilting his head, Aldo said, "No, it doesn't. It looks ragged. Like it hasn't seen a barber. Ever."

"No, I meant..." Stiliano shook his head sharply. "I meant it's not grey. Mine's grey."

"Sure."

His father walked to the other side of the table, turning to face him when they stood on opposite sides. "When did you... I mean, how long have you been back?"

Aldo took a deep breath. "Seven months ago."

"Good. That's good."

"Is it?"

Stiliano swallowed. "I mean it's good that you're back. That you got to come home."

"I don't really have a home, dad." Aldo leaned forward, bracing his hands against the back of the chair. "I went back to our old flat."

"Oh yeah? Is Aniya still there?"

"The flat isn't there. Burned down sometime between when I walked out that door and when I came back. Hard to tell when, exactly. That's a lot of years to account for."

Stiliano had a strange forced smile on his face. Whenever Aldo spoke, his eyes reacted as if he'd been struck, but the smile remained, like a rictus. Aldo found it grotesque. "The Nest never stays the same for long. I'm sure they built right over the ashes."

"Is that it?"

"What?"

"I grew a beard? The Nest doesn't stay the same?" Aldo had pictured this moment, pictured the heroic effort it would take to keep the rage from his voice. Instead, he just felt deeply tired. "Almost fifteen years, and that's what you have for me?"

The grin stayed fixed in place, as if it had been nailed into the bones of his skull. "You told them I was a friend."

"I did," Aldo said. "I'm guessing that you haven't shared with them what happened to your kid. Didn't feel like that was the best way to kick off this reunion."

"No, yeah. Yeah, that was smart." He shook his head. "They don't know. Anything about my life before."

Aldo nodded slowly. "I can imagine that would be a difficult thing to explain. Difficult enough that you're standing here asking me about my fucking beard."

The profanity seemed to finally peel the grin away. Stiliano's face collapsed like a rotting shed. "You never cursed. Before."

"Mom didn't like it. After she died, it felt disrespectful," Aldo said.

"That's good. That's a good thing." He looked around. "Are you hungry? They feed us well here." His face suddenly lit up for a moment. "I know!" He practically ran over to a table at the end with several crystal trays and bowls. Stiliano picked up a small one, and returned to Aldo's side, offering it. It was full of small clusters of golden crystals.

Aldo stared at the bowl, slowly raising his eyes to his father. "This isn't food."

"It's honey candy!" Stiliano plucked one of the clusters out, popping it in his mouth. "You love honey candy."

Aldo's mouth opened, then closed. He shook his head slowly. "I don't want any candy."

"But you love honey candy."

"I loved honey candy, yes. I loved it because you would buy some for me after we finished a job. But considering I waited for fourteen gods-damned years after my last piece, I've lost my taste for them."

Staring down at the bowl, Stiliano nodded slowly. "Yeah." He set the bowl down on the table. "Yeah, okay." He pulled out a chair, and sank into it. "Look, Aldo, what happened..."

Aldo held up a hand, and Stiliano fell silent. Reaching down, he picked up the bowl, and walked to the end, returning it to the spot it had been. He went over to the chair opposite his father, and sat down. "I've had a lot of time to imagine what you'd say. A lot of time. Time enough to go through every scenario, every possible reason why you didn't..." He trailed off for a moment, trying to collect himself.

Give the whistle. I'll come running.

Aldo felt a maddening urge to whistle, see what the man would do. He pushed it aside.

"It was a lot of time. I thought it over from every angle. And I realized something."

His father wasn't looking at him. His grey eyes were fixed on the table, hollow.

"There's not an answer. Not a combination of words in this or any other language that will make it okay," Aldo said. "There's nothing you can say that will give me back the time I lost, make everything that happened not happen. So let's just skip that part. Let's skip the excuses, the reasons. Because there's nothing down that road that's going to do either of us a fucking drop of good. So just... don't."

Stiliano nodded. "Why are you here, Aldo?"

"Because I don't have anywhere else to go."

"What happened?"

"I got over a dozen fucking fishhooks tattooed on my arm." There was no anger in Aldo's voice. "I walk around with marks that make damn sure that any job that pays enough that you won't starve won't have anything to do with me. I tried working the piers." He held up his hands. Stiliano's eyes widened as he saw the map of scars chronicling a fourteen year nightmare. "Between the broken bones and the hooks taking pieces of my flesh to chum the water, I can't carry shit all day. My hands swell up, stop working. I got hungry. I tried the canneries, tried even getting a spot on a real fishing boat. Nothing. I got hungrier."

He dropped his hands to the table. "I went to the brothels. The dockyard ones, where a small stack of grey will get you an hour of whatever you want. They wouldn't have me. Seemed convinced I'd rob the customers. I got even hungrier."

Stiliano seemed to shrink into himself as Aldo spoke.

"I got hungry enough that I went to the guard. Told them where to find someone who attacked a merchant's son. They gave me five ducats for squawking," Aldo said. "Enough to eat for two days. Then I did it again, because I didn't want to be hungry again. And I made the wrong people angry, so I had to leave the city."

He leaned back in the chair. "You know Amon Lawson?"

Stiliano looked up, eyes red. "Amon? Yeah, he does seasonal work for us sometimes."

Aldo nodded. "I ran into him. Down in Lofland Fork. He bought me a drink. I hadn't had much more luck finding work. They don't like Vetticcians that much, least not those without any coral. But he said I might find something up here. Said the captain of the guard was even Vetticcian. When he told me your name, I thought for sure it had to be a mistake."

"If you thought it was a mistake, then why..."

"Because I was hungry." Aldo shrugged. "You do stupid shit when you're hungry, hoping that maybe, despite every day of your fucking life arguing otherwise, you might have a bit of luck. And I thought that if it really was you, maybe there was enough of a father left in you to help me."

Stiliano straightened up, nodding. "I have money. Not much, but enough to get you wherever you want to go. It's yours."

Aldo tilted his head. "Just like that?"

"It's yours," Stiliano said.

"I don't want your money."

"But you said..."

"I don't want your money. I want a job," Aldo said. "I want to work and not starve. I want to survive."

"You want a..." Stiliano frowned. "You're not a rancher."

"Neither were you, but here you sit."

Stiliano shook his head. "No, that's..." He cleared his throat. "I can help you. I can."

Aldo lifted an eyebrow. "Really?"

"Really." Stiliano cleared his throat. "Just north of Galen's Crossing, there's an orchard. Big. Pears and apples. They always need pickers, and they pay well. Room and board, too. The foreman knows me. Owes me. I can..." He trailed off as Aldo shook his head.

"I told you. I can't carry shit all day. Don't know how much he owes you, but how long do you think it'll take him to bounce my ass once he realizes I can't go more than two, three hours before my fingers swell and I can't make a fist?" Aldo pushed up his sleeve. "How long before he sees this? Even people up here know what that means."

"Then what..."

"I can't carry a basket all day. But I can carry a crossbow over my shoulder, and I can walk," Aldo said. "I can walk every inch of this ranch, as many times as you want."

Stiliano stared. "You want a job as a guard."

"Why else would I be talking to the captain?"

"Aldo, I want to help. I really do. But that..." He shook his head. "I don't hire the guards. Naath does. And he's careful. Particular."

"How particular could he be?" Aldo scoffed. "You got hired."

"I got hired by Naath's father, before he died," Stiliano said. "Naath is different. And even if I could get you a job, you don't want one here."

"No, I don't," Aldo said, coming to his feet. "I don't want to work here. I want to work somewhere where I'm not reminded of the worst day of my life every time my boss asks me to do something. But I got nowhere else to go. This is what I've got."

"Aldo, this place..."

"This place pays you. Feeds you." Aldo's hands closed into fists. "I hate that I'm here. Hate that I'm begging you. Hate that I'm giving you another chance to leave me swinging. But I have nothing and no one left."

Stiliano stared at the wood, and slowly rose to his feet. "Follow me."

"Are you going..."

"Aldo, just... just follow me. Please."

Naath was waiting outside, speaking to an older man. When he heard the door open, he nodded at his companion, who walked away as Naath turned to face them. "Well! A good chat, I hope? A chance to catch up?"

Stiliano came to a stop in front of him. "I need a favor, boss."

Naath nodded. "Anything, Stilts, you know that."

"Titus has been walking the east border on his own for two weeks. He needs a backup." Stiliano gestured back to Aldo. "He's solid. Needs work. I'd take it as a personal favor."

Naath's smile didn't fade, but his eyes narrowed. "That's not how I like to do things, Stiliano."

"I know. But I owe him." Stiliano didn't look back as he spoke. "He saved my life. Back in the city. Ended up doing time on a penance barge while I walked away."

Raising an eyebrow, Naath nodded slowly. "That is a very large debt indeed." He glanced over at Aldo, and said, "I don't judge. You having been imprisoned, I mean. That's not why I hesitate. I take the safety of these animals, and the people who service them, very seriously."

Aldo nodded. "I can respect that."

"Can you." Naath considered him. "Stiliano, please go for a walk. I'd like to talk to your friend for a bit."

Woodenly, Stiliano nodded. He glanced at Aldo, but his eyes dropped, and he walked away.

***

Naath tilted his head towards the house. "I have an office inside. We should talk."

"Yes, sir." Aldo's father disappeared around the side of the building as he followed Naath. They walked past the dining room to stairs, at the top of which was a small, spartan room with a desk and several chairs. The surface of the desk was completely bare, as were the walls. There were no windows.

"It's simple, I know," Naath said as he watched Aldo take in the room. "But I prefer a lack of distraction. They're more than ample outside." He gestured at the chair. "Sit down."

Aldo did, swallowing as the door clicked close. "I could have handled this better. I know."

Naath offered a very slight smile. "You could have. I find myself in a difficult position. I don't know that I could run this place without Stilts. How long did you two know each other?"

"Quite a while," Aldo said.

"Well, it's fairly clear that you aren't fond of him. Which speaks to your desperation. I'm going to guess you don't have too many options if I was to send you on your way."

"I'm going to guess that's not going to play into your decision."

"You may be surprised." Naath settled into his seat, and considered Aldo. "I've heard stories about Vetticcian penance barges. None of them make the experience sound pleasant."

"They're not."

Naath nodded. "May I ask how long you spent on board?"

"A long time." Aldo shifted in his seat uncomfortably, but Naath simply watched him, and after a few moments, Aldo sighed and pushed up his sleeve. The fishhooks were tattooed in two rows, thin faded blue ink marching from his wrist up to his elbow.

Naath's eyes brushed over them, lingering as he counted. His eyebrow raised, and he exhaled slowly. "You are a lucky man, my friend."

"That's what they tell me." Aldo pushed his sleeve back down. "After the fifth year, simply managing not to die didn't feel like the windfall everyone made it out to be."

"I would imagine, but you misunderstand me." Naath tapped his fingers on the surface of the desk. "An experience like that changes a person. It shapes them. Teaches them."

"And what was freezing half to death in soaking wet homespun before I had hair below my belt meant to teach me?"

Naath shrugged. "I have no idea. Each experience like that is different, each lesson imparted different. But we don't get to escape those kinds of lessons. Most people spend their lives doing everything they can to do so. That city you call home, those who rule. They wrap themselves in obscene wealth, using it to shield themselves from anything and everything that might cause the slightest discomfort. They hide from what this life is meant to be, and they don't change. They don't develop calloused, scar tissue, don't grow."

The rancher tilted his head, asking, "Were you ever taught as a boy not to drink water from a stagnant pond?"

Aldo shook his head. "We don't really have ponds in the city. We drink from the rain barrels."

Naath nodded. "It's something we teach children here from a young age. If they can smell it, if they see flies, if they see a slick on the surface, they stay away. Without turbulence, without current rocking them from stone to stone, they don't change. They stagnate. They fester. And just like that festering, stagnant pool, those who hide from the lessons of this life offer nothing but disease and filth."

Lifting his own arm, Naath let the sleeve of his tunic fall. In the same spot that Aldo had his fishhooks, Naath had his own marking, a shepherd's crook. But this was no tattoo. It was a brand.

Aldo's mouth went dry as Naath asked, "Do you know what this means?"

Slowly, Aldo nodded. "I think so."

"And?"

"You're a Confessor."

"I am," Naath said.

"I thought..." Aldo swallowed. "I thought the Confessors all moved to Cicerone after the secession." It was about the kindest thing that he could draw from his limited knowledge of the religious sect. If any Confessors had found their way into the city, he hadn't heard about it. From what little he knew about them, the city was better for their absence.

"Many of us, yes. But many have been called to serve in other ways." Naath stood up, and came around to sit on the desk in front of Aldo. "I was in the holy land, studying to become a Shepherd. I thought I knew what my path would be. But when the grey fever came, when my family fell one by one and this ranch was in danger of falling to ruin, I was tasked to come back, to see this place thrive."

Aldo wanted to push the chair back, to create a bit of space between the two of them. He also knew there was no way to do so without making his discomfort clear.

"I do my duty to the church," Naath said. "But I haven't forgotten the role I hoped to play." Reaching down, he took Aldo's wrist in a firm grasp, and pushed his sleeve back up. He brushed his fingertip over the faded blue ink, and Aldo couldn't help the shudder that rippled up his arm. He could remember the men holding him down, the needle dipped in the blue mash made from the urchins that clung to the lines, the sting as it slowly dug into his flesh again and again.

If his reaction bothered Naath, it didn't show. "I called you lucky. But it's not because you survived. You endured. You experienced pain, and fear, and all of the things at the core of the time we spend in this world. Like pig iron brought to the forge, it burned away the parts that make you impure, that make you unworthy to take the next step."

He spoke in the soft tones of a prayer, the words clearly having passed his lips many times. Aldo met those wide eyes and couldn't look away.

"I call you lucky because most go their entire life without truly experiencing what we must to move forward, to break free of this perdition and realize where we were meant to be," Naath said. His thumb traced from one to the next. "You stepped onto that ship broken, rotten, contaminated like all of us. You stepped off as something very different."

Releasing his arm, Naath touched two fingers against the shepherd's crook burn on his wrist. "Do you understand?"

Aldo shook his head, a sharp, quick shake. He wanted little more to be out of this room.

"That's all right." Naath offered a kind smile. It did nothing to calm Aldo's nerves. "It's a very big truth to take in. I've tried my entire life, and still know there's so much for me to learn. But the pain we endure in this life, it's not without purpose."

"If there was a purpose to that hell, I can't see it," Aldo spat. His voice trembled, and his cheeks burned in humiliation. "I was a child."

"So were we all."

Aldo shook his head. "You can't know what it was like."

"I don't know your lyrics, but the melody of pain is one that we all can sing from memory." To Aldo's horror, Naath pulled his tunic over his head. His chest was a mass of scars, dozens, each one a perfect rectangle of raised flesh, precise, regular. He crouched down, and turned, brushing a finger against his right shoulder blade. "Do you see that?"

Among the tapestry of scars, a bulge sat on his back, just near his shoulder. Aldo nodded, and realized Naath couldn't see with his back to him. *Gods, Nicolette, you couldn't have warned me?* "I see it."

"I fought for Duke Snowsill when I was young. Seventeen. I was an archer, like most everyone else, but in my first battle, a skirmish with Duke Aldrich, an arrow punched through my chest, through my lung, through my ribs, and through my shoulder blade." He flexed, and Aldo could see the mass shift beneath the skin, and Naath sighed, almost in pleasure.

"They left it in?"

"I left it in." Naath stood back up, pulling his tunic back on. "They broke free the shaft, pulled that out. I lived through the days following, when fever burned through me and fire filled my breast. Once I was strong enough, the anatomists offered to remove it, but I refused. Its kiss reminds me of why I wake each morning, why I endure being away from the rest of my church to toil away here."

He offered an oddly sad smile. "I feel like I understand something about you many would not, Aldo. I'm inclined to let you stay."

Aldo blinked. "I... I appreciate it."

"It doesn't take much to see the bad blood between you and Stilts. Is that going to be a problem?" Naath asked.

Aldo shook his head. "I just want to do my job. Earn a fair day's wage."

"Then you can do that. But to be sure, I believe I'll put you with Titus tomorrow. He's the second in command of our guard force, and has been here longer than anyone. It might be best if you didn't test your patience with your old friend."

Naath walked back to the door, and pulled it open. "Welcome to the Vorchese Ranch, Aldo Fisher. I'm eager to know you better."

Chapter 9

Aldo followed Naath downstairs, staring at the back of the rancher's head, trying to collect himself after the unsettling discussion. When they stepped out onto the large wraparound porch of the house, there was no sign of his father, but Ian was waiting for them.

"I have a fair amount to do, so I'll put you in Ian's capable hands," Naath said. He nodded to Ian, who wore a somewhat less hostile expression on his face now that Aldo had been welcomed. "Ian, show Aldo to the barracks and get him set up with a uniform. He'll be working with Titus on perimeter patrol in the morning. You have it?"

Ian nodded. "I do, boss."

"Good." Naath nodded at Aldo, and headed into the house.

"Sorry about earlier," Ian said. "It's kind of our job to be inhospitable."

Aldo touched a finger to his forehead. "And you excel at the position."

Ian grinned. "I'll give you some pointers. Come on." Aldo fell in beside him as they walked toward the long unpainted wooden building he'd noticed earlier. "You missed evening chow, but there's always some rolls and dried meats. Breakfast is at sunrise in the barracks, dinner right before it gets dark, in the house."

Glancing around, Aldo asked, "Do I need to know what all these buildings are?"

Ian shook his head. "You'll pick it up. Besides, you won't need to know any of them. You're going to spend twelve hours a day riding." He glanced over. "You can ride, right?"

"I was riding when you first met me."

"You were clinging to that half donkey half coyote monstrosity that dragged you up here."

"His name is Stuart, thank you very much, and he's just so much worse than you can imagine."

Ian made a face. "Don't be so sure. I had to drag him to the stable. When I left, he was shrieking at the other horses and biting the groom."

"That's just how he says hello," Aldo said. "If he ends up in the stewpot, I won't be that upset."

"I can't imagine he'd be any more palatable in the bowl."

Aldo paused for a moment, and grinned. "Do you have anyone heading to Lofland Fork anytime soon?"

Ian nodded. "We send a convoy every two weeks with cheeses and milk. One leaves tomorrow."

"Think they'd mind bringing Stuart to the city? Dropping him off with a friend of mine?"

"They might, but if it gets that thing off this ranch, I'll make sure of it."

Aldo nodded. "I'd appreciate it."

Pulling open the door, Ian allowed Aldo to step through first. The interior was long and cavernous, a row of bunks stretching from one end to the other. A half dozen men were pulling on boots and rubbing sleep from their eyes. Several crossbows were mounted in racks on the wall, but they were far outnumbered by the unstrung longbows that seemed to rest against every bed. "Are you people issued those damn things when you're born?"

A nearby guard gave Aldo an odd look. "Try to forgive him," Ian said. "Aldo's from Vetticci." Looking back to Aldo, he said, "We all owe three years in a Ducal army when we turn sixteen. Almost all of us are trained as a longbowman. They let us keep the bow when we leave."

"Aren't those worth some money?"

"We're not allowed to sell them," Ian said. "Makes for a convenient conscription force in case the Dukes start squabbling again."

Aldo raised his eyebrow. "That happen a lot?"

"Not so much here," Ian said. "Few of the other duchies don't go more than a year or two without a skirmish." They got about halfway down to a bunk with blankets neatly folded on the end. "This is you. Not a lot of space, but it's free and you get fed." He shrugged. "Not the worst deal. You get coin at the end of each day. First year, thirty marks a day. Once you're here a full year, it goes to forty."

With the conversion, that was less than Aldo had been making on an average day on the docks. *Of course, you don't have a price on your head here, asshole. And if this plays out the way it should, it won't matter.* Aldo set his saddlebags down on the bed. "That works."

"Titus!" A burly man had just come through the door, tugging off a pair of rough leather gloves. He glanced over as Ian called his name, and tromped over, his heavy boots leaving bits of dried mud in his wake.

"I'm not doing it."

"It's not night watch," Ian said, waving him off. "This is Aldo. He's going to be with you moving forward."

Titus glanced at Aldo, who offered his hand. Titus stared at it as if not sure what it was. "I thought the boss said we weren't hiring more until the end of season."

"Old friend of Stilts," Ian said. "From before."

"Before?" Titus' eyes widened. "Oh. Before here?"

Ian nodded.

"We have questions," Titus said.

"Many questions."

Aldo shook his head. "I'm not the one to ask."

"Not quite sure who else would be the one to ask."

Aldo shifted, uncomfortable. This possibility hadn't come up in his planning with Nicolette. "Look, that was a very long time ago. He's different now. And I'm not sure that he'd want me dragging any of that shit up."

Titus considered this, and nodded. "Fair." He stuck out a meaty hand, and Aldo took it. As he did, Aldo's sleeve pulled up, revealing the first rough fishhook tattoo. Ian's eyes widened.

"Is that..." Ian raised a hand as if to point, then lowered it again. Titus looked down, and raised an eyebrow.

"Yeah," Aldo said. "Naath knows. Said it didn't matter."

"That means you were on one of the punishment boats, right?"

Aldo pushed his sleeve back down. "The penance barges. Yes."

"How long?"

"A long time."

Ian opened his mouth, and Titus smacked him on the arm. "What?!"

"Pretty gods-damned sure if I'd done something like that, I wouldn't want to jaw about it with someone I just fucking met."

Ian frowned. "Fair." He glanced over at Aldo. "Sorry."

"It's fine."

Titus turned to Aldo. "You can ride? Know there aren't a lot of horses in Vetticci."

"Rode a donkey all the way up here."

"That thing is not a donkey," Ian insisted.

"It's donkey-adjacent," Aldo said. "But yeah, I can ride."

Titus raised an eyebrow. "Bit of a difference between an ass and a Snowsill nag."

"I'll learn."

"I'll remember you said that when you're complaining of bruised balls and walking like I just punted you 'tween the legs," Titus said. "We'll be riding all day."

"I'll be fine."

***

He was not fine.

The sun had yet to reach its highest point in the sky, and Aldo's hips felt like he was being tugged apart like a wishbone. The horse beneath him wasn't nearly as obstreperous as Stuart; indeed, she was fairly calm. He suspected they'd chosen her to forgive his lack of experience, but he was still sore, and the day wasn't halfway done.

They were currently riding next to a herd of about thirty cows, keeping their distance. When they'd first approached, Aldo had done his best to keep his hands from trembling. If he'd thought they were big from a distance, this close they seemed like lumbering buildings, their big flat feet smashing down the grass beneath broad coal-black hooves. Their movements were slow and deliberate. They would lower their massive heads down, taking a big mouthful of grass, tearing it out by massive clumps, dirt raining down from the roots.

"Do they ever get spooked? Stampede?" Aldo watched them nervously from his saddle, balancing the crossbow on his legs.

Titus shook his head. "Don't think I've ever seen one run. Not sure they can." He shrugged. "I know they're big, but once you get used to them, they're pretty dull. Last year, we had a bad storm. Lightning split an oak right next to six or seven of them. Scared the hell out of me, but they didn't even blink. Like they didn't know it was going to happen."

As the day went on, Aldo saw how true that actually was. They wandered from point to point, encountering herds ranging from a handful of the massive creatures to over one hundred, a horde of cattle that left the ground a churned ruin in their wake. No matter how many they numbered, they had virtually no reaction when the men on horseback rode up, even when Titus took them in the midst of a herd, weaving in between animals towering just as high as the pair on horseback.

"Look, for the most part, this is an easy gig," Titus said. "Most of your days will be boring. You'll ride for ten hours, check fences, and that's pretty much it. Three rules to keep in mind."

Aldo made a face as one of the cows slowly swung its big head to stare at him as it dropped a pile of droppings the size of a small sheep. Aldo's horse nickered, stepping neatly around the manure. "Why doesn't it smell worse? The few times we had manure brought down to my part of the city, it stank to high heaven."

Titus shrugged. "Don't know. I know it's worthless for fertilizer."

"Weird," Aldo said. "Sorry, I interrupted. It's a distracting sight. Three rules."

"First. If you see or hear something strange, you send up the alarm." He pointed at the whistle hanging around Aldo's neck. "We all have them. Doesn't matter if you're not sure if it's anything serious or not. Sound the alarm. You don't know shit, so you can't know if something's off or not." Aldo nodded, but Titus fixed him with a stare. "Not a joke. No one's going to say word one if you blow because a cow farted a bit loudly. But you hesitate and one of these animals gets hurt, I promise, they're worth ridiculously more than you are."

"I hear you."

"Good. Next is just the other side of that coin. You hear a whistle, you run. If you have a weapon nearby, grab it, but otherwise, get moving. If you're taking a shit, wipe your ass on the way. If you're bleeding to death, knock it off and move your ass," Titus said. "If you're first on the scene, do whatever you can until someone who knows what the fuck they're doing shows up."

"What kind of emergencies come up?

"Poachers, trespassers. Mostly, it's a calf getting stuck in a fence or on a tree. If that's the case, just keep clear until one of the ranchers show up. The calves are smaller, but they can move a bit faster, and you don't want to make it worse."

Aldo frowned. "I haven't seen any calves. I think." He wiped a few beads of sweat off his brow. "I'm not entirely sure that I'd know one if I saw it."

"You'd know it," Titus nodded. "They look pretty much the same as any other calf. They only start to grow once they get old enough to be moved into the main pastures. But once they do, they grow fast. But you won't really see any until the fall. Breeding season."

"That's got to be something to see," Aldo said. "If this is how badly they tear up the ground when they're snacking, I can't imagine what a pair of these things could do while romantically entwined."

Titus raised an eyebrow. "Not sure why you'd want to see that. Least not unless you had one of those glass things they made down in your end of the continent."

Aldo frowned. "Glasses?"

"No," Titus shook his head. "No, it's long? Makes stuff far away closer?"

"Oh, a scope."

"That's the one. Anything to give me distance. 'Sides, I'm not judging, but watching two cows roll around in the hay isn't exactly how I choose to spend my days."

"I just meant it would be a spectacle."

"Sure." The corners of Titus' mouth twitched. "Well, I hate to disappoint you, but that's not how it works."

Aldo raised an eyebrow. "Admittedly, it's been a while, but I thought I had a pretty good grasp on how babies are made."

"Things get a bit more complicated if you weigh a couple dozen tons," Titus said. "Not to mention that from everything I've heard, putting the bull in close proximity with anything breathing is a good way to change that particular condition in no time at all."

"Naath said they were territorial, but even around their own species?"

"Especially then." Titus shook his head. "They figured that out a long time ago. They've never had that many bulls in the first place, and they don't want to risk the animals that way. Brings us to the third rule. There's a reason the fences around the Promenade are over a mile back. Cows do not cross that fence. Any closer, we risk the bull catching scent. Bull catches scent of a cow, he's going to want to mate, and not a goddamn thing is going to get in his way."

Aldo raised an eyebrow. "The paddock won't hold him back?"

"Probably, but even if it does, think Naath would be happy with his prize bull smashing itself against the walls over and over?"

Aldo nodded. "So how do they..." He made a gesture with several fingers, and Titus frowned.

"The fuck is that supposed to be?"

"You're an ass."

Titus grinned. "They don't. Naath and several of the ranchers bring the bull into the harvesting shed, doped up with this powder. Made from urchins down in your hometown."

Aldo frowned. "Dezma urchin powder is illegal."

"Not here. Not for the Vorchese. Doesn't knock the beast out, but mellows it enough that they can let it scent a bit of the female's urine, which gets things moving, and they..." He made his own gesture, and Aldo made a face.

"You can't be serious."

Titus grinned. "As a broadhead to the spine. Take comfort in the fact that you don't have the worst job on the ranch."

"So someone just goes in and... grabs the bull by the horn?"

"That's horrible. I'm sure there's more to it than that, but it's not a process I've ever been much inclined to observe." Titus glanced his way, chuckling. "That being said, given what we've discovered during this conversation regarding your viewing habits, might be the next best thing."

"Not going to drop that, are you."

"Doesn't seem likely, no," Titus said. "Sorry to disappoint, but the harvesting shack is off limits. Even the smell of any other creature's liable to send that bull into a frenzy if the doping doesn't take. We're not allowed to so much as touch the door. For most of us, that's not a rule we really care to argue against, given that watching the ranchers give a bull the one-handed ovation isn't high on our list of priorities."

"Fair."

"Although if you ask nicely, maybe we can have someone draw you some pictures."

"I'm going to push you off your horse." Titus grinned, and Aldo asked, "Why do it so close to the other buildings, if it's that risky?"

"Once they've collected the..."

"Bull batter?"

Titus made a face. "Heard it, didn't like it any better the first time. Once they collect the sample, they only have a short amount of time before it goes bad, can't be used any more. There's a cave underneath the harvesting shed, underground stream going through. Nice and cool. Keeps the samples cold until they're ready to use it on a cow."

"That's lucky."

"They built the whole Promenade around it. Paddock, husbandry shed, all of it. Five minutes after they've collected the sample, it's colder than a winter night."

Aldo didn't let his dismay show on his face. *Really hope you thought of that, Nicolette.* "Any other areas I should know about that I'm not meant to be?" Aldo asked. "Don't want to run afoul of the boss day after I get this job."

"Not going to be much opportunity for that," Titus said. "If you're not sleeping, shitting, or eating, you'll be riding with me." He shrugged. "First floor of the house is open to anyone. Anything upstairs is off limits to anyone without this ranch's name following their own. Harvesting shack, we talked about. Husbandry building, cold storage, armory without Stilts or Naath's permission. They've got the only keys, so not much you could do without them."

"So... Naath." Aldo glanced over to see Titus' reaction. "He's not what I expected."

Titus nodded. "Guessing you've not come across a Confessor before."

"Not really common in the city, no."

"Not all that common around here. Not anymore, anyway," Titus said. "Once Cicerone declared itself independent, pretty much everyone with a crook on their wrist packed up and headed to the holy land."

"He's a little intense."

"That he is." Titus chewed on his lip for a moment. "For the most part, Naath is fine. He leaves the guard force to Stilts and doesn't interact much with us. His focus is on keeping the cattle healthy and signing the trade deals. But you need to remember, this isn't just a job for him. A quarter of every mark that this ranch earns goes to the Church, and that's a lot of money. He sees this place as a holy mission, and you do not want to fuck with that."

Aldo nodded, watching a pair of birds land on the back of a cow drinking from one of the streams winding its way through the landscape. The cow didn't react. "I'll keep that in mind."

"Do your job, you'll be fine. I've been here longer than anyone, never had much of an issue." Glancing over, Titus asked, "So you and Stilts go back, huh?"

Aldo shifted, trying to get comfortable on the saddle. "We do."

"What's his favorite food?"

Aldo had spent the last few days rehearsing the answers to questions about his father's past. That had not been on the list. "What?"

"His favorite food?" Titus asked again. "Stilts doesn't say shit about himself. He's a locked box. Next year marks ten years since he started working here. Cookie wanted to do something special, but none of us know what he likes to eat. Just shovels down whatever's provided. Eats like someone shoving logs into a furnace."

"Oh." Aldo shook his head. "Uh, I'm not entirely sure. His tastes could have changed. I know he used to like pickled eel."

Titus made a face. "Please tell me you're making that up."

"You've never had pickled eel?"

"I've never had eel. Can't say I've spent any sleepless nights wondering what a slimy swimming snake tastes like."

"It's..." Aldo tried to come up with a good description. "I don't know, it tastes like vinegar and eel and whatever spices that cannery got a good deal on that week. Last time I ate it, they'd apparently got a shipment of peppers from somewhere. Nearly blew my sinuses out."

"You ate it willingly? Or did someone force you to do that?" Titus assumed a sympathetic expression. "You can tell me if someone forced you to eat spicy slime fish."

Aldo shook his head. "No one forces us to eat in the city. We get the chance, we eat."

"Thought every one of you Vetticcians was rich."

Aldo snorted. "I mean no offense, but if I was rich, I wouldn't have bruised my balls for three hundred miles on the back of the worst creature the gods ever created for the pleasure of your company." Something buzzed around his head, and Aldo waved it away.

"Vetticci is supposed to be the richest city in the world."

"And this ranch is supposed to be the richest ranch in the Dominion," Aldo said. "Once we're done here, will we be retiring back to your summer estate, or is it too early in the year for that?" Titus snorted, and Aldo said, "The Five Families are richer than gods. There are a few dozen other families that live in the Perch that have more money than they know what to do with. The Guilds, the Colleges, they all have accounts at the Bank that probably require a team of calculators to track. But there are four million people in the city, and most of them are rolling dice on what their next meal is going to be."

Titus nodded slowly. "Seems that's the way things work most places."

"Stiliano liked pickled eel because it was different than the salted cod and sea grass that most people eat for most meals," Aldo said. "But he's spent the last nearly ten years eating like you people do up here. Fruit. Meat that didn't come out of a net. Bread. Gods, bread." He shook his head. "I didn't know bread could be soft until I came up here."

"What else would it be?"

"Flat. Hard. They mix flour with wood pulp and rendered whale fat, bake it until you could tile a floor with it, and hand it out in the Nest," Aldo said. "We called them shit bricks. They tasted like burned bark. We ate it anyway." He shrugged. "Ten years away from that, and you're asking me what his favorite food is? If he hasn't found fifty meals up here that would make anyone in the Nest cry just to smell, I'll kiss one of those cows on the mouth. You and the other guards, you know him better than I do. We only worked together for a bit."

Titus nodded. "Fair." He glanced over at him. "Does bring up another question, though."

"What's that?"

"I'm not a calculator, but I can count backwards," Titus said. "Stilts has been here for near on ten years. But you say you worked with him before. You're not that old. Couldn't have been more than a kid."

Aldo grunted. "There a question in there?"

"What did you and Stilts do back then?"

Aldo reached down, pulling the water skin they'd given him from the saddlebag. He took a long drink. Wiping his mouth with the back of his hand, he said, "Nearly ten years, and Stilts hasn't told you?" Titus shook his head, and Aldo said, "Don't figure it's my place to break his streak, then. He's not interested in telling you, I'm not going to take that choice away from him. We worked together, until I got pinched. Last time I saw him was when the city sentries were taking me to the stockades." He shrugged. "Like I said, you and the others know him a lot better than I do."

Titus nodded. "I can respect that. We like Stilts. He's quiet, but he's fair, and a good boss."

"Good to know." Aldo glanced over. "Question for you?"

"What's that?"

"No one's asked me."

"Asked you a lot of questions, to be fair. Might need be more specific than that."

Instead of answering, Aldo pulled his sleeve up, just enough to show the first few tattoos.

"Ah," Titus said. "Well, that's kind of an unspoken rule around here. You're not the only one here that's had his share of troubles. The boss doesn't care about that. You do your job, carry your weight, what came before doesn't matter. You want to talk about it, we're happy to listen, but..." He glanced at Aldo. "I meant what I said to Ian before. What little we've heard about those boats doesn't sound pleasant. Not sure I'd want to be jawing about it."

Aldo nodded. "Appreciate that."

"But however bad it was, it can't be worse than pickled eel."

Aldo grinned. "If I'd known how curious you'd be, I would have brought some up with me. Let you sample a Vetticcian delicacy."

"Then I'll be tumbling to my knees tonight to thank the gods you didn't know," Titus said. "We're having chicken tonight. And it won't be pickled."

Aldo opened his mouth to reply, but was interrupted by a piercing squeal from the east. Titus cursed, shouting, "Follow me," and dug his heels into the flanks of his horse. The chocolate brown animal snorted and broke into a gallop, and Aldo did his best to keep up.

Chapter 10

I f riding had been uncomfortable, galloping was an entirely new torment. Aldo tried to ignore his discomfort and focused on keeping pace with Titus, trying to mimic the way the other man rose up in his saddle for the ride. Their horses flew over the grassy fields faster than Aldo had thought they'd be able to manage, and as they rode, the odd warbling squeal grew louder and louder. As it did, Aldo realized that he'd heard that sound before.

The pair crested a hill and came to a halt. At the bottom, nearly half a mile away, Aldo could see the long fence line marking the western border of the Vorchese ranch stretching out impossibly far in either direction. Titus pointed. "There." Aldo looked, and saw that the slats on a twelve foot wide section of the fence were lying on the ground, leaving a gap. He began to nudge his horse in that direction, but paused when he realized Titus wasn't moving.

"What are we waiting for?"

"The dogs."

Aldo frowned, and began to speak, but stopped as he heard the baying in the north. Titus said, "They're trained to come running when they hear the alarm."

"It's a Capresi alarm, isn't it?" The small artificer devices were popular intrusion alarms in Vetticci, manufactured and sold by the

College of Artificers. Aldo had been told once that the palm-sized devices were common tasks for apprentices studying at the school, given their simple design. Aldo's familiarity with them primarily came from teasing them open without setting off the alarm from a very young age.

Titus nodded. "They're all over the fence."

"You think a cow got out?"

"No." In the distance, a pack of small shapes appeared. The barking got louder. "The cows don't like going near the fence. We bury green pepper in the soil. It gets into the grass. The cows hate the flavor." He pointed. "Besides, the slats aren't broken. Someone pried them out."

"Hard to imagine someone stealing one of these bastards."

Titus began to respond, but the dogs had arrived. The Breguet scent hounds were well known, although this was the first time that Aldo had seen one. Long floppy ears framed mournful faces, and black noses pushed deep into the dirt as the eight dogs scattered, sniffing the ground furiously, tails wagging. After a few moments, one of them let out a long, shivering howl, and the others immediately flocked around him. The pack all looked up to Titus, nearly trembling with excitement, and Titus barked out, "Go!"

On his command, they began running north along the fence, occasionally dipping their big heads to the ground to sniff, correcting their course every few moments. Titus and Aldo followed close behind. "That thing loaded?" Titus shouted.

Aldo shook his head, and fumbled a thick iron bolt from the quiver strapped to the saddlebags. The crossbow wasn't a Vetticcian design, but he'd taken a few moments to familiarize himself with its function before they'd left. He had not tried to do it from the back of a running horse, and the first bolt bounced from his fingers to fall into the dirt. Cursing, he managed to fit the second in place. He didn't lever the string back yet, though. He was worried he'd drop the whole damn thing.

Through the baying of the hounds, another sound began to take shape, a high keening. The dogs became frenzied, scrambling over the ground as they broke into a dead sprint, bodies low to the ground, ears flowing back behind them. Titus gestured to Aldo. Before Aldo could express that he didn't know what the signal meant, the other man peeled off to the right, taking his mount in a long arc. Aldo didn't know whether to follow or not, and elected to stay with the pack. Titus didn't scream anything at him, so he figured he'd made the right call.

Behind a cluster of young oaks, Aldo spotted a huge shape, lying in the grass. It was a cow. It was flopped on its side, and he could see a black tangle around its hind legs, and several arrows sticking out of its flank. Two men were crouched over it, their hands bloody, and they stumbled to their feet, turning to run, but the dogs were faster. Within moments, the pack had surrounded them, barking loudly, and Aldo cursed under his breath as he saw one of them reach down and pick up a battered spear. He grabbed the loading lever, pulling it back until he heard the *click* of it notching into place. The butt of the weapon found his shoulder and he sighted down, shouting, "Drop it!"

There was a second spear, leaning up against the moaning cow, but the second man made no attempt to reach for it. Titus appeared around the back of the trees, closing from an oblique angle, crossbow leveled. The first man glanced between the two, and let the spear clatter to the ground, holding his empty hands out to either side. "You have us," he said, glaring at them.

"Keep them covered," Titus barked. "I'll bind them." He drew a coil of braided cowhide cord from his saddlebags as he climbed down. Setting down his crossbow, he pulled a short sword from a scabbard and began stalking forward.

He'd asked Aldo before they'd left if he wanted to carry a sword as well. Aldo quickly had said no. He didn't know how to handle a blade. He didn't know how to handle a crossbow, either, but he kept it pointed in their direction and did his best impression of competence as he climbed down from the horse.

Aldo kept his eyes fixed on the pair as he moved over to stand near Titus. They looked enough alike that he guessed they were related, probably father and son based on the age difference. The father stared daggers back at him. The son was more nervous, glancing from Aldo to Titus, back to Aldo, to the trees, back to Aldo.

Wait.

Aldo tilted his head. "Titus?"

"Just keep them covered." Titus reached the younger man, and roughly pulled his hands behind his back. The man winced, and his eyes flickered back to the trees outside the fence line. Aldo turned to follow the direction the young man had glanced. Just outside the fence was a thick cluster of trees and brush. It was a windless day, but Aldo saw the leaves shiver.

"Titus, DROP!" Aldo didn't wait to see if the other guard reacted to his shout. He slammed his shoulder into the older man as something flashed in his vision and tore a searing path across the meat of his upper arm. He threw himself backwards, and rolled until he had placed the supine cow between him and the tree line.

A second musical zip sang through the space which his head had just occupied. Aldo rolled to the crossbow, which he'd dropped when moving, and snatched it up. Miraculously, it hadn't triggered, and Aldo sighted in on the bushes and fired.

He didn't see if he'd hit anything, but heard a shriek as he sank back behind the cow. Another arrow zipped past as Titus sprinted over to crash down next to him, his blade dripping red. The older guard cursed as he brought his fingers up to the bloody cut on his ear. "You okay?"

"What?"

"Your shoulder."

Aldo glanced down, and felt light headed at the deep cut across his shoulder and the scarlet spreading steadily over his tunic sleeve, but nodded. "Yeah."

"You see them?"

Aldo shook his head. He began to crane his head around the side of the cow's flank to peer into the bushes. An arrow smacked into the cow, less than two feet from his head, and he jerked back into cover as the cow moaned in pain again. "They're in the bushes. Saw them move. But couldn't see anyone."

Titus nodded to the crossbow. "Don't suppose you have the quiver."

Aldo shook his head. "Didn't have time to grab it."

"Fuck." Titus touched his ear, bringing back fingers sticky with blood. "We can't stay here. They're going to move, get an angle on us." Leaning his head back, he bellowed, "HOME!" The dogs whined, but all broke into a dead sprint back toward the center of the ranch. No arrows chased them. Seeing Aldo's confused expression, he said, "Trackers, not fighters. I'm going to run for those trees over there. When I say, come up and point your crossbow in the direction of those bushes. They don't know you're dry."

"That's a terrible idea," Aldo said.

"I know. NOW!" Titus burst up as Aldo muttered a curse and swung the crossbow around. He saw a skinny man in mottled clothing holding a longbow running in a crouch to the left. The man spotted Aldo, saw the crossbow in his hand, and let out a squawk as he dove to the ground. Aldo almost grinned, but any sense of accomplishment was interrupted by another arrow singing past his head. He dropped back behind the cow.

"There's at least two!" he shouted. He couldn't see if Titus had made it, but he also hadn't heard the man scream.

"More'n that, friend!" The accent coming from past the fence was thick with the country. "Want to know just how many, how's about you poke that pretty face of yours up and say hello?"

Aldo looked back at Titus, who had made it to the trees, and was hunched behind a thick oak trunk. He held his short sword, which seemed laughably useless at the moment. Trying to stall, Aldo shouted, "I'd love to, but some ass keeps throwing arrows this way! I'm afraid it'll muss my hair!"

A chuckle floated over his way. "That'd be a shame. Tell you what. So long as that crossbow I saw you clutching finds its way out 'fore you do, I believe we might see our way to not killing you right away."

Aldo looked down at the empty crossbow. "I don't think you'd want it. It's awfully heavy. But if you come any closer, I think I can make it a bit lighter."

"Maybe. But those things take about nine hours to reload. You fire, the rest of us'll have time to feather you enough you'll think you can fly."

Aldo looked at Titus, mouthing, "*What do I do?*" Titus spun his finger, nodding, giving a *keep going* gesture.

"I do suspect that'll be little comfort to whoever catches this bolt," Aldo said. "These things are designed to pierce armor. I'm not sure it'll even stop once it hits you."

"Feeling confident about your marksmanship, are you? Think it's likely you'll get that lucky again?"

Again? "I'm the best shot on the ranch," Aldo said. "Well, second best. Fucking Doug."

A long pause. "Is Doug the other fellow in the trees?"

"What? No, Doug's on holiday." Aldo saw movement from the corner of his eye as the man who'd dived to the ground earlier poked his head up. He leaned around, leveling the crossbow, and the head dropped back down immediately. "Tell your friend to stay put, or he'll learn why I'm nearly as good as Doug!"

"You shoot him, I kill you."

"You really want to give Doug that satisfaction?"

"I don't know who Doug is!" The voice was beginning to bleed irritation.

"I told you, he's the best shot on the ranch!"

"Fuck this." Another arrow zipped past Aldo's head, and he sank as low to the ground as he could. He could hear mumbled conversation. His heart sank as the man rose to a crouch and began running to the left. He looked over at Titus, who clutched his sword, jaw set tightly.

Titus, I really fucking hope you're right about people responding to alarms. He tried to estimate how long before they could expect reinforcements, but gave up almost immediately. *If they kill you, you don't have any options.* Making up his mind, he shouted, "Okay! I'm throwing out the crossbow!"

"Careful now! Wouldn't want to make me nervous."

"I can promise you, avoiding that is fairly high on my list of priorities." He threw the crossbow as hard as he could. Given the weight of the weapon, it wasn't very far, but it clattered to the ground.

"On your feet, now. Easy."

Aldo slowly stood, hands outstretched. To his left, he saw the man in the mottled tunic cautiously lean out from behind a tree. Someone was crouched in a shallow ditch to the right. Aldo could only make out red hair. From that direction, he heard, "Now your friend! The one in the trees!"

"We're not really friends," Aldo said cautiously. "He's actually my boss. I'm not really allowed to tell him what to do."

"If he's got an interest in your blood remaining inside your body, he'll come out."

"Just met him today," Titus shouted. "Not really that invested in his safety."

Aldo turned to glare back at him. "You'd be so quick to lose your second-best shot?"

"I'll still have Doug."

"Well fuck you too!" Aldo turned back to the red hair. "Are you hiring?"

"What?"

"I'm not risking my life for this asshole," Aldo said. "And like I said, I'm a really good shot. I could be valuable to your organization."

"Sure," the red hair replied. He poked his head up enough for Aldo to see green eyes in a sea of freckles. "Go stab your boss, and you're hired."

"He's got a sword."

"I don't care." The man rose up, sighting in on Aldo with a long-bow. To Aldo's left, he heard the creak of wood as a second bow was drawn. "If you want to live, you'll…"

What Aldo was meant to do should he want to live would remain a mystery. He barely registered the whisper in the air before a sickening crunch marked the unfortunate moment in which that red hair and an arrowhead briefly occupied the same space. A shaft sprouted from the top of his forehead, quivering slightly as the man dropped bonelessly to the ground.

With a cry, the other man raised his bow to fire at Aldo, but his aim was spoiled by the pair of arrows that drove deep into his thigh and belly. He fell to the ground, howling like a wolf, and Aldo felt a wave of relief as three men on horseback galloped toward them from the east, following the hounds baying as they led the riders to them. On the top of a small hill nearby, he saw Ian and another guard he didn't know, nocking their next arrows.

Titus came out, running towards the fence. "Aldo, with me!"

Aldo had no interest in following, but it seemed like the only thing to do. His upper sleeve was sodden with blood, and he gritted his teeth and followed Titus, clambering over the fence.

The wounded man writhed on the ground, gasping in pain. Titus walked over to him, and said, "Check the others. The bushes, too." Aldo nodded, and ran over. The redheaded man stared up at the blue sky, eyes wide and unblinking. Sticking out of the bushes was a pair of booted feet, toes pointed up. Aldo carefully approached, spearpoint trembling, and used the weapon to push aside the brush. A third man lay unmoving on the ground. A crossbow bolt was buried deep into the hollow of his throat, less than an inch of iron protruding.

Aldo stared at the dead body, his brain scrambling to reconcile what it was seeing. When the hand gripped his shoulder, he jumped, nearly stumbling.

"Easy!" His father held up his hands, eyes wide. "Easy, Aldo! It's just us!"

Aldo nodded, letting the spear fall to the ground.

"Gods." Stiliano pulled a strip of cloth from a pouch on his belt, and began tying it around Aldo's arm. "Is it bad?"

Aldo shook his head. "I don't think so." Before he could say anything else, there was a choked off scream. Titus came back in their direction, wiping his blade with a cloth. The gorge rose in Aldo's throat, but he pushed it back down.

Ian and the other archer came jogging up. One of the other guards was pulling the arrows from the cow, tossing them to the ground beside it. Stiliano was still watching Aldo, worry creasing his face, and Ian called out, "Stilts!"

"Hmm?"

"What do you want us to do?"

"Oh." Giving his head a sharp shake, he said, "Take Aldo and Titus back to the house. Make sure they're okay. Faralt, you and I will clean up here."

Aldo began to speak, but was interrupted by the cow mooing loudly. The guards stepped quickly back, giving the animal space, as it clambered back to its feet. The massive animal stumbled, blood dripping from the wound, but it kept its footing.

Stiliano tightened the strip around his shoulder, and tied it off. "You and Titus. Back to the house, now."

Titus took Aldo by the arm. "Come on. Let's go."

***

The adrenaline began to fade on the ride back to the ranch complex. Aldo's shoulder was pulsing in steady waves of hot agony. He kept replaying the events in his head, trying to piece together what had happened.

"Who were they?"

Titus glanced over at him. The older man had been quiet as they rode, his hand resting on the hilt of his sword. Aldo's eyes kept being drawn to the flecks of dark blood staining the leather wrapping of the hilt. "Poachers. The meat from these animals sells for a high price. They can't really steal the cattle, so they hamstring them and butcher them where they fall, try to get as much as they can before we get there."

"Seemed like they were waiting for us."

Titus nodded. "Ayuh, that was an ambush, plain and simple. We've been pretty rough on them the last year or so. Guess they finally decided to see if they could push back." He considered Aldo for a moment. "You kept your head. Did well." He paused, and said, "Probably saved my life. That arrow was meant for me."

Aldo shook his head. "I didn't really think. I had no idea what I was doing."

"You stalled long enough for help to arrive."

"I didn't even know help was coming," Aldo admitted. "I was just trying to stall until I could figure something out."

"Vetticcians don't have mandatory conscription, right?" Aldo shook his head, and Titus said, "I'm guessing that means you haven't seen battle."

"You have?'

Titus nodded. "Border skirmishes, mostly. Stuff that the history books call 'minor action'." He snorted. "Never feels minor." He shrugged. "What you just said, doing whatever you can until you figure something out, that's combat. You just hang on and hope the hammer falls on someone else."

Aldo brushed his fingers reflexively over his tattoos. "I can relate."

"Was that your first?"

"Fight? I thought we'd established that."

"No."

"Oh." Aldo shifted in his saddle. "No. It wasn't my first."

Titus nodded. "Roland will look us over. Make sure you're not going to bleed to death."

Aldo glanced down at his soaked sleeve. "I don't think it's bleeding any more."

"Still. He'll clean it, stitch you up."

It took nearly forty minutes for them to reach the center of the ranch. Several figures were waiting at the closest gate in the internal fence. Naath and a young man with a bag over his shoulder came up to meet them, holding their reins while the pair dismounted.

"You two okay?" Naath asked. "I heard the alarms. Sent everyone I could."

Titus nodded. "We're good, boss. Poachers. Five of them. Laid a tidy little ambush for us." He jerked his head towards Aldo. "New guy got kissed by a broadhead. Stilts bandaged it, but thought Roland could take a look."

"Roland," Naath said. "Take Aldo back to the house, make sure he's in one piece." He glanced back the way they'd come. "Stilts bringing the prisoners?"

Titus shook his head. "They didn't survive."

Naath scowled for a moment, but the disapproval was gone as fast as it arrived. "Fine. Aldo, go get patched up."

"Boss?" Naath turned back to Titus when he spoke. "He did good. Kept his cool. Would have been bad without him."

Naath nodded. "Stilts seemed to be right about you, Aldo." He offered a half smile. "We'll talk more later."

"Enough jawing. Let's go." Roland took Aldo by the arm, and led him toward the house. He was a burly man, less than thirty years of age. His tunic was covered in small pockets, and the crossed wings of an anatomist was stitched into his breast pocket. "Can you move your arm?"

"I can."

"Any tingling in your fingers?"

Aldo shook his head. "Hurts like hell, but that's it."

"I'd expect so." They made their way up the stairs into the house, turning right away from the dining room Aldo had seen previously.

The east wing was lined with several doors, one of which was open. Stepping through, he pointed at the bed up against the wall. "Sit. Let's see the arm. Take off your shirt."

He hissed when he pulled the blood-stained cotton tunic over his head, a spike of pain needling through his shoulder. Roland raised an eyebrow as he probed the deep bloody gash, much less gently than Aldo would have preferred. "Next time, don't try to catch the arrow."

"Thought it might look impressive."

"Funny." He slowly lifted Aldo's arm. "Does that hurt?"

"It all hurts."

"It's really just so easy to diagnose and treat a patient when they're being vague and unhelpful."

He raised an eyebrow. "You're an anatomist?"

"Why the surprise?"

"No reason. Just thought people in your line of work were kind and nurturing."

Roland raised an eyebrow. "I don't seem kind and nurturing?" He unscrewed a jar that stank of alcohol, and dabbed it on the wound, drawing a hiss from Aldo.

"No, you're a warm hug."

"I'm a combat anatomist," Roland said. "In Duke Snowsill's army. My captain sent me here to recover."

"From what?"

"An arrow in the ass."

Aldo winced. "That had to be fun."

"Sure, sitting at a permanent lean was a fucking delight." He set down the cloth, and pulled out gut and a needle. "I'm going to guess by that patchwork of scars on your arms you're not a stranger to stitches."

"No."

Roland glanced over one long jagged scar on his forearm. "Whoever did this was either blind or drunk."

"He did his best."

Roland shrugged. "Do you want willowbark?"

Aldo made a face. "I hate the taste."

"No shit. It tastes terrible. But this is going to hurt like a bastard." His eyes fell to Aldo's forearm, and he raised an eyebrow. "Although based on your decoration, I'm guessing you and pain are old friends. One per month?"

"Per year."

"What the fuck did you do?" Before Aldo could answer, Roland held up his hand. "Never mind. It's not my business. I didn't think many people survived that long on board those barges."

"Yeah, they're dangerous," Aldo said.

"So how'd you keep from going tits up?"

Aldo shook his head. "I didn't do anything special. I just didn't die." *A scream punching through the howling winds of a squall and past small hands clapped tightly over ears.* He tried to push the memory aside.

"Bullshit," Roland said. "I'm not saying you probably didn't get lucky once or twenty times. But no one gets that lucky for that long. If you're not keeping your head up, sooner or later, you get a bad roll of the dice. It's the way it works in the middle of a battle. I'm willing to bet it's not that much different on a prison ship."

"By that argument, everyone who didn't make it did something wrong?"

"Not always. But yeah, most of the time."

Aldo stared at him. "You're a bit cold-blooded."

Roland chuckled. "I've been stitching men back together since I was fourteen. I promise you, there's not a lot you could say that could surprise me."

"Maybe not, but that doesn't mean that I have any fucking interest in saying it."

"Fair enough," Roland said. They fell silent while Roland worked, Aldo fixing his eyes at a point on the wall while the needle bit again and again. The bite was horribly familiar, and despite the man's gruff demeanor, far more gentle than any of his previous stitches. He didn't make a sound. If Roland was impressed, he gave no indication.

Roland tied off the end, and snipped the thread. "You can put your shirt back on. You're going to be hurting for a few weeks. If it gets too bad and you realize you're being an idiot about willowbark, find me." He was gone before Aldo could respond.

Aldo pulled his shirt back on, and stepped out into the hallway. Naath was waiting.

"Any permanent damage?" he asked.

Aldo shook his head. "No, sir. He said I'll be hurting for a few weeks."

"Glad to hear it," Naath said.

"He's... interesting," Aldo said, staring down the hallway where he'd left.

Naath snorted. "He's abrasive and altogether unpleasant. I don't particularly like him, but he knows his trade, and we needed an anatomist. Duke Snowsill offered him until I can find someone permanent." He waved his hand. "Go get some rest. We'll bring your meal to the barracks tonight, you and Titus. He told me what happened. You did well."

"Is there going to be trouble?" Aldo asked. "I mean, with those men dead?"

"They were trespassing on my land," Naath said. "You and Titus were doing your duty. Besides, no one's going to miss them."

Aldo frowned. He knew Naath meant it as reassurance, but it only served to remind him that no one would care if he disappeared either. He nodded. "Yes, sir."

***

Aldo's first shift had been ignominiously cut short. Naath instructed him to rest for the remainder of the day, but after three hours in the barracks, he became sick of the curious stares of guards he didn't know as they came and went. The light had begun to dim outside when Titus returned as several stewards were setting up an assortment of food on long tables near the barracks entrance.

"How's the arm?" Titus asked.

"Stitched shut," Aldo said. "Your man seems to know his trade, even if he's a bit sour."

"Not really our man. Just on loan. By the end of the week, he'll be heading back to his regiment."

"What do you do if someone gets hurt?"

Titus shrugged. "The best we can. If you get sick, Naath'll send you down to Galen's Crossing to see the anatomist there. But we don't usually have one on site. Lucky you."

"I wouldn''t call being ambushed and feathered a windfall of good fortune."

"It barely grazed you."

"I lost a lot of blood."

"You've got plenty." Titus gestured at the bread rolls and stew. "Eat something, you'll be fine."

Aldo watched four men leave the barracks together. "Thought change of watch wasn't for a few hours."

"Huh?" Titus looked to see where he was staring. "Oh, them. They're not going to take the watch. They're going for the Accounting."

"I don't know what that is." Aldo had heard the word before, but there was something about the way Titus said it that made the capital letter clear.

"Service. For the Confessors on the ranch."

"I thought Naath was the only one."

Titus shook his head. "Naath's the only one who studied the catechism in Cicerone. But there are still some who follow the doctrine, at least a bit. Naath holds an Accounting a few times a week for those who want to go."

"Is it private?" Despite himself, Aldo was curious. His only experience with religion was a few visits to temples as a child with his mother. He didn't remember much. There was no worship on the penance barge. The gods had no more interest in being out there than anyone else.

Titus shook his head. "You want to go watch, you can. I've attended one or two. Never found much need to do more than that."

Aldo walked out the doors of the barracks. The sun had begun to set, spilling golden light over the rolling hills to the west of the Promenade. He could see a cluster of massive silhouettes moving slowly on the crest of a hill far in the distance.

The shadows had begun to fall over the compound, but lamps on the front of the main house had been lit, throwing the dozen or so figures sitting on the grass before the porch into sharp relief. On the porch, Naath stood, speaking softly enough that Aldo couldn't hear what he was saying. Aldo walked over, finding a drooping willow less than thirty feet away. He ducked beneath the hanging branches and leaned against the trunk, listening.

"There's fear in not knowing," Naath was saying. His eyes flickered over to find Aldo, and he offered a slight nod before he continued to speak. "None of us can truly know what lies beyond the last time those who have truly lived close their eyes. We only know what lies in store for those who hide from pain, from the tempering that this world offers those of us with the courage to endure."

He gestured around. "More of the same. More suffering, more want, more of the understanding deep inside our breast that this life is not right. It's not what we're meant for. We are in this world to be purified, to be boiled and cauterized until everything broken and foul within us is burned away, and we stand ready to step into what comes next."

If that's the case, I'm all set. Aldo brushed his fingers against his sleeve, against blue ink that lay beneath the homespun cloth.

As if he'd heard his thoughts, Naath turned his gaze to Aldo. "Our pain is a gift. We come together to share that pain, to share the steps that we take towards that final reward." He gestured at one of the men sitting before him. Aldo couldn't see their faces. "Basil here broke his leg last year. We didn't have Roland's services at the time, so it wasn't set as it should have been. So every step is painful." He smiled, white teeth reflecting in the lamplight. "How many steps today, Basil?"

The man's voice was rough and weary. "Over two thousand, boss."

"Two thousand. Two thousand steps, two thousand marks towards your ascension." Naath walked down the steps, and gripped Basil's shoulder. "Well done, brother."

He looked back to Aldo. "Would you care to share your pain, Aldo?"

Faces turned towards him as Aldo felt his stomach fall. He shook his head. "It was just a scratch. Roland sorted me out."

Naath's expression didn't change, his eyes locked on Aldo's. "You know that's not what I'm speaking of." When Aldo didn't respond, he said, "Our new friend here has had a singular experience. One that very few of us north of the Myre Wood can share. He spent time on a Vetticcian penance barge. How long, Aldo?"

Aldo didn't want to meet those eyes. He wanted to be anywhere else. "Fourteen years."

Naath nodded. He stepped down from the porch and began weaving between the men, eyes never leaving Aldo. "Fourteen years. Do you remember the first time you were injured during your time?"

The cable sang as it snapped, hissing through the air.

Aldo swallowed. "I don't like talking about it."

"It can be hard," Naath said, drawing closer. "But when you remember the pain, when you share it, you help us all understand your journey. Tell us."

Fuck right off, you lunatic. The words caught behind Aldo's clenched teeth. *And I'm gone, and Nicolette finds a ranch with me nowhere to be found.* His jaw worked. "A line snapped. One of the mains. Caught my leg."

Naath was ten feet away. "Did it bruise you? Break the bone?"

A song of a butcher, like a blade sighing through a thrashing fish.

"It tore. Ripped my thigh open," Aldo could hear his voice trembling, furious that he couldn't keep steady.

"It hurt?"

"Yes, it fucking hurt," Aldo snapped. His fingers ached, and he realized how tightly he was squeezing his fist. *His own keening shriek, echoing over the deck and blending with the howling wind.*

"Tell us." Naath reached out and gripped Aldo's shoulder. Aldo shook his head, and the grip became tight. "Tell us."

"It hurt then. It hurt the next night when the fever dug in. It hurt for the weeks after when they boiled seawater and poured it in the wound," Aldo said. His voice was reedy and thin. He doubted anyone but Naath could hear. "It still hurts now, when I think about it."

Naath closed his eyes, and nodded slowly. "You're a lucky man, Aldo. Thank you for accounting your path."

Aldo said nothing. He didn't trust himself to speak, didn't trust himself not to burn the plan to the ground with his words. He watched Naath walk back among the gathered faces, eyes silently darting between the rancher and the trembling Vetticcian. When Aldo finally met their stares, most had turned to listen to Naath, who had quietly begun to speak once more. One lingered.

Aldo met his father's eyes for just a moment. He couldn't tell what lie behind the hollow expression on Stiliano's face.

I don't care, either.

Aldo turned, and walked back towards the barracks.

***

Between the ambush at the perimeter fence and the experience with Naath, Aldo spent the next few days with every muscle tensed, waiting for either event to have consequences. He'd seen Naath several times since then, but other than a polite nod or a quick, "Good morning, Aldo," there was nothing in the Confessor's demeanor to give away any hostility.

It also didn't help that Aldo kept waiting for the hammer to drop on them for the violence at the border of the ranch, but that fear also seemed unfounded. There were no guards or seekers poking around asking questions. He hesitantly broached the topic with Titus the day after the service. It had seemed odd to be back on the same patrol, the same horses, as if nothing had happened, and he said so.

"We're paid well," Titus said. "There's a reason. Poaching used to be a smaller issue, but as the family makes more and more trade deals, as more people find out what these animals can do, we're seeing a lot more raiders and thieves." He shrugged. "It happens."

"Yes, but... five dead? And nothing?"

"Who's going to come?" Titus asked. "The magistrates, the militia, they all report to the Duke. And Duke Snowsill lets the Vorchese do as they like. This ranch brings in a lot of money, Aldo."

"Seems odd."

"Way of the world. This place makes money. Money buys a lot of looking the other way."

Aldo didn't say anything for a moment, and said, "Seemed a bit cold."

"What's that?"

"You, uh..." He swallowed, and said, "You killed those men. After it was done."

Titus nodded. "They wouldn't have been gentle had it gone the other way," he said. "Besides, there are worse things than a quick death."

Aldo thought about the expression on Naath's face as he brushed his thumb over Aldo's tattoos. *What would Naath have done with them?*

He had more questions, but Titus' tone made it clear they'd reached the end of that particular conversational journey. In any event, a low moaning reached their ears, drawing their attention. Titus started looking around, squinting in the bright morning light. "You see it?"

"See what? What is that sound?"

Titus leaned forward, staring into the distance, and pointed. "There." Aldo spotted a large animal lying in a heap next to a tree, and the hairs on the back of his head raised.

"More poachers?"

Titus clicked his tongue, bringing his mount up to a cantor. Aldo fell into position beside him. "Not this far in, no. I think she's sick."

Sure enough, as they drew closer, they could see the cow, sprawled out in the shade of an oak. It was panting slightly, eyes big and glassy, and every few moments, it would let loose a low, baying moan, running its broad flat tongue over its mouth.

Titus climbed down, and approached the animal carefully. "Help me look for wounds, anything unusual."

It took a moment to find. Perhaps subconsciously, Aldo was looking for deep cuts and obvious wounds, as they'd found yesterday. When he spotted the rash on the animal's abdomen, he pointed. "Is that normal?"

Titus came around, and clucked his tongue. "No, she's sick. I need to go get Roland. You stay here. Don't touch her, just make sure nothing comes along and bothers her."

Aldo eyed the massive animal, uncertain. "She's not going to die on me, is she?"

"No. Give her a few hours she'll be back on her feet. But it's an opportunity," Titus said. "I'll be back."

Aldo nodded, and watched as Titus mounted up and rode back east the way they'd come. They'd maintained a steady pace for the time they'd been out. It would be a while before he made it back.

He stared down at the unmoving cow. *What the hell do I do now?* The sun was beating down on his face, and he pulled his water skin from the saddle bags, taking a long drink. Mid swallow, he glanced down. "You've got to be miserable in this heat. Can't even find shade," he muttered. He glanced down at the water skin, and said, "Well, shit."

He climbed down from his horse, keeping his movements slow and steady as he came around to the animal's head. It tracked him with big, deep black eyes, blinking wetly, and he crouched down in front of it. "How you doing, girl?"

The cow mooed softly. When she licked her lips again, Aldo could see it was dry and white.

"Wonder how long you've been here," he mused. He pulled the cork from the water skin. "I don't have much, but you're welcome to share." He dribbled water down onto the cow's mouth. The big, flat tongue came up to catch the drops, the moisture absorbing into the tissue as if it was a sponge. Hesitantly, he reached out and stroked the fur of the animal's head. It was coarse, but the cow let out a long sigh, and seemed to relax for a moment.

"Tough life you've got here," Aldo said. "Someone's not trying to carve steaks out of you, you're getting sick."

The cow mooed again.

"Exactly what I'm saying," Aldo said. He shifted to sit in the grass next to the cow, gently stroking its head. "If you were a bit smaller, we might be able to find our way to sneaking you back to the city." He looked around. "Course, you wouldn't have nearly as much space. And I can't guarantee that people wouldn't want to eat you. Come to think of it, that's a terrible idea." He shook his head. "I'm talking to a cow. Nicoletta, I don't know where you are, but you need to hurry up. I don't want to be here a minute longer than I have to."

The cow seemed to agree with his assessment of the state of affairs. Aldo fell silent, dripping water into the animal's mouth occasionally while watching the tall yellow grass wave idly in the warm breeze. Nearly an hour had passed before he heard hoofbeats, and climbed to his feet, wincing as his knees popped. Titus and Roland dismounted about twenty feet away. He had his bag over her shoulder, and jogged up to the animal.

"Show me the rash."

Aldo walked around and pointed out the patch of red streaks. "I think she's thirsty. I gave her a bit of water. Hope that's okay."

Roland nodded. "Dehydration is a common symptom when they contract this."

"What is it?"

"Called the phage. It's not fatal, but it makes them lethargic for a bit."

"Can you treat it?"

"I look like a fucking naturalist to you?" Roland asked. "One of the perks of being assigned to this place. I get to be the one to take advantage of this situation."

He reached into his bag, and pulled out several glass jars. Pulling out the stoppers, he rolled his sleeves up. "You two can go."

Aldo frowned, but turned and walked away, joining Titus. The pair resumed their ride, Aldo glancing back every few moments. "What's he doing?"

"Collecting," Titus said. "Remember when I told you that we use the urine to put the bull into heat for harvesting? They get sick every now and then. It's not serious, but it's the easiest way to collect the urine. Apparently, since they're dehydrated, it makes the scent stronger."

"So I really don't have the worst job."

"Don't feel too bad," Titus said. "He makes about five times what you do."

"He earns it."

The rest of the day passed with no issues, and they returned to the stables just as the sun was setting. The main house's windows were alight with cheery yellow light, and as Aldo handed his reins off to the stable master, he could hear voices drift over the twilight air to them.

When they walked into the house, there were already about two dozen people milling about in the entryway in groups of three or four, chatting and laughing. The smell of roasted meat and bread set Aldo's mouth watering, and he and Titus went into the dining room. The large table had been set with several huge platters of food: golden brown pigeons roasted and piled high, ears of corn the color of butter, fruit, roasted greens, and more. A stack of plates were at the front of the table, and Titus grabbed one, piling it high with food. He saw the expression on Aldo's face. "What's wrong?"

"Nothing," Aldo said. "Just still getting used to this."

Titus grunted. "Food, we have. Most of this comes from the farms and ranches nearby. It's why we don't have potatoes. No one around here grows them. They all come from up north, near the Breaking. We see them every now and then. Usually when a shipment bound for Vetticci comes through." He glanced over. "What do ya'll usually eat down there?"

"Fish. More fish. And for dessert, some fish," Aldo said, and Titus made a face.

"I hate fish."

"We hate empty bellies more." Aldo shrugged. "Lots of zucchini and squash. Anything that grows well in the gardens." Titus raised a questioning eyebrow, and Aldo asked, "Have you ever been? To the city, I mean?"

"You kidding?" Titus asked. "No, I haven't been to Vetticci. Less someone works a trade route, it's too expensive."

Aldo nodded. "We grow as much as we can from containers. Broken barrels, pots, crates, canvas sacks'll even work in a pinch. Compost everything we can, mix it with whatever dirt we can find. Most plants don't really take to that, but zucchini and squash like it just fine." He pointed. "What's that?"

"Hmm? Oh, apple brandy. We have peach and apricot, too," Titus said. "You have duty tomorrow, though. You're only allowed to drink if you have the next morning off."

"Gods." Aldo stared at the bottle. "You know how much that would go for in the city?"

"That's nothing," Titus said. "Boss has two casks of Campelli brandy."

Aldo's eyes widened. "How the fuck did he get his hands on two casks?!"

"That Vetticcian family? The one who bought the cows? It was part of them trying to convince him to meet with their man." Titus shrugged. "Wasted effort. Boss doesn't drink. So he's just got a small fortune's worth of booze locked in his office."

"Gods." Aldo looked at another dish. "What's that?"

"Apple pie. It's good." Titus grabbed himself a big slice. "Stilts never talks about the city. Gotta say, you don't make it sound great."

Despite himself, Aldo felt an odd flash of annoyance, and the urge to leap to his home's defense. "It's just what we're used to." He nodded at the massive pile of food on Titus's plate. "Can you really eat that much?"

"This is just my first pass."

Aldo snorted, and began to say something else, but someone cleared their throat loudly, and the room fell silent, everyone turning to face the front door.

Naath nodded, saying, "Don't mean to interrupt your dinner, but I wanted to touch on a few things. First, nice work to Titus and Aldo. That mess the other day with the poachers could have gone very badly. I would have been annoyed to have to hire your replacements." A chuckle rippled through the assembled guards. "For those of you who've yet to meet Aldo, he's an old friend of our good captain from back in Vetticci. And while I know that hiring Vetticcians is never the best idea, his quick thinking makes me think that he's another exception. Both of you will have a bit extra in your pay this week."

Aldo glanced over at Titus, unsure if he was meant to say anything. He was spared from having to guess when Naath continued speaking. "Stilts, want to bring them in on the other items?"

Stiliano stepped forward. Aldo hadn't seen him when they came in, but he'd been standing by the staircase, alone. He cleared his throat before speaking. "We have two cattle down with the phage in the western pastures. You all know the drill. Let us know if you see any growths. Hopefully, we won't lose any animals this year."

"We doing inspections?" someone Aldo couldn't see asked.

Stiliano shook his head. "Odette says it shouldn't be necessary yet, but that may change. Just keep an eye out." The gathered men murmured assent, and Stiliano continued, "Next note. We're expecting Her Excellency back again tomorrow." A groan rose from the men, and Stiliano held up his hand. "Get that out of your system now. This is the fourth time she's been here, so there shouldn't be any surprises."

Aldo did his best to keep his expression even, but inside, he breathed a long sigh of relief. *Thank the gods.*

"Who's the lucky winner this time?" Ian called out, and Stiliano turned to fix a baleful stare at him. The younger man's face fell. "Aw, Stilts, come on. I was with her the entire godsdamned week last time."

"And we didn't have any issues," Stiliano said. "Seeing as you did such a good job, we'll give you another opportunity."

"But…"

"She heads back north without complaining to me more than a dozen times a day, you'll get time and a half," Stilts said mildly.

"She makes it more than an hour without complaining, we can mark that as proof of divine inspiration," Ian grumbled. He shook his head. "She still in the guest house?"

"Yes," Naath said, stepping forward. "Remember, she's to be shown every courtesy, but the house is off limits, as well as the usual. Also, keep her away from the western fields. Last thing we need is for her to see a cow with the phage, start asking questions."

Stiliano said, "Ian, you'll be on the front gate tomorrow until she arrives. The boss and I will be waiting. The rest of you, remember: her title is Your Excellency. We all know she has a short temper, but if this goes well, she and the boss can finalize this deal and we won't have to deal with her any longer."

"We've been working on this trade deal for almost six months," Naath said. His voice was mild, but his eyes had grown hard. "Things go smoothly, we'll all see the benefits. Things go any other way, I will know why, and I won't be happy."

Heads bobbed up and down. Satisfied, Naath waved a hand toward Stiliano, who said. "That's all. If you see anything strange out there, call for help right away. I won't be upset for a false alarm, and after yesterday, I think we all need to step a bit more carefully." He nodded. "Enjoy your meal."

Ian came their way, a foul expression on his face. "Is there pie left?"

"If there isn't, you can have mine," Titus said, a sympathetic expression warring with a grin tugging at the corners of his mouth.

"It's not funny."

"I mean, for those of us who don't have to deal with her, it's a little funny."

"What's the problem?" Aldo asked. "Who is she?"

"Oh, don't worry," Ian said, shoveling a piece of pie on his plate. "You'll see her. Easy to spot. Just look for the walking tree of a woman with her foot planted firmly in my asshole."

"Trade liaison, from north of the Breaking," Titus clarified.

"Imperial?" Aldo asked, raising an eyebrow. "I didn't know this ranch traded the Empire. Didn't think anyone south of the Breaking did."

"Ever since they finished up the bridge, it's a whole new world," Titus said. "Every single duke is scrambling over each other to be the first to sign a permanent trade deal with them. So far, it's just been one-off deals, but one of the..." He frowned. "What are they called?"

"Archerons," Ian mumbled around a mouth of baked fruit and pastry.

Titus nodded. "Yeah, that. One of the archerons in Kaani got wind of the Vorchese cattle, and sent a liaison about six months to hammer out a deal."

"What the hell is an archeron?"

"Something like a duke, maybe?" Titus shrugged. "Important enough to negotiate a deal, and Naath really, really wants it."

Ian snorted. "That's an understatement. Every one of us has to spend the entire time she's here with our lips planted firmly on her ass."

"Ian." Titus shook his head, staring at him intently. "I know you're pissed, but if Naath hears you talking like that..."

"I'm not stupid," Ian said.

"It's that important?" Aldo asked.

Titus nodded. "Not a rancher, farmer, merchant, or duke in the whole of the Dominion that isn't drooling at the chance to sign a deal with someone other than Vetticci. A few hundred years of your people fucking us right through our breeches because we didn't have any other trade partners is more than enough, thank you."

Aldo snorted. "You seem to be doing just fine," he said, gesturing at the heavily loaded plate.

"Yeah? What's the exchange rate for coral to marks now?" Titus shook his head. "Everyone owes the Bank, the families own the Bank, so they get to dictate whatever terms they want. If we didn't grow so much food, we'd be in trouble."

"The Vorchese family's about the only ranch in the entire duchy that isn't in deep to the Bank," Ian said around a mouthful of apples and pie crust.

"How'd they manage that?" Aldo asked.

"Sold a few head of cattle," Titus said. "To one of the rich families. Charged them a gods-damned fortune, too." He shrugged. "Anyway, Naath wants the deal, so if you run into her, keep your eyes down and pucker up. She won't make it easy."

"That bad?"

"Worse," Ian mumbled. "Nothing's right. The guest quarters are always too hot, but she won't take off the godsdamned Imperial wools. The ranch smells funny. It's too far a ride. We don't have the brandy she likes, we don't have the food she likes, there's not enough light for her to read the books she brought, her tea's too hot, her tea's too cold..."

Titus' eyes widened, and he made a quick cutting off gesture, but it was too late. Ian turned to see Stiliano standing behind him, arms folded.

"Stilts. I wasn't..."

"You were," Stiliano said. "If I didn't know that you'll do the job when it's time, I'd kick your ass. Suck it up, earn a few hundred extra marks, and make her happy enough that the boss can finalize this deal and we don't have to deal with her anymore." He stepped closer. "And before you open your godsdamned mouth, make sure that no one's around to hear you. If the boss heard you talking like that…"

Ian swallowed. "I get it. Sorry, Stilts."

Let's see if this works. "I can do it."

The three men turned to stare at Aldo, who shrugged. "If it's that bad, let Ian and me trade. He can ride perimeter with Titus. I can kiss ass. I've had to do it before."

"I knew I liked you, first time we met," Ian said.

"Didn't you threaten to shoot me."

"Doesn't mean I didn't like you." Ian turned to Stiliano. "What do you say, Stilts? He's offering."

Stiliano shook his head. "No."

"But…"

"He doesn't know the ranch, not yet. She's going to ask questions, and if the only answer she gets is, 'I don't know, I'm new here' she's going to be irritable," Stiliano said.

Ian frowned. "But the boss said that I'm not supposed to answer any questions. That's what he's there for." He gestured to Aldo. "Only difference is, he won't be full of shit when he says he doesn't know."

"Job's yours, Ian."

"But I don't mind…" Aldo started to say, but fell silent as Stiliano shot him a hard glare.

"I don't care if you don't mind. Ian did the job last time, so we know he can do it. Two days on the job doesn't mean shit, and this is too important to trust to a greenhorn," Stiliano said, his voice flat. "Your job is to stick with Titus, learn, and make mistakes in a place that won't blow up a deal our boss has been working on since last harvest."

Aldo gritted his teeth, slightly surprised at the flare of anger that burst to life. "Awfully quick to assume I'm going to fuck it up."

Stiliano fixed his stare on him. "It's my job to keep things on this ranch running smooth. I've been doing that job for nine years. You've been here for two days."

"Sorry," Aldo shot back before he could stop himself. "I was a bit busy, otherwise I might have joined you."

Before Stiliano could respond, Ian grabbed Aldo's shoulder. "It's okay, Stilts," he said quickly. "I'm just grumbling, that's all. I'll make sure everything runs smooth." He dropped his plate on the table. "Titus and I are going to take Aldo for some fresh air."

Stiliano swallowed. His face had lost a bit of color. "That's a good idea." He watched as Titus and Ian marched Aldo out the front door, several people watching them go with raised eyes.

They reached the top of the stairs, and pushed him roughly down the two steps. Aldo nearly stumbled, and turned to snap at them, but Titus had his arm in a vise grip as the pair dragged him to the side of the building. The harvesting shed loomed large behind them, butting up against the side of the bull paddock, but there were no windows. The spot they found was dark and quiet.

"The fuck is your problem?" Titus snapped.

Aldo yanked his arm back. "I don't like being treated like I'm an incompetent."

"You are a fucking incompetent," Titus said. "I've got a bunion that has more time on this ranch than you do, you ass."

"Handled myself okay the other day."

"You got lucky. We both did," Titus shot back, while Ian nervously looked back to see if anyone was following them. "If they hadn't been idiots, we'd be buried in the north field."

"He's right," Ian said. "You haven't seen half the ranch yet. Took me a year before I knew my way around."

Aldo's jaw worked, but he nodded. "Fine."

"I don't know what kind of history you and Stilts have," Titus said. "Thought you two worked together, but it doesn't take a genius to figure that it didn't end well. But get this." He stepped close, jabbing his finger into Aldo's chest. "Stilts hired Ian. Gods, he hired nearly every guard on this farm. He looks out for us, makes sure we're healthy, have what we need. We know him. We don't know you. So before you start any shit, know that there's not a gods-damned man or woman on this ranch that won't put you in the dirt if you talk to him like that again."

"He looks out for you," Aldo said. *Must be fucking nice.* He shook his head. "Good to know." He took a deep breath, and nodded. "Sorry. I was out of line. Won't happen again."

Titus nodded. "Like I said, I don't know what happened between you two."

"Nothing worth getting into." Aldo held up his hand. "I was an ass, okay? I'll apologize next time I see him." *The fuck I will.*

"Okay." Titus relaxed somewhat. "I meant what I said. You did good with those poachers. Just don't fuck it up for yourself over something that happened long ago, okay?"

"Yeah." Aldo nodded. He realized he was clenching his fists, and forced them to relax. "You got it."

Chapter 11

For a moment, Aldo thought that there had been a terrible mistake. He and Titus had been near the front gate when he heard Ian and Luca mutter the same curse at the same time. About a hundred feet down the road, a woman on a charcoal grey horse rode toward them at a steady cantor. A flash of panic ran through him as he stared at her, not recognizing the rider in the slightest. Titus reached over and nudged him.

"She doesn't like people staring, Aldo."

One of the first skills learned by anyone who has served time is the ability to carefully watch without staring directly. Aldo's chin dropped to his chest, but in the corner of his eye, more details came into view. The raven black hair that tumbled down past her shoulders and the unfamiliar tattoos crawling over her brow and down alongside her left eye threw him for a moment, but finally he recognized Nicolette's jawline and pale green eyes peeking past the disguise. He exhaled silently.

Ian stepped forward, and bowed deeply. "Your Excellency. Welcome back to Vorchese Ranch."

"Oh, get off it," she snapped. The timbre of her voice had pitched slightly upwards, and an accent clipped her consonants in an unfamiliar way. "I'll be baffled if you haven't figured out by now that the ride to this backwards place is exhausting." She looked over the others. "Why so many guards today? Something I need to know about?"

Ian shook his head. "Absolutely not, your Excellency. Our perimeter guard was making their rounds. They arrived here at the same time as you."

"You." Aldo lifted his head to find her steely gaze fixed on him. "I don't know you. You weren't here last time."

"Aldo just joined our guard force this week," Titus said. "Our captain vouches for him, ma'am. Aldo, this is Subarcheron Noya Illych Greystone of the Alddarri Empire."

"An honor, your Excellency." He attempted to bow further in the saddle. It wasn't easy.

"You're Vetticcian." It wasn't a question.

"I am, your Excellency."

She clucked her tongue. "I don't like surprises." Shaking her head, she peered up at the sun overhead. "But I like your unnatural heat worse. Which of you is my nanny this trip?"

"I have the honor of serving as your escort, your Excellency," Ian said.

Nicolette waved a gloved hand. "Let's go. I need a cold drink and to get off of this beast."

The others watched them ride away, waiting until they'd crested the hill before saying anything. "He's earning that bonus pay," Luca said, shaking his head. "You know last time, she had him stay up half the night cleaning the mud off her boots?"

Titus nodded. "Said she wanted no reminder of this place, not even on the soles of her feet. Fucking Imperials."

"Don't think she likes me all that much," Aldo said. "She seemed less than pleased to know I'm Vetticcian."

"I wouldn't take it personally," Titus said. "Far as the Empire's concerned, if you're not from north of the Breaking, you're not worth their time. Fairly sure if I was Duke Snowsill and you had a seat at the Table, she still would have acted like an ass." He jerked his head. "Come on. Let's keep moving. I'm sure you'll see more of the Sub-archeron tonight."

As they rode, Aldo asked, "Does she treat the boss like that?"

"Not far off," Titus said. "He hasn't told us how big this trade deal could be, but we can make an educated guess based on how much he's willing to put up with her. If it was a normal trade deal, I'm pretty sure he would have buried her in the back acreage the first time she asked him why he smelled like that."

"You're kidding."

"Nope. Boss just pasted on a smile," Titus said. "Pretty sure that's why he's so eager to get it done. Half the money, half not having to deal with her any longer."

"She won't still be a part of things?"

"I don't know the details, but apparently not. She just arranges the deal. Once they're in agreement, she'll fuck back off across the Breaking, and the Archeron will come down to sign the deal with the Duke."

"Huh." Aldo scratched at his beard. "Might be a tactic. She shows her entire ass the whole time she's here, makes the boss more likely to agree to less than favorable terms just to be rid of her."

"You think?"

Aldo shrugged. "Wouldn't be the first time I've seen that kind of game."

"Huh," Titus said, considering. "Well, thankfully it's not our problem."

***

"You had to open your mouth."

Aldo looked up at Titus, mouth full of potatoes. He'd never had the tiny purple root vegetables before, but they'd quickly become his favorite. "What?" he mumbled, and forced himself to swallow.

"This is why you never speak up without talking with me first," Titus said. He was holding a large tray with a carefully arranged place setting atop, a tin dome covering the plate. He set it down onto the table next to Aldo. "Someone needs to go relieve Ian so he can get some chow. That same someone needs to also bring the Subarcheron her dinner. Since you spoke up yesterday, that gets to be you."

Aldo looked down at his still-full plate with dismay. "We've been riding for twelve hours, Titus. I'm hungry."

The older man shrugged. "Your food will still be here when you get back."

"It'll be cold."

"I'm sure you've eaten worse."

Aldo scowled, but nodded. He stuffed a pair of soft rolls into his pocket, and Titus said, "You'll have the shift for two hours, long enough for Ian to eat and change his clothes. He'll have the night watch."

"When does he sleep?" Aldo picked up the tray carefully, sniffing at the unusual odors wafting from beneath the tin cover. "Also, what is this?"

"Imperial food. Or as close as Cookie can come," Titus said. "Naath and Stilts will be escorting her around tomorrow for most of the day. Ian can rack out then."

"That'll put him awake for over a day," Aldo said. "We sure that's a good idea?"

"It's a shit deal, but it's what we've got."

Aldo shook his head. "Give him four hours. He can eat, grab a few hours sleep, then come back and relieve me. I'm going to guess him falling asleep on watch would not be good for his career prospects."

"That's generous. What's the deal?"

"I can't just be a nice guy?"

Titus raised an eyebrow. "You're Vetticcian. You people won't piss on a burning man without submitting an itemized bill per ounce afterwards."

"We would not!" Aldo grinned. "It's a flat rate for that. No need to itemize." He shrugged, the silverware clinking softly on the tray. "I'm still new here. Faster I can prove my value, the better. Right now, I got the job because Stiliano owed me a favor. Sooner I can show I belong here, the better."

Titus considered this, then nodded. "Okay, four hours. I'll even let you be the one to tell Ian."

"You're a prince of generosity."

Aldo couldn't help but notice the expressions of sympathy and amusement from everyone he passed on his way out the door. It was a short walk down a narrow path covered in cedar chips to the guest quarters. The night here was quieter than the constant dull roar of the Vetticcian streets, but crickets screeched their songs out in the tall grass. Out past the fence line in the eastern field, Aldo could hear the faint mooing of one of the cows that had been relocated earlier in the day.

Ian was leaning up against an oak tree planted in front of the small but neat guest house, rubbing the bridge of his nose, tossing sticks into a metal brazier that was merrily burning in front of the guest house. He spotted Aldo, and straightened up. "I thought they might fob this off on you."

"Part of my training, I suppose." Aldo grinned. "That'll teach me to volunteer for things here." He nodded at the brazier. "Little warm for that, isn't it?"

"Sun's setting soon. Naath and Stilts want a clear view of this place all night." He gestured at a pile of split wood. "Don't let it go out. They'll be annoyed." Ian jerked his head back to the house. "I'll walk you in. She's going to keep you in there while she eats. I think dishing out verbal abuse helps her digest. I'll be back in a few hours."

"Four hours." Ian frowned in confusion, and Aldo said, "I told Titus I'd keep the watch long enough for you to get a bit of sleep."

Ian's eyes narrowed. "How much?"

"Gods. Just because I'm Vetticcian doesn't mean I'm constantly trying to take your coin."

Ian considered this, and said, "Well, if you think I'm going to argue, you're an idiot." He glanced down. "You're not armed."

"Handed in the crossbow at the end of shift."

Ian nodded, unbuckling the leather belt he wore. A scabbarded short sword hung from it. "You know how to use one of these?"

"Not even a little," Aldo admitted as Ian set it down to take the tray from him. "I've used a boning knife quite a bit. Anything like that?"

"Sure, if someone tries to assassinate the Subarcheron, you can filet them," Ian grinned. "If Her Excellency asks, you're a master swordsman."

Aldo buckled the blade to his hip, and took back the tray. Ian went to the door, knocked three times, and said, "Your Excellency? We have your dinner."

"I can't eat it through the door," came the harsh clipped syllables. "Bring it in."

Ian opened the door for Aldo. Nicolette was sitting at a desk, a pen in one hand and a stack of paper in front of her. She hadn't changed her clothes from the severe, heavy woolen outfit she'd been wearing earlier, and the dark black strands of her wig were plastered to her sweaty forehead. She didn't look up until she'd finished writing, but when she did, her eyes narrowed. "Oh. The Vetticcian."

"Aldo here will have the watch for the next few hours, ma'am," Ian said. "If you need anything, he's your man."

"I desperately hope not." She waved her hand. "Set it at the table, and don't bother me until I'm finished." She lowered her head back over the desk, the pen resuming its scratching over the paper.

Ian mouthed, "Good luck," and Aldo gave a small head nod. The door closed, and he set the tray down on the table as Nicolette got up and walked to the widow, peering through the curtains.

"We good?" he asked softly. She held up a hand for a moment. After about thirty seconds, she nodded, turning back to him.

"I'm going to take off this gods-damned tunic before I collapse. Give me a moment." She disappeared into the next room.

Aldo went over to the window and glanced through the curtains. He could see the lights of the house, and spotted some figures trudging towards the barracks, but no one nearby.

Nicolette came back out, wearing a vest with her muscular arms bare, and sat down at the table, pulling the tray off. She wrinkled her nose at the dark red strips of meat atop rice. "Gods, I hate Imperial food." Her voice was still low.

"There's no one else close," Aldo said. "I think they're afraid you'll drag them inside and eat them."

She grinned as she took a forkful. "Over the top?"

"A bit, but it's working," he said.

"You can sit down."

Aldo shook his head. "Noya Ilych Imperial Whozit wouldn't let me sit down. Someone looks through the window, it'd raise questions. Thank you, by the way, for picking the longest name in history."

She took a forkful, and raised an eyebrow. "You doing okay? Overheard something about an issue a few days ago."

Aldo nodded. "I'm fine. Poachers laid on an ambush at the border. None of the ranch's people got hurt."

"What happened to the poachers?"

Aldo shook his head.

"Huh." Nicolette took a bite. She winced, and reached for her mug of water. "Tracks what I've heard. Duke looks the other way when poachers or raiders go missing near this place. Only ones who ever ask questions are rangers."

Aldo's head snapped around towards her, eyebrows lifting. "I do not want to deal with a ranger."

"Neither do I, but I don't think it likely," she replied. "There aren't that many of them, and there isn't one assigned to this area." Leaning back, she asked, "So how many problems do we have?"

He grunted softly. "First one is my posting."

"What do you mean?"

"I'm on perimeter watch," Aldo said. "Twelve hours a day on horseback, with one of the more senior guards. Training. By the time we get back, there's just enough time for chow and sleep. I'm nowhere near the ranch complex."

"Can you slip away at night?" she asked. "We'll have to hit the cold storage after everyone's asleep anyway."

"I'm in a barracks with forty other people," Aldo said. "If I get up to take a piss, someone'll notice. If that happens right before things go sideways..."

"Yeah." Nicolette scratched at her head. "Damn wig itches. Can you get transferred to a different post? I was hoping as the new guy, they'd have you as my guard. That's the idea behind me being such a bitch. I was hoping they'd hand it off to you."

"I figured. Nice work on that, by the way. Everyone here hates your guts." Nicolette offered a mock bow, and Aldo said, "Unfortunately, that doesn't matter. Naath wants you happy until the trade deal gets signed, and that means they don't want to assign someone who just got here a few days ago as your escort. I tried to push for it. It didn't go well."

She raised an eyebrow. "How bad?"

"Lost my temper," he admitted. "It's not easy. Seeing him."

"You going to be able to keep it together?"

He nodded. "Like you said. It'd be weird if I wasn't angry with him. Haven't crossed any lines." *Closer than you would have liked, though.*

"That's a problem, but we can figure something out. How long do we have tonight?"

"Some good news there. I bought us four hours," Aldo said. He explained, and Nicolette nodded.

"Okay. You said multiple problems. What else?"

"Something Titus said to me. The semen has to stay cold, otherwise it dies in less than an hour," Aldo said. "Even if we can get it out of the cold storage, it'll take weeks to get back to the city."

"We're not meeting DeLuca in the city. The handoff is in Lofland Fork. But your point stands." She pointed to her desk. "Grab my dagger, will you? It's over there."

He obliged, handing her the sheathed blade. It was large, with a dark black blade and a stag horn hilt. She gripped the hilt tightly, and twisted. Nothing happened at first, but a click issued from the dagger, and the handle came away from the blade. She handed it to him.

Aldo looked down at the hollow cavity within. He brought his fingers up to brush the odd metal lining the interior, and his eyes widened. "It's cold."

"DeLuca had already thought of that problem," Nicolette said. "She had that made by her household artificer. The interior is some metal from the Empire. I don't know how, but she said it doesn't really change temperature. It's going to stay cold for a long, long time. Long after when we've handed it off to her." She pointed at the hilt. "The space is supposed to fit the vials they use here. I'll have the unviable sample in the hilt. We get into the storage room, make the swap, get out. I always have the dagger on me, so no one will say boo."

His eyes widened. "Seriously? Why aren't they using this everywhere? Fishing boats spend a fortune on ice."

"Based on the way DeLuca talked about it, that little sleeve of metal is the most expensive investment she made on the job, our pay included." Nicolette took the hilt back from him, and snapped it back onto the dagger. The craftsmanship was flawless, the seam disappearing the moment it had been reassembled. "Probably too expensive or too rare. Have you gotten a look at the lock yet?"

"On the cold storage?" Aldo shook his head. "That's the other problem. It's under the husbandry building, two guards on it at all times. That building is off limits to anyone but Naath and the guards assigned to it. I could probably get down there, but if they saw you, they'd sound the alarm."

"You know which guards?"

"I can find out."

Nicolette nodded. "Okay, one problem at a time. First thing first. We need to get you assigned as my escort."

"I told you, they're not going to go for that."

"They will if I demand it."

"And how is that not going to raise suspicions?"

She looked uncomfortable for a moment. "I have an idea about that. It's not ideal, but it'll give me an excuse to make the request. But we have to give them a reason to replace Ian."

Aldo nodded slowly. "If he screws up, pisses you off in some way, that could do it. Naath wouldn't hesitate to replace him."

"I could throw a fit, claim he's not..." She trailed off. "No, it needs to be someone else's idea to replace him. If it's mine, and I then request you as his replacement, that's too obvious."

Aldo raised an eyebrow. "What if he got drunk? They serve beer with dinner."

"He'd have to drink a lot to get to the point where he screws up that badly."

Aldo grinned. "I think I can manage that."

Chapter 12

There wasn't a designated time in which members of the guard force had to go to bed, no lights-out period. But it was generally accepted that anyone making excess noise after the night watch laced up their boots and left the barracks would have something heavy thrown their way. By the time Aldo returned to the barracks, having been relieved by a bleary-eyed Ian, it was well past that hour, with most everyone sleeping.

A handful of people were still awake, including Luca, who sat up against the wall carving what looked like a small model ship, lit by the greasy orange light from a whale-oil lamp. He raised an eyebrow as Aldo approached. "Your tunic is torn, Vetticci."

Aldo scowled at him, peeling the damaged tunic over the top of his head and grabbing a folded one from the shelves next to his bunk. "I don't want to talk about it."

Luca set the model aside, brushing wood shavings from his tunic, and sat up. "You got ambushed by poachers three days ago, and didn't get much more than some mud stains. But you come back from babysitting her Excellency..."

"I said I don't want to talk about it."

"Because it looks like she kicked your ass."

Aldo let out a long breath. "That would have been preferable." He let out a long sigh. "Between you and me?"

"I mean, if the ranch is about to burn down..."

Aldo waved him off. "You know how it looked like she didn't like Vetticcians?" Luca nodded, and Aldo said, "That's not exactly accurate."

Luca frowned for a moment, but an expression bloomed on his face that was a mix of horrified and delighted. "She didn't. YOU didn't."

"Of course not!" Aldo shook his head. "I was worried the boss would bounce me right out of here if I crossed any lines, and that one's painted in blood red paint. Marked with torches. With a McElroy screamer bellowing at me to turn the fuck around."

"So then how did..."

"Her enthusiasm was unbridled by such petty concerns as whether or not I was interested." Aldo fingered the tear in the tunic he'd tossed on the bed. "I'm going to have to pay for a new tunic."

"Ask the Subarcheron," Luca said. "I'll bet she'll buy you something pretty."

"This isn't funny."

"You sure? We could poll the others."

Aldo shook his head frantically. "Gods no. Please, I don't have to see her again, and nothing good will come of Stilts and the boss finding out this is happening. Please, I'm begging you, you have to keep this quiet."

Luca grinned. "You know, I really do hate cleaning duty."

"What?"

"Cleaning duty. Once a week, Stilts has half of us spend three hours cleaning the barracks. We just did it, but I'm scheduled for the next time. You're not."

Aldo shook his head. "I'm sure you're mistaken. I saw the posted schedule. You're not scheduled, I am."

"There's a posted schedule?"

"You keep your mouth shut, I'll make one for you."

Luca nodded. "Well, then, your secret is safe with me."

***

"So word has it that our guest tried to take your virtue last night."

Aldo froze next to the spread of baked bread, jams, and butter that was laid out next to the doors of the barracks the following morning. He wasn't sure what he would have done had he misjudged Luca, and was gratified he didn't have to find out. Assuming an annoyed expression, he turned to Titus, who was waiting patiently behind him in line with his plate, a grin pasted on his face. Aldo bellowed, "Luca!"

Further down in the barracks, Luca popped his head up and yelled, "I like cleaning!"

"I could have told you not to tell Luca anything you wanted quiet," Titus said.

Aldo's shoulders slumped. "Wonderful. Can I at least trust you not to say anything?"

"Absolutely," Titus said. "I hate gossip."

Another guard Aldo had yet to be introduced to poked his head out of line. "Hey Aldo, want to borrow some of my trousers? They're a bit smaller than yours. Really showcase the goods."

"Omar loves gossip, though."

"Is there anyone who doesn't know?"

Titus shook his head. "I doubt anyone will be very eager to share that particular tidbit with Naath. He's uptight about that kind of stuff in the best circumstances. Otherwise, I'd put good money on it being a topic of discussion in Lofland Fork by now."

"Shit."

"It's going to be fine," Titus said, grinning. "You're not on escort duty, and we'll find someone else to relieve Ian for the rest of the time the Subarcheron is here. Best way to prevent this from being anything more than a funny story we'll be telling for a long, long, LONG time."

By the time they were saddling up their horses in the stables, Aldo had been treated to a series of suggestions as how he could better tempt their Imperial guest, much to Titus' amusement and his annoyance. As he tightened the straps, he heard someone say, "Aldo?"

"For the gods, please give it a fucking break. It's not funny, and..." He trailed off as he saw Stiliano standing a few feet away.

"I tend to agree with that," his father said, face impassive. "I think we need to talk."

Titus glanced between the two of them. "Stilts, I really don't think he actually did anything."

"I would hope not, but we still need to talk."

"Want me to..." Titus asked, and Stiliano nodded.

"Please. Aldo should know your route by now. I'm sure he can find you."

Titus nodded, flashed Aldo a sympathetic look, and climbed on his horse. Stiliano didn't speak until Titus was out of the stables. He turned to his son. "Aldo..."

"He's right. I didn't do anything," Aldo said, his voice flat. "She made her interest clear, but I explained I was on duty."

"I heard your clothes were damaged."

"She made her interest very clear."

Stiliano sighed, running his hand through his hair. "This is not good. If she was offended..."

"She seemed to think it was funny." Aldo scowled as he spoke. "Said something about us resuming the conversation later."

"That can't happen."

"I know your knowledge of me as a person ends about the same time my freedom did, but I'm not an idiot. I came all this way for a job. I'm not going to risk it by doing something that stupid."

Stiliano shook his head. "I didn't mean..."

"It's fine," Aldo said brusquely. He didn't want to push it too far, but he could feel his blood thundering in his temples with every word his father said. "I'll be on watch the rest of the day. Titus said that we can just have someone else relieve Ian if he needs it. I'll stay in the barracks when I'm not on watch. She doesn't go there, does she?"

"No. She saw them during her first visit. Was not impressed." Stiliano pursed his lips, brow furrowed with worry, but nodded. "It's the best we can do. But if it happens again, we're going to have to go to Naath, and he's not going to be happy."

"I'm not jumping with glee myself."

"I'm much more concerned with the boss' reaction." Stiliano ran his fingers through his hair. As he did, the top of his tunic slid aside, and Aldo's eyes widened at the sight of the wooden shepherd's crook hanging from his father's neck.

"You have to be kidding me. I know you were there the other night, but I thought..."

Stiliano adjusted his shirt, scowling. "It's nothing."

"Nothing?" Aldo stared at him. "You're a fucking Confessor?"

"No. Yes." Stiliano shook his head. "It's complicated."

"Is it?"

"We're not all..." He swallowed. "I needed something. After..." Stiliano trailed off. "I needed something to believe in. Something to tell me that there was something behind everything that had happened."

"Gods." *Please, gods, make him shut up. Just let me get out of here.* "I just don't fucking care. Are we done? Can I go do my job?"

Stiliano nodded slowly, and Aldo turned back to the saddle. He could feel his father's eyes boring into the back of his head. As he began to guide his horse out of the stall, Stiliano said, "I quit drinking."

"What?" Aldo stopped, turning back to him.

"I stopped drinking. When I started working here." His father cleared his throat, eyes not quite meeting Aldo's. "I had my last drink about eight years ago."

Aldo's jaw worked. "Why are you telling me this?"

"I just wanted you to know."

"Great. I know. Can I go?"

"Aldo..."

"What do you want from me?" Aldo said. "I told you. I'm not looking for an apology. I'm not looking for anything other than this job, and I'm doing the best I can. If you have a problem with how I'm doing that job, we've got something to talk about. But you setting down the bottle? It's surprising as anything, but it's just trivia. Got nothing to do with me."

"It does. It has everything to do with you," Stiliano said, desperation winding through his words. "I just need you to understand. I'm not that man anymore."

"Gods." Aldo spun on his heel to face him. "I. Don't. Care. What else do I need to say? I don't want to have this discussion, and you sure as fuck don't want to have this discussion."

Stiliano seemed to shrink into himself, but he shook his head. "I'm not that man anymore." He repeated the words like a mantra.

"Congratulations, you're not the fucking drunk who left me twisting before I knew how to shave." The words clawed out from between his teeth before he could stop them, reaching out to dig deep in his father. "That's why I have a beard, by the way. I don't know how to shave. Think you can reason out why that might be the case?"

"I can't change that."

"Hey, we finally agree on something." The horse behind him nickered nervously, but Aldo didn't turn. "What do you want from me? You're not drinking. Amazing. You took your last drink eight years ago. Hope it was delicious." Aldo reached down and pulled up his sleeve. "I already had four of these when you were deciding to better yourself." He touched a jagged scar next to the tattoos, nearly three inches in length. "I probably got this about the same time you were embarking on on your journey of personal growth. Know what it is?"

Stiliano's eyes traced over the row of fishhooks. He shook his head.

"It's what happens when a number nine hook snags your arm," Aldo's finger tapped against the scar as he spoke. "Digs into the bone. Want to know the process for removing it? What was happening while you were congratulating yourself on doing the bare fucking minimum?"

He bore down on his father with a hard stare as he kept speaking. "You have thirty seconds. That's how long the overseers will give us to get the hook out. Thirty seconds. After that, the line goes into the black, and you with it. So while every other prisoner kept working, bent over their lines and pretended not to see a teenage kid screaming and bleeding all over the deck, one man pulled out his boning knife, cut my arm open, and ripped the hook out so I didn't drown."

The blood drained from Stiliano's face. "Gods."

"They weren't out there with me," Aldo said. The voice in his head that knew what a bad idea this was was mute, batted aside by the white hot rage clawing its way out of the box he'd kept it inside for so very long. "You sure as fuck weren't out there with me. I was alone, and the only reason I didn't end up chum was because a man earning his tattoos after beating someone to death didn't want to find someone else to warm his bunk at night. That's the man who did more for me than you ever did. Burned the wound with a hot iron so it didn't sour. Bound it for me. Made sure I had almost a full day to writhe around in pain before I had to be back on the fucking lines."

Stiliano took a step back, as if physically repelled by the venom in his son's words. "I didn't mean…"

"You meant to make yourself feel better," Aldo spat. "To find absolution in your personal growth. But as you pushed that bottle away, did you once think about what your only son had paid for you to reach that point? You're making amends for you, not for me." Blood thundered in his temples as his fingers curled into fists. "I'm so fucking glad you stopped drinking. But don't delude yourself into thinking it changes a single moment of the fourteen fucking years I spent in the nightmare you shipped me off to. Drink. Don't drink. Makes no difference to me, because you're a gods-damned stranger."

He swallowed, trying to shove the lump in his throat down. "You have to be. Because I can speak to you, work with you, if you're a stranger. If you're my father…" His voice choked on the word for a moment. "I'll drown. No different than if that hook had dragged me into the water, I'll drown. My lungs will fill with my hatred for that man, and I'll drown."

Stiliano said nothing. His eyes were dead.

"May I please, for all the mercy of the gods, go do my fucking job?" Aldo's voice broke as he spoke. He hated himself for it.

Stiliano gave a single, jerking nod, and Aldo turned and left.

Chapter 13

Titus didn't ask what he and Stiliano had spoken about. Aldo didn't know if the expression on his face was enough to deter questions, or if Titus just didn't care, but he was grateful whatever the reason. They spoke little as they rode.

Aldo knew that this was just a temporary role he was playing, but he was quickly coming to appreciate the quiet of this job. He had never known this kind of solitude. It was impossible to find inside the chaos of the city, even when he'd left the stinking cells and packed decks of the penance barge. Millions of people jostling and shouting over one another meant that silence was an abstract, never actually realized.

Here, the world just sprawled. It spread out, luxuriating in the rolling hills and empty plains, dotted with trees and placidly chewing cattle. Titus wasn't much for idle chatter, and the two rode often for hours without exchanging a word, eyes roaming over the gently waving butter-yellow grass, listening to the birds and insects lend their voice to the gentle breeze. The air was warm, and smelled of hay and honeysuckle, and while he knew his presence was a lie, he was grateful for the moment.

Could this be my future? Can I really find peace at the end of this, be out from under everyone's thumb? He pushed the thought aside, but the closer they came to their goal, the more it scratched at his subconscious.

Time was counted by landmarks. They rode along the thin sliver of space between the northeast and southeast fields, a track of land churned up by thousands of massive blunt hooves over the years. It took hours to reach the eastern fence, stretching impossibly far to the north and south, and they turned to ride alongside it. Each time they would approach a cluster of trees or a spot they couldn't easily see from far off, Aldo would wordlessly cock his crossbow and fit a bolt into the slot while Titus did the same. Each time, they rode past with nothing to interrupt them.

It wasn't until well in the afternoon that hoofbeats drew their attention; not from outside the ranch, but from the direction in which they'd come. A guard Aldo had not yet met rode towards them at a full gallop, one hand gripping the reins while the other held a broad straw hat secure to his head. Titus frowned, hand falling to the hilt of his weapon.

"Something wrong?" Aldo asked, eying the rapidly approaching rider.

"Don't know. Didn't hear the bells, and he's alone. Can't imagine why."

They didn't have long to wonder. The rider drew close, and Titus raised his voice to shout. "Long way from the house, Macon," Titus said. "What's the fire?"

"It's Stilts," the man said breathlessly, wincing slightly as he adjusted in his saddle. "We're not sure... we don't know what to do."

"Is he hurt?"

"No," Macon said, shaking his head. "He's drunk."

"What?" Titus' eyes widened.

"Swear it, Titus. He's blackout, three sheets to the wind."

"Godsdammit," Titus said, glancing sideways at Aldo, who shrugged helplessly while his skin went cold. *Fuck.* "Does Naath...?"

"We have him in the armory. The boss is with Ian and the Subarcheron in the calf fields. Not supposed to be back until dinner."

"Did anyone else see him?"

"Just our people," Macon said. "He won't talk to us, Titus. No one knows what to do. We tried to take the bottle from him, but he won't let us. You've worked with him longest. We thought you could help."

"Okay." Titus thought for a moment, then growled under his breath. "Gods. Macon, you know the route for this week?"

"I think so."

"North to the feed stations, then cut back west until you hit the north access trail, then back this way." Titus made Macon repeat it back to him twice until satisfied. "You run into anyone that's not one of ours, come up with something. Tell them I got sick or some shit." Macon nodded, and Titus said, "Aldo, you're with me."

As soon as they were out of earshot, Titus snapped at Aldo, "The fuck did you say to him?"

"Nothing!" The words sounded hollow as soon as they'd left his lips, and Aldo could tell they'd not been remotely convincing. Titus's warning from the other night rang in his ears. *Fuck the job. He might actually bury you for this, moron.*

"Fucking hell." Titus dug his heels into his horse, which snorted in protest before leaping into a gallop, dirt spraying from its churning hooves. Aldo fell in behind him. "Keep up. You're helping me fix this," he shouted over the hoofbeats.

Aldo would have responded, but he instead focused on staying on his horse, the wind stinging his eyes.

Even at these speeds, it took nearly a half hour before they reached the ranch complex. Two other guards were waiting, running up to take their horses. "We got them. Just go," one of them said urgently. "In the armory."

They jogged over to the squat stone building. The armory was slightly larger than a small house. Where most of the other buildings in the complex were made of clapboard, the armory and the harvesting building were made of slabs of granite, mortared together. A small window had been Aldo's only exposure, at which his crossbow had been handed to him each morning before they rode, and where he returned it at the end of the day. The door was blackened oak, and had always been locked, but it swung open as they approached. Omar waved them over.

"How bad?" Titus asked, coming to a stop.

"Bad. We found him in the barracks," Omar said. "Titus... He took a bottle from the house. It's rye."

Titus muttered a curse. "Okay. Do you know if he got any of his checks done?"

"I don't think so."

Nodding, Titus thought for a moment. "Okay, first things first. Once Bern and Simon get the horses sorted, you two get to everyone who saw him this morning. He got sick. Collapsed in the house. We'll get him to the barracks, get him in bed."

Omar shook his head. "If they think he's sick, they'll get Roland. He'll figure it out."

"Roland's in Galen's Crossing, picking up supplies. We have seven, eight hours to get him sobered up."

"What about the bottle?"

"I don't know, godsdammit. First things first. Go." Omar looked unconvinced, but he took off at a jog.

Titus spun to face Aldo. "I haven't dug into what went down between you and Stilts because it's been none of my business. But if

Naath finds out Stilts was drinking, let alone on the job, it'll be worse than you can imagine. Whatever shit you have against the man, I need you to fucking stow it, because we have to sort this out. If you have a problem with that, tell me."

Aldo swallowed, glaring back at Titus. *I've done my time taking care of his drunk ass*, he thought.

Titus narrowed his eyes. "Keep something in mind, Aldo. I'm second in command. If Stilts goes, I take over the guard force, and I can promise you that the very first thing I do is can your ass. I'll make damn sure no one in the entire duchy hires you."

"I'm not the one who stole a fucking bottle that wasn't mine and got drunk!" Aldo blurted.

Before he could say anything else, Titus had the front of his tunic in a grip and slammed him against the stone wall. Aldo's eyes widened as the older man snarled. "Eight gods-damned years, I've never seen that man take so much as a sip of beer. You're here for three days, and he's half in the bag. If it's not your fault, it's a hell of a coincidence. We watch out for each other here, you ass. We have to. The rest of the guys think you're not willing to step up when needed? You might not make it off this ranch at all."

Shit. Aldo stopped struggling and gritted his teeth. Slowly, he nodded. "Let me go."

"You going to help?"

"Can't do much with you trying to bash me through this wall, can I?" Titus' fist relaxed, and Aldo straightened his tunic. "Let's go in. You take the bottle back to the house. Once you're sure no one's around, smash it next to wherever it was sitting, along with a few other bottles. Clean up most of it, but leave a few bits of glass. We'll tell them he collapsed, knocked it over."

Titus narrowed his eyes. "They'll take it from his pay."

"And you'll take it from mine," Aldo snapped. "It explains the bottle."

"But why break the others?"

"Three, four bottles is an accident. One is an obvious excuse." Aldo thought for a moment. "Mustard seed. Does Cookie ever use mustard seed when he cooks?"

"The hell do I know?" Titus shook his head. "Probably. We have mustard flowers in some of the pastures."

"Mix up ground up mustard seed, a lot of it, in water. Bring it back here. He'll puke up everything in his stomach if we give him that. It'll look like he ate something that put up a fight."

Titus considered him, then nodded. "Let's go."

The walls of the armory were fitted with wooden racks, filled with short swords, crossbows, and dozens of unstrung yew longbows. There was a table in the center of the room with an assortment of tools, a half-assembled crossbow scattered over the surface. In the far corner, Stiliano was slumped against the wall. He looked unconscious, the bottle clutched in his hands nearly empty.

"Stilts." Titus crouched next to him, giving his shoulder a little shake. Stiliano mumbled something under his breath, but didn't seem to respond. "Shit. He reeks of whiskey."

"Just go. Make sure everything is good out there. I'll handle him." Titus raised an eyebrow, and Aldo said, "I understand what's at stake, okay? I'll get him cleaned up and back to the barracks."

Crouching down, he tried to take the bottle from Stiliano's hand. His father offered little reaction, but his grip was tight around the neck of the bottle, and he wouldn't give it up. He said nothing, but Aldo could see that he was awake, looking at him from eyes smeared with tears and alcohol. He turned away, looking up at Titus. "I'll get the bottle before you get back." The older man nodded and left, pushing the door closed behind him.

Still in a crouch, Aldo let his weight pull him back until he was seated on the floor about five feet away, staring at the near-catatonic man. He found it difficult to maintain his anger. That flame needed something upon which to feed upon, and Stiliano offered nothing. He wasn't avoiding Aldo's gaze. He wasn't meeting his stare. His expression was hollow, empty.

They sat like that for a while, Aldo staring at Stiliano, Stiliano staring at nothing. Finally, Aldo spoke. "What is this?"

Nothing.

"I thought you were done with the bottle."

Silence.

"Are you even there? Or are you too drunk to even know that I'm here?" Aldo was surprised at the lack of heat in his words. Instead, he felt a weariness settle down over his shoulders, slumping them down. It was difficult to reconcile the man he'd spent so long feeling such fury towards with the miserable individual slumped against a worn stone wall. He opened his mouth to reignite that anger, to lash out, but that's not what came out.

"Where were you?"

Aldo's voice was small, as if coming from some hidden dark corner deep inside him. Slowly, his father's wet eyes came up to settle upon him as Aldo spoke again.

"Why didn't you come? Where were you?" He felt the old ache inside him as the memory of the empty door in the tribunal swam up in his memory. "I just thought... Where were you?"

His father swallowed, blinking several times. When he spoke, his voice was flat. "Does it matter?"

"Does it matter?" Aldo's breath slipped free of his trembling chest. "You were supposed to be there. You promised. You told me, over and over, that if anything happened, you would be there. I waited. I kept waiting. All the way up until the bumboat pulled away. I stared at the pier as it got smaller and smaller, looking for you. It mattered to me."

Stiliano nodded, a slow, jerking bob of the head. "I know. I thought about it. Every day. Every night since then, I think about it. I picture you in my head. I imagine all the things I could have done, could have said. But I didn't, and I wasn't, and at the end of things, does it matter?"

"Fourteen years is a long time not to know why your father left you to twist."

"See, though, that's the thing," Stiliano said. "The reason why doesn't matter. I put you there. So I can tell you any reason in the world, but I'm still the reason you were in that house when they found you. You broke into that safe for me. Because I asked you to. Just like every other time. Every time you could have been caught, and it would have been my fault. I was playing a game of dice and putting my son up for stakes." His eyes brimmed with tears. "What kind of man does that? What kind of man gambles with the life of all he has left?"

His head lowered, and his shoulders started to tremble. Aldo watched him. He could have reached out, could have said something. He didn't know if he wanted to.

When Stiliano started speaking again, it was so soft Aldo had to strain to hear it. "I saw the guards coming. They were moving right towards the house, like they'd been called. I broke a window, like we'd talked about. To bring them to me. But they barely looked over. Knew you were there. I panicked."

"You ran?"

If he took offense at the suggestion, Stiliano didn't show it. "I threw a rock. Hit one in the face. Broke his nose. That got their attention. They chased me. I tried to lose them. But I was never..." He let out a shuddering breath. "They caught me a few blocks away. Beat me. Broke my nose, broke my fingers. But they didn't bind me. Left me there, bleeding. Hurt, but I'd pulled them away. Once I could pick myself up, I made my way back to our apartment."

The anger flared again, like embers fanned back to crackling life. "Don't lie. Please. Not now, not about this."

"Not lying."

"The guards didn't chase you," Aldo said. "They came in. They were waiting, at the bottom of the stairs. Four of them. They were on me before I knew what was happening."

Stiliano nodded. "Took me two, three days to find out what had happened. Had to bribe a few people. Borrow money I couldn't afford to do it." He wiped the snot from his nose with the back of his hand. "The safe was rigged. An alarm. Brought some guards that were waiting."

"There wasn't an alarm. Wasn't any sound."

"Not audible," Stiliano said. "Visual. Don't know how it worked. College-made. Expensive. Not anything I'd taught you to look for. Not anything I'd ever heard of." He swallowed. "They had half a dozen guards watching that place. Didn't see us go in, but the moment the safe was open..."

Aldo remembered the shock, hands falling on him, wrenching the leather tube from his hands, pushing him roughly to the floor. He'd spent so long pushing that moment away, burying it under anything that could keep it from swimming to the front of his mind. He felt the familiar pit in his stomach as he remembered, but now, among the sick feeling, he remembered something else. "The lamps. The lamps downstairs were lit. I thought the guards had lit them when they came in, but why would they..."

"They wouldn't." Stiliano shook his head. "They must have come on when the safe opened. It's how they knew."

"So the two that chased you off knew they could."

"They knew that the others would take the house. I don't know. Maybe there was a way to stop them, to get you out. I've replayed it a thousand times."

Aldo ran his fingers through his hair. "Why? Why so many guards? Why were they waiting?"

"Something in the safe. The tube you stole. It was a Table communique," Stiliano said. "Found out months later. It's why you got fourteen years."

Aldo looked up. "What?"

"You had to wonder. Why a kid got so much time for burglary."

"They never said. Or if they did, I didn't hear."

"Asked around. Said if the seal had been broken, you would never have made it to the barge."

Aldo shook his head. "Vetticci doesn't execute people."

"Not officially." Stiliano gave a half shrug, blinking bleary eyes. "Accidents happen."

"If that's true..." Aldo trailed off. Finally, he gave a sharp shake of his head. "Okay. Even if I believe you, even if I believe that there was nothing you could do to stop me from getting pinched, that doesn't explain..."

"When you didn't show up, hours later, I started looking for you. Asking around. Didn't take long to find out what had happened." He wrung his fingers as he spoke. "I made arrangements. Asked Aniya to take you in. I was going to buy your sentence."

"You never showed, though. The arbiter waited. Longer than he should. I don't think even he expected a father to just let his son..."

"I was drunk." He said it as a matter of fact, as if the words weren't a condemnation of all he was. Stiliano's eyes were bleary and red as they came up to meet his son's. "I made the arrangements. Got everything set up. It was still a day until your tribunal. I just kept thinking. Knowing what was coming. Wasn't trying to avoid what I had promised to do. Just trying to numb the fear. So I found a bottle. Found the bottom of it." He blinked slowly, tears in his eyes. "You were waiting for me. I was lying in my own vomit. I didn't wake up until hours after you were gone."

The bottom dropped out of Aldo's stomach. "You were drunk."

The older man let loose a chuckle that was half sob. "Of course I was drunk. I was always drunk. Too much to think I'd stay straight for the one time I really fucking needed to."

Aldo wanted to turn and walk away. He wanted to hit him. He wanted to do a thousand things, but his limbs refused to move, his eyes refused to turn. Instead, he stared at the old drunk weeping in front of him. He saw the grief and guilt etched into every line on the weathered face, and knew that as painful as it was for Aldo to see him, it was harder for his father to come face to face with everything that had haunted him.

"So this is what?" he asked, voice rough. "Just you hiding in the bottle again, after so many years trying to be more?"

"Maybe." Stiliano wiped his eyes with the back of a rough hand.

"Bullshit." Stiliano didn't look up at the flat response, but his hand tightened around the neck of the bottle. Aldo's voice was tired as he spoke. "You're a fool. But you're not fool enough to think this changes anything. Whatever Naath does to you, it doesn't change what happened to me. What you did."

"I know. It's why I tried to find something. Tried to find this." Stiliano reached up to brush his fingers around the crook hanging from his neck. "I wanted to believe that pain and loss have a purpose, that it's not just random chance. That something, anything could come out of this disaster." His father finally lifted bloodshot and tired eyes to meet those of the son he abandoned long ago. "But who am I to find peace when I stole it from you?"

Aldo opened his mouth, then closed it again. He knew what he should say. One word of forgiveness would be a life preserver to a drowning man, a sign that there was some future in which he looked at his father as something other than the garrote that had been strangling him since before he started growing hair on his face. There was a job to do, people depending on him. But even the thought of offering a sliver of retribution made him tired. Exhausted in a place no sleep could touch.

He sank down to sit against the wall next to Stiliano, saying nothing for a long while. His eyes fell to the faded blue hooks tracing a path from his wrist to elbow, the first now merely a blur. Aldo brushed a thumb over the faded tattoo. It would never be gone. But every year, it was a bit more ephemeral. Swallowing, he said, "I can't forgive what you did."

Stiliano nodded, a short jerk of the head.

"I can't forgive. It happened, and there's nothing that can change that, not in that bottle, and not at the end of what unthinkable thing Naath will do to save your soul." He rubbed his eyes. "I served my time, time I didn't deserve. Time I shouldn't have carried. Maybe this is yours. Maybe it's right that your time kept going after I stepped off the deck. But there's no way to cheat your way out of your time. No way to end the sentence early." He reached out and took the bottle. This time, his father didn't resist. "There are people here, people who see you the way I used to. People who count on you. Who believe that you're the man you say you are."

"It's a lie."

Aldo couldn't help the wry chuckle that slipped past his lips. "I mean, yeah. You're a thief, and you've always been a liar. But somehow, you've found a way to make the lie work for someone other than you."

Stiliano shook his head. "I can't do it."

"You can. And you will. That's your time. That's your penance. Maybe the gods or the universe exact their cost for our sins in their own time, at their own pace. I earned my redemption in cold waves and biting hooks." Aldo raised an eyebrow. "All that stuff, about earning your salvation. Everything that's supposed to stand for." He pointed at the wooden crook hanging around his father's neck. "You really believe that?"

Stiliano stared at nothing for a bit. "I don't know. Maybe. Maybe I'm just trying to convince myself that there's something to be found at the end of all the pain I put you through."

"Yeah, well, if the only reason you wear that shit is to make yourself feel better about me riding the deck, then it really is nothing but self-serving bullshit," Aldo said. "I don't do faith. Never seen that it leads anywhere but pain. But even I know that any faith you use to excuse the hurt you've done isn't worth a gods-damned thing."

"So what's the point?"

"Maybe there isn't one. But if I was the believing sort, I might suggest that trying to earn your place in the next world off the pain you caused your son is a stretch even by the lunacy Naath spits. Maybe your pain, your penance, is knowing what you've done, every fucking day. I don't know if there's an ounce of salvation at the end of this road, but if there is, maybe you have to earn yours knowing the cost of the last time you picked up one of these." He gestured with the bottle. "You get to spend your life knowing that escape, no matter how destructive or foolish, lies at the bottom of this bottle, and making the choice to turn your back on that escape day after day after fucking day."

A tear ran down Stiliano's ruddy cheek. "I don't know if I can."

"You don't have a choice. None of us do." Aldo stared down at the bottle in his hands. "We all ride the deck for the time we have. Only way off is overboard."

Rough hands came up to brush against the crook. "I might have fucked myself. I stole a bottle."

The door opened, and Titus came through, a small bowl in his hands. He muttered something to someone outside, and shut the door before looking down at the pair. "We good here?"

"Not even a little," Aldo said. "That the mustard seed?"

"Mustard seed?" Stiliano asked as Titus nodded.

"You're sick. Collapsed in the house, broke a few bottles. But if you're sick, you need to be really fucking sick."

Stiliano recoiled from the bowl Titus offered. "I don't know..."

"No matter what I think, here's what I know," Aldo snapped. "There's a fucking half dozen people running around trying to save your ass. So unless you want them all to go down with you, drink."

Stiliano grimaced, but he took the bowl and drank in two quick swallows. Aldo clambered to his feet. "Let's go. We've got about three minutes before things get messy."

He and Titus each took an arm, hauling the older man to his feet. Stiliano's face was already turning a bit gray. As they emerged from the armory, two other ranch hands were keeping watch, and one waved them on, whispering, "It's clear. Get him to his quarters. We'll handle the rest."

Stiliano vomited twice before they'd finished the four-minute walk to the small cottage, and curled up on his side on a straw bed, wrapped around a bucket. Titus turned to Aldo, and said, "You need to not be here when Roland comes. It's no secret you two have a history. I'd rather your name not even come up when he starts asking questions. Go find Macon, relieve him."

Aldo nodded. "Got it."

Titus jerked his head at Stiliano. "This going to happen again?"

"No clue," Aldo said. "But if it does, it won't be because I showed my ass again."

Titus grunted. "Go. We'll talk later."

Chapter 14

B y the time Titus crested the hill near the eastern fences, Aldo was so tired he was struggling to keep his eyes open. He'd been awake for nearly 32 hours, riding the perimeter alone, and doing his best to keep the exhaustion from blunting his perception of the trees outside the fence.

Titus grunted as he drew alongside him. "You look like shit."

"Feel like it." Aldo raised an eyebrow. "We good?"

"Roland gave him something to settle his stomach."

"Think he smelled the booze?"

"Hard not to, but we explained that he broke the bottles when he fell. Besides, this place reeks of vomit right now. We've got all the windows open. Roland said it might be something he ate." Titus glanced over at him. "So we need to talk."

Aldo sighed. "Can it wait until I get some sleep?"

"What do you think?"

"Yeah." Aldo nodded. "Yeah, okay."

"You know how bad it would have gone if the Subarcheron had seen that?" Titus' voice was even, but his expression was as hard as granite. "Not just for him. For all of us. Everything Naath's been working for over the last six months has been in service to this trade deal. If it goes up in smoke because you and Stilts have history, the shit's going to land on all of us."

"I get it."

"You don't." Titus shook his head. "Might have done you a disservice, keeping you in the dark. You know what the boss is, right? What he believes?"

Aldo nodded. "He made it clear from when we first met."

"Do you know what that actually means?"

"I know Stiliano wears the same crook. That's about it."

Titus snorted. "A quarter of the men on the ranch wear the crook. But there's a difference. Naath is a Confessor to the bone. He believes. Hard. He believes in that more than anything else."

"Why isn't he in Cicerone?" Aldo asked. "I thought most of the dyed in the wool Confessors left when Cicerone broke away."

"They did. But the church asked Naath to stay. Keep running the ranch." Titus shrugged. "Holy or not, the church needs coin, and this ranch produces a lot of it. I don't know how much of the profits make their way into the Confessor coffers, but it's enough that Naath sees running this place as a holy mission, and that's not something you fuck with." He stared at Aldo. "So I need to know what the problem is between you and Stilts. And I need to know whether I need to escort you to the nearest gate and kick your ass off this ranch right the fuck now."

Aldo shook his head. "It's not..."

"I swear by all the gods I can name that if you say it's not important, I'm going to stab you. Not somewhere fatal, but it'll fucking hurt."

"That wasn't what I was going to say." Aldo saw the expression on the older man's face, and quickly said, "That wasn't exactly what I was going to say."

Titus glared at him. "First thought that you two worked a job together. But even assuming you're older than I think you are, and taking into account the number of decorations you've got on your arm, that would make you awfully young to be running scams on the streets of the Ruins."

"You really haven't been to Vetticci, have you?" Aldo muttered.

"So not too young?"

"Depending on the part of town, some infants have their hand in the midwife's pocket while she's trying to cut the cord." Aldo nodded slowly. "Yeah, we worked together."

"He leave you to twist?"

"Something like that."

"Then why would you godsdamned come here?" Titus said, frowning. "I don't figure you mean to put steel between his ribs. You've been alone with him enough, and if there would have been a better opportunity than in the armory earlier, I can't really think of it. If he's the reason you ended up pulling fish out of the sea, why would you..." Titus went pale.

Shit.

"He's your gods-damned father, isn't he."

Aldo sorted through lies one after another frantically, trying to figure out how to slide around this, but the longer he was silent, the more storm clouds gathered on Titus' face. Finally, he sighed. *She's gonna be pissed.* "Yeah. He is."

Titus stared for a long moment. "And you getting bound. His fault?"

"Pretty much." Aldo's mount nickered softly beneath him as a quartet of cows crested the hill a mile away. Even at this distance, he could see the grass tremble under their broad feet. "How much is up for debate. Things went sideways. He always promised he'd be there. He wasn't."

"Gods," Titus said. "Always figured he had reason not to talk about the city. But didn't think..." Looking back up at Aldo, he said, "He doesn't talk about it. Vetticci, I mean. Guess I know why."

Taste of the truth, now feed him the shit. "Work's been harder and harder to come by in the city. Canneries getting too good, too many College devices meaning one man can do the work of five. You have one hook on your arm, takes a minor miracle to find a way to put coral in your pocket and fish in your belly." Reaching down, he pushed his sleeve past the elbow, one hook after another appearing. "Tried. For months, tried to find anything, something. But I was fourteen when I went on the barge. Everyone I knew was either gone or didn't remember. I had no one, and no chances for honest work. My hands were no good after the hooks and the lines, so even dishonest work was hard to come by."

"How'd you afford to make the trip up here?" Titus asked.

"Don't care to provide details on that," Aldo said. "But there's always something a person can trade. Even if it leaves them feeling dirty inside and out."

Titus winced, but nodded. "How'd you know? That he was up here?"

Careful. "Convoy came through, about four months ago. Brought down rye and wheat from one of the farms up north. One was chatty. I asked if there was any work to be had for Vetticcians up here. He said no, that the only Vetticcian he knew of ran the guard force at a ranch up here." Aldo shrugged, trying not to watch Titus' face too intently for any sign of doubt. "Stiliano's not that common a name. I asked more questions. Figured it out."

"And thought you could cash in a very old debt." Titus watched the cows as they moved to a patch of grass and began eating, the sound of their smacking teeth wet and loud. "Look, you got a raw deal. But you have to figure out what's more important: being angry at him, or keeping this job. Because there's no room for both." He shook his head. "You've been here for less than a week, and a man who's been the godsdamned rock of this place is in ruins. Smart money is to send you packing."

"So why don't you?" Aldo asked.

Titus took a deep breath. "There's a lot I don't like about the boss. Naath. But whatever shit he believes, he don't hold a man's past against him. Not a one of us came here with clean hands. But all of us have a home, a job, and a meal at the end of the day. They took a chance on us. Figure I can do the same for you." He paused for a moment, as if debating whether or not to continue. "My father was a cast iron bastard. Never gave me anything but bruises. If I came face to face with the son of a bitch, not sure I'd be able to keep things locked down."

"So you get it."

"I get it. Doesn't mean you get a pass. Like I said, it's a shit deal, and I'll give you credit for keeping things as locked down as you have. But if it's him or you, it's him. Every time."

Aldo nodded.

"You saved my life. That counts for a lot. I'll do everything I can to keep you here, so long as you do everything you can not to take the choice away from us." He held up his hand. "You're out of second chances. Things go sideways in the slightest and I get a whiff of you on the trouble, there's only two paths for you to walk. Out the gate or in the fucking ground. You get me?"

Aldo nodded. "Yeah. I get you."

"Good. We're done talking about it, then. Far as anyone's concerned, Stilts got sick, and you two are old friends. The handful who know that he got soused know to keep their mouth shut." He jerked his head back towards the center of the ranch. "Go. Get some sleep. You're relieving Ian again tonight, and you're not falling asleep on watch."

Aldo knuckled his forehead, and brought his horse around to canter away.

***

Only a handful of men were in the barracks as he settled down on his cot, each studiously avoiding meeting his eyes, whether they knew what had actually happened between Stiliano and Aldo. He didn't mind the silence. It kept him from having to dance around the truth with anyone else.

In other circumstances, sleep might have proven elusive, but Aldo had long since learned the value of claiming what sleep you could in any opportunity you found, and it felt like only moments after his eyes shut that a pair of knuckles rapped gently against his foot. Outside, the golden light of the sunset was fading from the windows. He nodded at the ranch hand's whispered wakeup call and began pulling on his boots. As he headed out the door to the house, his eyes brushed past his father's empty cot.

Dinner was in full swing in the main house when he arrived, slabs of fried dough piled high with roasted corn and pork. Aldo spotted a few sideways glances, but did his best to ignore them. He saw Titus sitting at the end of one of the long tables, methodically demolishing a stack of food, and settled in across from him.

The older man grunted. "Eat fast. You have to relieve Ian in fifteen."

Aldo nodded, and silently began eating. Around a mouthful, he said, "Can we make a tray? Something he can eat at the barracks? The sooner he gets to crash, the more sleep he can get."

Titus raised an eyebrow. "Trying to earn points?"

"I've got plenty I need to earn." Aldo didn't look up. "Telling me I'm wrong?"

"Nope." Titus waved at a younger stable hand Aldo didn't know. "Ethan, go get a plate ready for Ian. Aldo here's gonna bring it to him. No peppers. Ian hates peppers. No need to make his day any worse than it is." The kid nodded and left. Titus glanced back at Aldo. "And there going to be any issues with Her Excellency?"

"Not on my part," Aldo said, feeling his cheeks burn slightly. "Can't make any promises on her behalf."

"Stay outside as much as you can. Don't give her a chance to set up a problem."

"That's not really that helpful."

Titus shrugged. "Well, apparently she asked about you several times today, so picking someone else really isn't an option, even if I were of a mind to do you a favor. Which, you know..."

"Yeah, I get it. I can handle it." Aldo swallowed a bite, and asked, "How long am I going to be in the shithouse?"

"That's gonna be interesting to find out."

Aldo frowned, but finished eating as quickly as he could, mind racing. He didn't like the idea of moving forward with the plan after the disaster of the previous night, but as he cycled through alternatives in his head, they each fell apart under the most minor of consideration. Try as he might, he couldn't think of an alternative. *It's a lot riskier now, but there's nothing else, not unless we're willing to wait.* He shook his head as he stared down at his food. *Been here less than a week, already put my foot in it. The longer I'm here, the more likely it is that this blows up in our face.*

He was swallowing the last bite when a plate piled high with food and a mug of beer was set on the table next to him. He nodded at the unspeaking guard who'd brought it to him, picked up the tray, and headed outside. *No moves left. Let's see how this goes.*

As he stepped outside, Aldo muttered a quick thanks for the moonless sky overhead. He gave the area a quick scan, and saw no one within eyeshot. In case he was wrong, he fumbled briefly with the dishes in his arm, muttering a soft curse as a bit of beer sloshed over the lip of the pewter mug. A line of feed barrels dotted the pathway between the main house and the guest house, and he set the dishes down.

As he brushed the drops of beer off of his tunic, his hand came back up with the small folded paper packet. With quick, practiced fingers, the grey powder dusted down onto the foamy surface of the beer as he picked the food and drink back up. He frowned, considering for a moment whether it would be enough. Shaking his head, Aldo dumped the entire packet of isleweed into the drink. He resumed his walk, eyes flicking down to see if the powder had dissolved yet, but it was too dark.

Ian raised a hand as he approached. "I think you have a fan."

"Oh?" Aldo had to fight not to look down at the beer as he stepped into the lantern light. He offered Ian the food. "Glad someone here is."

"Yeah, what in the gods happened?" Ian asked, passing Aldo the sheathed short sword and accepting the plate and mug. "I heard Stilts got sick, and that Titus has a bug up his ass about you. You've been here less than a week. How'd you already get on his shit list?"

"Natural talent, I suppose," Aldo said. "I don't want to talk about it. Titus took a few strips out of my ass. I was going to ask that someone else relieve you tonight, but as things stand..."

"Wouldn't have mattered if you'd been everyone's golden boy," Ian said, a smirk on his face. "She's been asking about you all day. Think she would have been upset if anyone other than 'that Vetticcian boy' showed up, and we know the boss wants to keep her happy." He took a long sip of beer, and made a face. "This home-brew batch is shit."

"Want me to take it back?" Aldo asked, trying to keep his voice even.

"Stop trying to stall," Ian said, grinning before taking another sip. "Bad beer's better than the night you're about to have."

"Yeah, yeah." Aldo scowled. "Go get some rack. Four hours, right?"

"May the gods protect your virtue."

Aldo offered a rude gesture, to which Ian bowed and walked into the darkness, chuckling softly, food cradled in his hands. After a few moments, he heard a voice bark, "Vetticci! Get in here!"

Assuming a properly dismayed expression, he turned and walked into the guest house, closing the door behind him. "We're clear."

She sat in a broad backed chair, back in the sleeveless tunic she'd worn the previous night. "Any issues?"

"With the drink? I hope not. He didn't like the taste, but from what I hear, the home-brew they get from the other farms tends to vary pretty wildly in quality."

"How long will it take to kick in?"

"You've never used isleweed?"

"Can't say I've had the pleasure."

Aldo grunted. "An hour, maybe more. I gave him quite a lot. He'll be asleep, and it should keep him that way until well after he's supposed to relieve me."

"After which I throw a fit, decry the unprofessionalism of my assigned escort, and demand that my new favorite southern ranch hand assume the escorting duties for the remainder of my stay." Nicolette nodded. "How bad will it be for him?"

Aldo shrugged. "Can't imagine they'll give him too much grief for oversleeping. Besides, everyone's too pissed off at me at this particular moment." He sank down in another chair, scowling.

Nicolette raised an eyebrow. "Anything I need to know about?"

"Probably." Aldo scratched at a rough spot on the arm of the chair. "Titus knows I'm Stiliano's son."

Her expression didn't change, but the big woman's eyes hardened. "That seems like a problem."

"Yeah, it wasn't my first choice."

"Wait, you told him?!" She leaned forward. "What in the gods happened?"

"Short version? Stiliano pissed me off, and I lost my temper. He, ah..." Aldo swallowed. "He got drunk. For the first time in years."

"Shit." Nicolette rubbed the bridge of her nose. "You couldn't keep it secured for two more days?"

Scowling, Aldo snapped, "I told you it was a bad idea, me being here. You didn't really offer me a lot of choice. All things considered, I think I've been about as even tempered as could be expected around him."

Nicolette held up her hand. "Calm down. I just need to know how much damage was done."

Still glaring, Aldo shook his head slowly. "I don't think we have to worry. It was always a possibility. I don't think we look that much alike, but Stiliano could have just blurted it out when I arrived. It might work for us. I'm supposed to flip my shit in a few days and storm off the ranch, right?" Nicolette nodded, and Aldo said, "Makes it easier. I can just go to Titus the day after you leave, and tell him that I don't think I can work with Stiliano any more. If it's a choice between dealing with more shit and keeping the peace, he'll walk me to the gate and wish me luck. They'll be relieved to lose me."

She nodded slowly. "Fine. Any progress on the guards for the husbandry building?"

Aldo nodded. "Apparently it's a pretty sought after assignment. I have the names. Problem is, they work with a different group. Different dining schedules, sleep in the main house. Even if the plan were to dose them, I don't see a way I could get close." He tilted his head. "Don't suppose you go to the main house during your time here."

She shook her head. "Even if I did, if I'm not in this building, I have a shadow. Even if it's you, I can't figure a reason we'd have to go there." She glanced at the windows, and scowled. "Move to the couch."

"What?"

"I'm supposed to be laying siege to your virtue. If someone looks in the window, we should at least be sitting next to each other."

Aldo raised an eyebrow, but they settled side by side on the leather wrapped bench. "I'm, uh, I'm not sure how far we should take this particular ruse."

"Calm down," Nicolette said. "Even if you were my type, there's no way a subarcheron would actually cross a line like that. I figure the good Mistress Greystone might enjoy the flirting, but we can keep it at you looking uncomfortable and me looking smug."

"Oh good, so the usual."

She grinned. "We still have to figure out how to get past the guards."

"We could knock them out."

"Could we?"

"You could knock them out."

She snorted. "Be a bit difficult to explain that particular circumstance. Remember, they realize what we've done, they'll have our scent in the nose of every hound on this ranch, not to mention Mistress DeLuca will cut our throats the moment we step into the city."

"I'd rather avoid that."

"I thought you might."

Aldo thought for a moment. "Okay, what about this?" He explained for a few minutes. Nicolette's eyebrow climbed higher and higher with every sentence. When he was done, she shook her head.

"The point is to be subtle."

"Subtle's not going to do it," Aldo said. "We need time to get past the guards, get into the basement, past the lock on the cold storage, time to make the swap, and time to get out without anyone realizing what happened. Even if everything lines up the way it should, the chances that someone walks in and spots us are way too high. Unless their attention is focused on something else."

Nicolette considered this, drumming her fingers on the arm. "Okay. So things go sideways, we get in, make the swap, and get out in the chaos. That might work. They'd likely decide to cut my trip short while they repair the damage. If it's their idea that I leave, all the better."

"I think that's pretty gods-damned likely. The only thing they're more worried about than pissing you off is giving you a less than sterling impression of the ranch and the operation." He paused. "Speaking of... What's going to happen when they don't hear anything from the Empire for months and months, and send a letter asking if the trade deal is still a going concern?"

"Thought of that. Before you leave, I need you to steal something. Anything. Doesn't really matter what, so long as it's valuable and not something they'd realize was missing for a few days. Think you can manage that?"

"Probably. But why? They're going to assume it was me."

"Not for long." There was a tall glass of water on the table next to them. Nicolette took a long drink, wiping sweat from her forehead. "Gods, it's like breathing soup here." She took another drink before continuing. "I've got a connection. Out east, in Havensport. One of the town militia. About a week after I'm gone, he's going to send a letter to Naath Vorchese. This letter will explain that they caught someone impersonating an Imperial Subarcheron while trying to scam a courier service. The letter will also note that before this foul degenerate was hanged, they found certain goods on her that they believe may have come from this ranch."

Aldo slowly nodded. "That's... that's not actually bad. But what if they dig deeper? Send someone to figure out a bit more of what's happening?"

"If so, there's not much to find. But I'm willing to bet they're not going to be wiling to let word get out that their security was breached. In fact, my money is on Naath telling them they're not missing a gods-damned thing, telling them they made a mistake, and pushing the entire thing under the rug." Nicolette shrugged. "The best cons are the ones the mark hides for you. A desire to avoid getting embarrassed is highly motivating."

"Okay." Aldo considered for a moment, and nodded. "I think I know. And, if we set things up properly, they may not even realize that it's been taken." He explained about the Campelli brandy, and Nicolette nodded.

"That's perfect. Easily identifiable, and worth enough to make wearing this many layers worth it." She raised an eyebrow. "So when do we move?"

"I need a few more days. Figure out the angles, the right timing, find what we need to rig up the pillars." Aldo considered for a moment. "Assuming everything with Ian plays out the way we think? Five days. Maybe six."

"I don't want to push it too long," Nicolette said. "The longer we're here…"

"I know. Believe me, I don't want to be here any longer than we need to be," Aldo said. "But you dragged me out here. We're going to do this right."

Nicolette grinned. "You still salty about that?"

"We Vetticcians aren't really known for letting things go. But I suppose if the payout is what you say it is, that buys a lot of forgiveness."

Nicolette started to say something, but shouting brought both their heads snapping around to the front window. Aldo was on his feet first, hand falling to the hilt of the sword, running over to the window, and he felt his stomach drop. "Shit."

Nicolette joined him. "Oh, shit."

"ALDO!" The bellow was loud enough that it easily reached their ears, despite Ian still being nearly a hundred feet from the front door. He was weaving back and forth, struggling to buckle on a belted sheath, as he shouted again. "Aldo, I'm not tired! I got this bitch!"

"This fucker's going to wake up half the ranch," Nicolette hissed.

"Half, my ass. They're going to hear him in Galen's Crossing," Aldo said, trying to see if the lamps in the barracks had been lit. "Wait here." He ran out the front door, boots pounding on the wood of the deck, and sprinted over to Ian. The younger man's eyes were bleary and unfocused, and he came to a halt as Aldo approached him, then grinned.

"I tried to sleep, but I'm not tired," he said. His words were slurred, and his cheeks were bright red. "You go sleep. I've got this shithead. I'm getting extra pay."

"Ian, what the fuck are you thinking?" Aldo said. "You're drunk. You have to get out of here before anyone sees you!"

"Drunk my ass. 'M had one beer." Ian shook his head sharply, as if trying to shake off an insect. "Don't want you to have to deal with her."

"I'm fine, Ian." Aldo spotted the flickering, greasy light of lanterns in the dark windows of the barracks. "People are waking up. We have to get you back."

"No!" Ian jerked his arm out of Aldo's grip. "My job. My bonus."

"I don't give a shit about the bonus..."

"The hell is this?!" They both spun, Aldo more quickly than Ian, and saw Stiliano running towards them. His eyes had deep dark bags beneath them, but they were alert and narrowed as he approached. From the barracks, Aldo spotted Titus and two others come out the door, and begin heading their way.

"He's fucking drunk," Aldo said, grabbing Ian's arm again. "We need to get him back to the barracks before..."

"What is this?!" They all turned to find Nicolette standing in the doorway, silhouetted against the lanterns inside the guest quarters. She was back in her Imperial wools, and wore the familiar mixture of irritation and outrage on her face.

Inwardly, Aldo cursed at her timing, but knew that it would have drawn more attention for her not to react. Stiliano came up on Ian's other side, taking his arm. In a low voice, he snapped to Aldo, "Go handle her. I'll get him back to the barracks."

Aldo nodded, and ran back up the stairs. "Your Excellency, my apologies. My colleague is unwell. I'll remain as your escort for the rest of the evening while he recovers."

Nicolette stepped forward, craning her neck to look around him. "He's not sick. He's drunk." She glared down at Stiliano. "You send a man half in his cups to serve as my guard and escort?"

"Ma'am, I assure you, that we didn't want to..."

Nicolette pointed at Ian. "He's drunk." She pointed to Aldo. "He's not. He's my escort, from now on. I'll not have my safety in a man who can't keep the bottle from his lips."

"Your Excellency, we'll have to discuss that with Master Vorchese, and..."

"We're not discussing shit." Ian scowled up at Nicolette. "It's not an escort, you bitch. It's babysitting. Playing wet nurse to an arrogant Imperial shit who thinks we work for her." Stiliano tightened his grip on Ian's arm, but Ian shoved him. Aldo didn't know if Stiliano was still weak from the hangover or if his feet got tangled up, but his father stumbled backwards and fell onto his ass.

Titus and the other pair began running faster, but Ian moved quicker than Aldo would have thought possible in his current state. Aldo managed to grab his arm, but not before Ian got within two feet of Nicolette, who brought her hand up just a bit too slowly. The spit struck her face right below her left eye just as Aldo yanked Ian back.

Everyone seemed to freeze for a moment as Aldo stared in horror at Nicolette's stunned expression. The gravity of what had just happened seemed to pierce through the drug-enhanced haze, and Ian blinked several times. "I... Uh, I don't know why..."

Nicolette blinked, raising a hand to wipe away the spittle, and her eyes flicked to the left. Aldo saw the brief moment of panic skitter through her eyes before the stone mask of her character slammed back into place, and in tones icier than the north of the country she claimed to be from, she said, "Is this the kind of treatment Imperial authorities can expect in the Dominion?"

"Certainly not." Aldo shut his eyes at the voice behind him, flat and hard. "Subarcheron, please accept my most sincere apologies. My man appears to be inebriated, and is not in his right mind." Naath came up to stand the opposite side of Ian from Aldo, his hand falling on Ian's shoulder.

"Your man. Your responsibility."

"Indeed."

Nicolette raised a hand, finger outstretched. "He will not come near me again."

"He will not," Naath said. "Please, tell me how I can make this right."

"The Vetticcian will be my escort for the remainder of my time here," Nicolette said. "And the Vorchese family will assume all transport costs to the bridge. Every single mark. They will also insure the value of every shipment."

Naath frowned slightly. "Your Excellency, that is irregular. The costs would be..."

"Hire guild guards. Put the cost in escrow in an account from the Bank. Figure out a way to fly it to us. It matters not, but you will see our concerns laid to rest," Nicolette snapped. "I no longer have faith in your ability to keep your people at heel. Why should the Alddarri Empire extend faith in your ability to protect our goods?"

Naath turned to look at Ian. Aldo braced himself for the fury that he was certain was coming. He had to fight not to recoil from the flat, empty eyes that found the wide-eyed ranch hand. "Indeed." Back to Nicolette, he said, "We will insure all shipments for the first three seasons. After that, we may revisit shipping costs and processes. Once we've demonstrated our reliability to the Empire."

Nicolette glared, but gave a sharp nod. "You'll make the adjustments to the contract."

"You'll have the revisions by sunset tomorrow."

"Fine."

"Now. May I leave these two," he gestured at Titus and Stiliano, "to stand watch outside your quarters for a brief time? I must speak to Aldo before he assumes full escort duties." He looked down at Ian, who was a shade of grey and getting worse. "I also need to address this one's actions."

Nicolette was good. She didn't let her eyes flick over to Aldo once. "Do what you must. But when I wake in the morning, I expect him on guard and well understanding his place."

"Excellency." Naath gave a slight bow, and Nicolette spun on her heel and went inside. Slowly straightening back up, Naath said, "Aldo."

"Sir."

"Bring Ian to the harvesting building. He is not to leave. I will meet you both there in five minutes."

Aldo nodded. "Yes, sir."

***

Naath turned and walked in a slow, methodical pace back towards the house. As soon as he was out of earshot, Stiliano stepped forward. "What in the gods happened?"

Aldo shook his head. "You saw." He tried to ignore the pit in his stomach. "He's drunk. She's been shitting on him for days. He lost control."

"Gods." Stiliano looked at Ian, his face pale. "This is bad. This is very, very bad. I'm shocked she didn't torch the entire trade deal. As things stand..."

"As things stand, I'm guessing we're all standing on a very slick deck in a very bad storm," Aldo said. "I'm new. I'm not stupid."

"Whatever happens in there..." Stiliano swallowed. "You're in a very bad spot, Aldo."

"Stilts, Aldo, I get that this is complicated, but we don't have time," Titus hissed. "If they aren't in the harvesting shed by the time the boss gets back, Aldo's paying the price too. You need to move, now."

Aldo's mind was whirling, but he nodded, and took Ian by the arm. "Come on."

Ian didn't resist. He was confused, tears brimming in his eyes. "What did I do?"

"We have to move, Ian. Now." Aldo couldn't look at him.

It took longer to reach the harvesting shack than it should have. Ian stumbled several times, and Aldo had to haul him back to his feet, desperately trying to ignore the pit in his stomach. They reached the big windowless building built flush with the massive palisade surrounding the bull pen. It took Aldo a moment to realize the pair of guards he'd always seen on either side were nowhere to be found. Their absence didn't feel like an accident. Aldo half expected the single door to be locked, but when he pushed on the weathered oak, it swung open.

The interior of the building was cavernous, the ceiling nearly thirty feet off the ground, massive timbers crisscrossing over their heads, black iron bolts and railings bolted into the dark wood. The ground was packed dirt, and a long fenced chute ran from a pair of huge doors in the far side, framing a serpentine path ending in a pen near the center of the room, above which was a series of hooks and chains hanging from above. Two panels of iron-banded wood flanked this space, each the size of a dining room table set on its side.

Ian's arm still in his grip, Aldo quickly scanned the rest of the room. His eyes quickly found a set of stairs on the far side of the building, descending below the building. There was no sign or marker, but his eyes lingered on it for a moment. Next to the stairs, he saw a shelf with several glass jars, sealed with wax, filled about halfway with an amber fluid, held in wooden racks.

The sound of the door opening brought his head around. Naath had changed. He was shirtless. A thick cowhide apron hung around his neck, and he was tying the cords behind his back as he approached. "Thank you, Aldo." He nodded towards the center pen. "This is our harvesting station. Those panels squeeze the bull, help keep it calm along with the sedative we provide."

"You're not..." Aldo swallowed. "You're not going to feed him to the bull, are you?"

Naath shook his head. "Don't be absurd. I just need you to bring Ian into the breeding pen." Reaching into the pocket of the apron, he pulled out a pair of iron manacles. "There are hooks set into the top of the compression box. Secure his hands, if you will."

Aldo took the manacles, but shook his head. "Sir, I understand there need to be consequences, but I'm not... This isn't my job."

"None of us know the part we have to play in this life, Aldo." Naath's face was blank, his tone oddly pleasant. "You may refuse this role, but I can't say that you'd find the alternative more to your liking." He stepped closer, bringing his hand up to rest on Aldo's shoulder. "Right now, I need only a witness. If you wish to play a more... active role, we can realize that."

Aldo tried to keep his eyes locked on Naath, who was standing far too close, his hand tight on Aldo's shoulder, but he couldn't look at those terrible empty eyes any longer. He lowered his gaze, took a deep breath and nodded. "Yes, sir."

Ian didn't struggle. He was weeping silently, confusion and fear battling on his face. He didn't struggle as Aldo pulled open the gate, steel hinges squeaking loudly enough that they both winced. He didn't struggle as they stepped between the two panels, boots crunching in dirt much darker than the rest of the room. He didn't struggle as Aldo affixed the manacles around his wrists and hooked the chain over a hook, extending Ian's arms above his head. It was only when Aldo stepped back that he raised reddened eyes to meet Aldo's, whispering, "Please. I don't know why I did that."

"I know," Aldo said, keeping his voice low enough that Naath couldn't hear. "I'm sorry."

Ian shook his head, tears plopping into the dirt at his feet as Aldo stepped back and left the pen. Naath was waiting outside, and shut the gate as Aldo stepped through.

"Do you know why we do what we do here, Aldo?" Naath pulled a pair of leather gloves from his pocket and began tugging them on.

"Sir?" Aldo's eyes were flicking back and forth between Ian's wild expression and Naath's calm demeanor. "The ranch?"

"The ranch, yes." Naath walked over to several long loops of chain extending up from the ceiling, and tugged on one. There was a brief squeal as the pulley the chain was looped around resisted before turning. Naath frowned. "Please take a note, Aldo. Someone needs to oil the rigging gear."

He began pulling on the loop of chain, and a series of gears overhead rattled into motion. The two panels trembled, and began sliding towards one another, Ian's feet dragging in the dirt as the bound man began to hyperventilate.

"It's been my family's livelihood for a very long time, but the money it brought was empty. It did nothing. It disappeared, but there was always more to pour into pockets with no bottoms." The panels were now less than two feet apart. Ian's breath was that of an animal, cornered and bleeding, terrified gasps of air sucked between teeth. "When the grey fever came, it left only me to carry on the Vorchese name, the business." He turned his eyes to Aldo, not pausing in his efforts. "Nine brothers and sisters. My mother. My father. My grandfather. All burned from this life by fever, leaving only me remaining. I don't believe in coincidence. Do you, Aldo?"

The panels were now so close together that Ian had his cheek pressed against the wood, head turned to the side as the second panel came to rest on his chest, pinning him between the two. Aldo could barely see him, but Ian's wild panicked eyes were still locked on Aldo.

"I asked you a question, Aldo," Naath said, and Aldo tore his eyes away from Ian to look to the rancher.

"I... yes. I think I do."

"I don't believe you." Naath paused for a moment in pulling the chain, the deafening rattle falling silent, the only sounds the silent clinking of steel on steel and the desperate gasps of a man pinned like an insect. "How many others stood on the same deck as you? How many others bigger, stronger, older, smarter, more sure-footed stood next to you, only to find themselves dragged down into the cold black, while you survived? So many deaths, so much pain, all stones in the path you took to stand here, now. Before me. Do you know the odds? The chance that you would survive the sea, that I would survive the fever, for us to stand together here and now?" He shook his head, his black hair falling over his brow. "No. I was meant to survive. I was called to realize the true value of what we do here."

His grip was white on the cold iron of the chain, his eyes wide. Naath stepped closer, and the chain shifted just barely. One click, and Aldo heard Ian's frantic gasping race up an octave to a wheeze, a reedy whistle of desperation.

"Sir, I don't... Please, we can just fire him. Send him away." Aldo shrank in on himself under Naath's stare and how small his voice sounded in the massive building.

Naath continued as if Aldo hadn't spoken. He still hadn't raised his voice. No anger or frustration tinged the words. "This place, this ranch, these animals, each of us, they are a blessing. And that coin, that money that vanished for so long into the grasping fists of those with no path, no purpose, it now goes to something bigger than you, bigger than me, bigger than all of us. It funds those who walk this earth to guide the lost to a world better than this, to shepherd them from this life of blood and pain to where we are meant to stand."

Naath now stood mere inches from Aldo. Every fiber in his body trembled in a desperate urge to pull away, but Naath's eyes pinned Aldo in place just as iron-banded wood pinned Ian. "I begged. I pleaded to take my place alongside those Shepherds, to do my part in this life to guide others to the next. But I was denied. I was told that my calling was different. I fund those who do what I know, what I am certain I was called to do, and I must have faith in the wisdom behind my denial. So here I stand, playing my role. There Ian stands, playing his. And here you stand, playing yours."

Leaning forward, Naath pressed his sweaty forehead against Aldo's, and a quaking moan slipped from between Aldo's lips before he could choke it back. He took Aldo's hand, and lifted it up, as if drawing Aldo in for an embrace, placing his fingertips on the bulge over Naath's shoulder blade. When Naath rolled his shoulder, Aldo could feel it grind against the bone beneath the skin. He could feel the sigh slip from Naath's lips. It was obscene and horribly intimate.

"We each carry our pain, you and I more than most. So you will bear witness. You will see the scope of my devotion, of my insistence. Because if I cannot pave the path to salvation with my coin, I will ease that journey with their screams."

He pulled the chain.

The wheezing gasps exploded from Ian's lungs as a howl, driven forth by the sound of cracking bone. Aldo couldn't look, couldn't turn away from the empty black eyes burning into his.

"I told you your pain, your ordeal was a blessing." Another pull. Something else snapped, and the scream cut off into wet gasps. "A fire, burning away all that ties you to this misery, this cruelty, leaving you naked and pure to step into the light." Another pull. Aldo cried out, hands flying up to clasp over his mouth, shoving the scream back down his throat as Ian howled through the ruin of his chest. "Ian risked everything I am called to do. But please know, I bear no anger, no ill will. Instead, you and I together are tempering him, driving out his impurities, cleansing his corruption and sin with the purifying gift of pain. He leaves this life ready to step into the next, ready to leave this vale of misery behind him."

Naath twisted his head, turning those eyes towards the sliver of light left between the panels, blood already painting the wood. "I forgive you, Ian. Be at peace."

With both hands, he hauled the chain as hard as he could. Ian's last scream died in a crunch of bone and one last spray of scarlet sheeting out from the panels. Blood no longer trickled onto the dirt, it poured like juice from a fruit crushed within a fist.

Aldo felt urine warm his legs. His heart hammered in his chest as if trying to break through. Naath released the chain, the clinking of the steel almost obscenely cheerful as the smell of shit and iron filled the air. He turned back to Aldo.

"If the Subarcheron cancels the trade deal, I will have failed in my calling." He tilted his head slightly to the side, blinking slowly. "And I will have to find another, and Ian will not be alone in moving forward. Do we understand one another, Aldo?"

Aldo nodded.

"Good. Clean up this mess. Clean up yourself. And go do your job, please."

Chapter 15

Aldo had been on the penance barge for two days the first time he saw a man die. He saw two men argue over a cup of homebrew green, saw the sharpened spike of wood come out moments before it vanished into the belly of a man whose name he did not know. He sobbed as he saw the body cut to pieces, added to the barrels of chum that brought the churning schools of fish to the surface, but he quickly stopped. It was the first time he had to lower a filter over something his mind couldn't come to terms with, to let himself go numb.

The same filter came down as he wrenched the bull compressor back apart. It kept him numb as he heard the sounds, smelled the blood. Kept him numb as he dragged what little remained of the body onto a sheet of canvas, as he scrubbed the wood with water and lye, the chemicals burning his hands. It let him focus long enough to finish the job, and to walk over to the racks of bottles, pulling one from the bottom row and hiding it inside his tunic.

That numbness kept him dull as he left the shed, up until the moment that his father and Titus said anything to him. It felt as if his legs were moving of their own accord. It wasn't until Titus reached out and grabbed his shoulder, saying his name, that the world snapped back into focus, sound and realization rushing in on him as if filling the space that had been hollowed out by what he'd seen.

He blinked once, twice, and raised his eyes to look at the pair. "What?"

"Are you all right?" Stiliano was speaking faster than normal, looking quickly between Aldo and the dark building his son had come from.

"I'm not hurt." Aldo's hands had begun to tremble. He clenched them into fists, willing the shaking to stop.

"Aldo. What happened?" Titus asked.

"Ian's dead."

If either were surprised at the news, their faces didn't show it. "Are you good? Do you need..." Stiliano trailed off, clearly at a loss for what could possibly be of any use at the moment. "We can hold the watch for a few hours. Let you collect yourself."

Titus and Aldo shook their heads at the same time. Aldo glanced over at Titus, who said, "After everything, I can guarantee you the boss is going to be combing over everything with a fine-toothed comb. If he doesn't see Aldo at his watch when he's supposed to, there are going to be questions, and this feels like a really gods-damned bad time for him to be asking questions."

"He's right." Aldo's voice was dull even to his own ears.

Stiliano looked as if he wanted to argue. Titus didn't give him the chance.

"I don't know if anyone else has figured out the connection between you two, Stilts, but if he wasn't who he is, you would have already told him to hold the watch and to do his job," Titus said. "This is bad. We've seen bad before. We have a gap in our roster, and it's your job to sort that out. Everything else, we can deal with later."

Movement caught their eye, and the three turned to see a pair of guards walking back towards the husbandry building. One had an armful of torn cotton rags. The other carried a bucket brimming with soapy water. Dully, Aldo said, "Finishing the cleanup."

Titus muttered a curse. "I don't know when we'll be able to relieve you," he said. "I'll make sure someone brings you chow in the morning."

The thought of food sent Aldo's stomach twisting again. "No. I... No."

"You might feel different later. Stilts, we need to go."

Stiliano stared at Aldo for a long moment, but finally nodded. "Shout if you need us."

"I don't." He had not meant for the words to sound as harsh as they did.

Stiliano nodded, and the pair heading back towards the barracks.

Aldo took his position on the porch, back to the house, unblinking eyes sliding mechanically back and forth over the dark ranch buildings. He didn't look directly at the pair of guards resuming their post and studiously avoiding eye contact with each other. He didn't watch closely enough when Naath came by hours later, nodding at Aldo as if nothing had happened before wordlessly disappearing into the darkness.

The night was quiet. Occasionally, an owl would hoot mournfully from somewhere in the dark. There was no moon tonight, and it was impossible to know how much time had passed. Aldo had not spent an evening awake in the center of the ranch yet. He was ready for this to be among his last.

By the time the sun began spilling light over the rolling hills to the east, silhouetting the huge shapes of cattle on the crest of a ridge a mile away, the ranch was already bubbling with activity. Men began spilling out of the barracks, most heading towards the main house for food, others scattering in different directions to realize different purposes.

Aldo could see the difference in their faces, blank masks around eyes that seemed to go anywhere he wasn't. He wondered how many times they'd woken to one of the beds empty.

The day had well and truly started by the time that Aldo spotted Luca, walking slowly towards him with a covered tray balanced in his hands. The man's face was impassive. "The Subarcheron's breakfast. There's a plate for you, too," Luca said. Aldo nodded as he relieved Luca of his burden.

"Titus wanted me to tell you. The boss is going to come in a few hours, personally escort her around today. Try to mend some fences. Any sleep you're going to get, you need to get it then. There won't be an evening relief. We're going to be short-handed for a bit," Luca said. He rubbed the bridge of his nose. "Fucking mess."

"Yeah," Aldo said. "Hey, has the boss..." He trailed off at the expression on Luca's face, but swallowed and continued. "Has that happened before?"

Luca scowled, but he nodded. "Been a while. And we don't talk about it. Never thought Ian would..." He shook his head. "Didn't think he'd be the one to stumble. No offense, but my money was on you."

"And you all stay."

"I'm thinking you know a thing or two about doing something you don't want to do to keep your belly full," Luca said. "The pay's good. The food's good. Place to sleep. None of us have to worry about a Duke hauling us into their battalions to go fight some horseshit border skirmishes over a grain mill. We do our jobs, we live our lives." He folded his arms. "Ian fucked up. He knew better than to get drunk."

Aldo's stomach was a lead ball. He didn't trust himself to speak.

"Eat. Make sure the Subarcheron is up, let her know the boss will be here soon. Get some sleep."

"Not sure that's in the cards for me."

"Figure it out," Luca snapped. "You understand now. You don't want to fall asleep on watch tonight. We're carrying Ian's load now. Don't leave us to carry yours." He turned, and stalked away, fists clenched at his side.

***

She didn't say anything as she held the door open for him. Aldo came in and set the tray down on the table as the door closed behind him, arranging the plates with more deliberation than was needed as she came up to stand beside him. She wasn't meeting his gaze.

"We go tonight."

Nicolette took a deep breath. "Aldo, are you..."

"Tonight." He didn't let her finish.

"Okay." She nodded slowly. Her face was grey. "Ian's dead, isn't he?"

"Yes."

"Gods." Nicolette ran a trembling hand through her hair. "I didn't... I planned this out. No one was supposed to get hurt."

"Funny how that works," Aldo said, the bitterness thick in his mouth. "Nothing's ever supposed to go wrong. We fucked up. And Ian paid the price." He shook his head. "We're doing this."

"This... This isn't what I intended."

Something in her voice drew his attention. "You plan jobs like this. People had to have died before."

She shook her head. "I plan so no one does. I've never..." Nicolette swallowed. "How are you so calm?"

"I'm not calm. I'm just…" He trailed off. "I'm numb. I've seen more men die than I can count. This was the first that was my fault, though." Aldo pointed. "You need to eat. If they look in, you should be eating."

Nicolette and sat down to her meal. "Are you sure everything's in place?"

"We'll improvise."

"I thought you said to never improvise."

"I don't give a shit what I said. We can't stay here."

Nicolette considered him, and nodded, picking up the sticks and beginning to eat, mechanically. She gestured at his plate between bites.

"Eat."

"I am so far from hungry."

"Yeah," she said. "But if we're going tonight, we need every single edge. You're going to eat. You're going to figure out a way to get some sleep today."

He scowled, but sat. "Naath is relieving me in a few hours. He wants to escort you personally today. Try to mend fences."

"Good." She watched him as he began to mechanically shovel rice and vegetables into his mouth, eyes fixed on the wood of the tabletop. "I still think it's a good plan, Aldo."

"It's a shit plan. But it's what we have." He swallowed, and said, "I managed to get a urine bottle. Didn't have a lot of time to look around. Thought about looking downstairs when he left me to clean, but thought that'd be a bad idea."

"Most likely," she said, nodding. "Did you see the entrance?"

"I did." He shook his head. "If we get down there and the vial's not a match, what do we do?"

"I don't know." The big woman ate like a machine, her plate already empty. Setting down the sticks, she said, "We can delay a few days.

See if we can somehow get a look down there..." She trailed off, Aldo already shaking his head. "Look, Aldo, if we rush this..."

"We might survive," Aldo said. "Every day that we're here, the odds of that happening drop. Naath is not what you think."

"I told you. He's an extremist."

"No." Aldo shook his head sharply. "You said he was crazy. He's not. He believes. He believes in a way that will never bend. Doubt or pity or sympathy mean nothing to him. I just watched him murder a man while calling it salvation, and if we give him the slightest reason, he will take us to pieces and expect us to thank him." He leaned forward. "We have to go. Tonight. We have to put this place behind us and disappear."

Nicolette nodded slowly. "Tonight. You have what we need?"

Aldo nodded.

"Okay." She took a deep breath. "Let's get it done."

Chapter 16

Despite everything, Aldo slept, drawing on what he'd learned at sea to muffle the screams and find slumber. He'd gotten more than he'd expected, too. By the time another ranch hand shook him awake, it was late in the afternoon. "Boss set up a dinner for the Subarcheron," the man said. "Said to get food, meet them back at the guest quarters by last bell."

Aldo nodded his thanks, and got dressed. There were a few others in the barracks, but no one was saying much, the mood subdued. Someone had stripped Ian's bunk, emptied the foot locker at the end of the bed. Aldo had a strong feeling that Ian's name would become something not spoken. He knew well how much easier it was to pretend things like that hadn't happened.

Rubbing the sleep from his eyes, he tugged on his boots, and headed out the door. The dinner service was already in full swing. He could see Luca and a few others sitting outside, eating and talking quietly as they enjoyed the mild weather. The wind blew through his hair, carrying the sweet scent of honeysuckle along with it.

Luca nodded as Aldo passed. "You have a bit. Boss and the Imperial just sat down. He had her all over today. Showed her just about everything she wanted to see. I think he's relieved she was still here this morning." He raised an eyebrow. "You have something to do with that?"

Aldo shrugged. "Did what I was told. Figured that's the only right way forward."

"Not the worst strategy."

Dinner was roasted chicken and tiny blue potatoes. As usual, there were a lot of them. Aldo piled his plate high, trying to ignore the pit in his stomach cheerfully insisting that he should enjoy this while he could. He found a spot at the end of one of the tables, alone. No one came to join him. Aldo was fine with that.

He ate mechanically, shoveling the food in his mouth while his mind darted over the layout of the ranch compound, the path from paddock to husbandry shed, the route he'd seen guards and ranch hands take at different points. He spotted dozens of potential fail points, countless opportunities for things to fall to pieces.

If you were smart, you'd wait. He snorted softly under his breath. *Fuck, if I were smart, I wouldn't be here.*

Titus sat down across from him, pulling Aldo from his musings, and Aldo sat up straight, nodding at the older man.

"Thought we should talk before you take your post."

"Not a lot of competition. Doesn't seem like all that many people want to talk to me." Aldo glanced around at the void of empty seats that had formed around him.

"Yup. Between everything that happened with Stilts and last night, well…" Titus shrugged. "Not saying last night was your fault. But we've had a run of bad luck since you got here. Nothing to be done about it, just need to wait it out."

"Yeah." Aldo speared a potato. "Anything I need to know about tonight?"

"I'm going to send someone to bring you tea, maybe four, five hours into the shift." Titus sipped at his water. "I don't need you falling asleep. We're short handed now, and as soon as Her Excellency sees fit to head back north of the Breaking, you're back on perimeter watch."

"I can think of nothing I'd like more," Aldo said. *Shit.* "I, uh..." He shifted uncomfortably in his seat. "What if the Subarcheron feels the need for me to stand watch inside?"

"You mean what if she decides to take things past flirting?" Titus asked. He sighed. "I don't know. Normally, I'd tell you absolutely not, but as things stand..."

"Yeah. I heard the boss has been schmoozing her all day," Aldo said. "I'm going to guess he wouldn't be too pleased with me upsetting her."

"That's an understatement," Titus said. "I don't know. Maybe tell her you have a headache."

"Think that'd be enough?"

"You're going to have to deal with it, whatever happens," Titus said. "She's heading north in two, three days. We just need to get her to that point, and things will settle down."

"I'll handle it." Titus raised an eyebrow, and Aldo said, "I mean it. Sooner we can get things back to good, sooner people will stop treating me like I've got the grey fever."

"Okay. Anything you need?"

Aldo started to shake his head, and stopped. "No... wait, yes." *Careful.* "Her boots. The heavy ones, with the fur at the top?" Titus nodded, and Aldo said, "The sole's coming loose. She said it happened the first day here. I mentioned I could fix it, and she said I should do so. But I need tools."

"You know how to cobble?"

Aldo shifted uncomfortably. "A bit. Back on the barge, if you could figure out a trade, some way to be of use to people, your life got a touch less miserable. Prisoners are a bit more hesitant to throw you overboard if you can fix their shit. I learned from someone there." He shrugged. "Besides, if I'm fixing her boots, I can't be doing... other things."

Titus raised an eyebrow. "Cobbling. Huh. Figures. Yeah, I think we have something that will work. I'll have one of the boys bring them to you before nightfall."

"Thanks." Aldo didn't let his relief show. "Few days, right?"

"Few days." Titus stood up. "Might want to head over. Wouldn't want to be late."

***

Aldo stood outside the guest quarters for nearly half an hour before he saw Naath and Nicolette riding up. Naath was quietly talking, while Nicolette was sweating through her Imperial wools. As soon as they reached the hitching post, Nicolette clambered off, waving her hand towards Aldo. "See to him, Vettician. I have to get out of these clothes before I smother. How you can choose to live like this..." Her voice trailed off as she went inside.

Aldo tied the horse to the hitching post while Naath did the same. He didn't meet the rancher's eyes, but took a deep breath when Naath quietly asked, "I hear you asked for tools." He pulled a leather roll from his saddlebag.

"Yes, sir," Aldo said, working to keep his voice even. "Her Excellency damaged one of her boots yesterday. I thought I might be able to repair it."

"Don't try if you're not sure," Naath said. "I've spent most of the day ensuring that yesterday's untidiness doesn't derail the progress we've made. She's still in a fairly unpleasant mood."

"It's not a problem, sir. Just a bent nail. Won't take but a moment."

Naath nodded. "Very well." He handed Aldo the roll. "You've eaten? Had sleep?"

"I have."

"Good. Give my regards to the Subarcheron." Without another word, he turned and began walking back towards the house, hair ruffling in the breeze. If what he'd done the night before weighed on him at all, Aldo couldn't see it.

He didn't know how long it would be before Nicolette called for him, how long she would feel was safe before bringing him inside. Aldo watched ranch hands and guards leave the house after eating, most back to the barracks, several heading out to take over the perimeter watch. None looked his way. It was as if the guest house and all around it didn't exist. Aldo was fine with that. He didn't know what he would say even if someone had tried to spark a conversation.

The sun had nearly disappeared behind the western hills, spilling deepening orange light over the gently waving grass and throwing deep black shadows off of trees and buildings, when he heard the door click open. He didn't turn until she spoke. "Vetticcian. It's going to be difficult to fix my boot from out there."

Aldo shut his eyes for a moment, taking a deep breath. "Yes, your Excellency." He turned, walking past her without looking up. He tossed the bag on the table as the door shut behind him.

"Are we clear?" she asked, her voice low.

"We're fine," he said. "No one wants to have anything to do with either of us, now."

She settled into the seat across from him. "That works out for you, I think. No one's going to argue much when you leave." He didn't respond. She reached out as if to touch his hand, but thought better of it. "Aldo…"

"It won't be much longer," he said, acting as if she hadn't spoken. "The guard change will happen soon. I can go after that, and we can get it done."

"Aldo, what happened yesterday…"

"Don't."

She looked stricken. "We did that. We got Ian killed."

"We did. And now one of the only men here to treat me with kindness since the beginning is dead," Aldo said. He could hear how hollow his voice was. "He died confused, and he died scared, and I have to live with that. You have to live with that."

"You don't think I know that?" Nicolette snapped. "I liked Ian. I had to treat him like garbage, day in, day out, and I helped make the decision to get him killed. I did that. Me. I killed a good man, and this…" She trailed off, and shook her head. "Do you want to walk away? It's dark now. The dogs know you, they won't make noise. You can be off the ranch before sunrise, and given the last few days, I don't think anyone would blame you."

"Just like that, huh?"

"Why not?" Aldo looked up, expecting anger, but instead, saw just exhaustion on her face as she spoke. "There are still a dozen ways this can go badly. If there's a time to bail, this is it. You have a good reason. I don't think they'd come looking for you. And none of this has gone the way we thought."

"You can still turn me in."

"We're hundreds of miles from the border," Nicolette said, rubbing her forehead. "The Dominion is huge. No one's going to spend money sending a tracker after you. No one cares."

"But you said…"

"I know what I said." She leaned forward. "I don't want you to go. I think we can still do this. I think we can both have the kind of future where we're not looking over our shoulder every few moments, where we don't have to worry about the next job, the next meal. But…" She shook her head. "I don't know what happened in that harvesting shed. I expect you don't want to talk about it. But I know what I saw in your eyes after you came out. Man sees something like that, it has a way of changing his priorities, right?"

Aldo couldn't meet her eyes. "Want to hear something strange?"

"I suppose."

"I don't see them. The nightmares." He brushed his fingers along the scar near his elbow. "The first time the hook caught my arm. I know there must have been blood, but I can't picture it. Can't see it. It's the sounds. The sounds stick in my ear, like they've taken root. I close my eyes, and I can hear the metal scraping my bone. Hear my voice fail because I'd screamed so loud and so long that my throat bled. Hear the sound flesh makes when you drag half-inch thick steel through it. I hear it, just as if it's happening now. Years and years pass, and I can still hear it." He let loose a shuddering breath. "How long will I hear Ian?"

Nothing was said for a long while. There was little too say. But finally, he brushed the tear away from his eye. "I'm not leaving."

"Aldo…"

"I have to carry this with me. Forever. So do you. But we're not the only ones who put Ian in the ground." Aldo turned his eyes to the wall, as if he could burn a path through walls and space to stare down Naath. "You said he was a fanatic. You were wrong. He's a gods-damned monster. I don't know if there are other Confessors like him, but if he didn't have that gods-damned church, he'd find some other reason to justify his cruelty. I saw him, saw the look on his face while we heard that man's bones break. He walked away from what he did without a mark to show for it, without a doubt in his mind." He clenched his fist. "If DeLuca gets the sample, the families, they'll breed Vorchese cattle, right?"

Nicolette nodded. "She will."

"Then they'll do the same thing every Vetticcian family has done for centuries. Strangle their competition, one by one, choke them off until they can gobble him up," Aldo said. "He won't know. Won't know that we were the ones who took it away, who led him to fail that fucking church he's so eager to butcher for. But I'm going to play my part in tearing it all down around him."

Chapter 17

A ldo stepped outside, and began walking slowly, deliberately around the side of the guest house, letting his eyes move over every window, every rooftop. He didn't think anyone was up and watching, but if they were, they'd see a dedicated guard inspecting the perimeter of the building they were assigned.

Behind the building was a black well of shadow. The bulk of the guest house blocked the greasy light from the gas lanterns that lined the road, and threw an inky black passage connecting him to the edge of the bull paddock. His impulse was to crouch as he got close, but Aldo resisted, instead stepping forward casually until he was at the looming wall of the palisade.

He ran his fingers along the rough pine trunks, finding the heavy iron nails driven deep into the wood. The nails had no head, and had been driven in flush with the wood. Aldo'd seen that construction approach before. Those who built with this technique didn't want someone prying the nails out. In Vetticci, they did it because people would steal any metal they could get their hands on to sell as scrap.

Aldo paused for a moment, listening for any sound that might indicate someone had spotted him. Finally, he risked a glance in either direction. He spotted a tawny owl, perched on the top of the palisade, staring balefully down at him, but no other witnesses were visible. "Okay," he whispered. "Let's see if this works."

He splayed his fingers over the head of one of the nails, keeping a hair's-breadth of separation between his skin and iron polished smooth from years of the elements. Aldo started to close his eyes, dismissed that as a terribly foolish idea, and instead stared down as he focused. The shivering sensation slowly built, millions of tiny legs brushing against his skin, and he felt the first invisible band snag the iron, then another, then thousands more, imperceptible connections leaping the millimeter between flesh and metal, binding them together. Exhaling slowly, Aldo willed those connections to shorten.

The sensations doubled, then doubled again, and Aldo could see a visible ripple roll over the back of his hand as something pulled against his arm, like a rope tugging him forward. He braced the toe of his boot against the palisade wall, grunting softly with the effort, and tried to pull his hand back slowly, his eyes fixed on that iron dot beneath his fingertips. He felt beads of sweat burst into life on his forehead, and pulled harder, but the nail didn't move.

Gritting his teeth, he decided to risk closing his eyes. A voice in his head brimmed up, rough and run through with salt. *To the lines, minnows!*

Aldo shuddered, remembering the smell of fish and cold salt, the feel of thick hempen rope on his calloused palms.

Take hold!

Without thinking, he turned his body sideways, bending at the knees, his left hand coming up to meet his right, as if grasping an invisible line between them.

Brace!

His boot drove into the dirt, wedging itself firmly against the base of the wall.

Now fuckin' earn your sunrise and PULL, MINNOWS!!!

Muscles in his back and arms tensed and flexed, remembering the motions that defined over a decade of his life, and Aldo seized hold of the invisible line in his hands, and pulled. For an impossibly long second, the nail remained motionless, but Aldo gritted his teeth and doubled his efforts, and a shower of rust burst from the nail as it trembled once, twice, and slowly began to ease from the wood in jerking, tiny bursts.

Pull!

One inch of black metal slipped free, then two, and with little warning, the nail shot out as if hammered from the other side, flying into Aldo's hand and coming to an abrupt halt between his palms, quivering without quite touching him. Releasing his powers, the nail fell into his hand, and Aldo stared down at the ten inch spike lying in his palm. "Well," he muttered quietly to himself. "Actually fucking worked."

He dropped the nail on the ground, where it landed with a soft thump, and looked up, eyes tracing over the dozens more in this section of the wall. Nodding, he got to work. The second seemed easier than the first, though not in terms of physical effort. Each of the nails had been driven deep, and clung to the wood stubbornly, but the growing pile of nails at his feet was a constant reminder that it was possible. The growing ache in his back and arms was a familiar one, and one by one, the wood surrendered the nails to Aldo.

Flexing his arms to try to shake loose some of the strain, he unrolled the pack of tools that Naath had provided him. The steel pry bar was nestled between a small hammer and an awl. Ignoring the rest, he set the roll on the ground and wedged the pry bar between the edge of the first post and the heavy pillar driven deep into the ground. The wood had been in place long enough that it resisted at first, but after a few tries, it popped loose, and Aldo caught the post on his shoulder before it toppled to the ground. The rest came easier, and soon Aldo stood before an eight-foot wide gap in the palisade wall, the dark open field of the bull pen spread out before him.

He stared into the darkness, heart thumping inside his chest like a triphammer. Aldo could see the outline of the copse of trees at the top of the hill, but even if there was movement, he couldn't make it out. The insects had fallen silent, the only sound the wind whispering around him.

Swallowing, he muttered, "Okay. Let's see if this works." He withdrew the jar from inside the bag, and carefully unscrewed it. Inside was a wad of cotton, about the size of a fist. The sharp scent of ammonia stung his nostrils as he used the pliers from the tool roll to pull it out. He dabbed the wet cotton over the fence, then quickly walked back over to the guest house.

The two horses were still tied to the hitching post out front, and he untied the dusky grey nag that Naath had ridden up. He brushed the cotton all over the animal's flanks. The horse nickered softly, but offered no protest. When he was done, he tossed the cotton into the burning brazier next to the entrance.

The door creaked open, and Nicolette stuck her head out. "Problem?" she whispered, and he shook his head.

"Nothing yet. I have another cloth, but I don't want to go into the paddock if I don't have..." He trailed off, and gagged slightly at the intense odor pouring off of the flames.

"Gods," Nicolette choked, covering her face with a cloth. "It smells like a tannery. But worse."

"I didn't think it would smell that strong," Aldo said, panicking. He glanced in the direction of the husbandry shed. "What if they smell it?" He looked up at the leaves of the willow next to the guest house, each of which was gently bobbing in the direction of the paddock.

"Can you put it out?"

"I don't know!" Aldo glanced around, spotting the horse watering trough, and said, "Do you have a bucket inside?"

"Maybe. I'd have to check..." The words died in her throat, and they both turned looked at each other with wide eyes at the rumbling sound echoing from behind the house.

"Uhh... Aldo? Is that..."

"I don't know." Aldo walked around the side of the guest house slowly, Nicolette falling into step behind him. The fire from the brazier had burned their night vision away, and once they stepped back into the shadows, it took a moment for their eyes to adjust. Nicolette spotted the gap in the paddock, and cursed.

"I didn't realize you were going to take the whole gods-damned section out."

"Shhh..." Aldo held up his hand. "You hear that?"

They fell silent. Moments later, the sharp crack of a snapping branch echoed from the paddock. Not a twig breaking beneath a boot, but the splintering crash of a limb splintering into pieces. Aldo heard muttered voices, and he spotted motion from the other side of the house. Motioning frantically to Nicolette, the pair flattened themselves against the clapboard. Aldo peered around the corner, and saw a figure walking along the paddock line, fifty feet from the gap.

The angle in the wall kept it from his view, but in twenty seconds, they'd see it. He turned to whisper something to Nicolette, but before he could speak, another, louder crash issued from the darkness, followed by a rumbling sound getting closer and closer, thunder hammering into the ground. A shape took form beyond the gap in the paddock, hulking and swelling in the night. As the ground began to tremble beneath his feet, he turned frantically and began sprinting back towards the horses, Nicolette hot on his heels.

The crashing hoofbeats were deafening now, and a deep roar rumbled through the night. Aldo could see lights coming on in the barracks. *No keeping it quiet anymore.* He reached the horses, who were thrashing and rearing, trying to yank free of the hitching post, eyes wide with panic at what was drawing closer. The sword was in his hand, and he brought it slashing down through the reins. Both animals reared up, hooves slipping in the dirt, and bolted west, their hoofbeats barely noticeable in the oncoming din.

Aldo began to turn to say something to Nicolette, but a splintering crash echoed across the buildings of the ranch, and he looked up to see a massive log from the palisade flipping through the air like a thrown toy. Without thinking, he threw himself into Nicolette, the pair crashing to the dirt as the log tumbled into the roof of the guest house, shattering clay tiles and spraying them like shrapnel as it smashed the building like a child stomping a toy. The front window exploded outwards, four feet of the log bursting through.

He vaguely heard someone shout, but there was no time. The next roar split the world. It was louder than anything he'd ever imagined, and he turned to see the Vorchese bull exploding through the paddock wall.

The animal was massive, almost double again the size of the rest of the cattle. A pair of curled, twisted black horns jutted from either side of the enormous head, and the eyes were wild and blood red. It opened its mouth wider than should have been possible, and bellowed again, an unearthly scream of fury, hooves slamming against the ground as it charged forward. It started to turn, to run to the opposite side of the guest house from where Aldo and Nicolette lay stunned, but its momentum carried it forward, and its shoulder struck the corner of the building.

Brick and wood exploded in a crash, the entire side of the building disintegrating like ceramic hurled into a brick wall. With a groan, the remainder of the roof collapsed, the entire house smashing down only to be blasted apart by the bull sliding through. Its hooves found purchase, and it came to a halt, roaring once more as it lifted its head, inhaling through black flared nostrils, sniffing the air with whooping gasps. It swung its head through the wreckage of the home, hurling plaster and brick in a shower over Aldo and Nicolette, who curled up and covered their eyes as debris rained down. Through the din, Aldo could hear shouting, and lifted his head enough to see a half dozen guards in various states of undress, standing in front of the barracks, eyes wide.

The bull sniffed once more, and stepped forward, nose shoving over the hitching post. Its eyes bulged, and it roared again. Aldo clapped his hands over his ears. At this distance, the sound was physical, hammering into his skull. The bull's head tracked west in the direction the terrified horses had fled, and it burst into motion, moving far faster than anything its size had any right. Four bounding steps brought it to the side of the barracks, as men scrambled and dove to get out of the way. Aldo couldn't make out who it was who failed to move quickly enough, but a scream was cut short with a sickening wet crunch as they disappeared under the barrel-like hooves.

The long clapboard building didn't slow the animal down in the slightest, as an entire third burst apart in a splintering crash. Before Aldo could come to his feet, the bull had barreled over the fence line, charging up the hill into the night, roars echoing over the hills.

Aldo stumbled to his feet, ears still ringing, staggering a few steps forward as he looked around. The ranch complex looked as if a tornado had barreled through. The guest house was gone, fragments scattered all over, some having tumbled through windows on the main house. Dozens of men were scrambling out of the ruined wreckage of the barracks, and Aldo spotted Titus lifting a beam, and pulling Stiliano to his feet. His father looked dazed, blood running down the side of his face, but waved off whatever Titus was saying to him.

Aldo turned to Nicolette, who had sat up, and was blinking slowly. "Are you okay?" he said, and winced at how loud his voice was. She nodded, and accepted his hand, coming to her feet. Plaster dust showered down from her hair.

"What the hell happened?" Aldo turned to see Titus jog up. The older man looked relatively unharmed.

"I think your bull got out," Nicolette said, her voice a bit dreamy.

"I don't know. We were inside, and heard the noise," Aldo said. "Came around the corner of the porch just in time for the fucking place to come down around us." He waved back towards the paddock. "How the fuck did it get through that wall?"

"The fuck should I know? I was asleep!" Titus spotted three more figures running towards them. Naath was shirtless, and Aldo's eyes darted down to the patchwork of scars on his chest.

"Titus! Where's Stilts?" he shouted.

"Getting everyone out of that disaster, boss," Titus said, waving towards the barracks. "He told them to get horses, as many as they can. But how in the gods are we supposed to stop it?"

"He can't keep that pace up for long," Naath said, shaking his head. "But we have to find him. Get ropes on his rings."

"Fast as he was moving, he could be anywhere," one of the men with Naath said. Aldo recognized him as one of the guards on the husbandry shed, and willed his eyes not to flicker to Nicolette.

"We need everyone on horseback, now," Naath said. He turned to Nicolette. "Your Excellency, I apologize, but we have to deal with this, now."

Nicolette waved her hand. "There's no deal if you lose your only bull. Do your jobs. I'll be fine here."

Naath bowed. "Thank you, your Excellency." He turned to Aldo. "Take her to the main house. Some windows were broken, but the rest is intact. Once she's safe, find a horse. Start checking the east field."

"What if it comes back?" Aldo asked.

"It won't. Not until we have him." Naath looked at the others. "Let's go." They took off in a sprint towards the chaos of the barracks, where men were already heading off in every direction.

"Come on." Aldo started walking towards the house, waiting until the others were out of earshot before saying anything. Nicolette beat him to it.

"Fucking hell," she breathed. "If that thing had gotten any closer..."

"I don't want to think about it." Aldo glanced out at the ruined barracks, towards the spot where he'd heard that abbreviated scream. "Gods, how many people aren't coming out of there?"

"I don't know. More gods-damned blood on our hands." She glanced around, and muttered, "It fucking worked, though. A bit like burning down a building to get past a door, but it worked."

"Yeah." Aldo swallowed. "Come on. Let's go."

Chapter 18

The pair climbed the steps to the front door, walking into the empty house. It was oddly quiet. Closing the front door behind him, Aldo pointed. "Back door's that way."

As they made their way through, glass crunched under their boots. Fragments of debris from the guest house had peppered the windows on the eastern wall. Aldo glanced out of one of the empty frames, eyes falling on the wreckage in the darkness. "The body count on this job is getting higher and higher," he said.

"Did you see who it was?" Aldo shook his head, and Nicolette swallowed. "I didn't think…" She shook her head sharply. "Come on. Let's get it done, and get the fuck away from this place."

Aldo said nothing, but the pair walked out the back door. The cinder stone lights over the husbandry shed were pale blue lights in the darkness. The door stood unattended as they approached. Nicolette tried the handle, and shook her head. "Locked."

"I got it." She stepped to the side as he came forward, pressing his fingertips against the metal of the keyhole. After the strain of pulling the nails, this was simple, the tingling sensation quickly flooding down his fingertips. He could feel the shape of the simple latch, and with a thought, he heard it click, and the door swung open.

They stepped through, shutting it behind them. It was pitch black inside. Aldo heard Nicolette rummaging in her pockets, and a pale blue light bloomed from her palm, just bright enough to send ghostly azure over everything within twenty feet. Aldo glanced over towards the paddock, but it was too dark to make out the spot where Ian died. "This way," he whispered, his voice thick in his throat.

They made their way over to the stairs, their steps obscenely loud in the cavernous space. Nicolette held the cinderstone out, throwing light down the steps that descended into darkness. Taking a deep breath, she started down them, Aldo falling in behind her.

The walls were supported with unfinished pine boards braced with thick beams across the ceiling, the stairs cracked and uneven. Aldo counted forty steps, and heard rushing water before he saw the stairs give way to a stone chamber. Nicolette held the cinderstone up, and the shadows gave way to reveal a bubbling stream at their feet, emerging from beneath the far side of the limestone wall. A set of several slabs had been set inside the stream, providing a path across to a shore on the other side.

The pale blue light from the cinderstone glittered off of thousands of reflective points in the walls and ceiling. As they stepped gingerly across the creek, Aldo realized that the light lingered even after the blue glow passed. He shivered slightly as the chill from the room raised goosebumps on his arms. "It's cold."

"That's a good sign," Nicolette said.

The shore gave way to a narrow passage in the rock that passed over small tributaries of the underground spring. They'd walked less than a hundred feet before spotting the heavy metal door, set in a thick oak frame. Nicolette approached it carefully, holding the light up. "They cut into the stone. Set the frame right into it."

Aldo nodded. "Even if you wanted to dig it out..."

"It would take days. Weeks, even." She lowered the light to the pair of keyholes set above a metal wheel. "Wait." Nicolette tilted her head as she brushed her fingers over the keyholes. "This is a Devresse."

Aldo nodded. "Yeah. It is." He thought back to the last time he'd seen one of those, in a dark room in a dark house. *Last time I touched one of these was the last time I was okay.*

She glanced over. "You've cracked one of these before, right?"

"I have." Nicolette looked relieved until he said, "When I was fourteen. And I got caught moments after."

"Oh."

"That about sums it up, yeah." Aldo crouched next to the lock, wincing as his knees popped, the sound feeling louder in the cramped space. "Give me a bit of space."

"Don't you need light?"

"No." Aldo pressed his palm against the metal, and shut his eyes.

The rush of victory that had followed pulling the nails from the fence had faded. That had been raw force, using his powers to grip the metal while his muscled did all the work. This was delicacy. He could feel the glass spindles nestled against the twelve metal pins, ready and waiting to crack at the slightest provocation. The tension spring resisted his every move, and to make matters worse, there were two separate locks, both of which were keyed differently and needed to be tripped at the exact same moment. They were said to be uncrackable. They were. Unless you didn't need tools.

Aldo didn't know that his powers had a name until he'd been using them for a long time. At first it was a game, pushing whatever bits of metal his father would bring home back and forth across the battered wooden table that was their only real piece of furniture, eager to find any way to pull a smile from his father's face in the dark years after his mother had died. Soon, Stiliano was bringing home small locks, disassembling them and showing Aldo how they worked, and together, they teased out how Aldo could pop them open without picks or key.

Those memories had made a home in the lockbox inside his mind. Aldo had learned at a much earlier age than he should have that it's not just the ugly, blood-soaked memories that could cause pain. Standing on the rain soaked deck, knees bent so that the heaving planks beneath him didn't rob him of his balance, Aldo had learned that even the happy memories of the time before the iron closed around his wrist and he left his childhood back on the pier could be painful. So he closed them away, put them somewhere they couldn't bite.

Now, as he knelt on hard limestone in a cave that smelled of moss, the burbling creek echoing around the dimly-lit cavern, he thought back to those lessons, to his father patiently showing him the intricacies of padlocks, safes, throw bolts, and anything else he could bring home. He remembered the first job, at the age of nine, and the delight that bloomed over his father's face as the simple cylinder lock fell open at his son's touch. He remembered the feel of loving the puzzle, and as the tingling bloomed in his wrists and hands, Aldo felt the vibration of the lock beneath his fingertips, and remembered what he'd discovered in the happy days before his world had come crashing down.

It was never about the lock. It was always about him.

The pair of clicks were simultaneous, sounding louder than usual in the cave, and he exhaled, rising to his feet. Nicolette glanced over at him, eyebrows furrowed. "Is there a problem?"

In lieu of an answer, Aldo spun the steel wheel, and with a loud thunk, the door swung open.

"Gods." Nicolette's eyes widened, and she shook her head. "I thought it would take longer."

"Be grateful it didn't," Aldo said. "Let's go."

"Right."

The room guarded by this elaborate and ultimately useless lock was smaller than Aldo had expected, no bigger than a large closet. In the center of the room was a slab of granite, about chest high, with dozens of holes bored into the top. Sitting neatly in nine of the holes were small vials, filled nearly to the top with a milky liquid.

"Watch the door," Nicolette said, drawing the dagger from her belt. In practiced movements, she unscrewed the pommel, and tilted the dagger up, the vial hidden inside falling out into her palm. She plucked out one of the samples from the granite, holding real next to fake, eyes darting back and forth as she muttered to herself.

"Are they a match?" Aldo asked, glancing back.

She nodded slowly. "I think so. If there's a difference, I can't tell." She made the swap, sliding the fake sample back into the granite block. Nicolette quickly reassembled the dagger, and placed it back into its sheath, and like that, it was done.

"Feels almost anticlimactic," Aldo said.

"Let's say that after we're back in Vetticci."

They closed the door behind them, Aldo spinning the wheel to bolt it shut once more. Resetting the lock was much easier, and he turned to Nicolette. "We're good. Let's go…" He trailed off as both turned toward the other side of the creek, eyes widening at the sound of voices.

Aldo couldn't make out what they were saying but the tones of alarm and anger were clear. He could hear Naath's voice snap out an order, and moments later, they could hear booted feet on the stairs leading down.

He looked at Nicolette. The woman's face was stricken, eyes darting back and forth. She had no weapons.

I forgive you, Ian. Be at peace.

Aldo drew his short sword. "Don't let them take you. Not alive. You can't..." He shook his head.

"There has to be something," she said, shaking her head.

"There's not."

"I'm sorry, Aldo."

"A bit late for that," he said. Aldo wanted to keep his voice steady. He couldn't. He knew what waited for them. Instead, he offered what he could. "You did what you had to do."

"I did." Her hand fell on his shoulder, and Aldo glanced over at the odd expression on her face. "But that's not why I'm sorry."

When he'd first met her, Aldo had recognized someone who knew how to handle herself in a fight, who knew how to throw a punch that landed like a thunderbolt. He didn't expect to get first hand experience. Nicolette's fist crashed into his temple like a sledgehammer. Lights exploded in his vision, and the brief flash of pain was driven out by a muted thundering in his temples as he crashed to the ground, head bouncing painfully off damp rock. Before he knew what was happening, her boot sank into his belly, deflating his lungs and sending a bloom of white hot nausea, sharp and brilliant, rippling through him.

His arms and legs wouldn't respond to commands. Pain settled over him like a stifling blanket, smothering everything but the sounds of boots splashing in water, of shouts and curses, of blows landing and blades scraping against leather scabbards. Aldo tried push himself up, but his body was devoting all of its energies to finding its breath again.

"Bind her! Bind her!" He recognized Stiliano's voice. "Don't hurt her, just bind her!" A hand fell on his shoulder. "Aldo! Are you okay?"

Even if he'd been able to answer, he wouldn't have known what to say.

***

She definitely hadn't pulled her blows. It took nearly five minutes before Aldo was able to sit upright with Titus and Stiliano's help. Every time he tried to speak, a bloom of pain sang out in his right side. Titus had offered him water, but even trying to swallow led Aldo to gag once more.

His head wasn't much better. The events of the past few minutes were jostling inside his head, and much as he tried, he couldn't arrange them in any way that made sense. He had seen Nicolette, wrists bound tightly behind her back, marched back up the stairs, firmly in the grip of several guards, Naath following them up. Stiliano kept asking Aldo questions that he didn't know how to answer.

"Give him a moment, Stilts," Titus said, as if trying to sooth an anxious animal. "She knocked the fuck out of him."

"His eyes..."

"His eyes are fine. He's going to be fine." Titus dribbled a bit of water over Aldo's face. It stung his eyes a bit, but succeeded in driving some of the fog away. He blinked twice, his eyes focusing on Titus. "There he is," the older man said. "Aldo. Are you with us?"

Aldo swallowed twice. He nodded slowly, wincing at the pain that drew from his jaw. "Think so. Hurts."

"Can you tell us what happened?"

That's a good fucking question, Titus. Aldo was momentarily grateful for the blow to the head. It gave cover to the long pause while he gathered his thoughts in his head. *Nicolette, what did you do?*

Even in his dizzied state, it wasn't difficult to piece out.

Gods.

"She said she needed a moment. In the house." Aldo could hear the slurring in his words, both from the ringing inside his skull and the pain in his jaw. "Didn't hear anything. Looked for her. Found her, but she..." Nausea choked off his words. He didn't know if it was from her boot or from what he had to say.

"Didn't think she had that in her." Titus shook her hand. "You slowed her down, anyway. Not sure what she thought would happen once she got to the door."

"She could have killed him," Stiliano said, his voice tight and clipped. "If we hadn't gotten here when we did..."

"Thought you were after the bull," Aldo mumbled. *Why the fuck are you back?*

"Mikel caught up with us," Titus said. "He saw someone over by the paddock wall. Couldn't make them out, but it was enough that Stilts here thought something was off. Sent most everyone out hunting the bull, but convinced the boss to come back with a few of us to check it out. When we didn't find you in the house, we went looking."

Aldo nodded. *Fucking rotten luck.* "Thank the gods you did. I didn't think she could move like that."

"She put up a fight, but we have her. Think you can stand?" Aldo nodded, and the two men each gripped an arm, lifting him to his feet. The room spun for a moment, but he gripped onto each tightly until it decided to stop spiraling. The three looked up at the sound of footsteps, and Naath came back in the room.

"Is he okay?"

"She beat the shit out of him. Rang his bell pretty good," Titus said. "He might have a busted rib. But I think he'll live. She gave him the slip, but he followed her down. Tried to stop her." Titus shrugged. "Might have stalled her long enough for us to get here."

"How did she get away from you?"

Aldo shook his head, regretting it immediately. "She said she needed to lay down. Must have slipped out the back door." He swallowed. "Should have made sure it was secure."

"Yes, you should have." Naath considered him for a moment, than shrugged. "But I should have thought of that too, reminded you. The chaos of the moment..." He turned to Stiliano. "Get him back to the house. Make sure he's all right. We've secured the Subarcheron in the armory. She's under guard until we can figure out what just happened."

"Why the hell would she do this?"

"I don't know," Naath said. "I would have marked this up to her trespassing someplace that she wasn't supposed to be, but she assaulted one of my men. I'll send a message back to the Archeron before we decide how to deal with her." He waved his hand. "Get him sorted, then set up a guard rotation to watch her. We found the bull. I need to go coordinate getting it back where it belongs."

"Yes, sir."

They took the stairs slowly. By the time they'd reached the top, Aldo's head had cleared enough that he could walk on his own. It was still dark, the wreckage of the ranch scattered about, enough that they had to be careful to step around debris. He didn't say anything. His mind was whirling.

Why did she do that?

They brought him upstairs in the main house to a small bedroom. It was spartan, only a bed, a desk, and a chair. Once he was settled, Titus said, "I'll go check on her, set up the rotation. You can stay here with him, if you want."

Stiliano nodded. "Thank you."

Once he was gone, Stiliano sat heavily in the chair. "Do you need water?"

Aldo shook his head. "I'm fine."

"You're not fine, you're hurt."

"I'm fine," he repeated. "It's not the worst I've experienced."

"No." Stiliano swallowed. "I suppose it isn't." He shook his head. "I knew this was a bad idea."

"What?"

"Bringing you on. I keep finding ways to put you in trouble's path."

"This one's a bit less on you," Aldo muttered. "If it wasn't me, it would have been someone else."

Stiliano didn't say anything for a bit. "When I saw you on the ground..."

"It's fine. I'm fine." Even to his ears, the word was losing its meaning.

"Yeah." Stiliano rose to his feet. "I need... I'm going to get you some water."

The door swung close behind him, and Aldo let out a long breath. He pulled off his boots slowly, and went to lay down, but something jabbed him in the lower back. He winced, and reached behind him, pulling out a sheathed dagger. Aldo stared down at the weapon in his hand. He didn't know when she had tucked it into his belt. To be fair, she could have buried it in his shoulder, and he might not have noticed after the blow she landed.

"Gods," he breathed out. "What do I do now?"

Chapter 19

A few hours passed. Stiliano came back with water, but fled almost immediately after. Titus came in to see how he was, but didn't stay long. He knew everyone was working to try to get the bull back to where it belonged. He also knew that they'd be inspecting the wreckage of the wall, trying to figure out how the animal had broken free.

But it almost doesn't matter. Anything they find, they'll put on her.

He didn't understand. He needed to understand.

Time seemed to move at a crawl. It felt like an eternity before light spilled through the small window in this room. It faced the wrong way to be able to see what was happening, but he could hear voices outside, feel the floor beneath him tremble slightly at massive footfalls. His curiosity got the better of him, and he came to his feet.

The fog around his head had mostly cleared. During his brief visit, Titus had checked his eyes, and deemed it unlikely that he would fail to wake if he went to sleep. The clarity brought a down side with it. The ache in his jaw had swelled to a throbbing, a deep pulse of pain that rippled through his face with each movement. When he spoke, it was in mumbles, the act of opening his jaw too far a spike of bright pain.

Slowly, he made his way down the stairs. The glass on the floor still remained, and he could see where they'd crushed it underfoot on their way out of the house. He came out on the porch, shielding his eyes from the bright light, and stared at the spectacle before him.

A dozen guards surrounded the bull, each clutching long ropes tied off to the huge steel rings in the animal's nose and ears. The bull's eyes were glazed, its head hanging low to the ground. In the light, the animal's fur was almost iridescent, blues and blacks shining in the morning light. He'd only caught glimpses of the creature last night, the dark and chaos shrouding any detail, but it was no less intimidating in the golden light of the morning. The twisting horns were the size of wagon wheels, dense and curled close to its skull. Its thick feet sank into the ground with each step, leaving behind table-sized indents full of crushed grass and debris driven deep into the ground.

Aldo watched the nervous men carefully guide the bull towards the open gates of the paddock. He looked over at the shattered gap in the fence, where a half dozen men were hammering scrap wood and planks into place.

"Are you feeling better?"

Aldo felt his muscles tense at the voice as the memory of clinking chains echoed in his ears. He did his best to keep his discomfort from his face as Naath came to stand next to him. He'd been so fixated on the scene before him that he hadn't heard the man approach. "I'll be all right."

"Good."

"Are you sure that's going to hold?" Aldo asked, gesturing towards the haphazard repairs.

"No. But it will do for the next few days. I've sent Luca to Galen's Crossing to get timber and other materials," Naath said. "The bull is always lethargic a week or so after mating."

Aldo glanced over. "So it did... I mean, it found a cow?"

"We have over six hundred. It didn't take him long."

"What happened?"

"We have a dead cow." Naath shook his head. "Expensive night."

"Yeah." Aldo swallowed. "Do you know how he got out?"

"Not yet. We asked her, but she hasn't said anything since we caught her."

"What's going to happen to her?"

"I've sent a message north, explaining her actions." Naath shrugged. "If they want her back, the terms of the arrangement will have to be adjusted to reflect the damage done."

"What if they don't?" The question was out of his mouth before he could stop it.

Naath gave him a curious look. "You think they won't?"

Careful. "I don't know. They might be angry enough to wash their hands of her." *Or they'll tell you they don't have a clue who this person is.*

"Perhaps." He nodded. "Unlikely, but if they leave her for us to discipline as they see fit, we can manage that." Aldo's blood ran cold at Naath's words, and Naath stared in the direction of the armory for a long few moments before speaking again. "It had to be impulsive. She saw an opportunity in all the commotion. Perhaps she thought if she brought..." He trailed off. "No matter. How long do you need to recover?"

"I think riding a horse might have to wait for a day or so." Aldo thought for a moment. "I can take a shift guarding her. I assume she's locked up?"

"Bound and locked in the armory. She's not going anywhere." Naath turned to face him, eyes blank. "It didn't exactly work out the last time you were watching her."

"I know." Aldo let his eyes fall. "I fucked up. I know it."

"Well." The bull snorted loudly, and both turned as everyone around the animal froze in place, gripping the ropes tightly, although Aldo didn't know what they would do if the bull decided to run. The big head swung slowly back and forth, slowly blinking huge glassy eyes, and it snorted once more before resuming its plodding path forward. Aldo could see the relief on the men's faces. Once he was satisfied no disaster was imminent, Naath spoke again. "I meant what I said. Considering the chaos, your error was understandable. And given the results, I think it unlikely you'll repeat it. Go relieve Luca. Tell him to help patch the breach."

***

"Wow." Luca raised an eyebrow as Aldo approached. "You look like shit."

"It looks worse than it feels."

"Really?"

"No."

Luca snorted softly. "Didn't think that she had that in her." He glanced back at the door of the windowless armory. "Gods, I didn't think she'd try anything like this."

"Yeah. She surprised us all, I think," Aldo said.

"You're lucky. She could have killed you."

"Think that might have been the plan, if we hadn't been interrupted." Aldo didn't trust himself to say more. "Boss wants you to help fix up the breach."

"You sure you're good?" Luca asked. Aldo nodded, and he said, "Okay. This is an easy one. Don't open the door for anyone but the boss. If you need relief, wave someone over. We'll be around."

"Understood."

Luca nodded, and headed towards the distant sounds of hammers and curses by the paddock. Aldo waited until he was sure the man was out of earshot. Leaning back against the door, he rapped his knuckles several times against the wood. "You alive?" he asked, his voice low.

He could hear the sound of shuffling inside, and a thump as someone leaned against the other side. "Hey." Her voice was barely loud enough to hear.

"Gods, Nicolette." He ran his fingers through his hair. "What the fuck were you thinking?"

"Didn't have time to think of much," she said. "Hope I didn't break anything too valuable."

"You could have told me what you were planning."

"If I didn't have time to think, I definitely didn't have time to loop you in," she said. "Besides, it needed to look real."

"Felt real," he muttered, prodding at his jaw. "But what about you?"

"We were caught," Nicolette said. "I keep waiting for the obvious solution we missed to pop into my head. But there was nowhere to go, no way out. I hoped that this would at least put you in the clear."

Aldo was quiet for a long few moments.

"Are you still there?"

"Yes." He sighed. "Why did you do that?"

"Seemed like a good idea at the time." She chuckled softly. "I made you come. You didn't want to do this, and I didn't give you a choice. It's my fault that you're here. At least this way, you had a shot. I assume that the fact that you're out there and not in here means they bought it?"

"You nearly took my head off my shoulders," Aldo said. "It was a convincing performance."

"Good. I was worried you would fuck it up, be too confused to see what I was doing."

He didn't know how to respond, didn't know how to ask the question. Didn't understand why she'd made this choice. The sum of his life's experiences left him looking for her angle. The reality of the woman he'd come to know made it plain there wasn't one.

"Aldo? You still there?"

"I am. Nicolette..." He took a deep breath, wincing at the pain in his gut. "They sent a message north. To the Archeron. Letting him know what happened."

"Yeah. I kind of figured that'd be the next step."

"Do you know what's going to happen? When they find out you have nothing to do with the Empire?"

"Suspect you've got a better sense of that than I do," she replied. "But I don't figure it'll be good."

I forgive you, Ian.

Aldo clenched his fist. "We have to get you out of there."

"I think you've tempted fate enough, Aldo," she said. "That's not going to happen."

"Nicolette..."

"I kicked this whole thing off," Nicolette interrupted him. "The plan was mine. The idea to drag you into this was mine. You did everything I asked of you and more." There were several thumps. He didn't know if she was slowly bouncing her fist or head off the other side of the wall. "You have the dagger, right?"

"Yeah."

"Good. Get off this ranch, and make your way back to the city."

Aldo turned, as if she'd be able to see his glare through the heavy oak door. "I'm not..."

"Shut up." There was no anger in her tone. "You'll need to get to the DeLuca estate. The contact in Lofland Fork won't meet with you, not without instructions. You need to get in front of Mistress DeLuca. Turn in the vial. She'll make the payment. Go find Auggie, go live your life."

"I'm just supposed to leave you here?"

"If it was you in here, I'd already be gone."

Aldo shut his eyes. "You should have left me alone."

"Lot of things I should have done," Nicolette said. "Too late to change what's happened. At least I can get this one right." Another thump. "You're a good man, Aldo."

"If I was a good man, I wouldn't walk away."

"So be a selfish man. At least long enough to find your way out of this place. You've paid your dues, enough for the sins of a lifetime. You deserve a chance to be safe."

He didn't say anything. She was offering him everything he'd wanted. All he needed to do to take it was to be his father's son.

After a long few moments, she spoke again. "You told me. If you had the chance to walk away, you told me you were going to take it. So take it."

***

He found his father by the barracks, sifting through the wreckage. It was late. He'd stood watch for nearly ten hours, Nicolette refusing to speak after her last command to him. Aldo had tried to engage her in conversation a dozen times, but other than the sound of her walking away and sitting down, nothing came from the armory but silence.

The bull had been returned to the paddock, the damaged spot patched up. They'd done a surprisingly good job, given the extent of the damage. They'd had plenty of materials scavenged from the ruins of the guest house and barracks. Naath had ordered bedrolls set up inside the house. It was cramped. Men would have to sleep on the floor and lined in the hallways until the barracks could be rebuilt.

As Aldo approached Stiliano, the man was pulling blankets from the rubble, dropping them in a pile. He spotted his son, and nodded. "How are you feeling?"

"Like shit."

"Yeah." Stiliano paused, wiping sweat from his head. "I was surprised. That you wanted to get back to work so quickly."

"Didn't really feel like I had a choice," Aldo said. "Not much use for dead weight around here."

"You're not dead weight."

"A good thing, too. I've seen what Naath does to those he has no more use for." Aldo glanced up at his father. "How do you work for him? You know what he is, what he's done."

"It's not that simple," Stiliano said.

"Yeah? How long did you work with Ian?"

His father's eyes fell. "Five years."

"Five years." Aldo shook his head. "You work with a man for that long, how do you just keep going on as if what happened didn't happen?"

"I would think you more than anyone would know about the things we do when we're desperate," Stiliano said. "How hard was it for you to come to me? Ask me for help?" He shook his head. "I know how much you hate me. How much you blame me for everything that happened. And I get it. But still, here you are."

"I didn't have a choice."

"I know. But you seem to think you're alone in that," Sitliano said. "When the one choice is starvation, there aren't many alternatives that don't seem preferable. And the promise of a full belly and a comfortable life have made a lot of men make choices they don't love."

Aldo shook his head. "I've been here less than two weeks. I've nearly been killed several times, and I've watched the man you work for murder someone in the worst way I've ever seen. How is it so easy for you to just pretend everything is fine?"

"People like us don't get fine," Stiliano said. "We grab whatever is available to keep our head above water. I can't bring Ian back."

Aldo stared out over the hills for a few long moments. He both wanted and didn't want to say what he knew he needed to. "Was it that easy for you to move on from me?"

"What?"

"Ian's dead, and you're moving on like nothing happened. Like a man you worked with day in and day out didn't just die screaming from the man who fills your purse," Aldo said, allowing venom that had bubbled inside him for a long time seep into his words. "How long did it take you to wash your hands of me? To find a life for yourself while I shivered on that boat?"

"That's different," Stiliano said, his face stricken.

"Is it? You've been here for years. How many people have you washed your hands of?" Stiliano didn't respond, and Aldo said, "You're not wrong. I do know what it is to swallow something bitter to give yourself a chance. But this place, that man..." He shook his head. "I can't. I can't keep working here, surrounded by people who mark the worst moments of my life. You were right. I don't belong here."

The silence that fell between them was nearly physical. Finally, Stiliano fished in his pocket, pulling out a small cloth purse. "Here. Take this."

"I don't want your money."

"Call it pay earned," Stilano said. "I don't know how Naath will react if you tell him you're leaving. Could be that he pays you what's yours and wishes you well. Could go a different way, and I'm not willing to roll the dice on your life. I did that once, and it didn't go our way." He tossed the purse to Aldo, who caught it. "It's not much, but it'll get you to wherever you want to go next. Maybe head east, to Havensport. You've worked docks before. You can find work there."

"What are you going to tell Naath?" Aldo asked.

"The truth, I suppose." Stiliano smiled sadly. "You thought you could work with me. You couldn't. And I owed you, so I let you go."

"What if he doesn't like that answer?"

"Then..." Stiliano took a deep breath. "Then I suppose I'll pay a bit of what I owe this world for letting you down. But I suspect it'll be fine. I keep his ranch safe. He needs me to keep his ranch safe."

The dagger felt very heavy on his belt.

"Go. Now, during the night. Cut through the pastures, walk to the fence. You should make it before morning."

"Yeah." Aldo stared at his father. "I..." He trailed off, not knowing what to say.

Stiliano smiled sadly. "Just go. Let me at least do this for you."

Chapter 20

It began raining when he was halfway to the perimeter. He walked through the fields, listening for the telltale sound of hoofbeats to indicate that Naath had not accepted his father's explanation, but the only sounds were the occasional hoot of an owl. When the rain began pattering down, plastering his hair against this forehead, he drew his cloak tight over his shoulders, and kept moving forward. Aldo's hand rode on the hilt of the dagger, a fortune nestled in the hilt.

By the time he reached the fence lining the southern border of the ranch, the light sprinkling had turned into a downpour, rumbles of thunder echoing over the sprawling dark plains. The fence slats were easy enough for him to slip between, and just like that, he was no longer on Vorchese land. It didn't make him feel much better.

He continued south for a while. The solitude did him no favors. His mind kept darting back, pulling up moments from the past few weeks to hold up to the light, really letting him inspect them from every angle as he worked over what he could have done differently. He knew how little it mattered, but Aldo couldn't help explore these other worlds, worlds in which he knew Nicolette would be waiting for him in Galen's Crossing. Worlds in which she'd left him on the pier, in which Auggie didn't find herself in the back of that wagon.

Worlds in which he'd grown up with his feet on solid land, with a father who had showed up.

He shook his head, surprised at the well of anger that bloomed inside him. He didn't know who he was angry at, but it sat deep in his gut, following him as he made his way through the woods surrounding the ranch. It was still there when he found the stone span of the Duke's road, when he flagged down a passing wagon, offering a handful of coins for a spot in the back, nestled among crates of turnips and barley. It was still there when he clambered off the wagon in Galen's Crossing. Aldo wondered if it would always be there.

He found the inn they'd stayed out the night before they'd split up. A few words with the innkeeper, and Aldo found himself at a table, silently eating a bowl of stew while waiting for a promised convoy heading south to Lofland Fork.

"Interesting tattoo." He looked up, startled, at the young barmaid holding a pitcher. "Ale?"

"What?" He glanced down at his mug, which was nearly empty. "Ah, I mean yes. Please."

As she poured, she nodded at his wrist. His damp sleeve had crept up, revealing the first of the blue hooks. "Not seen a tradesmark like that before. What's it mean?"

"It's not a tradesmark." He took a sip. "It's from south. The city."

"What's it mean?"

He stared down at it. "Nothing. Nothing worth talking about."

"Seems a bit strange. Putting needle to your skin for something you'd rather forget."

Aldo nodded. "Sometimes we don't get a choice of what we remember."

"Suppose that's true." She tilted her head. "You wanting company tonight?"

He shook his head. "No. Thank you."

She smiled, not unkindly. "You sure? Sometimes the only cure for the memories you'd rather forget is to build new ones to take their place. Ones that you'll be happy to remember."

"I'm sure." He offered her a half smile. "It's appreciated, though."

She tipped her head. "Oh. Simon wanted me to let you know. No convoys today. Raining too hard. They'll wait for the road to be a bit more welcoming."

"Damn." He rapped his knuckles against the table, mentally counting up his funds. "I'm guessing any horse in this town won't go cheap."

She chuckled. "Afraid not. Doubt there's a mount left. Harvesting season starts next week. Anything that can pull a plow has long since been sold. Well, except for the devil in our stables."

Aldo raised an eyebrow. "Devil?"

"Donkey. Some little shit sold it to Simon this morning. Neglected to inform him that it's half trijjat. Damn thing bites anyone that gets near."

Aldo came to his feet so abruptly that she took a step back, startled. "Who sold it to you?"

"I don't know! Some kid. Traded the donkey for a room and some meals."

"What room?"

"We're not supposed to say…" She trailed off as he produced a coral coin. Her eyes widened. Glancing around, she took the ducat. "Upstairs. Second door to the right."

Aldo was halfway up the stairs before she'd finished the sentence. He tried the handle, but it was locked, and he pounded on the door, heedless of anyone trying to sleep. "Auggie, I swear by the gods, if you don't open this door right now…"

He didn't hear anything for a moment, but just as he raised his fist to pound on the door again, the latch clicked and familiar green eyes peered out from the crack. "Aldo?"

"What... and I mean this sincerely... the actual fuck are you doing here?!" he snapped, pushing the door open. She stepped back, offering a toothy grin up at him that faded when she saw his face.

"I came to find you." She saw the storm clouds on his face, and said, "I knew you were coming here. I just... I wanted to find you."

"Gods." He looked around the room, realizing it was the same one he'd stayed in before heading to the ranch. "What happened? Did those people we left you with do something wrong?"

"Yes. They were boring." She shrugged her bony shoulders.

"They were boring."

She nodded.

"Auggie..." He glared down at her. "You were safe. You were finally safe."

"Safe to do what?" She stomped over to the bed and flopped down on it. "To stack vegetables? To take tin money from a hundred idiots a day? That's what I'm supposed to do forever?"

"It's a good life. You'd have been fed, had a roof over your head..." Aldo trailed off, and he shook his head. "And you'd have been bored." He walked over, and sat down next to her. "How much did you steal on the way out?"

She looked offended. "Nothing. I was bored, not mean. They were nice. They just... It just wasn't for me. I wanted to come north and find you. I didn't steal anything."

"So they gave you Stuart?"

"I stole one thing." She offered him a toothy grin. "I don't think they'll be mad. He kept biting the horses. And the stable hands. And I think a city guardsman lost a finger."

"Sounds about right." Aldo shook his head. "Why did you come up here?"

"I'm not an idiot," she shot back. "I can't go back to the city. And I don't know anyone else. I know you're on the job. I can help."

"Was. I was on the job." He brushed his fingers over the hilt of the dagger. "Job's done. And I'm heading back to Vetticci. You can't come with me. We've got to find something else for you."

She made a face. "No more inns."

"Fine, no more inns."

Auggie asked, "What about Nicolette? Is she coming back with you too? Is she downstairs?"

He shook his head. "No. Nicolette... she got pinched."

"What?" The young girl was on her feet before he finished the sentence. "Let's go!"

"Auggie..."

"What's the plan? How are we getting her back? How can I help? Do we need Stuart?" The questions tumbled from her mouth so quickly it felt like each was shoving the others out of the way in the rush.

"Auggie, calm down," Aldo said. "It's not that simple. We can't get her out."

She shook her head. "Bullshit."

"Language!"

"Fuck my language!" Aldo scowled at her, but she plowed forward. "You said you two were partners. You can't leave her behind."

"It's not that simple!"

"Sure it is." She shook her head. "You came to get me. I ignored what you told me, broke your rules, did everything you told me would get me caught, and just like you said, it got me caught. But you came. You came and got me, even though it meant you had to go. Even though it meant everything was ruined." To his shock, he saw tears begin to brim in her eyes. She swiped a hand over them angrily. "You came and got me, because that's what you do. That's what you said. It's what we do. So let's go."

He stared down at her, his argument burning away in the face of this child's righteous rage. *Is it that simple?* Aldo brought his hand to the hilt of the dagger, a fortune chilled beneath his fingertips. *She told you to go. She gave you her blessing. There's no reason in the world not to walk away, to take everything that's been stolen from you since you were a child. No reason at all. Except...*

It's what he did. The old anger was still there, but it was muted somewhat. *It's not as simple as you used to think, but it's what he did.*

And you don't have to.

Aldo met Auggie's eyes. "It's what we do, huh?"

She nodded.

"Fuck."

"If I can't swear, you can't either."

"I think we both know that's a lost cause." He ran his hand over his beard. "Even if I was to try, there's no guarantee I can get her out."

She folded her arms. "How do we do it?"

"Not we." She opened her mouth to argue, but he wouldn't let her speak. "Auggie, I'm serious. If I do this, you have to stay behind. This isn't Vetticci. If we get caught, they're not fining us or sending us to a penance barge. They'll hang us, and that's if we're lucky." She still looked rebellious. "Besides, we need an exit plan. That's you."

"What do you mean?"

"Let me think."

To her credit, she let him quietly roll over things in his head for almost five minutes before her impatience got the better of her. "Aldo!"

"We'd have to go now. Today," he muttered. "Any longer, and the window's gonna be closed."

"What are you talking about?" she said.

"It's not getting in that's the problem," he said. He wasn't really talking to her, he was just working through the problem. "It's big. The hounds know me, so they won't give off an alarm. I know the perimeter routes, I know where they're keeping her. It's getting out. Once I have her, there's only one place they won't look, and it won't be available for long."

"Okay, so we go now." She was nearly bouncing with excitement.

"Calm down." He thought for a moment, then pulled out a ducat. "Go downstairs. I saw dried firepeppers behind the bar. Buy four or five, and bring them back."

She grinned. "So I can help, right?"

"Yeah." He nodded. "Yeah, I'm going to need your help."

Chapter 21

For Vetticcians, who lived and breathed on what thousands of boats could pull from the water, storms were uniformly disastrous. They kept all but the largest fishing boats in, and every hour that a maelstrom raged on was that much closer to starvation for many of them. They knew it wasn't that way in the Dominion. The sprawling farms of the massive nation welcomed the rain in a way Vetticcians never would.

For the first time, Aldo felt more like someone from the Dominion than someone from the city.

The rain was a torrential downpour now, hammering into the ground with a constant steady roar, punctuated by the rumbling crash of thunder that followed the brilliant splinters of lightning on the horizon. He'd crawled back through the fence three hours ago, and moved as quickly as he could, the storm covering up what little sound he made squelching through the muddy fields. He was also grateful that the rain would wash away any tracks that he left.

Aldo knew that the perimeter guards would still be out, draped in the same oiled cloaks that he wore now. He knew that due to the limited visibility, they'd have the hounds with them, the soaked dogs plodding along next to them. But they were sniffing for traces of the unfamiliar, not someone they'd been smelling for weeks.

Every hundred feet or so, he would peer down at the compass he had nestled in one of several pockets. There were very few visual indicators that he was heading in the right direction. He'd chosen his new route in to avoid the roads that split the ranch. As he came over a hilltop, he dropped to a crouch, muttering a quick curse. Aldo had seen movement in the night, maybe four hundred feet distant.

It took him a moment to be sure that there were no smaller figures moving through the huge herd milling about at the bottom of the hill. At least a hundred Vorchese cattle moved as one, soft mooing echoing past the thrum of rain and crash of thunder. Aldo watched them for a few more moments, wanting to be sure he was right, and then grinned. *Okay. This will work.*

He jogged down the hill as quick as he could without losing his footing on the soaking ground. The cattle were big, but they moved at a steady plodding pace that he was able to catch up with easily. Aldo slowed as he drew within twenty feet of the cattle on the outside of the herd, staring up at the animals. They were still huge, their shoulder nearly six feet over his head, but compared to the terror that had come charging out of the darkness at him just days earlier, they seemed almost normal. One swung its big head around, mooing softly at him. He approached slowly, his hand outstretched.

"Easy... easy..." He got close enough that she was able to lower her head down to his hand, sniffing at him with big whooping inhalations. The cow considered him for a moment, then plodded forward to catch up with the others. Aldo carefully ducked underneath her, slipping below and around the thick legs until he was at the center of the herd. Once he began walking with them, tons of mooing cover moving alongside him, he let out a long breath.

The rest of the hike was a mixed experience. He was confident in his invisibility while at the center of the herd. The cows moved and shifted around him, slow enough that he could easily remain near the center, keeping him shielded from anyone's view. But the smell of the wet animals was overpowering, made worse whenever one would pause long enough to deposit a steaming signature the size of a small mattress on the ground. Several times, he had to nimbly step out of the way to avoid a fate he'd rather not ponder.

By the time he spotted the haze of lights from the Promenade, they were nearly to the interior fence, and he had to break off from of his herd. He dropped into a crouch, and ran up to the fence. He'd come up directly on the other side of the ruined hulk of the barracks. At some point in the last few days, more of the building must have collapsed. Only a small section remained, the windows dark.

Aldo moved as carefully as he could around the side of the barracks, keeping the ruins between him and the rest of the buildings. He could see the captain's quarters across the thoroughfare, and peered back towards the other buildings. The armory entrance was out of view, but he could see the flare of a match as someone outside the husbandry building lit a pipe. He waited patiently for a strobe of lightning. The jagged brilliant arc lit up the sky, flaring in his vision, as well as (he hoped), anyone else who was watching, and he ran across the road, bracing himself for a shout of alarm. None came, and he came to a halt behind the small house his father claimed.

He crouched next to the window, well out of sight, the rain deafening against the tiled roof. Leaning up, he peered through the corner of the window. The rain streaked over the cheap windows made it difficult to see, but he could make out his father, sprawled in a chair, staring at something in his hand. Aldo took a deep breath, and rapped his fingers on the glass.

Stiliano didn't hear him at first. The rain was loud, and the thunder chose that moment to roll over the hills and through the cluster of buildings. It wasn't until the second rap that he jolted, staring out the window. He was looking right at Aldo, but there was no recognition on his face. Slowly, he rose to his feet, and Aldo watched him pick up the sheathed short sword leaning against the door.

When he came around the corner, the blade gleamed in the flickering lamplight coming through the window as Stiliano's eyes fell upon his son, wrapped in a cloak, clothes plastered against him and waiting. His eyes widened, and he hissed, "What are you doing back here?!"

"We need to talk," Aldo said, leaning close. "Can we go inside?"

"Do you know what will happen if they find you here?" Stiliano said, ignoring Aldo's request. "Do you have any idea how hard it was to convince Naath not to set the hounds on you?"

"Inside. Unless you want me to be caught."

Stiliano muttered a curse, glancing around, and then nodded. Aldo followed him in, pushing the hood off his head as his father shut and locked the door. Spinning to face his son, Stiliano snapped, "Why are you back?"

"I came back for her," Aldo said. "I'm not going to let Naath take her to pieces."

"Gods." Stiliano shook his head. "I knew she had it for you, but I didn't think you'd let her get into your head like that."

"It's not that."

"You've known her for four days, Aldo."

"No." *Here we go.* "I met her almost a month ago. In Vetticci."

Stiliano opened his mouth, but whatever he'd been about to say died in his throat. Confused, he shook his head. "No, that's not... She's never been to Vetticci."

"She's from Vetticci. She's never been to the Empire," Aldo said. "Her name isn't Noya Greystone. She's not from the Empire. She's been casing this place. Planning a job. And a month ago, she recruited me to help."

Stilts stared. "You need to tell me this is a joke. Now. Right now."

Aldo brushed the water from his face. "Not a joke. She needed someone who had an in to get hired, and she needed someone who could crack a vault." He shrugged. "Two for one with me."

"A vault..." Stiliano shook his head. "What vault? There's nothing here to steal."

"There is if you're a Vetticcian family with a pair of Vorchese cows, and no way to breed them."

"Gods." Stiliano's face turned the color of milk. "You didn't."

"We did," Aldo said. "We didn't expect you and the others to come back so quickly. She had to improvise. She saved me. I'm returning the favor."

Stiliano moved quicker than Aldo would have thought possible. Before he realized what was happening, Aldo's back slammed into the wall, his father's fists bunched in his shirt. "You set the bull loose?" he snarled. "We lost two men! Four more are hurt!"

Aldo pushed him back. "I know. I have to live with that. It's not what I wanted, but it happened."

Stiliano started to snap back, and paled. "Wait. Ian... you didn't..."

Aldo swallowed. "Isleweed."

"Gods." Stiliano stepped back, horrified. "How could you do this?"

"I got backed into a corner," Aldo said. "I got backed into a corner, and talked into doing a job. And I did the job as best I could, in the only way I knew how. And yes, it blew up. And yes, people got hurt." He swallowed. "I liked Ian. I thought he'd pass out, be late for his shift. I didn't think..."

"You're fucking right, you didn't think, gods-dammit." Stiliano clenched his fists. "This is my home, Aldo. I had a place here."

"You did," Aldo said. "And if things had gone the way they were supposed to, I would have come and gone, and you never would have known the difference. But shit didn't go how it was supposed to, and you know a little something about that, don't you?"

"You think that makes it right?" Stiliano asked. "I fucked up. I know I did. And if you wanted payback, I get that, but this…"

"This wasn't about payback." He swallowed. "It wasn't all about payback. I have to admit, fucking you over had a certain appeal. I didn't want to come up here, but I did. I didn't want anyone to get hurt, but they did. And I had the chance to walk away, but I won't."

Stiliano recoiled as if struck. "I told you. I didn't mean to leave you hanging."

"I believe you," Aldo said, and to his shock, he realized that he meant it. "I think that given a thousand chances to redo that day, you would be there for each and every one of them. I think you've spent every day reliving that moment, wanting nothing more to be able to change the way things played out, to actually be there to save me. That's how I know I can't walk away. I can't live the rest of my life wishing I could change things, go back and do right by her. Because of the three of us, she's the only one who made the right call, who took the hit for someone else."

Stiliano stared at him for a long time. When he spoke, it was barely a whisper. "I can't take back what happened."

"I know," Aldo said. "And I can't take back everything that's happened here. But I can do everything possible to do this one thing right. We both have a chance here. It might blow up in our faces, but we have a chance."

Father and son stared across a gulf of decades in the small room. Finally, Stiliano said, "Do you have a plan?"

Aldo nodded. "It's a really, really bad one. But to be fair, the good one blew up in several fairly spectacular ways." He told his father the plan.

By the time he was done, Stiliano looked fairly green. "Gods. Are you out of your mind?"

Aldo shrugged. "Desperation and insanity are fairly close cousins. If it goes well, you don't have to come with us. You can stay, plead ignorance."

"I doubt it. The ice is cracking under my feet as it is, after you disappearing. This would cap the worst week this ranch has ever seen," Stiliano said. "Not likely to be a safe place for anyone if that happens."

Aldo nodded. "Then you can also come with us."

"You'd want me to come with you?"

"I don't know," Aldo said. "I don't know what would happen. I don't know if I can forget what happened. To be honest, I don't know if I want to. But whether you come or not, I'm going to try to make this right. You can stay here, or maybe you and I can see what happens next."

Stiliano stared at him for a long while. "I'm sorry I wasn't there."

"I know."

Taking a deep breath, Stiliano buckled the sword around his waist. "Okay. Let's see how bad this plan actually is."

Aldo tried not to let the relief he felt show. "How many guards are on the armory?"

"Just the one. It's Titus right now."

Aldo muttered a curse. "I was really hoping it'd be anyone else."

"Yeah." His father shook his head. "You got past the vault door, right?"

"I did."

"Good. Because I don't have a fucking key to the armory anymore."

Aldo raised an eyebrow. "Why not?"

"Naath took it. When I told him I let you go." He shook his head. "He's relieving me as captain. As soon as we get everything cleaned up. Titus is taking the job."

"Shit."

"What's the problem?"

Aldo shook his head. "Nothing. It'll be fine."

"Then we need to move. Before the storm lets up. It's the only cover we have." Pulling on his cloak, Stiliano said, "Just walk behind me. Casually. With your hood up, they won't be able to tell who you are."

The pair stepped outside, Aldo falling in behind him. The walk to the armory was a quick one. A flash of lightning threw Titus's face in sharp relief as they drew closer. Aldo was careful to remain behind his father as he drew the small cotton pouch from one of the pockets inside his cloak.

"Stilts? What's going on?" Titus asked. He was huddled back against the door, trying to use the small overhang of the armory roof to protect himself from the rain as much as possible.

"Naath wants to see you," Stiliano said. "Now. I have the watch until you get back."

Titus frowned. "He was just here. Ten minutes ago."

"What?" Stiliano paused, and Aldo muttered a curse. "I…"

"Who is that? Luca?" Titus leaned around, and Stiliano moved automatically to block his view. Titus's eyebrows raised, and his hand fell to the mace on his hip. "Stilts, who the fuck is that?"

"Titus…" Stiliano held out his hands. Titus drew the mace from its loop.

"Fucking hell, is that your gods-damned son?!" Titus stepped forward, raising the weapon, and Stiliano dropped to his knees just in time for the pouch to sail through the air. Titus tried to duck out of the way, but he had no time, and it struck him on the tip of his chin, the firepeppers he'd ground into a fine powder bursting out from the cheesecloth in a scarlet cloud. He choked and gagged, gasping, but even as his eyes clamped shut, Titus was swinging the mace in a flat plane.

Aldo shoved his father down even further, knocking him into the mud, and feeling the spray of water from the iron ball as it whipped past him. He threw a punch at Titus, but his balance was all off, and it glanced off the big man's shoulder. Titus shouted out, and swung again and again, Aldo stumbling back to avoid the heavy slug of black iron. His back came up against the door of the armory, and he cried out, dropping to his knees as Titus brought the mace crashing down at a steep angle. It slammed into the door with a cracking sound, glanced off, and smashed into Aldo's shoulder.

Aldo felt something pop with a white burst of pain, and couldn't help the scream that slipped free of his lips. Titus raised the weapon again, but Stiliano crashed into him from behind, bearing him down to the ground and raining blows down on the man's head. Only when he was certain that Titus was lying insensate did he look up, eyes wide, shoulders heaving as he gasped breath.

"There's no way that they didn't hear that," he wheezed. "You have to hurry."

Aldo struggled to his feet, his arm throbbing, and stumbled over to the door. In the distance, he heard shouting, and a bell began ringing insistently. He hammered on the door. "Nicolette!"

"Aldo?" The other side of the door thumped as the woman ran up to it. "What in the gods is going on?"

"We're getting you out, but once we do, we have to move." Aldo looked down, and felt his stomach drop. "Shit."

"What's wrong?"

The heavy iron of the lock was canted at an angle, dented from the impact of the lock. Aldo shook his head. "Lock's damaged." He splayed his fingers over the rough surface, trying to focus. The pain in his shoulder combined with the increased shouting that was drawing closer made it difficult, but he felt the shiver ripple down his arm, and shut his eyes as he cast out for the tumblers. He found them almost immediately, and nudged.

They didn't move.

"Fuck," he muttered, and tried again, pushing harder. He could feel the tumblers, feel each of the four pins, but they felt wrong. He tilted his head as he tried a different angle.

"Aldo..." His father's voice was urgent. "We have fifteen, maybe thirty seconds. I thought you said you could do this."

"The pins are jammed," Aldo said. He tried pushing harder, and felt two of the pins reluctantly click into place. He shifted his attention to the other two, and doubled his efforts. A squeal emerged from the lock, cold iron dragging against cold iron, and Aldo winced at the sound. He pushed harder, and the squeal raced up in volume until it suddenly halted, and the pins stopped as certain as they'd been fixed in stone. Aldo grabbed the handle and wrenched at it, but now it wouldn't even turn. "No. Gods, no no no..." he cursed, wrenching at it as hard as he could.

"Aldo?"

"The fucking lock is broken," he said through the door. "The pins, the bolt. They're bent. We're going to have to take this entire door apart."

"What?" Nicolette hissed. "Aldo, you have to go. Now."

"I can't leave you!" He stepped back, and kicked the door as hard as he could. It didn't move.

"If you don't, you'll be dead, godsdammit!" She pounded at the door from the other side. "I can fucking hear them coming, Aldo!"

"I can't..."

"You came back. You tried. But it's fucking over, and you're not going to help me if you're screaming under Naath's knives, you fucking idiot," she shouted, her voice cracking. "GO!"

Titus stirred with a groan, and Stiliano stumbled over, grabbing Aldo's injured arm. Aldo gasped, but Stiliano said, "She's right, Aldo. We have to go, now!"

Aldo turned to him, furious, and saw shapes dimly lit by torchlight running their way, shouting. Aldo bit off what he was about to shout, and laid his hand against the door. "I'm sorry!" Before she could say anything, he and Stilano broke into a run, sprinting around the building and doubling back, past the wreckage of the guest house.

They ran hunched over, keeping behind piles of rubble as much as possible. When they reached the stump of brickwork that was all that remained of the fireplace, Stiliano grabbed him, and pulled him down into a crouch. "Don't move!" he hissed. They waited, breathing heavily, hearing someone barking orders. Aldo couldn't make out faces, but torchlight broke in several directions away from the armory, bobbing orange flickers spidering off towards the pastures. None headed their way.

"They're not looking this way," Aldo said, his voice hoarse. "We could try to go back..."

Instead of responding, Stiliano pointed. They couldn't see the front of the armory, but they could see several figures standing beside it. "They're not leaving it unguarded. Even if we could..." He swallowed. "Can you get past the lock?"

Gritting his teeth, Aldo shook his head in one violent jerk. "The entire mechanism's fucked. Maybe if I'd been more careful..."

"It looked like someone took a battering ram to it," Stiliano said. "Even if we'd had the key, I don't think it would have worked."

"I can't leave her."

"You did what you could. But if we stay here, we're gonna be right there with her."

Aldo clenched his fists. "I can't leave her. I fucking won't!"

"Aldo!" His father grabbed him, staring at him with pleading eyes. "This isn't you blind drunk, leaving her to twist. This isn't you turning your back. You did everything I wish I had done. But if you were in there, and she was out here, you know what you'd want her to do."

Aldo shook his head again. "I can't."

"If we get caught, it's over. It's done. If we figure out a way out of here, we still have options." Stiliano swallowed. "I don't know what happens next. But I can't see you in irons again."

Aldo shut his eyes, heat flaming his cheeks at the realization that the stinging in them was tears. *I'm sorry, Nicolette.* "Let's move." He rose to a crouch, and, moving as quietly as he could, made his way through the dark night, his father close behind him. When they came to a stop thirty seconds later, the pair paused for a moment.

"Are you sure about this?" Stiliano asked, naked fear in his voice.

"Absolutely not," Aldo said. His shoulder throbbed, and his stomach was a ball of acid, but he took a deep breath, and squeezed through the space between the lower boards patching up the wall of the paddock.

Chapter 22

He knew that the temperature hadn't actually dropped in the few moments it took him to make his way into the bull paddock, but the adrenaline that flooded his system and filled his mouth with a bitter taste made gooseflesh erupt along his arms. Aldo heard his father grunt behind him, one of the boards creaking softly, and as soon as Stiliano's boots hit the ground, they flattened themselves against the wall of the paddock, flanking the large patched opening.

They could hear voices outside, and through the gaps in the patched section, lantern light shone briefly through in flickering shafts of orange light. Grass crunched under boots, and Aldo could make out snippets of barked conversation and orders. He held his breath until both the lantern light and the voices faded into the black night.

"Gods." He glanced over, and could make out his father, staring down at the ground. "I thought this was a bad idea before we actually crawled into this fucking place."

"And now?"

"Now I know it's even worse." Stiliano's eyes rose to the top of the hilltop, to the clustered copse of trees that towered high into the star filled sky. "No one fucking comes in here."

"That's the idea." Aldo tilted his head, and raised a finger to the air. "Hear that?"

"The crickets? Yeah, I hear that."

"When the bull came before, right before it smashed through the fence, they went silent," Aldo said. "Kind of like an early warning, maybe."

Stiliano nodded. "What's the plan?"

"We wait?" Aldo leaned to peer through the gaps. "Look for another chance to get her out."

Stiliano shook his head slowly. "Aldo, that's not going to happen."

"I told you, I'm not leaving her."

"You don't understand." Stiliano glanced back up at the hilltop. "Your timing is good. I think you're right, I think the bull is still worn out from mating. But he's not going to sleep forever. And when it wakes up, if he smells us in his territory..."

"So we go before then!"

"They're going to have a half-dozen men guarding her from here until they hear back from the Empire. And when that happens, they won't need any men to guard her." Stiliano swallowed. "I understand. Gods, I wish I didn't, but I understand. But the fact is, if we stay here much longer, we're dead, and if we go back into the compound, we're dead, and she'll still be locked up. It won't change a gods-damned thing."

Aldo shook his head. "You don't know that."

"I know that while you're sucking air, you have options."

"Like fucking what?"

"I don't know!" Stiliano's voice threatened to break the whispers they'd been hurling at each other. "I don't know. But they're there. If you get killed, they're gone."

Aldo shut his eyes, his mind sifting through angles and scenarios, one after another that ended the exact same way. The anger and helplessness solidified in a hot ball deep in his gut, and he pounded his fist slowly against his leg, tears welling in his eyes. "I can't leave her."

Stiliano stared at him, then nodded slowly. "Okay. Okay, I get it. I'll go."

"What?"

"If Titus is still unconscious, they don't know what happened. I can figure something out, send them away, try to get her out of the armory," he said. "But if you go, if anyone spots you, that's it. They'll sound the alarm and have a dozen guards on you before you can shit your pants." Stiliano took a deep breath. "Alone, I have a chance. You make your way to the fence line, make sure our way out is secure. I'll meet you there."

"Wait." Aldo shook his head, frowning. "Even if that's true. Even if Titus hadn't been stirring when we ran, even if his brains are so scrambled he thinks a godsdamned trijjat leapt from the trees and kicked his ass, the door's still jammed shut. And even if it wasn't, you don't have a fucking key."

"I'll figure it out."

"You'll…" Aldo said, raising his eyebrows. "How are you going to figure that out? If there was an easier way in, we'd be a trio right now. And you know as well as I do, Titus was waking up. He's already told everyone and their fucking dog that you attacked him, that you were with me. They'll be on you in seconds."

"Maybe." Stiliano shrugged. "Maybe not. I used to be a pretty good thief."

"You were a terrible thief."

"I might get lucky."

"You're going to get yourself killed, and she'll still be locked the fuck up."

The moon in the sky had slipped out from behind the clouds, throwing pale blue light over his father's face. "But you won't be."

Aldo's mouth opened, but he could think of nothing to say.

His father offered him a sad smile. "This is about fifteen years too late. But I can finally do what I always said I was going to do. I can't buy your time. But right here, right now, I can buy you time to escape."

Rising to his feet, Stiliano leaned down to begin to crawl back through the gap. He glanced up as Aldo grabbed his shoulder.

Aldo gritted his teeth. "You dying doesn't help her."

Stiliano slowly straightened back up. "But it could help you."

It should have been easy, trading his life for a chance to see her free. Aldo was amazed and furious that it wasn't. "Gods, I really hate you." Aldo glared at his father, but finally, reluctantly, he nodded. "Options. Okay. Let's get clear of the ranch, but then you and I are figuring out a way to get her back."

Stiliano let out a long breath, and nodded. "Agreed." He glanced back at the treeline. "You said you had horses waiting. Where?"

"North of the paddock wall. Only place I know they don't patrol." Aldo glanced back in the direction of the armory. *I'm sorry, Nicolette.*

"That's at least eight miles."

"Yeah. We have four hours until dawn."

Stiliano nodded, eyeing the hilltop fearfully. "We need to stay clear of..."

"I know." Aldo pointed to the right of the hill, a gully that traced a long path around it. "We can go that way. Stay low, out of site." He turned his back to the compound, and began walking quickly, the tall grass brushing the tips of his fingers. He heard his father fall in behind him, but they did not speak.

***

Clouds were scattered across the dark sky, the stars spilling through the gaps. As the moon wandered out from behind clouds and back again, pale light would spill over the rolling fields before them. Other than the cluster of trees at the top of the hill, the only vegetation was the gently waving grass. It tickled Aldo's fingers as he walked alongside the thin bubbling creek that traced the path through the gully.

Crickets eagerly filled the heavy warm air with their song, and several times, Aldo heard an owl's mournful hoot. He spotted one, far in the distance, silhouetted at the top of the paddock wall.

"I wish I knew how long we'd been walking," Stiliano said. He whispered, but his voice seemed almost obscenely loud in the quiet.

Aldo glanced up at the moon, holding his hand up to the sky, his thumb extended out. "About two and a half hours."

Stilano came up beside him. "That's some trick. I know I didn't teach you that."

"No." Aldo glanced over at him. "One of the other prisoners did. He was a sailor, on one of the Family frigates. Showed me how to navigate with the stars, that kind of thing. Never mattered where we were. But knowing the time was important."

"Why?"

Aldo muttered a curse as he stumbled briefly on a root. He waved off his father's outstretched hand. "We had twenty hours. Twenty hours each day to meet the quota. We needed to know how far off we were, whether we'd been lucky enough to be able to take a break, sit for a moment."

"Did that happen a lot? Getting a break?" Stiliano asked.

"No."

Stilano glanced over at Aldo's terse reply. "Sorry. I get you don't want to talk about it."

"It's not my favorite."

Stiliano nodded. "One of the men I traveled north with, when I left the city. He'd earned two hooks. Not on your ship. The Merino barge, I think. I asked him about it. He told a few stories. But after a bit, I asked him to stop," he said. Looking over at his son, he asked, "Do you remember Antony Pellen?"

"Who?" Aldo asked, then frowned. "Wait, the cooper? Lived next to that pub you drank at?"

Stiliano nodded. "That's him. He did eight years on a private fishing boat, saving up enough to open that shop."

"Yeah. Yeah, I remember. We used to bring him scrap wood and iron. He'd pay better than most in the Nest."

"He loved telling stories. Never shut up. Would tell you the same one five, six times, no matter how much you insisted you'd heard it before," Stiliano said. "But any time we'd ask about his time on the barge, he'd change the subject. Get a dark look in his eyes if anyone pushed the topic." Before Aldo could speak, his father held up his hand. "Not me saying I understand your reluctance. Not even me saying that he would. Imagine there's a vastness between his two fishhooks and your collection."

Aldo was quiet for a few minutes. Finally, he said, "Two or fourteen. Makes little difference. I was a changed person by the time the sun set on my first day on deck. Didn't really matter what happened after that, there was no going back."

Stiliano stared out into the dark night. Silence had fallen around them, and his voice was the only thing beyond the wind slipping through the tall grass and the gentle babbling of the creek. "I'm sorry. I'm sorry I took so much from you."

"Yeah. Me too." Aldo didn't feel angry. He just felt tired. "But it's in the past. Nothing that any of the gods can do to make it different.

Maybe it's just..." His voice trailed off, and he tilted his head as he came to a halt.

"What?"

"Shhh." *No no no...* "It's quiet."

Stiliano's eyes widened, and he turned to look up at the hilltop. The trees were bathed in moonlight, but if there was any movement other than the wind rustling the leaves, he couldn't tell. "I don't hear it. Can you hear it?"

Aldo pressed his palm flat to the ground, grass scratching his skin. He tried to ignore the pounding in his chest, and waited, ears straining for the rumbling and waiting for the ground to tremble beneath his sweaty skin. For several long heartbeats, he heard nothing, but a soft whistling sound brought his head around. "What..."

He didn't get to finish the sentence as his father smashed into him, slamming him to the ground so hard that his teeth snapped shut on his tongue, drawing the sharp taste of hot blood. The whistle terminated with a wet thump, and Stiliano screamed, his howl of pain echoing over the dark hills, and rolled to the side. Aldo pushed himself up, staring wide-eyed at the bloody arrowhead protruding from his father's hip. Another whistle rose up for just a moment, heralding a second feathered shaft that punched through Stiliano's calf, driving through deep into the dirt to pin him to the ground like an insect.

Aldo started to scramble to his feet, but a flat voice called out from the night, "Don't." His blood ran cold in recognition. From the east, out of the darkness, Naath emerged, an arrow nocked in the longbow leveled in their direction. "If you move, the next goes into his belly."

Aldo froze.

Naath made his way down the hill to the other side of the creek, his aim unwavering. There was no hostility in his expression, just the flat, empty eyes that had become so horribly familiar. "Titus is hurt quite badly. I must admit, I didn't believe either of you had that kind of will within you."

Swallowing, Aldo said, "We didn't want to do that. We didn't want anyone to be hurt."

"No?" Naath shrugged as he stepped over the creek, coming within ten feet before he came to a halt. "That's disappointing. Gave me at least some hope you were something more than a common thief."

"Where's everyone else?"

"Still searching. I thought it unlikely that you'd be foolish enough to come this way, and didn't want to waste the men. But I thought it best that I come make sure. Figured you'd take the easiest path and try to stay away from our sleepy friend there." He nodded to the top of the hill. "It was a bold plan. Just didn't quite work out as you hoped."

"No," Aldo muttered. "I suppose it didn't."

Naath tilted his head, the gleaming point of the broadhead unmoving. "Why did you think you could break into the vault? I assume you were in on it with the Subarcheron, although I find myself suspecting that title to be inaccurate."

Aldo was momentarily grateful for the arrow that kept him motionless. It kept his hand from involuntarily brushing against the dagger on his belt. "I used to crack safes. In Vetticci." He gritted his teeth. "She never said it was a Devresse."

Naath nodded. "Well. Were my father still alive, he'd be gratified to know that wasn't a wasted expense."

Aldo nodded his head towards the blood pooling beneath his groaning father. "Can I try to stop his bleeding?"

Naath shrugged. "Toss that dagger on your belt away, and you can try. May not matter too much, but I won't kill you yet."

Aldo did as he said, tossing the weapon ten feet away to splash into the water. It sank the foot or so to the bottom as he moved over, kneeling to check the wounds on his father. Stiliano's face was white, from fear or blood loss, Aldo didn't know. Stiliano gritted his teeth as Aldo checked the wounds. To his surprise, the bleeding had already slowed to a trickle.

"Moringa tree seeds," Naath called out. "I put a paste made from them on my arrowheads. Makes the bleeding stop." He stepped over the creek, standing over them. "Thought we might have a conversation. Difficult to have a really good chat if either of you leave the bulk of your blood in my bull paddock."

Aldo glared up at him. "The kind of chat that you had with Ian?"

"Possibly," Naath said. "Might be needed for your father. He's had his share of pain, his share of struggles, but if I'm going to be responsible for sending his soul to what comes next, I intend to make sure he's endured what's necessary for him to realize salvation."

"You're not taking him."

"I am," Naath said. "But you? Those marks on your arm tell me all I need to know. You've endured. You've been tempered. You've been ready to step out of this life, purified, since you were old enough to shave." He smiled in what he might have assumed to be a warm fashion. It was not. "It's a gift few get, and it will be my honor to help you take your last step."

Aldo burst into motion, but Naath's arrow tracked him steadily. Aldo heard the bowstring twang and braced himself for the broadhead tearing into his flesh, but to his shock, the arrow missed far to the right. Snapping his head around, he saw Naath bring his hand up to his cheek, a blood welling up from the small stone that Stiliano had thrown. It hadn't hurt the rancher badly, but it was enough to throw off his aim. Naath reached for the quiver hanging at his hip, but when he saw Aldo change direction and charge, he dropped the bow into the grass and lowered into a crouch.

Some part of Aldo's mind screamed at him that this was a mistake, while another cycled through every possible option and acknowledged he had no others. He balled up a scarred fist and drove a blow forward towards Naath's face.

The man moved faster than Aldo thought possible. One hand came up, batting aside the punch, and the other came up to catch his chin in a punch that cracked his teeth together with a loud clack that brought stars bursting into his vision. He stumbled back, bringing his hands up, but Naath moved forward, driving blow after blow in quick combinations. For every strike Aldo managed to block, two more hammered into his gut and head. He felt like a child against the onslaught, and Naath sank a fist into his gut. Aldo gagged, beginning to double over, and felt Naath grab the back of his head, driving it down towards the knee that smashed into his nose.

The pain was blinding. Aldo could taste the blood from his broken nose flood back into his mouth, and he fell back, vomiting over the front of his tunic. Naath knelt over him, raising his fist to strike again, and another rock struck him in the shoulder. Stiliano was trying to stand, but his legs buckled under him as he tried to reach his son.

Naath sighed. "Apologies, Aldo. I'll be with you in a moment." His knuckles smashed into Aldo's jaw like a hammer, and Aldo felt a tooth crack as his vision greyed out. He could just barely make out Naath rising to his feet, stepping over, and kicking Stiliano in the stomach. His father gasped out a reedy scream, and fell back, and Naath reached down, grabbed the shaft of the arrow in his hip, and twisted. Stiliano shuddered, his eyes bulging in agony, and collapsed into a shaking, sweaty heap.

Naath rose to his feet, watched Stiliano for a moment, and nodded. "That should keep him calm while we finish up." He stepped back over to Aldo, and knelt down, his knee pressing down into Aldo's sternum. Aldo feebly tried to push him away, but all the strength seemed to have drained from his body. "Calm, Aldo. You're done," the rancher said, in the same tone he'd use to sooth a restive horse.

Tears bloomed in Aldo's eyes. He didn't know if they were from the pain or the realization that Naath was right.

Naath reached into his pocket, and pulled out a glass bottle. "Recognize this?" Aldo blinked through the tears, and Naath held up a hand. "I'm sorry, Aldo, that's rude. You're probably a bit rattled at the moment. Let me help you. This is one of our urine collection bottles. I noticed we were missing one. It doesn't take much to reason that you borrowed it to encourage the bull to go on his nighttime stroll. Am I right?"

Aldo tried to glare. He didn't know if it came through.

"We'll call that a yes," Naath said. "I don't blame you for this part, Aldo. You couldn't have known. But it's very difficult to collect this. Takes time, effort." He waggled the bottle in his hands. "The bottle you stole is the result of a great deal of hard work."

"Add it to my fucking tab," Aldo croaked out, blood foaming at his mouth.

"No need. This one is my gift to you." Naath smiled, white teeth glinting in moonlight. "You see, I'm going to take Stilts back to the harvesting room. We're going to have a long discussion. It's going to take days, but I don't mind. Stilts served me long and well, and he deserves every chance to ascend, and I promise you, I'm going to give him every single one of those chances." He tilted his head. "Titus told me that he's your father."

Aldo gritted his teeth, wincing as the cracked portion of his molar broke free.

"I thought there was more to your relationship than you admitted." Stiliano reached out, gently cupping Aldo's face, brushing a tear away with his thumb. "My last gift to you, Aldo, is a promise. After the others come and load your father onto a stretcher, after I cut your heels and pour every drop of this bottle over you, after the bull has left nothing of you but a smear..." He leaned close, lips brushing against Aldo's ear in a hideous intimacy. "Your father's screams will be his sacrament. I will walk him into the next life, peeling every bit of flesh from this body to guide him to his next. I... will... SAVE HIM."

"Fuck you," Aldo spat, wrenching away. "He saved me, you bastard." His hand came up, not in a blow, but fingers splayed wide across Naath's chest. He leaned up, bloody spittle painting the Confessor's face as he hissed, "My fucking turn."

As the tingles surged into his hand, he cast forward, tracing a line past the breastbone, past the heart steadily beating beneath his palm, past the spine, to the arrowhead that had been nestled in Naath's back since a long forgotten skirmish. He seized the small piece of twisted steel, and pulled. There was a sound like a knife crunching into a melon, and a spray of hot blood bathed Aldo's palm right before the arrowhead ripped through and came to rest in his hand.

Naath's eyes widened, and he stumbled back, blood fountaining from the jagged open wound in his chest, spraying over Aldo. His legs failed him, and he crashed to the ground. Aldo crawled forward, squeezing the arrowhead tight so that it didn't slip out from the blood. Naath's eyes found his, and his mouth opened and shut several times, but if he had last words, Aldo had no interest in hearing them. He drove the jagged edge of the arrowhead into the flesh beneath the man's right ear, and dragged it in one vicious tearing motion in an arc across his throat.

The spray of blood was not as strong as he had expected, but a scarlet pool spilled forth, and Naath blinked once as he choked. Moments later, he gasped, blood bubbling up through the ruin of his throat, and slumped to the ground, eyes wide towards the cloudy sky.

Chapter 23

A ldo stumbled back over to his father, his guts roiling, and dropped to his knees next to him. Stiliano was glassy eyed, but the bleeding seemed to have stopped. He looked over his father, who opened his eyes, and muttered, "Well. That was fairly terrible."

Aldo couldn't help the deranged laugh that slipped free of his chest. "You think?"

"You really do look awful."

"At least I don't have a pair of coat racks sticking out of me." Aldo reached for one of the arrows before thinking better of it. "I'm guessing whatever he put on the arrowheads isn't going to be enough to keep you from bleeding out like a butchered pig if I tug on those, so I think I'm going to leave them be for the moment."

"I think…" Stilano winced, sucking air through his teeth in pain. "I think that's a good idea." He glanced down, and his already pale face went a bit closer to white. "I don't know that I'm going to be walking out of here."

"What, you think you might be able to jog?"

"Sure, just give me five minutes."

Aldo looked back at Naath's corpse. "Long way to come on foot. We can attest to that. Think he rode?"

"Didn't hear hoofbeats. But seems likely." Stiliano waved a hand to the east. "I know there's a gate on the east side of the paddock. We never use it, but he could have ridden up through there, tried to get ahead of us." He gritted his teeth. "Gods, this stuff might stop the bleeding but it's doing fuck all for the pain."

"Well, I don't think you're going to drop dead. Not immediately, anyway." Moonlight glinted off something in Naath's hand, and Aldo felt his stomach lurch as he recognized the urine sample bottle. He rose shakily to his feet, and picked it up, checking the seal. "Let's not break this." He handed it to his father, who tucked it into his shirt pocket.

Aldo scanned to the east, but it was still too dark to make out anything. "Okay. I'm going to go see if I can get lucky, find his horse."

"What if you can't?"

"Maybe I can make a stretcher or something to drag your ass on."

Stiliano shook his head. "We're still miles away from the perimeter."

"Yeah, and then you'll really owe me. Best hope I can find a horse," Aldo said. "Now shut up and make like a log. He said he came alone, but if the others decide to come see what's taking him so long..."

Stiliano nodded, and Aldo walked over to the creek, bending down to pluck the dagger out of the crystal waters. It was cold. Aldo tried to inspect it, but he hadn't been able to see the seams in the hilt when Nicolette had shown him in the cabin. In the dim light, it was impossible. He slid it into the sheath, and began walking to the east.

He hadn't realized how close they'd gotten to the eastern wall of the paddock. The stream they'd been following had curved further and further from the hilltop at the center, and Aldo was sure he'd been walking for less than twenty minutes before the large log palisade took shape in the distant dark. The moon had slipped back behind another cloud, so it was impossible to make out details, but he heard something, and froze.

A few long, breathless moments later, he heard a soft nicker from the north. A few moments later, he spotted the grey mare, and let out a soft chuckle of relief. He approached the animal slowly, hand out. She stepped away at first, chuffing nervously at the smell of blood, but he managed to get the reins and murmur soothing words to the horse while stroking its neck until she calmed.

"Holy shit, I didn't actually think you'd find her." Stiliano was propped up on his elbow. He'd torn strips from the few sections of Naath's tunic that weren't covered with blood, and was carefully wrapping his wounds around the arrows.

"About gods-damned time we were due for a bit of luck." Aldo hopped down. "How are we going to get you up on her?"

"I'm going to say carefully."

"Funny." Aldo paused for a moment, then crouched down next to his father. "Throw your arm over my shoulder. Let's try to get you up first. And no screaming, please. You're right next to my ear, and they're still ringing from that lunatic kicking my ass."

As soon as they rose, Stiliano let out a shriek. Clapping a hand to his mouth, he choked out, "Sorry."

"Probably bit of an unreasonable ask anyway," Aldo said, wincing at the growing headache that was blooming inside his skull. They stumbled to the side of the horse, and with a combination of awkward lifting and sobbing, after a few minutes of difficulty, his father was straddling the horse at an odd angle. "Scoot back, if you can." Stiliano did his best to comply, and Aldo climbed up and got as comfortable as possible.

"This is not going to be a fun ride," Stiliano said, voice reedy with the pain.

"Better than walking." Aldo thought for a moment, staring down at Naath's body. "Give me the jar."

"What? Why?"

Aldo nodded down at the corpse. "That's very clearly a murder victim. We need things to be a bit more ambiguous."

Stiliano looked confused for a moment, then his eyes widened as he passed his son the jar. "Are you sure about this?"

"We're going to have to ride pretty quickly once we do this," Aldo said. "You going to be okay?"

"You do what you need to do. If you open that bottle, I want to be as far away from here as possible."

Aldo nodded, and very carefully, pulled the cork stopper out of the bottle. He really didn't want to spill a drop on them. Reaching out so far he was leaning off the horse, he poured the contents over Naath's body, dropped the bottle, and dug his heels into the side of the animal. For her part, the mare seemed quite eager to vacate the area, whether due to Aldo's urging or the scent of the urine, and Stiliano let out a gasp of pain as the horse leapt into a gallop.

After hours of walking, the new accelerated pace seemed almost as if they were flying. After a few minutes, the pair had arranged themselves in a position that was merely painful instead of blindly agonizing, and they clung to the horse as it bolted north. When they heard the first roar, neither looked back. Instead, they leaned forward, keeping a good grip as the mare was stirred forward by the trembles in the ground beneath her hooves.

Despite the discomfort of their ride, Aldo was grateful as he tracked the moon's movement over the sky. It became apparent very quickly how far they'd still been from the northern palisade. There was no way they'd have been able to make it before sunrise, but an hour after they abandoned Naath's corpse to whatever fate the bull had in store for him, the wall rose up in the distance. Aldo scanned the length of the wall, not spotting what he was looking for at first. But when the moon slipped behind a cloud, darkening the sky, the faint orange glow far in the distance behind the wall came into view, and Aldo nudged their horse in that direction.

They arrived at the wall, riding alongside it until they reached the huge gate. Gritting his teeth from the pain, Aldo climbed down from the horse, muttering, "Wait here," to his father. Stiliano nodded, his eyes glassy.

Aldo walked over to the gate, and softly knocked twice, then twice more. From the other side, he heard Auggie say, "What took you so long?"

Aldo let out a long breath. "Stopped for tea. Hang on."

It took him a few moments to collect himself long enough to focus, but the bolt lock on the gate was simple, and it thunked open. He pushed it open, the hinges squealing from disuse, and Auggie poked her head through.

Her eyes wide, she said, "Hey Aldo?"

"What?"

"Your face is smashed."

"Thank you, Auggie," he said, his voice weary.

She pointed at the horse. "That's not Nicolette."

"Thank you, Auggie." He shook his head. "We tried. But we couldn't get her out."

Auggie looked rebellious for a moment, and he held up his hand. "We'll figure something out later. For now, we have to go. Go bring the horse. Stiliano's hurt."

"Who the shit is Stiliano?"

"Language." Aldo rubbed his forehead. "He's the reason I got out. He's coming with us." Stepping through the gate, his face fell. "You didn't." Stuart was lashed to a wagon, glaring balefully at Aldo.

"I asked how much to buy him back, and they told me I could just take him," Auggie said, bringing the horse through the open gate. "I'm pretty sure I could have negotiated them paying me to take him, but I knew we were in a rush."

"Fantastic."

They got Stiliano down from the horse together, gently laying him in the back of the wagon. He laid back and shut his eyes, mumbling, "I'm going to nap now."

"Yeah. Sounds good." Aldo turned to Auggie. "You drive the wagon, I'll ride alongside."

"Okay," Auggie said. "Where are we headed?"

Aldo took a deep breath. "To get help."

Chapter 24

Toni DeLuca hadn't spoken more than a few words for the last hour. Instead, she'd listened attentively as Aldo told his story, detailed out everything that had taken place at the Vorchese ranch. When he fell silent, she nodded slowly. "Do you have the dagger with you?"

Aldo glanced over at the pair of house guards standing behind him. "I do. I didn't think it the wisest choice to draw a weapon without the appropriate context."

"It's good to see that you have the capability to properly think things through." She waved her hand. "He's going to pull out the dagger. Don't kill him, please."

He set it on the table in front of him, and she picked it up, inspecting it. With practiced motions that belied familiarity, she clicked the hilt open, and a burst of white condensation hissed forth as she slid it apart. The vial fell into her hand, frosted around the edges, and she held it up to the light, nodding.

"Where is your father?"

"The guards took him inside. His injuries... They were worried they would draw attention you wouldn't like."

DeLuca nodded. "Steven, please go ask my aide to contact the Pallia Clinic, have an anatomist sent over to treat Aldo and his father." One of the guards nodded, and headed towards the house as DeLuca spoke to Aldo. "Your nose needs to be set. I'm not an expert, of course, but we'll see you sorted out."

"That's not necessary, Madame..."

She waved him off. "Mister Marini, you look as if you've just been beaten half to death. I intend to set you right before you leave." He nodded his thanks, and she continued. "The contract may have been with Miss Saffman, but the terms were clear. Payment upon delivery, regardless of who provided said delivery," she said in clipped tones. "Do you have an account with the Bank?"

Aldo shook his head. "I don't, but..."

"You should open one. I can make arrangements. I don't believe you'll want to travel the streets with that much coral, not without some substantial security."

"Madame DeLuca, with your permission, I'd like to ask for an amendment to the contract prior to payout," Aldo said, speaking faster than he had intended.

DeLuca raised an eyebrow. "Given that you were not an original signatory, I'm not certain you have the right. But I'll admit to some curiosity."

Aldo swallowed. "I recognize that. But the original contract specified a payout of 800,000 ducats, correct?" DeLuca nodded, and he said, "I'd like to modify that total."

"Be very careful how you proceed, young man." Her voice remained calm, but her eyes were hard. "What amount do you feel acceptable?"

"Zero."

DeLuca blinked. "I believe you should clarify."

"You have a great deal of influence in the Dominion," Aldo said. "All the families do. Most of the Dukes have substantial debt to the Bank, which means they owe the families."

"Need I remind you, I do not have a seat on the table," she said.

Aldo nodded. "I know. Nicolette was fairly sure that was by choice. I don't know if that's true or not, but you have a better chance of influencing the Dukes than I ever will, whether or not I have that money." He leaned forward. "I want to find out if Nicolette is still alive."

DeLuca considered him for a moment. "Interesting."

"I know it's not easy, but we could negotiate for part of the funds if you could find out..." He trailed off as she held up his hand.

"It may not be particularly Vetticcian of me, but I'm inclined to offer this information at no charge. Nicolette Saffman is still alive. She's being held in Snowsill pending trial on charges of murder, property destruction, and attempted theft," DeLuca said. "After the death of Naath Vorchese after he foolishly ran afoul of an angry bull, the remaining staff at the ranch were unsure what to do with her, even after the Empire sent word that Miss Saffman's was unaffiliated with their government. They handed her over to the local sheriff, who brought her to Snowsill to be judged by the Duke. That happened yesterday."

Aldo's eyes went wide. "How do you know that?"

DeLuca simply looked at him.

"Right. Ah, okay." He swallowed. "I want you to get her back to Vetticci. Out of Dominion custody, charges dropped. You do that, you keep the vial and the money. We're free and clear."

DeLuca considered him for a few moments before speaking. "It might have been more prudent for you to negotiate. You're talking about giving up a fortune, young man."

"Technically, I have no legal standing to propose a change in the contract," Aldo said. "You could charge me with violating a contract right now, have me in irons. I didn't feel like this was the right time to be negotiating."

She nodded slowly. "It's a good offer, I'll grant you that. But don't you think Miss Saffman might be a bit perturbed if she returns to the city with no payment for the job done?"

"Not as perturbed as I suspect she'd be at the end of a rope."

"Duke Snowsill doesn't like hanging. He prefers beheading."

"A distinction I think that might be lost on Nicolette."

"I suspect you're right." DeLuca shook her head slowly. "I would be happy to accept your offer, Aldo. But what influence I do have is far from enough to wipe Miss Saffman's slate clean. While the Duke remains blind to what was taken from the ranch, the simple reality is that the Vorchese ranch has suffered major losses. Several animals, substantial property damage, and the death of the only remaining Vorchese family member familiar with the animals. It will take years, if not decades, for the ranch to recover, which means substantial losses for Duke Snowsill. To put it simply, he's furious, and Miss Saffman is currently the only target for that anger. I cannot simply wave my hand and make that all disappear."

Aldo shut his eyes, despair flooding him. "Damn." He shook his head. "I suppose the original contract, then. Maybe I can find some guild mercenaries to help me..."

"I'm going to stop you before that path of thought finds you in some very shark-filled waters, Aldo," DeLuca said. "No guild would ever consider hostile action against a Duke without the Table's consent, which would absolutely be withheld. And should you attempt to employ less reputable sorts, I can promise you that I will take any and all action to stop you. While Miss Saffman's fate is regrettable, we cannot risk our relations with the Dominion, particularly in light of the Empire's efforts to establish more trade with them."

"You can't expect me to do nothing," Aldo snapped.

"If I have any concern that you might do anything to jeopardize our relationship with Duke Snowsill, I can assure you that the anatomist will be wholly unnecessary." There was no hostility, no anger in DeLuca's tone. Simply a matter of fact statement of the reality before Aldo. "You've done well. Take the money."

Aldo could feel the stare of the guardsman behind him, but he shook his head. "I can't leave her. She saved my life. How can I turn my back on her?"

"Loyalty is admirable, but it can be expensive." She tilted her head. "Are you sure you are prepared to pay what it costs?"

"I have to help her."

DeLuca considered him for a long moment. When she opened her mouth to speak, Aldo was fairly convinced that she was going to order the soldier behind him to strike, but instead, she said, "There might be another way. But as I said, it will cost."

"I told you, I don't want your money. I just want Nicolette free."

DeLuca nodded slowly. "I cannot make the charges against her go away. However, I could issue a warrant for Miss Saffman on charges here in the city."

Aldo frowned. "What charges? She didn't do anything."

"On the contrary," DeLuca said. "I have a witness sitting in front of me that has attested that Miss Saffman aided in the escape of three convicted criminals, bound for terms on a penance barge."

His mouth went dry. "I broke those prisoners free. Nicolette had nothing to do with it."

"She knew what you'd done, and helped smuggle you and one of those prisoners out of the city," DeLuca said. "She broke the law. And because she broke the law, I might be able to demand her extradition to Vetticci, to stand trial here. Duke Snowsill might accept that, so long as she's being punished."

Aldo sat back, blinking slowly. "Those are serious charges. Years on a penance barge."

"But no execution." DeLuca raised an eyebrow. "So long as she's alive, she has options."

"If she goes on that boat, her odds of staying that way drop fairly fast," Aldo said. "But it's better than the noose." *You believe that, Aldo?*

"Indeed." She sat back. "You are correct. You have no standing to modify the contract. However..." She paused. "How much money do you have on you at the moment, if I may ask?"

Aldo shook his head. "Sixteen ducats. All we have left after getting down here."

"You fulfilled the contract. Your net worth is currently 800,016 ducats. So I propose a new contract. For a fee, I will attempt to arrange the extradition of Miss Saffman to the city."

"Let me guess," Aldo said. "The fee is 800,016 ducats."

She nodded. "Payable only upon the successful extradition. If the Duke declines to extradite, you'll keep the money."

Aldo was about extend a hand, but paused. *How far are you willing to push that?* "I've heard that wealthier families can... I've heard there's something else you might be able to do."

DeLuca raised an eyebrow. "I've made an offer for her extradition. I've told you the price. I know what else you'd like me to do, but that does not come cheap. Unless you have something else to offer, I'm afraid Miss Saffman will have to take her chances with the adjudicator."

Aldo stared down at the scars crossing over faded blue ink. *How far are you willing to go, Aldo?* He took a deep breath. "I have one more thing I can offer."

"What might that be?"

"My token."

For the first time since he'd met her, he saw a look of surprise cross her face, and felt a perverted sense of pride he'd managed to shock the indomitable woman. "Very few people do tokens any longer."

"I know it's rare, but if I'm not mistaken, the laws are still on the books," he said. "You stand for her now, and I'm your man, until you declare my debt cleared."

DeLuca considered him. "Do you truly understand what you're saying?"

"I do."

"I wouldn't have thought a man who had been through all that you have would be that eager to hand his fate back over to someone else."

"I'm not," Aldo said. "But at least this time, I'm the one making the choice."

She considered him, eyes boring into him, and finally, she nodded. "One token," she said. "I will leverage every bit of my influence in your favor now. But you are mine, any time I choose from now until your death. Are we in agreement?"

Aldo shut his eyes, and nodded. "With one small addendum."

"Fond of pushing your luck, aren't you?"

"It's Auggie." Aldo swallowed, and glanced back at the young girl who was still methodically demolishing the plate of food set before her. "She can't stay in the city."

"From what you've said, she didn't do particularly well outside the city either," DeLuca said. Raising her voice, she called out, "Young lady. Come here, please."

Auggie paused, a forkful of fish halfway to her mouth. She looked at Aldo, who nodded. She finished her bite, and stood up, shuffling over to stand before the table, fidgeting.

"What is your name?" DeLuca asked her.

"Auggie."

"There are very few things that I believe to be true with absolute certainty," the older woman said, grey eyes fixed on the skinny young girl. "One that I know for sure is that no parent would willingly name their child something so absurd. What is your name?"

Auggie looked rebellious, but quailed in the face of DeLuca's hard stare. "August. My mother's name was Liana Sindhi."

"August Sindhi." DeLuca nodded. "Is that the name you gave the adjudicator?"

"No." DeLuca blinked slowly, and Auggie quickly said, "No, Mistress. I told them Auggie. They didn't ask any more questions."

"Good. Auggie has a warrant out for her immediate arrest. August Sindhi does not, particularly if I vouch for her." DeLuca nodded. "You'll stay with me. I believe we might be able to find a place for someone like you."

Auggie scratched her head. "Will it be boring?"

For the first time, Madame Toni DeLuca allowed the ghost of a smile to cross her face. "No, my dear. It will not be boring."

***

Aldo had experienced a moment of apprehension that today's events would be adjudicated in the same narrow, dank room in which he had waited for his father so many years ago. Even with all that had changed, he wasn't certain he was ready to confront that place again. He needn't have worried. Extradited prisoners were judged at the Table Exchange, the center of Vetticcian politics.

"Was it like this? For you?" Stiliano kept picking at the clothes he wore. They had spent a fair amount of the limited coral they'd been able to scrape together on outfits that wouldn't make them seem even more out of place then they were. The cloth was much finer than the homespun they'd both worn for their entire life, but it felt strange.

"No." Aldo glanced around at the marble floors and carved oak pillars spanning overhead. "The Ruins adjudication hall was in a warehouse. It stank like rotting crab." He glanced over.

Stiliano nodded, and shifted, wincing.

"You okay?"

"I'll be fine."

Aldo knew he was lying. The anatomist summoned by Toni DeLuca had removed the arrows, and packed the wounds with a poultice that kept them from going septic, but the damage to the hip and leg would never fully heal. A sturdy cane rested against the seat between them. His father would use it for the rest of his life. He'd feel the wounds for the rest of his life as well.

For his part, Aldo was nearly fully healed. His nose still whistled softly every time he exhaled.

The doors at the end of the hall opened up, and father and son turned to see Nicolette Saffman enter the room. Her hands were manacled before her, and she was dressed in the white canvas tunic and breeches Aldo had worn for fourteen years. Her jaw was set, and she walked in, eyes forward, as the bailiff called out, "Lot 4455, Nicolette Saffman, extradited from the Snowsill Province in the Dominion."

"So received," intoned the adjudicator. She was an older woman, in her late fifties, snow white hair cut close to her scalp. The bailiff handed her a folder, which she opened and scanned as Nicolette came to a halt before her.

"Nicolette Saffman, you have been charged within the Dominion on the following violations," she said. "Mayhem, impersonating a foreign dignitary, destruction of property in excess of limits, the assault of several Dominion citizens, and murder. Does anyone speak on your behalf?"

In the bench at the front of the room, Aldo saw Toni DeLuca rise to her feet. "The DeLuca family speaks to the charges."

The adjudicator bowed her head. "Mistress DeLuca, we are honored by your patronage. To confirm, you requested the extradition?"

"We did."

"Primary reason for extradition?"

"The prisoner possessed information of value to Vetticcian interests. Her execution would have incurred an unacceptable cost," DeLuca said. "Duke Snowsill accepted a 0.5% reduction in interest rates on his outstanding debts to the bank in exchange for her extradition to Vetticci, which has been approved by the Bank."

"Thank you, Mistress." The adjudicator made a quick note. "Are all charges being transferred over?"

"No." DeLuca produced a sheet of paper, handing it to the bailiff to bring to the adjudicator. "The Dominion failed to produce compelling evidence or renumeration to properly quantify the scope of damages done. Without proper accounting, we cannot recommend retention of the destruction of property charges."

Nodding, the adjudicator made a note. "The Table declines to accept the charge of destruction of property."

A second piece of paper came out. "The Dominion failed to produce compelling evidence or testimony that Miss Saffman's actions directly contributed to the death of Ian Montague or Naath Vorchese.

Given this failure, we cannot recommend retention of the murder charge."

"The Table declines to accept the charge of murder."

A third. "The Dominion's definition of the crime of mayhem is vague and unspecific. We have no interest in processing charges that hold no basis in Vetticcian law. We cannot recommend retention of the mayhem charge."

The adjudicator frowned, and read over the paper. After a few moments, she hesitantly said, "With all respects due to the DeLuca family, the Table finds sufficient parallels of the mayhem charge to Vetticcian law. The Table accepts the charge of mayhem."

If DeLuca was angered by this decision, Aldo saw no sign of it in her disposition. "The charges of assault and impersonating a foreign dignitary are sufficiently documented and reflect parallel charges in Vetticcian code. We recommend retention of both charges."

The adjudicator looked relieved. "We thank Mistress DeLuca for her thorough consideration. Upon further review, in appreciation of her role in this extradition and the preservation of diplomatic relations with Duke Snowsill, we will moderate the mayhem charge by fifty percent."

DeLuca didn't hesitate. "Seventy."

"Sixty."

"Sixty-five."

"The Table accepts a moderation of the mayhem charge of sixty-five percent." The adjudicator made a note. "Total penalty assayed, fourteen months, six days service upon the DeLuca penance barge."

DeLuca tilted her head, and sat down. Nicolette's jaw worked, but she stared forward, unblinking.

The adjudicator signed the paper before her. "We will now accept any offers of purchase. Does any individual in attendance wish to negotiate for assumption of penalty?"

"I do."

Nicolette spun on her heel, and the bailiff stepped forward, alarm on his face, but she didn't move from her spot. Her eyes found Aldo, and widened. Aldo could feel the eyes of the attendees on him, but he ignored them, and said again, "I wish to negotiate for an assumption of penalty."

"Step forward, please."

Aldo didn't look down at his father, but brushed his hand away as he made his way to the center aisle to come stand before Nicolette. "Didn't quite work out how we thought, did it?" he muttered under his breath.

"What the hell are you doing?"

"The accused will remain silent," the bailiff barked. Nicolette glared in his direction, but his hand fell to the truncheon on his belt, and she closed her mouth.

"Name?" the adjudicator asked.

"Aldo Marini."

"Are you of sound body, capable of fulfilling the contracted penalty?"

"I am."

"State your offer."

Aldo's head was spinning, but he considered quickly. " Eighteen months."

"Thirty-six."

"Twenty."

"Thirty."

"Twenty-four." Before she could respond, Aldo rushed on. "I can provide a higher than average return."

The adjudicator raised an eyebrow. "Explain."

He rolled up his sleeve, and the eyebrow climbed higher. "Experience."

She considered him for a moment. Finally, she picked up a small pot of wax bubbling over a candle, pouring a dollop over the document before her. "The Table accepts the purchase offer of twenty-four months made by Aldo Marini for the original fourteen months, six days. Will you sign?"

Aldo started to step forward, but Nicolette spun to stand in his way. "I can't let you do this," she said under her breath.

"Bailiff!" As he stepped forward, Aldo raised a hand.

"If I could beg the Table's patience for a brief moment."

The adjudicator glanced over towards Toni DeLuca, who offered a slight nod. "Please proceed quickly."

"Thank you." Aldo leaned in close. "I don't like being in debt."

"What?"

"You saved me. If you hadn't done what you had, we'd have both been caught."

Nicolette glared. "If you tell me you didn't have anything to do with me being dragged back here, I'll call you a fucking liar. If you hadn't, I'd be at the end of a rope."

"Duke Snowsill doesn't like hanging."

"What?"

"It doesn't matter." Aldo shook his head. "We're both here because of what you did. I have faith in you, Nicolette, but the fact is, I know how to survive out there. You don't." He offered a faint smile. "I've never had someone who mattered. Who thought that I mattered. You're my friend. And more than that, you... You're a better person than I thought you were. But if you spend more than a week out there, that'll be burned out of you. And even if you survive, you won't come back the same." He shrugged. "There's nothing out there I haven't seen. But I can't..." He swallowed. "I don't want you to end up like me."

She shook her head. "It's not right."

"First right thing I think I've ever done. And it's my choice," he said. "That matters more than you know." He glanced back over his shoulder. "Do me a favor. Keep an eye on Stiliano. He's going to be a bit slow for a little bit. I'd like to know he's with someone I trust."

Nicolette shook her head. "I don't..."

"It's okay." Aldo smiled softly. "I've done this before. I can do it again."

Epilogue

I
t was raining.

The bumboat had a tendency to bob in the water, but its flat deck let the rain drain off the side. The crew had waxed canvas ponchos, but the prisoners weren't offered. Until his boots hit the pier, that's what he was. A prisoner.

His hair was plastered against his head, and he idly reached down and rubbed the raised reddened bumps of his new tattoo. It had been a week since the hook had been added to its fifteen companions. He tugged down his sleeve, and peered through the mist covering Pallia Bay in the early morning hours.

The lantern lights of the piers slowly emerged from the mist, a faint orange glow that grew brighter until he could make out the silhouettes of longshoremen waiting to unload the barrels of fish packing nearly every square inch of the deck. As they drew closer, features emerged, until he saw them both, waiting.

Aldo let out a long breath, and waved.

Acknowledgements

This is the sixth book I've written. I keep thinking that I'll figure this out, that I'll reach a point in which this becomes easy, but in the moments in which I'm actually honest with myself, I know that's never going to happen. Learning to tell stories is a never-ending chase for the next milestone, but every time you realize one of those milestones, you learn just how much more there is for you to know. Writing Extraction was hard. I'm proud of this story, but it demanded a lot from me, and reminded me of one very simple truth. Nothing worthwhile is ever achieved alone, and I have a lot of people to thank for helping me bring Aldo home.

To Nephi, Owen, and Brian. This last year has been a lot. But it's been a good reminder that no matter how long we go between seeing each other, I've got the best brothers and sister in the world. Thanks for being there for as long as I can remember.

To Bennett. I still remember meeting you at Walgreens to hand you the thick stack of paper that was my very first book. You've believed in my ability to do this as long as anyone, and I can never say how much your love and support have mattered.

To the writing community of TikTok. I have no idea why so many people have offered kind words and support of all kinds while asking so little in return, but I'll never be able to thank you all the way you deserve. I don't know how long this little oasis of nerds will endure, but I'm so grateful that I found it.

To Libby. I couldn't ask for a better critique partner, but even more, I couldn't ask for a better friend. Thanks for helping me slog through the beginnings of this story, and thanks for bringing Mason to life. He's still my favorite.

To Cee. I'll bet you didn't realize when you agreed to edit a book about some frosty boys and their hijinks that you were committing to editing a nine book series, but you're stuck with me now. You're an amazing editor and an even better friend.

To Cassie, Taylor, Adrienne, Mel, and Cate. My favorite quote from my favorite book by my favorite author talks about friends being "the people who build their houses in your heart," and goddamn if you nerds didn't build a whole subdivision. I am in awe of each of you, of your ability to tell stories that break my heart and make me grin, and I'll forever be grateful to get to be a small part of the journey of such astonishing writers. But even more, I'm grateful to have found friends as weird, chaotic, and ferociously kind as the five of you. I love you all.

To the best dogs in the world: Patton, Charlie, and Pickle.

To Emi and Hannah. Nothing in my life could have prepared me for the journey of being your dad, of seeing you grow into two of the most incredible women that I've ever known. I won the lottery with you two. Emi, you are one of the kindest, most fearless women I've ever seen. You love ferociously and relentlessly, and I can't wait to walk you down the aisle. Hannah, you have the drive, brilliance, and focus to do anything that you want, and you've chosen to put every ounce of that drive, brilliance, and focus to helping those most in need. I'm so proud of you, and I know that this world will be so much better for having a woman like you in it.

To Josh. You got the dedication, so the only thing you get here is this: I still think the Zune should have been a bigger hit.

To Toni. This is where I'm supposed to say something funny, to tease you or make a joke, but I'll do that the next time you sit and give me shit while I'm cooking. You're my best friend, you're my family, and this book simply would not have happened without you in my life. Thank you for pushing me when I needed a push, for listening when I needed to talk, and for believing in me even when I didn't. Love you, and I still owe you a cherry pie or three.

To Jen. You have had my heart since the moment I first laid eyes on you. You make me smile, you make me laugh, and you make me happy. You're my person, my partner, and the best part of every single day, and I'm going to spend the rest of my life loving you just as hard as I possibly can. Thank you for loving me, thank you for believing in me, and thank you for being my wife. You are my very favorite person, the love of my life, and yes... you're funnier than I am.